FREE FALL

(FREE FALL 1)

LETA BLAKE

An Original Publication from Leta Blake Books, LLC

Free Fall Written by Leta Blake

Cover Design by Dar Albert
Cover Art by LCheery
Formatted by BB eBooks

First Print Edition, 2025

ISBN: 979-8-88841-074-5
Print Edition

Other Books by Leta Blake

Contemporary

Will & Patrick Wake Up Married
Will & Patrick's Endless Honeymoon
Cowboy Seeks Husband
Bring on Forever
Stay Lucky

Sports

The River Leith

The Training Season Series
Training Season
Training Complex

Musicians

Smoky Mountain Dreams
Vespertine

Dark
The Difference Between

New Adult/Coming of Age

Punching the V-Card

'90s Coming of Age Series
Pictures of You
You Are Not Me

Only You
My Skin Begs You Please

Winter Holidays

North's Pole
My December Daddy

The Mr. Christmas Series
Mr. Frosty Pants
Mr. Naughty List
Mr. Jingle Bells

Omegaverse

Heat of Love Series
White Heat
Slow Heat
Alpha Heat
Slow Birth
Bitter Heat

For Sale Series
Heat for Sale
Bully for Sale

Fantasy

Any Given Lifetime

Re-imagined Fairy Tales

Flight
Levity

Paranormal & Shifters

Angel Undone
Omega Mine

Horror

Raise Up Heart

Audiobooks
letablake.com/audiobooks

Discover more about the author online

Leta Blake
letablake.com

Gay Romance Newsletter

Leta's newsletter will keep you up to date on her latest releases, sales and deals, future writing plans, and more from the world of M/M romance. Join Leta's mailing list today.

Leta Blake on Patreon

Become part of Leta Blake's Patreon community to support her indie publishing expenses and to access exclusive content, deleted scenes, extras, and interviews.
patreon.com/letablake

Leta Blake's Shop

Find special editions, book-inspired spicy art, merch and more! Leta's shop is growing, so check back regularly.
payhip.com/letablake

Acknowledgments

Thank you to Robin Covington, Jordan B, and Cecily Green for their excellent editing skills. Thanks to Mia for wonderful climbing and general beta reader input. Thank you to Clara and Aimee for their input on adoption. Thank you to the climbing community as a whole and to many individual climbers for providing inspiration as well as easy to locate resources in the form of movies, books, and YouTube videos. Specifics are mentioned at the end in the author's note. Thank you to Willow for using her eagle-eyes to seek out hero-typos and other mistakes. Thank you to my husband for his support and love, my parents for their generosity and encouragement, and my daughter for her unending delight in my writing career. Most of all, thank you to the readers. I hope you love this book as much as I loved writing it.

Dedication

For Moonbin—beautiful memories always stay.

PART ONE

CHAPTER ONE

Dan

Sunday, Aug 22, 2021
9 weeks until free solo ascent

MY EARLIEST MEMORY is of eating rocks. I was six years old, sitting on the driveway leading up to our trailer, putting handfuls of gravel in my mouth. I remember the grind against my teeth, the metallic taste, the dirt coating my tongue. Once they were slick with saliva, cleaned of whatever dust made them taste so appealing, I spit them out again. I remember the dark, gray wetness spattering against the pale, dry rocks, followed by the sensation of being smacked on the back of my head.

"You little idiot! What's wrong with you? Mamaaaaa!" a temporary "sister" screamed for my foster mother. "He's doing it again!"

It wasn't my first time.

And not my last either. Though this mouthful isn't voluntary.

Hanging against a rock wall on the western side of Lower Cathedral Rock, over three hundred feet in the air, I spit out a bunch of tiny gravel pieces.

"Dan? You okay?"

I give a thumbs-up to Peggy Jo. She gazes worriedly down at me from where she's climbing higher up the wall, her GriGri acting as a self-belay device.

"Fine. Just got a mouthful of dirt." I kick off the wall in front of me, swinging out over the exposure, enjoying the morning breeze.

"Hell if I know how, though."

"Climber above," she says, peering up. "Kicked some shit down. Some got on me too."

"Ah." That explains it. I'd been in a precarious position on the pitch when suddenly a shower of dirt and gravel hit me and I lost my grip. The jerk of the rope had hurt as my GriGri engaged, but it's always a reassuring pain.

"They okay?" I ask.

If the climber above sent that much crap raining down on us, it's likely they've lost the wall too. Probably they're fine. Simul-climbing with self-belay systems on a route like this one is reasonably safe for experts like me and Peggy Jo, but freak accidents can happen.

"Still moving. All's well," Peggy Jo says, cupping her hand over her eyes to get a better lock on the wall above and the climber and their belay partner. "You sure you're good?"

"Yup."

"Well, come on then. We got a lot of ground to cover this morning. The sun's only going to get hotter and the rock slippy-er."

Slippy-er.

I'm not sure that's a word, but I learned ages ago not to give Peggy Jo—or anyone—grief about whether their sentences make grammatical sense or if their word choices are actually in the dictionary. It just makes people mad, and disgruntled people don't want to help me achieve my goals.

And I *really* want to achieve my goals, whether that's climbing this rock, the next rock, or getting a decent shower before bedding down in my van for the night. As much as I don't like it, my personal concept of success involves other people.

Maybe that's part of why I prefer to free solo. Then it's just me, the rock, and the sky. No one else matters at all.

The rest of our ascent goes well. It takes some doing since we chose to simul-climb instead of belay each other, but it's nowhere close to hard for me. Each piece of rock is gone over three times so we can free the anchor at the bottom of the rope. It's child's play for me, but given how Peggy Jo is huffing and straining, I'm not sure another outing like this is in our future.

I've been climbing with Peggy Jo since I was fifteen years old, and she's getting to an age now where I wonder if she's starting to slow down. Maybe this "easy climb", one we're both familiar with and didn't use to trouble her in the least, is her way of starting to admit that to herself—and to me.

Although, Alex Honnold's mother climbed the Easy Rider route on El Capitan at age sixty-six, and I think if Peggy Jo stays fit and doesn't get injured, she could do that too. She's only sixty now. She's limber, strong, and tough. She just needs to train more regularly again to keep up her stamina. I'll bring that up to her.

The chiming of our clanking cams and carabiners bounces off the rock, an ever-present "birdsong" as we make our way up. At the top, the view is nice. My muscles don't even burn; that's how easy the climb is for me, but when Peggy Jo sighs, I suddenly wonder if there's another reason she's taken me up such easy pitches. One I might like even less than the idea that she's slowing down. Maybe she wants to *talk* with me.

I take a long swallow of water and steel myself for it.

"So…" she begins.

Ugh. I knew it.

"I've spoken to Henry…"

I wipe sweat from my brow. It's more from the sun that's shining hot and bright than from exertion. From the looks of the wide open sky, it's only going to get warmer.

"Did you hear me?"

I shrug. If Henry's talked to Peggy Jo, it's probably not great news. I avoid his calls typically. He insisted a few years back that I set Peggy Jo up with financial power of attorney for a reason. This one, I guess.

"He says at this rate you've got, at most, a year of cash left before that trust fund is gone."

I frown. "Money is meaningless."

"Until you need to replace something on the van or you want food in your belly. Come on, Dan. All he's suggesting is that the time has come to look into sponsorships, writing journal articles, speaking engagements, that sort of thing. Your reputation is strong enough now. The community will vouch for you. Even if they think you're odd, they're going to admit you're one of the best."

"I don't climb for money."

Peggy Jo sighs. "Fine, but you can't climb without food, gear, gas…"

I wrinkle my nose in distaste. It's true, but I don't want to hear it. Worrying about things like that is a distraction. Distractions slow you down or fuck you up, and free solo enthusiasts can't afford either. A distraction at the wrong time can be life-ending. I'd ended up with a mouthful of dirt earlier, hadn't I, all because of some other climber's distraction. Up until now, I've been lucky to have the trust fund—weird as it was to receive initially—but I've never felt attached to it. The money's always felt unearned and undeserved.

"He can talk to me about it again when I've sent the route." I scratch an itch behind my ear. "For that, I only need a few months."

Peggy Jo glances at me sharply. "You're still determined to do it this October, huh?"

"I am."

"You're insane."

I shrug. I hear that a lot. No one has attempted what I'm going to do and it's arguable no sane person would. So, yeah, maybe I am out of my mind. "We'll see."

"The weather isn't even optimal for it. August and September, the wall's still too hot for reliable training."

"I'll send it in late October or early November. It'll be fine."

Peggy Jo's expression grows grim. "Are you *planning* on dying in the attempt?"

"No." Though it can't be ruled out, and designing my life around some nebulous future, jumping through hoops to get sponsorships or speaking engagements—both of which I'd suck at—when I'm not even sure I'll make it to Christmas seems arrogant. Better to live tightly focused on the present. Better to plan for no future at all.

"Then you're gonna need money."

"I'll deal with it after."

Peggy Jo groans, throwing her hands at the sky in frustration. "Sometimes I wish I'd never taken you up on that first wall."

"I'd have found someone else to do it."

"I know you would have." Laying her arm across my shoulder, she squeezes me. Her fingers are chalked up, warm, and familiar. She's one of the only people who ever touches me—aside from the men I hook up with. I'm not fond of the backslapping, hugging culture of climbers, and they've all learned from my cringes that I'm not interested in hugs *or* in them. But Peggy Jo never holds back. She treats me like a mother would.

Ha. A mother.

Like I even know what that means…

"Henry said you have a year of money left *if you're lucky*. Look, I could place a few calls. A sponsorship would be the easiest to get. All you'd need to do is agree to use sponsored gear and allow some photos to be taken while you're climbing with it, and—"

"I don't want to do that."

"You don't want to do what you love? Paid for by a company with nothing to lose but cash? And your picture splashed over a major advertisement for some teenager to see and be inspired by?"

I shake my head. "The last thing I want is teenagers looking up to me."

"Why? You looked up to Alex when you were younger. That's what started all this, remember?"

"Of course, I do. But this is *my* journey. Mine. It's important that I keep it that way."

"I know you're fiercely protective of your climbing experience," Peggy Jo says. "But I don't understand. Climbing should be a communal thing. You make it as private and solitary as you can. Where did I go wrong?"

She uses her arm still around my shoulder to shake me slightly. "I got you into this to give you community and friends, and you just…" She throws up her free hand.

I extricate myself from her hug. "I'll make more friends when I'm finished achieving my goals."

"You'll never be finished, so you'll never have any friends."

"You act like no one likes me," I say. "I have *some* friends."

"Who?" She tilts her head, a dare in her eyes as if I'm lying.

"I have you, and Lowell, and Rye." I count out three fingers. "And I'm on speaking terms with plenty of climbers. It's not like they shun me. I've even climbed with some of the bigger names a couple of times."

I haven't climbed with Alex Honnold, though. The worst thing I can imagine is getting to know the guy. There's no way he'll be everything I want him to be, and I'd rather not be disappointed. I know enough from his books, interviews, and the documentaries and clips I've seen of him anyway. That's all I ever need to know.

When I was younger, I mapped out my own career based on his. I've already done most of his documented North American climbs except for some of his harder free solos. I'm not sure why I feel the need to best him at least once, to do something even *he* hasn't tried.

But I do.

Peggy Jo sighs. "Lowell isn't a friend; he's a search and rescue ranger who helped you when you got hurt."

"He gets coffee with me sometimes."

"And Rye isn't at your level."

"He doesn't need to be. He's a good belayer."

Rye has a lot of room to grow as a climber, sure, but Peggy Jo shouldn't be so hard on him. I hope she isn't coming down on Rye for the reason most people judge him, because I really want to think better of my mother-figure and mentor. But old people are set in their ways, including ignorant ones and, as I've mentioned, Peggy Jo is getting old. There's no ignoring that fact.

"You're so alone, and you don't even know it." She sounds sad, and I don't get it. If I want to be alone, why does it bother her? "When's the last time you were with someone? Someone you cared about?"

I snort. "Uh, never? I never care about the people I get with."

I say *people* because, technically, I'm bisexual, but really, at this point, functionally, it's just men. I avoid sleeping with women because…

Well, there are a lot of reasons.

One, I live out of my converted van, and most women lose interest in even a quick screw as soon as they figure that out. Two, it's not fair—or even true, maybe—but I assume women are looking for a relationship, and I'm not interested in one. Three, women are…well…

Peggy Jo will say I need therapy if she ever finds out, which she won't, but fucking women makes me feel sad inside. I can't explain it. When it's over and done with, I just feel like weeping, and I hate that. Maybe it's because of my childhood and how messed up it was. I really can't say. But anticipating the post-coital fallout is a real mood-killer every damn time. Also, women don't like it when you cry after screwing them. Men probably don't either, but it doesn't happen with them.

Besides, I really like how men fuck. It's hard, fast, and there's almost no expectations built in around it. It's typically good enough, even when it's bad, and hardly any guys want to stick around after. It's just golden gravy on top of delicious biscuits that I never find myself crying afterward or lying there with a grinding pit in my stomach and a hole burning in my heart.

Don't get me wrong. I don't think it's *women* who are the problem. Women are great. Obviously, the problem is me.

"Hookups can only go so far in building a life, Dan."

"I don't want to build a life. I want to free solo Heart Route."

Peggy Jo takes a swig from her water. "Until you complete that, nothing else matters to you, does it? Much less a relationship."

"Exactly."

But she doesn't let it go. "Humans need other humans, and I hate to break it to you, kid, but *you're* human. You *need* relationships."

"I like getting off sometimes with a hot person, but otherwise, no. I don't need anyone."

I hold back from saying *I don't even need you* because it seems hurtful, even if it's true. See? Peggy Jo has taught me *some* social niceties.

"Dan, I don't even know what to say to you."

"Say it's time to head down," I reply, kneeling up to gather our things. "I'm ready."

Peggy Jo doesn't argue and by the time we've rapped the wall and are at the base again, I can tell she's done with me for the day. I'm an acquired taste, and Peggy Jo is probably the only person on earth who's had the chance to really acquire it. But even she gets quickly weary of what she sees as my "bullshit." I'm hard to like, impossible to love.

I'm fine with that.

I prefer it that way.

Sejin

"GUYS, C'MON," I call into the café's break area without looking in. Lord knows I don't want to see anything if I can help it. I saw *way* more than I wanted to a few days ago. Still, Celli and Gage are good co-workers when they aren't in the back making out, leaving me to fend for myself with a shop full of customers.

Like now.

New love is cool and all, and one day I hope to experience it again for myself, but it's also annoying to literally everyone else in the lovebirds' lives. It must be, right? I can't be the exception.

"I only have two hands and feet, and the place is packed. Put your lips away and help me."

The only reason I refrain from telling them Pete doesn't pay them to kiss and play doctor is because there's yet another bearded, marginally dirty man standing by the counter looking greedy for caffeine.

The summer tourist season is wrapping up, and soon the autumn sports season is starting. The place is jammed with folks in from the campgrounds and freshly down from the granite walls of the valley. Chalk-dusted, calloused fingers distinguish the climbers from hikers usually, but so does the vibrant look in their eyes—an almost holy radiance like they saw God up there on the wall, and they're giddy from the vision.

Celli exits first, with pink cheeks and eyes that shine almost as much as the climbers' do. She's four years younger than me, short as can be, with curly, sun-streaked brown hair and a smile that crinkles her nose. I get what Gage sees in her, though I don't *get* it, being gay and all, but I can still fathom the appeal of her twinkling adorableness.

Gage, for his part, looks like a model or something, all cut cheekbones and dark, brooding eyes. His hair swoops down over his forehead, and he spends a lot of time tossing it back off his face. He moves like everyone wants him and if he were into me, I certainly would be open to a little bed-wrestling.

But alas. Apparently, straight *really is* a rating on the Kinsey scale.

Still, he's a good guy, and he's good to Celli. They make each other happy, that's for certain, and that's sweet. But it's *also* sweet when they do their jobs, and there's no time like the present. I give Celli a scolding shake of my finger. She smiles sheepishly and takes over the counter, freeing me up to make drinks until Gage comes out to deliver them to tables—which he does after a few minutes spent calming down his dick.

We work hard for about two hours and then things slow enough for us to get a break. Sitting out on the patio together, waiting for the next influx of customers, we sip iced coffees and eat yesterday's stale cinnamon rolls. We're allowed to grab them from where Pete tucks them away in the freezer when he closes the place at night. They're still tasty, and I love the texture of the icing when it's congealed.

"Y'all are gross," I tease as they steal a sticky smooch. "One day, I'll find a man, and what a glorious day that'll be!" I laugh. "Just wait. I'll give as good as I got with you two. I'll bring him to work, and you'll both see *so much*. You'll gag daily."

"She already does," Gage says with a snide eyebrow lift.

"Ugh!" Celli whaps his arm, and I do too, because seriously *ugh*. "And just for that, see if I 'gag' today."

Gage chuckles, unrepentant.

"You're nasty," I say and pull my long hair up into a fresh ponytail, enjoying the light breeze on the back of my neck. "I'll make you both pay."

"Just as soon as you get a boyfriend," Celli says on a laugh.

So much easier said than done. And maybe, just maybe, I don't even want one. I mean, the fall season *is* about to begin after all. Shortly there will be a flood of hot guys, some of whom will want to get busy with me after a day on the rocks. Why lock myself down?

Who am I kidding? I'd *love* a boyfriend. But I'll settle for hookups if I must.

"When are you going to download that app I was telling you about?" Celli asks, nudging me with her shoulder. "It isn't just for sex, but for, like, you know, people looking for real relationships."

"I already did. Set up the account a month ago." I grimace. "It's been useless. Maybe the het side of things is different, but for the gay side, it's just a bunch of locals getting into things I don't want to know about."

Gage pretends to puke, summing up my feelings eloquently.

Celli's eyes gleam. "Oh, yeah? Who?"

I shake my head. I'm not gonna out people who aren't ready. Not even when they're gross guys into skeevy stuff or married men who should know better.

"You're just in a lull right now. Summer tourists are leaving, but hey, climbing season's starting," Gage says, nodding his head toward the forest across the street. "Some new guys should be coming through soon."

"Thank God." Though I know it won't be much more than a series of hookups. I do really miss being in a relationship. It's been three years since I walked away from the mess that was my first love, but I still miss the way it felt to rest in Baylor's arms or to kiss his hair and feel that he was mine. I want that again but, you know, *not* toxic. I want something healthy and fun, like what Celli and Gage are growing between them, or what my parents had before…

I shut that thought off.

But whatever. If I can't have that, then I'll have to settle for a casual screw. It's been almost three months since the last time anyone touched me with intent, and my entire body is ready for some mindless sex with any number of the rough and ready men passing through Yosemite Valley. Never let it be said that I'm not easy.

"But hookups won't get you what you really want," Celli says, frowning so earnestly that the lines in her forehead cut deep grooves. "You need to find someone who wants to be serious. Someone who wants to date you, and love you, and treat you right. Not just"—she glances toward Gage—"gag you and move on."

"I gag a few of them too," I say. "Don't think I do all the work, and I hope you're not doing all the work either." I narrow my eyes at Gage. "She's not, is she?"

He smirks. "I put in my time, don't worry."

"Good."

Celli rolls her eyes. "Honestly, Sejin, I just want you to be happy. I can see in your eyes how much you need a man who gets you."

"Really? In my eyes?" I chuckle. Truly, she's so cute.

"Yes. You're desperate for it, and—"

I blow a small raspberry, dismissing her claims. I mean, she's right, but how embarrassing to have her point it out like that. Am I that transparent and pitiable? "Don't worry so much, Celli. As soon as a few queer climbers show up on the scene, I'll be too worn out from all the athletic bedroom shenanigans to want a relationship."

I press my middle fingers and thumbs together, closing my eyes dramatically and take a deep breath. Laughing on the exhale, I say, "Until then, I just need more practice with patience."

"And your hand."

"I wish I had enough privacy to even make good use of that." I groan and eye the van pulling into the parking lot. A man and a woman climb out first, and I wonder if they're part of the Quiverfull movement because they're certainly dedicated to popping out children if the *eight* exiting the vehicle are any indication.

Another van pulls up, this one full of Boy Scouts. And then a camper van, followed by a handful of trail hikers.

"This is it!" I announce, swallowing the last of my iced coffee. "Go time!"

"Promise me you'll give that app another try," Celli says, as we head into the coffee shop to take our positions before the next onslaught. "It's supposed to be for people looking for relationships. Not just sex."

I hate to burst her bubble by telling her that typically gay men don't use apps to find relationships; they use apps to fuck. Then, if the sex is good, *maybe* something else comes of it, but typically not. That's just the way things are. Especially here in Mariposa County.

"It's not like I deleted it," I reassure her. "I'm just waiting for someone to reach out to me first."

"But why? There are so many fish in the sea, Sejin. You just need to cast your line."

"Then there's no reason not to wait until the tide turns," I chirp.

"I know, it's just—"

The door bursts open, and the afternoon washes in a load of families and a handful of sweaty hikers. It's busy enough to keep my mind and body occupied until evening when I head out to my car, take out my phone, and to my surprise, discover there's a new notification.

Someone's messaged me on Celli's damn app.

Lo, *has* my tide turned?

Because from the looks of this guy's rather spartan profile, he is *fine.* Wide hazel eyes. Brown hair cut in close curls around his face. Smoking body. He sent a lame opening line, but that's common enough.

New in town? I respond.

My stomach twists with anticipation. Sex with strangers is always a little dangerous, but that just adds to the excitement. I hope he tops. No, I *really* hope he tops. Because I'm dying to be plowed hard by someone who knows what they're doing. It's been too long.

I rub my cock through my jeans and stare at the screen, willing his response to be not-creepy or otherwise full of red flags.

"Please let me get laid today; please let me get laid today," I whisper, relief flooding me at the entirely normal reply that flashes onto my screen. "Yes!"

Celli's right. I am desperate for it. But it's not a relationship I want right this minute. It's dick.

CHAPTER TWO

Dan

I MIGHT NOT be into love, but I'm definitely into sex.

So, after I've washed off in Peggy Jo's shower and driven my van back to the campground near Yosemite Valley where I've been parking the last few weeks, I climb into my very cozy bed wedged into the back and pull out my phone to peruse the local ass on offer.

There isn't much. Mariposa County is pretty rural, and I quickly grow frustrated. Hooking up isn't going to be as easy as it had been when I was staying closer to Vegas. Most of the guys on the app are okay, a few are even borderline hot, but too many of them also seem to be operating on the DL. One even has a photo of himself in a bathing suit, flanked by his wife and kids, their faces covered by emojis. Who does that? This guy apparently.

I almost resign myself to spending quality time with my hand and a porn site when I swipe to another profile that catches my attention. Young guy, but not too young—probably my age, so 25-ish—with long, black hair, skin the color of ocean-kissed sand, and a brilliant smile. Shirtless, yes, and looking sexy as hell with his finely honed, slim arms, and dark nipples. Most guys on these apps pose topless or otherwise show off their sex appeal, but most don't smile in the photos they upload. Or if they do, not like *this*.

This guy's smile is *so* pretty. The way his eyes curve up at the bottom, nearly eclipsing his dark irises, turns them into happy, upside-down half-moons. And then there are his teeth—so bright and shiny, and yet imperfect with a slight overlap between his front two. It's…what word would my third foster mother, Edith, have used? Charming. His smile is charming.

And I *am* charmed.

Charmed enough to want to see him naked and bent over my bed, at least. Would he object to me grabbing hold of his hair as I plow into him?

I click to the messenger side of the app, hoping I'll get to find out. If not tonight, then soon. He's not online according to the notification at the top of the screen, but I send a tentative message to feel him out. I'm not in any big rush. I'll be here all season.

Sup?

It's my go-to opener. Non-committal. Common. I've gotten it from other guys on apps when they're trying to pick me up, so I figure it's a safe and inoffensive way to get a guy's attention. I wait a few seconds to see if he's got notifs turned on, but his status doesn't change, so I put the phone aside and do some hang-boarding over the sliding door of the van.

I face outward, my feet lifted away from the ground as I work my arms. The night is pleasant, with woodsmoke in the air from neighboring campfires and the sky thickening with dusk. A breeze ruffles my hair, and I can hear the rustle of the aspen leaves and a squirrel scurrying nearby.

Ping.

I drop to my feet again, get back in the van, and collapse on my bed, phone in hand.

New in town?

I type out my response. *Climber. Seasonal. How 'bout you?*

I've been 'just passing through' for about a year and a half, so I guess I live here now.

Cool.

I don't really want to chat or get to know him. I'm more interested in seeing that smile in person and then getting naked, but I don't want to be rude or run him off. This is always the hardest part for me. Luckily, he takes the next step.

You have a place to hook up?

I let out a long breath. *Yup. It's not much. Just my van. But it has a bed.*

A bed's good but not necessary 

I laugh under my breath. So he's like that, is he? Perfect. I like a guy who's willing to get a little dirty in unconventional places. Not that I'll be hooking up more than once with—I glance at his username—SJWV? Okay, boring, but whatever. But then again… maybe I will. This is a sparse area. I'll be here for a few months. No reason to count him out when the pickings are so slim.

How do you want to do this? I ask.

I'm vers and willing to meet you wherever. I have a car, but no privacy, so…

My van's private, and I'm vers too.

Cool. What are you up for tonight? Do I need to bring supplies?

I've got condoms and lube.

So you want to fuck?

If you're cool with it, but hjs or bjs are fine too. Whatever. I just want to get off.

I'm dtf for sure. Been a while

What are you in the mood for?

I'd love to get plowed if you're up for that, but if you'd rather bottom, I can do that too.

I lick my lips, thinking of that long hair and imagining it wrapped around my fist as I fuck into what must be a decent-looking ass given the rest of this guy's body.

Topping sounds good.

Address?

I shoot him the location of the campground and give him the details on my van.

Great. Give me forty-five. I'll be in a green Versa.

See you then.

There isn't much to do about the state of the van. It's already pretty minimalist, but there's no denying it's cramped, and there's stuff everywhere. At least it's all strapped in with rope and cables so it won't go flying while I'm driving. Still, I go around tidying, and I sniff the bedding to make sure it's not too gross. It's sort of fresh. I just went by the laundromat a few days ago, and I've been showering consistently at Peggy Jo's house, the campground's showers, or beneath the waterfall I like. They're fine.

Especially for a quick hookup.

By the time headlights and the sound of spitting gravel alert me to the car that pulls in next to my van, I've been waiting and scrolling SuperTopo aimlessly for well on thirty minutes. The LED string lights I have inside the van are all turned on so it doesn't look quite so sketchy, but there's no stopping my worry that this SJWhatever guy will take off once he gets a look at my digs. Plenty of guys do. It's just a little too weird for them sometimes, and I get it.

Of course, lots of guys *don't* take off. I mean, a nut's a nut, and sometimes a guy's gotta get it, no matter the location.

When I throw open the sliding side door, the face that greets me isn't quite as easy-going as his picture. He looks a little skeptical, but when I hop out instead of immediately inviting him in, he relaxes some. He's gorgeous, dressed down in sweatpants, Birkenstocks, and a white t-shirt sporting the words "Red Velvet" in appropriate scarlet letters.

"Hi, I'm Sejin," he says with a smile that's about half the wattage of the one in his profile picture. I wish I had the ability to increase that glow, but I'm often accidentally a dick and sort of "on the spectrum" according to an official diagnosis in my teens, for whatever that's worth, so I doubt I'm gonna manage it, which is a shame.

"Like Seh Jin," he emphasizes, clearly accustomed to having to clarify.

"Dan," I say, nodding and shoving my hand out to shake like Edith taught me. "Like Daaaan," I draw it out, trying to be funny, but Sejin doesn't laugh. Which, again, is a shame, but I'm not surprised. My jokes often fall flat.

"I figured," he says with a small twist to his lips. I can't tell if he's pissed or just wary.

"So, uh, look," he says, glancing over his shoulder and then swiveling his head back around, trying to look past me into the depths of the van. "I don't know if this is like a fetish thing for you—" His accent is Appalachian and thicker than I've heard since I did some climbing out east. "—and I truly don't care if it is, but—"

"A fetish thing? No, I live here."

Sejin does smile then, but it's nervous and still not as shiny as I'd hoped to see in real life. "No, I mean, me."

"You?"

Sejin huffs out a strangled-sounding laugh. "Shit, sorry, I'm so bad at this sometimes. Out of practice, I guess. Small towns are hard to get laid in, yeah?"

"Sadly."

Then he *does* laugh, a real one, and it's like little bells ringing up my spine. I nearly shudder from the delight it evokes in me, and that's super weird. I'm not used to liking anything about a person before I get to know them, much less *two* whole things. But Sejin's smile and laugh are pretty special, and even I have to admit that.

"It's just...all right, so like... how I look—" He gestures at his face and then down his body. "Some guys are into...aw, hell, it's not like I even care. I only brought it up because I thought you were making fun of how I said my name, but now I think I'm just making it awkward. You just want to fuck, don't you?"

"Yeah," I agree, but now he's got me curious. "But, uh, what are some guys into? I mean, maybe I *am* into it, and I just don't know? I don't want to cross any boundaries with you. I like to keep things neat. Consensual. I'm not into kink during a first hookup, but…"

Sejin flushes and runs a hand through his thick, long, black hair, and I wonder if it's going to feel as smooth as it looks. "I'm not averse to a little kink with the right partner, but yeah, not on a first hookup," he agrees. "And, uh, I just meant some guys think there's going to be something special about fucking me because I'm…" He gestures at his face again.

I blink. "Because you're so pretty?" I'm baffled and really don't know what he's talking about.

He laughs again and, damn, I like it so much. "No, because I was born in Korea," he says finally. "Some guys think Asian men are different in bed…"

He clears his throat, clearly embarrassed, especially because this is a conversation he's brought on himself. I get it. I do dumb stuff like this all the time too. "We're not. I'm not."

"Why would you be? You're a human being." I'm so confused, but I remember a guy I met at Trillium Lake Crag telling me that women expected certain things from him in bed because he's Black, and when I was puzzled by that, he said that was my privilege showing. I guess Sejin, as an Asian man, deals with similar things, and since I'm just learning about it, I'm still privileged. White men always are, or so the Trillium Lake guy had said, and I'm obliged to agree because I don't know anything about being non-white.

"I'm sorry. This got so awkward," Sejin says, and now his smile is shy. "Can we start over?"

"Sure."

"Hi," he says, stepping closer this time and putting his hand out first. "I'm Sejin."

"I'm Dan," I answer, taking his hand and noting the cool, dry length of his fingers against mine. "Want to fuck?"

"I'd love to," he murmurs, and we kick off our sandals as I lead him inside.

Sejin

I HAVE TO duck my head to trail Dan into the decently-lit van. I'm glad there are plenty of lights so it doesn't feel quite as much like a bad idea to be getting all naked and vulnerable with a stranger.

Well, I hope we get naked and vulnerable. Some guys like a quick jerk-the-pants-down-and-go-at-it fuck, but I'm hoping for a little bit more than that to keep me sated for the next inevitable dry spell. Why did I move to Mariposa County again? Oh yeah, adventure! Escape! To live near my cousin. And be someplace new.

I never intended to stay here, though, but here I still am.

Currently, "here" is some kind of custom van that's actually tall enough for me to stand upright in, and that's saying something because I'm a slender six feet. My narrow hips and delicate bone structure make everyone treat me like I'm small despite my height, but I'm a good three inches taller than Dan, who looks to be around five-nine, at most. He's slender too, but in a different way from me. Every bit of him looks made of tightly-corded muscle, even his hands, which are firm on mine as he gazes up at me.

I take in the set-up of the van. His bed is tucked sideways on an elevated platform in the back with a TV screen bolted into the van-wall above it. It looks cozy with folded layers of quilts laid over smooth, clean-looking sheets. It's on top of storage containers, making it taller than usual, the mattress at waist-height for me.

When he'd said to meet him at his van, I'd imagined a dingy mattress on the floor, and while that should have scared me off, I'm just a big enough fan of risk to have thought it was likely worth it for a good fuck. Though not all fucks *are* good, and there's no telling if this one will be yet, I'm hopeful.

Along the wall of the van, opposite the sliding door, there's a wooden counter with a stove built in and all kinds of things tied onto it. Above the counter, there are cabinets with locks, and to the right is a blue fabric curtain that blocks off the front of the vehicle where the driver's and passenger's seats are. All in all, it's like the littlest tiny house ever, and a mobile one at that. I can't imagine living here, but at the same time, it doesn't seem too awful either. At least it doesn't smell bad. I wonder where he poops. Taking a piss is easy enough, but...

Dan's hands are calloused and rough on mine, and a sizzle of electricity seems to burn my skin where he touches me. Chemistry. There's no guarantee of it in a hookup, and no accounting for it either. I've felt it with a handful of men, and a few of them were...well, not the kind of guys I'd want to spend much time with. But all of them were heavenly fucks. In fact, one made me come without even touching myself, and that's an experience I'd love to have again.

But after the three long, sexless months I've had, just a cock up my ass and a shared orgasm seems like more than enough.

"There's a shower block and bathroom about a hundred yards from here," Dan says, letting go of my hand and shoving both of his into the loose pockets of his sweats. "I can show you the way if there's anything you need to take care of before we—"

"I'm good," I say, shaking my hair behind my shoulders, and taking a deep breath. "I handled everything before I arrived."

"I've got lube and condoms," he says, indicating the box and bottle by the bed. "Is there anything else you need before we get to it?"

His dark, hazel eyes are big, and wide-set over a straight nose, set into a thin face. His brown, curly hair is unkempt, but not overlong. It looks like he cuts it himself, what with his jacked-up bangs and the unfashionable shape, but he's still a handsome guy. His lips are well-made and not at all chapped, which surprises me since most of the climbers I've met—and living in Mariposa County, I've met a lot—have chapped lips from all the wind on the walls. His jaw is sharply cut with a dimpled chin that somehow, when combined with his ample mouth, almost makes him look like he's pouting.

Or maybe it's his big eyes making him look so oddly innocent while staring up at me, talking about condoms and lube and 'getting to it.' I don't know what it is about him, and maybe I'm foolish—everyone back home would say I am—but I decide to let down my guard and enjoy myself. This guy looks good for a few rounds if I play my cards right. So, I take hold of his chin and tilt his head up.

"I'm ready if you are."

And, *fuck*, he's ready. His mouth is on mine instantly, and he's not a shy kisser. My blood runs hot, and my nipples ache along with my thickening dick. I didn't even feel aroused a few seconds ago. Nervous, yes; anticipatory, yes—but now I'm like liquid heat. I mold against him, letting him take the lead as he turns me toward the back of the van and presses against my body with his own until I'm walking backward. I feel the raised platform and the mattress hit my ass, and I grin. It's perfectly positioned for what comes next.

Dan breaks the kiss, turns me around, and pushes me face down on the bed.

"This okay?" he asks, breathless, as his hands canvas up and down my back, sliding beneath my shirt to touch my skin. "Can I be like this with you?"

"Yes. Fuck, yes." I dig my toes into the soft wool rug he has next to the bed. "Oh, God," I whimper.

He chuckles. "Been a while, you said. Don't want to make you wait."

He's taking his time, though, sliding his rough hands all over my skin and pushing my shirt up so that the soft air of the van gives me the shivers.

"I've already waited way too long," I whisper.

"Let's take care of that."

I gasp as he shoves my sweats down to my ankles, and I kick them off. Pushing my feet apart, he insinuates himself between my thighs. I gulp when I feel that he's shoved his sweats down too. The heat of his skin against mine, and the soft, velvet slide of his cock as he rubs it against my ass cheeks makes me groan with anticipation.

"Fuck," he hisses. "Do you want to get this first one over with or make it last?"

First one? Fuck yes. He seems on the same page as me with regard to neediness, and the last of my reservations and tension bleeds out. I sink into the mattress and press my ass back against his thrusting cock, feeling it skim my crack as I knot my hands into Dan's soft blankets. It's been so long, and I'm not prepped, so it might hurt, but it's going to be worth it too. I just know it.

"You have more than one fuck in you?" I ask.

He chuckles again and slaps my ass lightly. "I can go all night if you want."

"Please do," I beg. My legs are already shaking, and my heart is beating double-time.

"You can change your mind at any time," Dan says, as he thrusts against me and rubs his hands over my hips and ass cheeks. "But for this first fuck, I don't want to wait."

"Me either."

The snick of the lube being opened reaches my ears, as does the crinkle foil sound of the condom as it's unwrapped. I can't believe I'm going to let this guy just push into me without any prep work, but I'm also so horny and pent-up that I'm not going to slow things down either.

I jump a little in surprise when I feel his fingers press around my hole, testing the give and tension of it. "Mmm," he murmurs. "You're tight. Want me to lick it?"

I can't help but whimper. I've been rimmed before, but never by a stranger. And since I've only fucked strangers for the last few years, it's been a long time. Dan must have taken my helpless noise for consent because he's on his knees with his tongue against me before I can grab hold of my scattered thoughts.

"Fuck!" I bury my face in his blankets and rake my aching cock against the edge of his mattress, moaning and writhing as I ride his shameless tongue. I whimper and groan as Dan works over my hole. Grunting and crying out like a virgin who's never experienced this kind of pleasure, I end up jamming a mouthful of quilt between my teeth to keep from getting loud enough to attract the attention of the other campers in the lots around us.

My legs tremble, my cock throbs, and I shout with the quilt between my teeth. I quiver with onslaughts of pleasure, and still Dan keeps going. If I had to give his tongue a service rating on Amazon, I'd go with five stars all day long, because *holy fuck*.

I'm on the verge of thinking I might come from this alone when he rises again, muttering, "Damn. You're hot."

There's another snick of the lube bottle, and I twitch against the mattress as he hooks his slicked-up, calloused thumb into me, stretching and probing my hole. "You're *really* fucking hot."

I squeeze my eyes closed, and the scents of sex mix with the detergent he uses on his sheets. I want to beg him to get on with it, but his coarse thumb pumping in and out of me, rubbing my hole and massaging me open, has me too incoherent to gather the words.

I know the moment he's decided to get on with fucking me because he pulls down on my hole, opening me a little roughly in a way that makes my knees give out and my cock flex. The wet quilt falls from my lips, and the van pulses with a warm, sexy energy. Removing his thumb, Dan lines up, and I feel the bluntness of his cockhead for only a moment before—

"Oh, sweet Jesus," I moan. The damp quilt rubs against my cheek as I squeeze handfuls of blanket and bear down to accept him inside. "Oh, holy fuck."

In my experience, scrawny, tight-muscled guys are always the most well-hung and, *shit*, Dan's thickness is going to leave some tenderness behind. Especially if we do this more than once like he said. And I *really* hope we do because I can already tell he's going to hit my prostate just right. I pant and whine as he slides in deeper, slowly, *slowly*. The gentle curve of his dick rubs over my gland and gives me a breathtaking, flashing warning that this fuck is going to drive me mad.

Dan clutches my hips and thrusts the final inches in all at once.

"Yes!" I cry, my asshole spasming around the base of his cock. I feel so full, so tight around him, like he's cleaving me in half and owning my ass entirely. The way his hands clench my hips, holding me tight and fast, keeping me from inching away from his fully-seated thrust is irrationally hot. He shuffles forward a little, closing all the space between us so I feel his hairy legs against my own, and his hip bones sharp against my ass cheeks.

"Like this?" he whispers.

"Oh, oh *fuck*!"

"Do you?" he presses.

I nod and whimper. Christ, do I like it. I like it *so fucking much* that my cock is *right there* ready to spurt. My balls are drawn up tight, and my hole convulses around Dan's dick, pulses of pleasure that threaten to swamp me. It really has been too damn long. I'm going to come before he's even made his first stroke.

"You're..." Dan gulps, his calloused fingers going impossibly tighter on my hips, holding me still. "So hot."

He doesn't seem to be able to say much more than that, and I get it because everything about this situation is adding up to make me explode without even working for it. Dan grips me tightly, shoves in deeper, and holds himself there for a long, beautiful moment before bending low to kiss my exposed shoulder blade. I tremble, and he nudges my shirt up a little higher with his nose to kiss the space between my shoulder blades too.

"You smell amazing," he murmurs, and then he leans back, gaining his footing again, and slides a hand into my long hair. "Is this all right? Can I hold your hair like this?"

I'm so stuffed with his dick and so aroused that my cock is leaking all over his quilts, but all I can think is that if he slams into me, holding my hair like that? He'll *own* me. I said I'm not kinky with strangers, but that may have been a lie because right now all I want is for him to dominate me, fuck me hard and rough until I shoot my load screaming.

"Yes," I manage to get out, though my throat is closing with excitement. "You can do whatever you want."

He hesitates, like he knows that's too much permission—and it is—but then he does take hold of my hair and wraps it around his fist until I feel a pleasant burn.

After a moment, he tugs hard enough to lift my head up from the mattress, forcing my neck back and my face forward. I open my eyes. Twinkle lights line the back door of the van and, for a moment, my attention locks onto the painted dark blue windows there. I dig my fingers into the blankets and groan. Tight on both ends now—tight around Dan's cock and tightly held by his fist in my hair.

"This too much?" Dan whispers. My stretched hole throbs with each thud of my heartbeat.

"No," I whisper back. "Do it."

"Alright, I will," Dan says, and he sounds like a man about to take on something daring, something terrifying.

But what he's taking is me.

The slide of his cock out is easy, making me twist as the sensation lights me up inside, but the drive in is hard, forcing me to grunt and convulse like an animal. Dan hushes me as he sets up a rough pace, his hips slapping crudely against my ass. My eyes roll up, the burn of my scalp growing as he tugs my hair, and my nipples ache and scrape against the soft material of my t-shirt. I wish I had clamps on them… or his teeth. I wish there was more of Dan to go around so that his hands could rub over my skin as he plows into me, and his teeth could bite my flesh, and his tongue could tease my nipples.

Overcome with need, I writhe against the mattress, trying to get enough friction on my cock, and I let him ride me hard. I gasp when he releases my hair, pulls free of my grasping ass, and hoists my lower half up so that my knees catch the edge of the mattress. He climbs on behind me, grips my hair once more, and pushes inside again. Face down, ass up, one of his hands on my hip, the other tugging my hair, I keen with pleasure. My fists grip and release the blankets and my toes curl as he rails me. I'm in hookup heaven. All my nerves are alight with lust, pleasure, and that special risky frisson that comes from being fucked by a stranger. And not just any stranger, but one who seems hellbent on making me lose my mind.

"Dan," I squeak out as he rubs past my prostate again. My thighs quake and my balls clench like I'm going to jizz everywhere without even getting one of his rough hands on my dick.

"Dan that's…that's…" I can't find the words to say how good it is.

But he seems to get the wrong message because he slows down, gasping, "I'm sorry. Is this too much?"

"Fuck no," I say, reaching back to slap his thigh with my palm. "More. Harder."

"Harder?" He seems skeptical.

"Harder," I demand.

I'm almost sorry I asked for it.

I've never been fucked like this before. Clutching at whatever I can get my hands on, I end up with his pillow smashed up against my howling face as I shake and shout. My balls draw up so tight I might pass out if I don't come. My God, I've never felt this kind of power in a man's body, and I think I might *actually* die if he stops, but I might pass out if he doesn't.

He jerks my hair, lifting my face up again, and my world goes white and wild. Nerve endings fire, my hips jerk and shake, and with a warbling shout I'm coming. I convulse beneath Dan's ongoing thrusts, and when I think my pleasure is going to be the end of me, I jolt through one last burst of orgasm. Crying out loudly and then collapsing, I reach back to touch Dan's thigh as he slams into me one more time and shoots into the condom with a comparatively calm little grunt escaping his throat.

"Well," he says, as he collapses against my back, a sweaty mess of skin and shoved-aside t-shirts, and quakes against me. "That was really fucking *good*."

I can't even speak. I've never shot harder and for such a long time. I can feel the slick of my come beneath me on the bedclothes, and the amount of it is astonishing, especially since I just jerked off last night. But Dan isn't the kind of guy to take silence as agreement, apparently, because he lifts up and whispers, "You all right? I wasn't too rough, was I?"

"I said hard," I scrape out. "You gave me hard."

"But…" He gently tugs out of me, and I moan as his cock

leaves my body, making me feel weird and gaped open. Dan kneels up, hunches over me, and spreads my ass cheeks with his palms to take a look. "Does it hurt? I've got some arnica and—"

"It doesn't hurt," I lie. Because of course it does, but I *like* how it hurts, and I really want him to get hard again before too long and see if he can bring me off at even half the strength of that last orgasm. Holy crap, coming out to this stranger's van has been the best decision of my entire sexual life, it seems.

That's confirmed when he says, "If you're sure," and then leans down and gently *kisses my asshole*, just a sweet press of his lips.

My hips twitch involuntarily, and I moan. He laughs softly, and then licks it lightly. "I don't taste any blood," he says, and then, with hands gentle on my ass cheeks now, he proceeds to rim me again.

His thick tongue. Slick lips. Sharp teeth. The works.

Tears well in my eyes as he pleasures my hole. I shake like a leaf, spread out on his mattress, pierced to the quick. I'm not sure what's going on in me, but tears slide down my cheeks as he works. Chills and pleasure almost too good to bear sweep over me and I groan and gasp.

Dan doesn't act like my tears are weird when he looks up from his dedication to my hole and sees them. He just runs his thumb through the wetness on my cheek, and asks, "These tears are good? Or bad?"

I whimper, "Good."

"Nice. I can't wait to fuck you again." But then he goes back to work on my hole, and I'm delirious by the time he finally slides into me for the second time. I'm dazed, muddled, and transported by pleasure. Somewhere deep inside, I recognize that I'm vulnerable and exposed. Dan could kill me right now, and I'd simply let him, drowning in my enraptured state.

But he doesn't. Unless you count the exquisite and painfully good *la petite morts* he subjects me to over the course of the night. And, in that case, he kills me three more times before the sun comes up.

CHAPTER THREE

Dan

I'VE FUCKED A lot of men, but Sejin is definitely the hottest guy I've been with in a long time. Maybe ever. As the night turns toward morning, I'm tempted to tell him that, but then I remember what he said when he first arrived, something about guys thinking fucking him is special because he's Asian. Fucking him *is* special, but I'm pretty sure it has nothing to do with him being born in Korea, and everything to do with what an open man he is in bed.

Some guys resist me when I want to lick their hole. They say it's dirty, or it's not right, or some other bullshit. I always stop, of course, and let them miss out on a great time. Consent is consent, and sex requires it. But I feel sorry for them for being so uptight.

Sejin, though, let me lick and suck and eat him to my heart's content.

I don't know why I like rimming guys so much, but I love it. The taste and scent of them, the way their asshole spasms against my mouth, and the little gasping sounds they can't help but make when I really go to town on their hole are divine to me. Like definitely better than anything I've ever felt in church, and almost as good as sending a big, new-to-me wall route.

Last night, I rang the bell of Sejin's body over and over and made him sing with pleasure all night long. It was so good I'd nearly come before I wanted to just from the wild noises he made. So sexy to hear that much gratification let loose shamelessly into the night.

It's sometime after four a.m. now, and I'm still high from it all. I start to protest when he gets up, but stop myself. Instead, I stretch out in the sweat-and-cum-stained sheets and watch him get dressed in his loose sweats and t-shirt. Licking my lips as he catches his long hair in a thick black band that looks like it's not strong enough to hold all of it, I feel my groin stir with blood even though there's no way I can get it up again this soon. He runs his hands through his ponytail and my fingers ache to touch the silkiness of all that hair again. But we're done fucking, so I don't have permission anymore.

"It was—" Sejin breaks off, turning to me, his eyes shiny from lack of rest and hours of hedonistic pleasure that's sent endorphins cascading through his system.

"Fun," I prompt. Because that's what you say to a guy you've hooked up with. You say it was fun, and they agree, and then they leave. And now Sejin needs to go because that's how hookups end.

Weirdly, though, I don't really want him to leave. I mean, my balls are empty, I'm fucked out, and my last orgasm actually hurt. We truly can't go again, so he should head out. What else am I going to do with him? I ought to get some breakfast in my gut and find some easier bouldering to do after my sleepless night. Training for the ascent. That's what I'm here for.

"Yeah, it was fun," Sejin says, but he sounds confused, like that's not all last night was for him.

Tilting my head, I take in his tall, lithe form. He's so gorgeous, like *dreamy* hot, with his beautiful skin and hair, his dark eyes, and his mouth all red from so much kissing. I wish I'd licked his pert nipples more before he'd gotten dressed. Now they're lost forever beneath his baggy t-shirt. What a shame. They're such a sweet size and a pretty brown color.

"You enjoyed it?" I ask because I need to make sure. Consent is something I'm big on. I'm not good at reading body language, so I try to always get it verbally when I can, but sometimes, during sex, things just go the way they go, and—

"Enjoyed it?" Sejin says with a strange laugh. It doesn't sound like the laughs that'd burbled out of him the night before when I stroked him in places that tickled, and it doesn't sound like the bells that made me shiver in delight when he first arrived. It's a hurt little laugh. I don't get it.

"Yeah, I enjoyed it." Sejin swallows and then shrugs, affecting a strange approximation of the smile I saw in his profile pic. The structure is the same—lips up, eyes going half-moon, but there's a certain *life* missing from it. "Best hookup I've ever had."

"Me too," I say honestly, because it certainly *was* the best hookup I've ever had. Best sex, period. Hands down. One for the record books. Or my journal, at any rate.

"Yeah?" His eyes take on a gleam that makes my tummy flutter.

"For sure."

"Yeah," he says again, nodding his head. "How long are you here?"

"Uh, until the end of October at a minimum," I say, and suddenly I think I know where this is going, and I'm just about to shut him down when *he really* smiles, and it's...

Oh.

It's still not like it was in the picture, but it's closer. And it's even more breathtaking in person. It's like when the sun breaks over a mountain, and I'm at the top watching it rise. *Jesus.*

"We could...if you wanted..." Sejin trails off, a hint of uncertainty tainting that gorgeous smile.

"We could do it again?"

Sejin nods, a lock falling from his ponytail to frame his face and those bow-shaped lips trembling a little, and I realize I forgot to get them around my cock last night. "If you want, I mean, if you're going to be around..."

"I don't usually do seconds."

"Oh." His shoulders drop, his eyes un-curve, and the smile vanishes. I hate that.

"But I'd fuck you again right now if my dick would cooperate."

Sejin's cheeks flush and he glances up with a smug expression. "I could fuck *you* if you wanted. I still have another round in me, I think."

I swallow hard. I'd forgotten Sejin had mentioned being vers. The idea of that long cock up my ass is fantastic, and I wonder what he's like when he's on top of a man. He lost control so beautifully on the bottom; how would he handle it when *I* came apart on his dick?

Would be cool to find out.

"Another day?" I suggest, standing up and pulling on my sweats too. "But, yeah, I'm in."

Sejin's sun-smile and moon-eyes make me feel dizzy, and he steps forward, taking hold of my chin to tilt my head up for a kiss. My knees go a little weak as he deepens it, and I remember how it felt to be buried inside his hot body last night while he'd kissed me desperately and moaned against my tongue.

He is a hot, hot, *hot* man, and his mouth is doing things to make my cock think it's ready to get hard again. But no, my balls ache, and if I want to climb today, I have to break this off now.

"Maybe this weekend," I say, pulling my mouth away from his. "We can meet again."

I can't do as much work on the weekends; the walls are crawling with tourists and the more casual climbers. They're both a pain to get around and a liability all rolled into one.

"I have to work in the mornings," Sejin offers. "But I'm free after that."

"Great." I put my hands on his shoulders and push him away. "See you then."

When I open the sliding door of the van, Sejin takes the hint and leaves with an awkward bend to exit. He doesn't feel that much taller than me when we're fucking—I guess because he's so lean—but when he kisses me, or now when he has to bend down to keep from knocking his head, I'm struck by his height. If he were broader, he'd make me feel small. As it is…

I don't know how to describe it, but I feel like we're well-matched physically. He might be taller, but I'm stronger, and he's so thin I can move him easily while we fuck.

I watch him go, admiring the way his ponytail swings in counterpoint with each step. I'm gripped by the fact that I still haven't seen him smile *exactly* the way he had in that picture. A certainty drops over me, a determination that should have alarm bells going off in my mind, and yet I tug it closer, a smug smirk stretching over my lips. It's like how I feel about Heart Route. I *will* make it happen. I will own that route, and it will be mine. And I don't know how, and I don't know when, but I *will* see Sejin's full-glory smile, and I'll see it while he's laughing, and it will be *all for me*.

The satisfaction that follows that thought is intense, like a calm, golden guarantee stamped over my heart and soul. Closing the door to the van and turning back to the messy bed, I wonder how I can get that smile from him during a hookup. I don't know, but I'm gonna figure it out. I'll see it before I make the Heart Route ascent.

Dead certain.

Sejin

I'D NEVER INTENDED to live with Martin, Leenie, and the kids for as long as I have. I'm just a little lost about how to proceed with my life from here. In my humble opinion, that's a perfectly normal way for a twenty-four-year-old to feel. Besides, their couch is as comfy as anywhere else I've stayed since I left my parents in West Virginia.

But you know what isn't comfy?

The sound of kids screaming at six in the morning when you've been out getting reamed like a wanton slut all night.

I groan as the screams draw closer, letting out a pained *oof* as a little body bounces onto my stomach. I peel my exhausted eyes open.

"Jeremiah, get off Sejin." Leenie sounds half-asleep and half-irritated—a typical morning mood for her—but also like she's not going to really *do* anything about her son bouncing on my belly. Probably because her hands are literally and figuratively full of Sarah Kate, who's as loud as a fire engine in full wail. Leenie's wavy, blond hair is mussed from bed, and she pads around the kitchen in just her pajama bottoms and a worn-looking concert t-shirt from an Avett Brothers tour. She's only two years older than me, but exhaustion paints her to look in her thirties. "I said *off*," she repeats with a tinge of warning.

"No," Jeremiah says cheerfully, curling up against my side and snuggling in tight. "Sejinie *loves* me."

Leenie huffs but leaves him and returns to pulling baby food out of cabinets and fastening the wailing Sarah Kate into her highchair.

Jeremiah rubs his little blond head against my chest. I typically don't mind his small body against mine, but after the long overdue satisfying of my sexual needs with a very hot stranger in his tricked-out van, I'd crept in as the sun crested the horizon and hadn't wanted to wake anyone by taking a shower. So I can't possibly smell nice.

"C'mon, buddy," I say, trying to extricate myself from his clinging hold. "I do love you, but I need to shower."

"Daddy's gotta go ta work. You hafta wait."

I haul myself up to sitting, dislodging him. Jeremiah doesn't seem to mind, though, at least not once Leenie opens the fridge and pulls out the jug of chocolate milk. That kid has a sweet tooth to rival my own.

I smooth my hair back and hoist it up into a ponytail with a band I find discarded on the floor. Hair ties are a choking hazard for Sarah Kate, so I need to be a lot more careful where I throw them when I take one off. But when I got in this morning, I'd been so fucked out I'd nearly fainted on my way to the couch. I don't even remember taking my hair down at all. The band probably fell out on its own.

Speaking of fucked out and exhausted, my legs quake when I stand up to snag the hallway bathroom to take a piss. I hear the water running from the bigger "master bath" off Leenie and Martin's bedroom, so I don't flush. I know from the last year of being dashed with ice-cold water every shower—because Jeremiah flushed a toilet, or Leenie started the washing machine—that their couch is comfy, but their plumbing is not. After all, the shoemaker's kids never have any shoes.

"Heard from Uncle Buck?" Leenie asks me when I return to the main rooms and seat myself at the counter between the living room and the kitchen area.

I rest my elbows on the cool laminate and watch her spoon green, soupy stuff into Sarah Kate's open baby-bird mouth as Jeremiah carefully prepares his own cereal with chubby, four-year-old hands. Leenie and I both watch with bated breath as he heaves up the half-liter of milk and shakily pours it into his bowl. This seems like a high-risk situation to me, and I don't know why Leenie's letting him do it, but she hasn't asked me to help so I keep my opinions to myself.

We both heave a sigh of relief when Jeremiah completes his task and puts the milk down with a little grunt.

"No," I say, when Leenie looks back my way, expecting some

kind of reply to her question about whether I've heard from my dad. "He doesn't talk to me much ever since…" I trail off. I don't want to say "since Mom died" because then I have to think about the fact that my mom is dead and I don't like to think about that. Especially not so early in the morning.

I'd rather think about the guy from last night, and how he'd railed me into next month, and the way he'd gripped my hips with such rough, calloused fingers, and—

"Sejin, you can't avoid him forever."

But the thing is… I can.

I can just *not* call Dad, and he won't call me, and we can both suffer our loss alone the way we prefer.

"I know. I'll call him soon."

Leenie raises her brow, but doesn't say anything else because Martin rushes into the room to kiss her cheek, kiss Sarah Kate's bald head, and run his fingers through Jeremiah's hair fondly. "Got any more of those granola-peanut butter thingies?" he asks, tearing open the cabinet where Leenie keeps stuff he can grab on the go. Because Martin is always on the go.

"Sejin, can you…" Leenie holds the spoon out to me, and I come around to take it from her. She wrinkles her nose when I get close and shudders.

"Good God, I don't even want to know," she mutters. "But shower as soon as I get Martin settled."

"Aye, aye, Cap'n." I sit down across from Sarah Kate and giggle at her little face. Her open mouth searches for the spoon eagerly. I fill it with more green goop and aim it into her wide gawp.

"You workin' both jobs today?" Martin asks me, scratching at his dark beard. His West Virginian accent rivals my own. His parents didn't move out to California until he was grown and Appalachian roots are hard to shake. "Paul says he could use you."

"I am, actually," I say, glancing at the clock. I could probably fit in some time with the plumbing company too, but I really hate getting down on my knees in other people's bathrooms. Since I'm working at the preschool in the late morning, and the coffee shop in the afternoon, I figure I have a good excuse to beg off. It's not like I'm being lazy, just not fully productive. But not taking advantage of every opportunity to earn a little cash always makes me feel guilty.

"S'okay," Martin says, glancing over. "Don't sweat it, man."

He gives me his reassuring smile, the one that's soothed my anxieties since we were kids. I've always looked up to him, especially back when he protected me from bullies who had something to say about the shape of my eyes or the color of my skin. Those jerks only ever said it once, though, because Martin "talked" to them with his fists. He's always had my back, and I know he always will.

I just hope I can move off his sofa before it starts to affect his marriage. Leenie's great, but having her husband's cousin crashed out on the couch for over a year can't be how she imagined her life would go when they moved into this little place just before Jeremiah was born.

But to move off their couch, I need a lot more savings, and the money-making opportunities in Mariposa are few and far between. Which is why I really ought to just move on entirely to somewhere that offers more job opportunities. It's what I've always planned to do anyway. But this place has me bewitched. I keep telling myself I'll go after one more month here, and then one more month, and now, somehow, I've slid through nearly two years already.

If I don't leave—and let's be real, I'm not going anywhere—I really should take Martin up on the plumbing work. Any money I can add to the shoebox of savings under the sofa will help me get a place of my own at least. How is Mariposa so friggin' expensive when no one really lives here at all? Just people passing through… And yet every apartment boasts a rent so far out of my league it makes my eyes water.

I tell myself there's no rush. Martin and Leenie's couch *is* comfortable, plus they get free babysitting out of me. I help with the dishes, the lawn, and the cleaning. I'm not an asshole roommate. Not me.

But still…

I really should get out of their hair soon. Any day now.

Leenie never complains. She takes my presence as easily as she takes everything else. Easy as pie, like my Grandma Helton used to say. I can still see her rocking in her La-Z-Boy chair, tinny gospel music playing from her old record player, explaining to me for the hundredth time how to crochet. "It's easy as pie, doll baby," she'd tell me. "Easy as pie."

I never got it right, though, so maybe that's not a good example.

But Leenie's never made me feel like she's in any kind of hurry for me to get out of here. That's all on me. I just know I should.

Martin and Leenie kiss goodbye. He pecks the kids' cheeks before sending me a salute. Then he's out the door, and I hand over the spoon to Leenie and hightail it to the shower to claim the next batch of hot water.

It pours down on me like a blessing.

As I wash, I briefly consider what Leenie said about calling my father. She's right that I *should* call him, but I'm right that I could just not, and we'd avoid another round of being awkward and sad together.

I hate awkward and sad.

After dismissing that train of thought, I tentatively feel my asshole. It's a little tender, and I smile remembering the way Dan took me at my word, fucking me like I was a rag doll in his hands. *Unnnfff.* So good. Dan hadn't seemed to think my height was any obstacle to manhandling my body into any position he wanted me. I'd felt breakable beneath him, like he could own me. Like he already did.

I shiver.

This weekend can't come soon enough. There's no way sex with Dan can possibly be as good the second time, but I'm willing to try. And it's embarrassing how relieved I am that Dan seems to want me again too. His "seconds" comment had sent my stomach swooping in disappointment and mortification, but when he'd immediately flipped and agreed to another encounter, I'd been dizzy with a renewed rush of excitement and lust.

Even if it's not as good as the first time, I'm certain there's still tons of fun to be had together. Things we haven't done yet. I haven't fucked *him*, for example, and I'm very much up for that. My dick, rising against the heat of the shower, agrees.

With my hand wrapped around the base of my cock, I admit the truth. Part of me—deep down, where some odd kernel of golden light has ignited—feels a kind of tugging sensation. It's hard to call it hope, but no other word comes to mind.

All I know is Dan—wow, I don't even know his last name—has beautiful eyes and powerful hands. I know the way I felt while he fucked me is different than any other hookup I've ever experienced. And I know the way he kisses after he's shot his load, all slow and hot and wet, is something I don't think I can ever get enough of…

And that's all I know. But I *suspect* so much more.

The seasonal tide is washing into Yosemite, bringing new fish into my figurative sea. Has it also brought me a seahorse? Only time will tell, but my heart whispers *yes*.

Dan

"OH HO HO, friend. You got *laid*," Rye says, laughing in that high-pitched way he hates. He's been working on vocal training to change the tonality of his voice with a lot of success, but his spontaneous laughter is something he's still wrangling.

"Yeah," I say, stepping toward our meeting point at the start of the approach.

"Look at that smile." He whistles. "Must have been a good night."

"It was."

The smile feels good on my lips. It's been a while since anyone or anything—aside from sending a fresh route—has made me feel this clear and pure inside. Like ice melt running through my body, all tickly and rushing. I can't stop thinking about Sejin, the sounds he made, the way he moved under me, and how his laugh had touched me like a physical thing.

There's a lot of untraversed ground to cover with Sejin's body, and somewhere on that ground must be the key, the one that'll open that special smile up for me. I want it, and I'm determined to get what I want. Just like I'm determined to free solo and send Heart Route.

So, if Sejin's game for another hookup or ten, then I'm game too.

I don't think other men have ever made him come the way he did last night. He'd seemed overwhelmed by it, taken by surprise. Just like me. I'm not usually big on surprises, but this one intrigues me and what harm can it do to work his body over again and again until we both get what we want? For him, that's orgasms that make him cry, obviously, and for me…

That smile. That particularly perfect smile.

"Anyone I know?" Rye asks.

I shrug. "Maybe. You know a lot of people."

"I do," Rye agrees. "I'm quite the slut these days." He chuckles, this time in the new, deep tone he's cultivating. "Between my sex work and hookups, my future memoir will need to be called 'Sex in Yosemite.'"

"Sex work, doesn't that make you a whore more than a slut?" I ask, hoping to get away from the inquisition about *my* sex life. Why talk about what I like to keep private if Rye's willing to talk about what he loves to share?

"I can be both." He grins proudly. "Why not? People are happy to pay for access to what I've got, and they'll pay me even more for the games I'm willing to play."

"Just keep it safe," I warn, never liking the idea of Rye's promiscuity as much as he does. He's small, lean, and light, and he tends to fuck guys twice his size, many of whom are into the fetishistic fantasy of screwing him more than they're into the reality of it. More than one encounter has ended with Rye bruised from their rough use. Cis men are assholes—I know because I'm a cis man— and I don't trust any of them not to hurt him.

"I just got free of all that bullshit," Rye proclaims. "Screwing as a gay man is a reve-fucking-lation, and I won't be going back into *any* kind of cage. Understood?" He chuckles again. "Cages are for my clients."

I huff a laugh, kicking off my approach shoes and putting on my rock shoes. "Clients are one thing. You're in charge with those. Randoms are another."

"Like you don't fuck randoms?"

I shrug. "Good point."

"Last night was a random hookup, wasn't it?"

"Yeah."

"Guy or girl?"

"Guy."

"Who was it? I wonder if I've had him."

I stop with my left rock shoe half on, a coldness washing over me. I cast my gaze up at the gray granite of El Cap as I ponder whether Rye and Sejin might have slept together before. I finish pulling on my shoe. The chances are good.

Unlike me, Rye resides in Mariposa all year and, as he's just been saying, while he's riding out this new testosterone-induced male puberty, he's *living* to get fucked in all three of his potential holes by whoever is interested. His business as a Dom has several regular clients and thrives on the kinky seasonal tourists who come and go. But he's told me many of his clients aren't even paying for penetrative sex. Sometimes they just want him to boss them around, or tell them to lick his feet, or order them to jerk off on the floor and then lick that up.

There's lots of licking involved in his work, from what he tells me.

Also, Rye craves *a lot* of sex. It's why he hooks up with random men all the time. After trawling that hideous app, I know for a fact there aren't that many options available for him here in Mariposa during the winter months, especially not with men who aren't awful, or assholes, or…

I swallow hard.

So, there's a strong chance, a very strong chance, he's had Sejin. Why does that bother me? It *shouldn't* bother me.

I shake out my arms and hands, trying to get the uncomfortable feeling in my chest to leave. Sejin and I have hooked up *once*. I don't even know anything about the guy outside of the sex. But that logic doesn't seem to matter.

I can even imagine them together. I can see how it would go—

Sejin on his knees as Rye fucks him with a dildo. Rye on his back as Sejin—he's vers, I remember—screws him to glory. Swallowing hard, I feel a little sick at the thought of Sejin being like that with Rye.

It's not jealousy, is it? It can't be.

For one thing, Rye and I haven't ever fucked. When we first

met, I sometimes wondered if he wanted to because he'd look me over with an expression that only made sense once I decided it was lust. But I'd always ignored it because a good belay partner is hard to find—especially for me—and I didn't want to ruin it by fucking him.

Luckily, as Rye got to know me better, those looks stopped. Now I don't think there's any amount of money he'd accept to have sex with me. At least, I hope not. Rye's great, cute, and fun, but he's my friend—no matter what Peggy Jo thinks—and I don't fuck friends.

So, I can't be jealous. One of the guys I don't even know, and the other is my friend.

The end.

If they've fucked… So be it. It's fine.

Except it isn't, and I really don't know why.

"What's wrong?" Rye asks. "Is there a problem?"

As always, he's attuned to me in ways I can't reliably reciprocate. I don't always know when *he's* upset, so why does he always see through me like this?

"I don't know," I say honestly. "His name's Sejin. Have you fucked him?"

Rye blinks at my bluntness, but he recovers quickly, accustomed to it for the most part. "Yeah, no."

My heart flip-flops so fast between the yeah and the no I feel dizzy. "Yeah, you've fucked him, or no, you haven't?"

"I haven't." Rye cocks his head. "Seems like you'd care if I had."

I shrug, relief running through me like cool water over a sunburn, shivery and right. "I don't know why I would."

But I did, and I do, and I'm *so glad* it's not an issue. "You don't know him then?"

"I didn't say that," Rye says with a smug grin. "I know him plenty well. He teaches Movement at Jeanie's nursery school."

Jeanie is Rye's daughter, though she lives with her dad these days, ever since Rye claimed his life as *Rye* instead of…well, the name he went by before. I don't remember it anymore, though I heard his mother call him by it once when we stopped by his folks' house after a climb to grab showers. I've never heard it since, and I don't care if I ever do again, given the way Rye's shoulders had slumped and his expression had fallen. I told him afterward he should never go back there if they don't respect him, and as far as I know, he hasn't.

Okay, maybe I *can* read him too, sometimes. I'm not a complete jerk after all.

"Movement?" I frown, trying to figure it out. "Like…baby PE?"

"It's more like baby dance," Rye says, laughing again. "It's so adorable."

He raises his brows, checking over his clips and hardware, making sure he's got what he needs for the climb. "And Sejin is adorable too. You should see him with the kids."

I think about the man I fucked. He'd been so open and enthusiastic about everything we'd done. A man so eager for joy is totally the kind of guy who'd teach dance to children. I bet he's cute with them. I feel the corners of my lips pull up with another irrepressible smile.

"Wow. He must be some fuck," Rye says, bewildered. He pulls the rope in smooth, clean loops around his shoulders, so it won't get tangled in our bags.

"Yes," I say again with another smile. "Yes, he is."

"You gonna see him again?"

I nod. "This weekend."

"Yeah? So soon?"

I shrug as an answer, then finish off my prep work and heft my bag up onto my back. "Ready to hike in?"

"Yup," Rye says. "Are *you* ready to put down a bet?"

"On what?"

The trees around us are beyond tall, and they sway in the wind with audible creaks and groans. The sandy earth beneath our feet lets off the reassuring smell of disintegrating leaves as we walk. I feel at home in a way I never do anywhere else.

"I bet you thirty bucks this weekend won't be the last time you see him."

I consider my memories of our night together and think of Sejin's naked body and all the things I haven't done with it yet. I remember the way he'd crooned like a wild thing as he surrendered to my cock, and think of that photo on the app, the smile in it that lights his face like a radiant, heart-stopping sunbeam. I remember the dimmed approximation of it I got to see last night and how beautiful it'd been too. "Nah, no bet."

"Why? You think I'll win?"

I shrug again. "I don't want to take your money. You need spending cash for your days with Jeanie."

Rye chirps another high-pitched laugh and then shifts it to a lower key. He elbows me lightly. "I see how it is. And speaking of Jeanie, I have her for a few hours this afternoon before Andrew gets back from Groveland. He had business there today. Wanna hang with the two of us?"

"You don't get a lot of time with her, do you?"

"No, but she thinks you're cool, and she'll be glad to see you."

I scoff. "Me? Cool?"

"I know. I don't get it either." Rye sticks his tongue out at me, and I laugh as we navigate the thicker vegetation and rocks that lead to the base of the wall.

"Okay, yeah. Let's grab some boba or something." I love boba with tapioca beads. The chewy texture is satisfying. "I saw they started selling it in the coffee shop."

"The coffee shop?" Rye asks, his eyebrow popping up. "That

where you met him?"

"Who?"

"Sejin."

"Oh, no. Hookup app."

"*Oh.*"

"You sound disappointed. Why?" I ask.

"Ha. I guess I am." Rye smirks. "I was hoping it was something more than a hookup for you guys."

"More than sex?" I blow a raspberry. "Why would anyone want more than sex?" Though I do. I want his *smile*.

"True. Casual sex is great," Rye agrees. "One of my favorite kinds. But *I'm* not lonely. *You* are. You need someone, Dan."

"Not this again." I roll my eyes. "I don't need anyone."

Rye looks me up and down. "If that's so true, why not make that bet? It's just thirty bucks."

"Nope." I think of Sejin's photo again and the smile he flashed me this morning. I don't make bets I'm sure to lose.

I gaze up at the granite wall of El Capitan ahead of us. It looms large. My gaze follows the lines of Heart Route. I take a slow breath and let it out.

I only make bets if I have a *chance* to win.

No matter how slim.

UP ON THE wall with Rye, the sky is blue above us, and the trees wave their green, bushy limbs down below. We get into an easy rhythm with Rye leading a pitch and me following him up, and then I lead a pitch and he follows behind.

"You sure this is the route you want to free solo?" he asks, gazing up at the wall ahead. "The roof over the Heart and that fucking dyno, man. That's…that's…" He stops just short of declaring it crazy.

I've heard it a million times before.

Well, I don't have enough people in my life for it to be even close to a million, but I've heard it a few dozen times at least.

"Yeah. This is the one."

I can't explain to him what it is about the route that's made me choose it. I've never been seduced into romantic feelings for any man or woman, but there have been climbing routes that've tugged me under their spell more than once. Heart Route, up the face of El Cap, has pulled me in like no other.

Just thinking about free soloing it this fall…my heart thrums, my skin feels electric, and my mind goes blank and calm in a pure, crystalline way that I crave more than anything else in life. That blankness has always been my goal. I love nothing more than when it descends on me while I'm climbing, and it's just me and glacial bliss stretching out forever. Glacial bliss on glacier-made walls.

No one else ever believes that blankness could be worth the risk of what happens if I make even the tiniest error while up there without ropes. But no one else really understands just how very little I have to lose either. Maybe that's the difference. They have so much on the ground calling to them, keeping them tethered. I have nothing meaningful down there. Everything of importance to me is up here.

Rye wipes sweat out of his eyes. "Sometimes I don't know why I'm helping you do this."

"Because you know I'd just rope solo it if you didn't."

"Or find someone else."

I nod.

"It's just… How will I live with myself if I've helped you prepare for this and then you—" He winces and the ropes shake from the force of it. "Look how far down it is, Dan. There's no living through a fall."

"You make it sound like that's the worst outcome possible."

"Isn't it?"

"For me, maybe, but not for you. You'll go on with your life. Jeanie will grow up. You'll have other friends who are a lot less troublesome than I am. It'll be fine."

"It really pisses me off when you say things like that."

"Why?" It's a mystery to me why he thinks he'd care so much if I kick it. I've seen it with my own eyes so many times in my life. People move on. They promise you're important to them, but then you just aren't. Not in the end anyway. The world keeps spinning.

Don't get me wrong. I'm not saying Rye won't care at all if I take a plunge off the wall, but he'll live. He's lived through worse, judging by the stories he's told me about his past, and I have too. All this drama around a little death. It's baffling really.

"You know why," Rye says, and takes off up the wall because it's his turn to lead the pitch.

There are a lot of things I don't know. I'm comfortable with a certain level of ignorance. And not knowing why Rye insists my death would be the worst thing ever is just another thing I'll never comprehend. It's fine.

I head up after him once he's linked into the next bolt.

"Here's the part where I'll have to be really wary," I say, running my hands over the smooth, slick, glacier-polished granite.

"Pfft." Rye kicks off it, swinging out into the air and bouncing off the rock again. "Yeah, this part is murder, but that dyno…"

"You and that dyno. It's not like I can't nail it."

"How? How can you ever be sure?"

"If I can do it a hundred times blindfolded without missing once, then I'll be sure."

"You can't climb this wall a hundred times this season."

Watch me, I almost say. But the truth is, I don't plan to and I shouldn't be defiant just to make a point. I plan to practice the dyno both up on the wall, like today, and off the wall at the climbing gym and at a low-to-the-ground boulder problem I've found with a similar dyno.

The dyno doesn't scare me as much as the roof of the Heart. That thing juts out and, even though I've found a place with a strong crack to climb, and I can do the crux in less than five moves, I'll still have to hang nearly upside down, gripping with just my fingers and toeholds, thrusting my hips up, fighting the weight of gravity on my back. It just gives me the heebie-jeebies. Way more than taking a short leap completely free of the wall, betting I can grab the hold across from me.

It's weird how some things scare a person, and some things don't.

I guess with the dyno, I figure if I don't make the jump, then I don't make the jump. But with the roof, I'll have a chance to really *know* before I go. I'll be hanging on, scrabbling, trying anything to keep from going down. That seems worse somehow.

Ugh, that roof makes me sweat just thinking about it. And yet…

"Your lead," Rye says, peering at me with his gray eyes that can twinkle like a sparkling sea or turn calm like the sky when it's flat and empty of clouds. Right now, though, his eyes are hard, a little anxious. I hate that. Climbing is supposed to be fun.

"Let's not stress about it," I say. "I'm not doing it any time soon. I have weeks of prep ahead. Months even. Maybe even years if I don't feel good about my chances." I chalk my fingers. "Look, I don't want to die. I want to live. I'm not, like, suicidal or anything. So, I'm taking this seriously. I want to have every move mapped out. Sequenced. Like choreography. I want to know I can nail it—"

"You can't know anything. It could rain—"

"There are satellite apps to watch the weather."

"It could still rain. Meteorology is barely a science."

"Hey now, be careful, you sound like me."

"Look what you've driven me to!" Rye smiles, though, and takes a swig of water from his backpack. "I'll stop. I know I can't talk you out of this. It's why I'm helping you. I guess, if you go down, I'd rather know I did my best to help you prepare than to think you did it all alone, without anyone on your side."

"You and Peggy Jo make me out to be friendless. I've got friends."

"Mm-hmm, and where are they today?"

"Busy."

"Whatever. You pulled me into this, and now I can't opt out. I can't un-know your plans."

"You could un-care about me."

Rye lifts a fist and mimes a punch. "I will pop you for real one day, I swear."

Rye will never pop me. I know that. Which is good because I've been at the receiving end of my fair share of fists. I'm not sure how I'd react to another one.

"Dan, could you just 'un-care' about me?" Rye asks impatiently.

I ponder the question, and that alone makes Rye huff. "Go," Rye commands. "Get on up the pitch."

See? This is why Peggy Jo is the only one who can stand me for very long, and why I might have a few friends, but most aren't very close. I'm apparently an asshole, and I don't know how to fix that.

CHAPTER FOUR

Sejin

"JEANIE, THAT'S PERFECT," I say as I watch over my herd of preschool dancers, twirling in the sparkling sunlight. I don't really have any qualifications for this job, but I do have a lot of self-confidence and zero fear of being told no.

Which explains how I marched into Tater Tots Preschool six months ago armed with my recently-issued ECE Associate Teacher license and said, "Do you have anyone teaching the kids Movement? Because if not, I'm your man."

Heather Tate, the owner-director of the preschool, had looked me up and down and said, "You're Martin Sutley's adopted brother, right?"

"Cousin. But, yes, I'm Sejin Sutley."

"Right." She'd given me another long once-over, and then asked, "What did you have in mind?"

I had my phone on me, and I'd cued up some of my favorite songs with easy or cute choreo. I showed her the dances. Most of them were from girl groups, so they were maybe a little feminine, but she didn't even blink at that.

"What language are they singing in?" she asked instead.

"Korean," I answered. "It's KPop."

"Whatever it is, the dances are cute. The kids will have fun, and if you can teach them a little Korean in the mix... *You're* Korean I take it?"

"Kinda? Like in one way yeah, but in most ways no?" I could see I was losing her. "But yeah, sure."

"Well, if you teach them some Korean along with the dances, I think I can sell it to the parents as a real value-added thing. So how about one dollar per kid per class?"

I'd swallowed, gathered my self-esteem, and asked for what I thought I was worth. Admittedly, it wasn't that much. "Five?"

"Three," she'd said, and turned her attention back to the papers on her desk, something very important and 'director-y' I was sure.

"Three it is."

So here I am, six months later, with a small squad of dancers singing along to "Fancy" by Korea's top girl group, Twice, while nearly nailing the choreo with their chubby little limbs. Well, kinda. Okay, not at all, but it's so cute I can't stand it, and I tell them they're nailing it even when they aren't.

And Jeanie Erickson is one of the cutest. Her rosy cheeks, shiny eyes, and thick, red curls just kill me. Holland, Griffin, and Tanner all knock my socks off with their enthusiasm too. And Natalie just rocks period with her powerful singing voice. She's memorized most of the words, even the Korean ones, and she's a real dynamo with her stage presence.

Jude, though, bless his heart, is just gonna have to accept that he has no rhythm in his soul. But I won't be the one to tell him. No sirree. No way.

"Mr. Sejin," Lila calls, panting as the song ends and I'm preparing to launch them into BTS's "Dynamite," which also has some very fun disco-themed choreo, plus Michael Jackson-inspired moves the kids love. "Gotta go pee!"

"Ahh!" I cry, pointing toward the door back inside. "Go find Miss Heather if you need help!"

She darts in, and I feel a little guilty starting up "Dynamite" without her since I know she loves it, but the day will end soon.

Today my Movement class is last on their schedule and designed to wear them out just in time for their parents to take them home, feed them, and then let them wind down for the rest of the afternoon.

"Ready?" I ask.

All ten shout back, "Yes!"

We've almost finished shining through the city with all our funk and soul when the first car pulls up. It's Jeanie's dad...er, mom, but dad? Jeanie still calls Rye by the term "Mommy," and it's a little confusing to me, even if it isn't to them, because I feel weird calling Rye by that title, but I can't exactly say, "Jeanie, your dad's here" because that's the other male parent in her family.

That's life, I guess. Hardly ever as tidy as we hope.

We finish out the dance, and I clear my throat. "Uh, Jeanie..." I just nod at the car.

She turns to look, grins, and shouts "Mommy!" as the driver's side door swings open. Then she shouts again as the passenger door pops open too. "Dan!"

She starts to run toward them, but I grab her up before she can get into the driveway area where other cars are already pulling in.

"Now, now," I gently scold. "You know you're supposed to wait."

My throat closes around the last words as my eyes lock with those of Rye's passenger. My heart kicks hard. It's not just any Dan coming to claim Jeanie with Rye today. No, it's my Dan.

My Dan? Ha! As if.

I mean, the Dan I slept with last night. The guy who screwed me so hard I can still feel it in my hamstrings and calves, and his passion still shows in the bruises that've come up on my hips, which I discovered in the bathroom earlier in the day.

"Hey," I say, dropping Jeanie so she can run to her parent.

Dan nods his head sharply.

I suddenly feel awkward in my sleeveless shirt, cut-off shorts, and sandals, and I don't know why. I wish I looked more put together. Sexier or something. It's not as if Dan looks like anything special in his nylon sports pants and chalk-dusted t-shirt, though, so I don't know who I want to impress.

Rye is busy kissing Jeanie's chubby cheeks, but then he glances up and says, "Sejin, I understand you know Dan?"

I cough, surprised Dan told Rye about hooking up with me, but I suppose I hadn't asked him to keep anything a secret, so it's fair game.

Dan's ears go a livid pink, and his cheeks flush with heat. He stares at me like he's daring me to call him out on his embarrassment.

Lucky for him, I won't do it. Mainly because there are children around, but also because his gaze is so piercing it's making me feel lightheaded. He's a little dorky-looking in some ways, I've noted, but he's also just…wow, smoking hot.

"We've met," is all I offer up, and Dan's Adam's apple bobs up and down once.

"Mr. Sejin?" Jeanie says, squirming out of Rye's arms and turning to me. "Can we show Mommy and Dan my favorite dance?"

I glance toward the other cars pulling up and figure any parent who doesn't want to see their kid dance to KPop songs is a sad human being. "Sure. Remind me which is your favorite."

She pops into the opening moves, crying out the first line of the song, which is in English.

"Right," I say, pulling up the song "Idol" by BTS. It's one of my favorites to teach the kids because they scream the lyrics of the chorus at the top of their voices every time. Listening to three-to five-year-olds yell about how no one can stop them from loving themselves is *pure joy*.

Everyone gets back into position and as soon as the music exits the speakers, the kids start moving, wriggling, twisting out their approximation of the complicated choreo. Obviously, I've toned it down for them quite a lot because it's not like I can actually do it myself. But I do like to make them exercise their bodies so I keep some of the more complex moves in too. They work hard for it and basically fail, but they all look adorable trying.

Out of the corner of my eye, I watch Dan watching the kids. The pink in his skin dies down, and I look for any sign that he doesn't like children. To me, fair or not, I have a rule—good to kids and good to animals? Good to me. And that's always been the case in my experience. Anyone who's shitty to kids or animals always ends up being shitty to me too. Like my toxic ex who was an asshole to his best friend's dog.

On her deathbed, my mom told me to find someone who loved me as much as she did and for me to never put up with my ex's brand of bullshit again. I'd made the promise, and I intend to keep it.

Not that I'm gonna fall in love with Dan or him with me.

It's just I don't have time for bad people in my life, period.

I don't really see any negative reaction in him, but I don't see a truly positive one either. Not until the chorus hits anyway, and then his lips pull into a smile, he chuckles softly, and his eyes grow fond.

All right. All *right*.

I can hook up with him again then without much worry now. I mean, I should have known he was okay with kids by the way Jeanie greeted him so enthusiastically, but you never know.

Maybe I should test him with a dog too, though? Just to be sure.

I cough lightly into my hand. What is *wrong* with me? I'm getting way, way, *way* ahead of myself. But why would Dan tell Rye about me unless he was thinking of the future too? I mean, there *has* to be something there, right?

Yeah, that I'm a good fuck.

That's about it. What else can he say about me? We don't know each other from Adam. I'm really getting loopy out here in the "wilderness" without a man to suck my dick regularly. One stellar orgasm—okay, four—and I'm practically buying wedding bands in my imagination.

Get a grip, Sejin! He lives in a van, for fuck's sake. There is no long-term potential here.

The kids finish out their song, and by the time they do, they're sweaty, pink-cheeked, and grinning. We're surrounded by applauding parents on all sides. Lila has returned, holding Heather's hand, and she stares sullenly at the other kids instead of clapping for them. I'm not surprised. Lila also loves this song and she missed it. Bodily functions! Always getting in the way of fun.

I'm inundated with moms and a few dads wanting to tell me stories about their kids dancing to the songs at home, or singing them in restaurants, or what have you. Taking out my ponytail, I shake my hair. The weight off my head feels amazing and the tickle of hair on my shoulders feels cool and soothing on my hot skin. I can feel Dan's eyes on me, and when I glance over, he's licking his lips. I laugh at something little Marshall Miller is telling his mom although I'm not even sure what it is. I'm so busy putting on a show for Dan's benefit of being the best preschool Movement teacher *ever* that it goes right over my head. But my reaction must be appropriate because everyone else laughs too.

I feel a rush of effervescent giddiness as I interact with the kids and their parents, and I hope that Dan finds me dazzling. I don't know why I suddenly feel like every move I make is exaggerated and enlivened by his attention, but I do. I continue on like this for four, five, maybe even eight minutes, until I finally dare to glance back to where he's been standing in order to gauge his reaction to me.

Only to find he's gone.

Yup, Jeanie, Rye, and Dan have all left the party, and I'm here being adorable for parents who already think I'm cute.

The let-down is accompanied by a rush of heat to my cheeks. I'm a fool. A silly, ridiculous, recently-fucked fool. At least I'm the only one who knows it, though. I can be an idiot inside my own head all I want. I just don't want to be an idiot outside my head. Much.

I suppose calling myself a Movement teacher and then helping preschoolers learn KPop choreo is pretty silly-looking to most outsiders, but it makes me happy and happiness is what matters most. Or so my mother told me near the end.

Why do I keep thinking of her today?

I try to keep my smile as light, twinkling, and charming as possible before I beg off from any more chatting with the moms and the sole dad who have stuck around. I have my next job to get to, and Pete will dock my pay if I'm late. Or at least threaten to...

Pete and Celli are working together behind the counter when I arrive at the coffee shop. I hustle in and check the schedule. Gage is off today so Celli is probably bummed. But, hey, Ashley will be coming in when Pete takes off around dinner time, and she always makes me laugh with her snarky observations of our patrons and I can't complain about that.

I head into the back room to quickly change into my work uniform—a turquoise blue t-shirt with *Papa Bear* in handwritten font on the front, alongside a drawing of a roaring bear over my right pec—and I make sure my hair is tied back tight. Then I hustle out to the front to ask Pete where I should start.

"Bus the tables," he says, nodding toward the café's lightly occupied sitting area. "It's been a busy day, and we've had no time."

"Aye, aye," I say, saluting him, and he rolls his eyes at me.

There are five booths along one side of the half-wall hiding the occupants from my sight. Next to them are ten scattered tables with a magnificent view of the mountains out the wide window behind them. Outside stand five wooden picnic tables and some round, metal ones too, with built-in metal chairs. But those often get so hot in the midday sun that we have to put out signs warning the customers to grab a pillow from the stack in a container by the door before sitting down at them.

I happily bus the cluttered tables. Ashley hates touching the used plates, glasses, and cutlery, but I don't mind too much, and it gives my brain time to wander without having to deal with customer demands. It also feels good to have "made something right" whenever I wipe down a table and leave it ready for our next customer.

As I finish in the main room, I turn the corner of the half-wall to work on the booths, and I stop in my tracks. My mouth goes dry. My heart kicks again.

Given the expression on Dan's face, he isn't expecting to see me so soon either. Rye, for his part, just smirks and goes back to helping Jeanie. She's tucked into the booth with her raggedy sheep stuffy, a coloring book, and a boba drink.

I crack a smile. "Are you following me?" I tease.

"No." Dan frowns, eyes wide, seeming a little affronted.

"I was kidding."

"Oh." Dan relaxes and then mumbles something I can't hear before sucking hard at his boba and chewing on the black tapioca beads.

I stand frozen for a second, confused, until Jeanie looks up, smiles happily, and breaks the silence.

"Dan is friends with Mommy," she says by way of explanation. To whom, I'm not sure. Herself? Me? All of us? Probably all of us. "Mr. Sejin is friends with *me*. We can all be friends together."

"Of course," I reply, stepping closer.

Why am I drawn in when this feels so awkward and uncomfortable? Why don't I just skedaddle? It was *one* fuck. Three. Four.

Whatever. A true count depends on the definition of "fuck," and I really don't need to be standing here figuring that out because it doesn't really matter.

Oh, my God, Sejin, please get it together.

I find myself saying, "We're all friends."

Dan's brows jump oddly, but he just keeps chewing.

Rye rolls his eyes at Dan and sighs. "I should have warned you, I guess."

Dan swallows. "That he works here? Yeah. That would've been nice."

"Trying to avoid me?" I cock my head. "Funny way of showing it. Turning up at both my places of business in one day."

"I'm not avoiding you," Dan says, his big eyes making him look incredibly earnest. "I'm surprised. That's all. I wanted to see you again."

He frowns and looks baffled by his own words. "But I don't..." He shakes his head. "You know. I don't... Do *that* with friends."

Rye and I bark with laughter at the same time.

"Excuse me," I say. "Is this your way of saying you don't want to be my friend?"

"If I'm your friend then we can't meet again this weekend, and I was looking forward to that."

Jeanie looks up from her drawing again, confusion in her eyes. "Being friends is good, Dan. Be friends with Sejin. Please."

"I can't," Dan says firmly. "Not if I want to be something else with Sejin."

"Something else?"

Dan nods.

"Like what?"

Rye gives Dan a sharp glance. "Yeah, like what, Dan?"

"Like climbing partners?" Jeanie asks with a sudden knowing. "You're Mommy's climbing partner. Do you want to be Sejin's climbing partner instead of friends?"

"Sure," Rye chimes in. "That's what he means, honey."

"Do you climb?" Dan asks me suddenly.

I've been up on a rock wall, but I don't love it. I'm not so great with heights. I've mainly done low-level bouldering because big walls are definitely not my speed. But why is he going on about how we can't be friends? What kind of asshole doesn't want to be friends with guys he sleeps with? What if little Jeanie is actually a *bad* judge of character? I already know Rye can be—look at his ex!

I wish for a customer to enter the shop right now with an overly friendly dog so I can see how Dan reacts to it. More than half the time, we have multiple animals in the place, but not today. Of course.

"I've been a few times," I say.

"Hm."

But that's all he gives me. He goes back to his boba, and I'm left hanging there like a fool.

Rye shoots me a wide-eyed look that communicates his own vague irritation at Dan's rudeness. But it's not his fault that the guy I hooked up with is so…whatever this is.

I shrug. "Well, yeah. Okay, see you around, Rye. See you for Movement tomorrow, Jeanie." I look at Dan who gazes back at me over his boba. "These tables won't bus themselves."

"We're still on for this weekend, right?" Dan asks as I turn away.

I stop and consider. Are we? This has been a painfully uncomfortable conversation. Will it be like this every time I see him outside of having sex?

Probably.

My heart sinks, but then I stiffen my back.

So, what if it is? Weirdness is a foregone conclusion now. He'll either avoid the coffee shop after this, or he won't. If he doesn't, then it's clearly going to be uncomfortable, and if he does, then fine. But none of that means he and I don't have great chemistry in bed. If we can fuck again like we did last night? Then I guess it's worth the awkwardness later. It's not breaking my promise to my mom if we're just fucking, right?

Because… damn, it was good.

Like really, *really* good.

I turn back to him and smile tentatively. He frowns like he's not satisfied by something about me or this interaction, but I don't know what or why since *he's* the one who's made it weird. "Yeah, sure."

Rye whistles under his breath. "Must've been out of this world then, because shit."

"Mommy, shit is a bad word," Jeanie pipes up.

"Oh, your father can bite me." Rye takes a slow breath and adds, "Thanks for telling me, Jeanie, but Mommy can say whatever he wants, alright?"

"Alright."

"Friday?" Dan says. "Or do you work?"

"I do, but I can come over after."

"Yeah. Do that. I'll be waiting."

I go back to bussing tables with my heart pounding so hard I feel dizzy. What is it about that weirdo that makes me feel like my soul is leaving my body? I don't know.

But no way is he a seahorse. No damn way.

CHAPTER FIVE

Dan

"Y OU BLEW IT back there," Rye says as soon as his ex, Andrew, pulled out of the Papa Bear parking lot with Jeanie in the back of his Subaru.

There'd been sticky, little kid kisses back and forth as Rye and Jeanie said goodbye, and Rye had teared up knowing he wouldn't see Jeanie again until Andrew needed childcare out of him. But today's separation hadn't been nearly as heart-wrenching as when Rye first lost custody to Andrew and was forced to make peace with not seeing his baby every day.

I was there that first week, helping Rye set up his semi-permanent site at Upper Pines Campground. It isn't that Rye disagrees with the court that a tent isn't a suitable home for a small child, but the fact that Andrew insisted on making his full custody *legal and permanent*, instead of just working with Rye until he could get back on his feet again, had been a betrayal of the worst sort. And, of course, Rye's family refused to help him keep Jeanie, saying it was exactly what they'd warned him would happen when he decided to transition.

I know how much it sucks to be alone in the world without any people to call your own or have your back. It's been sad to see the far-reaching effects of Rye's family's transphobia after he came out to them. Even his grandparents have abandoned him although he'd been their favorite grandchild before.

"Did you hear me?" Rye asks. "You blew it."

"Blew what?"

"Blew *it!* With Sejin!"

I grimace, shaking my head. "There's nothing to blow but his dick, and I'll do that this weekend. He's already agreed to it."

Rye crosses his arms over his chest, a frown on his face. "You are so short-sighted."

I frown too. This is bordering on a topic of conversation which Rye has already made clear upsets him—my plans to free solo Heart Route and what that means for my possible life expectancy. Why be long-sighted until I see if there's going to be a future to see into? It really is as simple as that.

"I live for the moment."

Rye quirks a brow. "Oh? Do you? Then what's with these dumb rules?"

"Like what?"

"Like 'I don't sleep with friends.' If you're really living for the moment, then shouldn't you be enjoying every last one of them as much as possible? And if you like someone—and you could like Sejin, he's *very* likable—then you should allow yourself to enjoy those people in as many ways as possible, right? To maximize the moment."

I contemplate that. It's not like he's wrong. It's just that it feels a little dangerous for him to be right. But danger isn't something I necessarily lean away from, if that isn't clear by now. Especially not when someone else shoves a challenge in my face and basically dares me to do it.

"Double-dog dare" is a taunt that got me into a ton of trouble in my foster homes as a kid.

Apparently, it's still a call I can't resist because Rye's comments, along with his pointed tone, are making me feel like I need to either defend my cowardice in this regard or rise to the challenge. One or the other.

I decide to try a defense first, though, just to see how it sounds. Because the idea of fucking someone I actually know and care about scares me. Maybe just as much as free soloing Heart Route scares me. Which is, of course, a kind of fear I like a little too much.

"It's dangerous to care like that about men I have sex with. Or women," I tack on, though they are few and far between. "It's a distraction from the pleasure, a distraction from my goals both in bed and out." Deciding to bring back that early conversation about the dangers of my free soloing plan, I go on, "I think we can both agree the last thing I need is a distraction of any kind."

Rye chooses to play dumb. "What's distracting about it?"

I snort. "That's pretty obvious."

"No, it's not. Spell it out."

I can tell Rye knows exactly why caring about someone I fuck is a distraction, and he's just making me say it. Why, I'm not sure yet, but *fine*. I'll spell it out like he's asked. "I don't need any more attachments to the ground when I'm free soloing up a wall. Fucking someone I like enough to call a friend could become a slippery slope to…"

I swallow, feeling sick.

"Something deeper." I put my hand over my heart like I'm trying to block any sort of wily, human attachment from hooking into me there. "The last thing I need is to get up there and feel held back by someone waiting down here for me."

"What if that's exactly what you need?" Rye insists. "What if you get up there and instead of doing something stupid, you play it safe because there's someone you care about, and you want to get back down to them?"

"I'm always considering safety when I'm on the wall."

Rye huffs. "Look, jackass, there are so many good things that come out of having friends, and if you insist that free soloing Heart

Route is your ultimate goal in life, then we have to accept there's a decent probability you'll die going for it. So, before you go out, don't you owe it to yourself to truly enjoy all the time you have left by spending it with people who make you feel good?"

"He can make me feel good without being friends with me. He already did."

Rye eyes me for a long moment. "Mm, okay, well…" He shrugs. "I can see there's no reasoning with you. As usual."

"I'm an incredibly reasonable person, and what you're talking about just isn't logical or judicious. What you're talking about is all feelings and emotions. Those get you killed when you're free soloing."

"Or they protect you. They can tell you 'No, this isn't worth it,' or 'This is too scary,' or 'This doesn't *feel* right.' Feelings and emotions can save your life, Dan."

I think about that and reluctantly agree. "I don't see why that means I have to be friends with a guy I fuck."

"Oh, for Christ's sake," Rye says. "Forget I brought it up."

"I will."

"Fine."

"It's forgotten."

"Liar."

I am a liar, because that mocking call of double-dog dare is in the back of my mind, as is my still unfulfilled desire to see Sejin's real, genuine, happiest of smiles directed at *me*. And despite telling myself enough orgasms will earn it for me, I'm not actually sure of that. The photo was taken outside, wading in a creek, and there's no indication that sex was in any way involved in the photographer capturing that look.

For whatever reason, I really don't want to die on Heart Route without having seen that smile. Just once.

Or twice.

Or a million times.

Fuck. See? Emotions really are dangerous, and I haven't even tried being friends with the guy yet.

Yet?

Oh, Rye, you asshole. What have you done?

CHAPTER SIX

Sejin

"DON'T WAIT UP for me," I say, kissing Sarah Kate's fuzzy head and handing her down to Leenie where she's sitting on the floor helping Jeremiah with some Legos. When I scrub my hand lightly through Jeremiah's hair, I'm met with a sweet smile that makes my heart squeeze fondly.

"Oh?" Leenie asks, looking tired.

Martin's still out, having picked up a hauling job at a plumbing client's house earlier in the day. The guy has a bunch of logs he wants moved from one end of his property to the other, and Martin has the brawn and the truck to make that happen. So, Leenie is still alone with the kids, though it's well after dinner. I feel guilty leaving her with them. I'm sure she could use a break.

But I've been working all day too, first at the preschool and then the coffee shop. The season has really started now, so the place is bustling.

Plus, I'm going to get laid. So…

Sorry, Leenie! Happy parenting!

"Yeah. I'm meeting with a…" I hesitate. Dan made it quite clear at the coffee shop the other day that he's not a friend, but I'm also not going to call it what it is in front of Jeremiah. "A friend."

"You have a friend?" Jeremiah asks.

"I have lots of friends, buddy."

"Don't you just," Leenie says casually, and I snort.

If she only knew the "friends" I'd made as I travelled across the country from West Virginia, crashing on hookups' and even strangers' couches—or in their beds—until I could scavenge enough money to continue on my journey here. There were even a few guys I let pay me for, well, things we did together because I needed the cash and they wanted to give it to me. But who cares? Here I am now in Mariposa, and I'm sure Leenie loves having me on her sofa.

Ha.

"I might be in really late or even not until morning," I warn her.

"Have fun," Leenie says, wiping snot from Sarah Kate's nose and checking the time on her phone. "Martin should be home soon. Don't worry about us."

"Alright." I bend to kiss her forehead. She looks up, surprised. "Thanks for letting me stay here so long, Leenie. I promise I'll get out of your hair as soon as I can save a little money."

She grabs my hand and kisses the knuckles. "You're fine. Go have fun tonight."

I accept that response and as I'm driving toward the campground where Dan is staying in his van, I think about the journey that's brought me here. The tug of adventure. The need to escape. The sense that no matter how much I love West Virginia, and love my family, it isn't really *mine*. Those enthusiastic phone calls from Martin, who'd made his way here four years prior after a stint in a trade school in Albuquerque and marrying Leenie there. He'd lured me in, convincing me to come out and join him. Then came my mom's death…

Nope. Nope, nope, nope.

I'm about to get laid. I am not thinking about her, or *that*, or the fact that it's been five weeks since I last called my dad. We've texted, but he's worse than Martin when it comes to texts that hold any meaningful content. Our last interaction essentially went—

Hey, Dad, I miss you. How are you?

Fine. You?

Good. Doing great.

Great.

That had been it. I could have tried harder, but it's like pulling teeth. Phone calls aren't much better. Face-to-face, we do okay. I can read his body language, and he can read mine. It's the distance that's killing our relationship, and maybe the grief. And maybe the fact that I left at all. I don't really know how he feels about that. I don't really know how he feels about anything.

But I need to stop thinking about him now because I'm turning into the campground. The lights are on in Dan's van and I wonder what it's like to live in it. Is it really that different from living on someone else's couch? At least he has space to call his own. I'm still packing my clothes in and out of a duffle bag that gets shoved behind the curtains in the living room when I'm out of the house.

I sniff my armpits, suddenly worrying I forgot deodorant after my shower. I'd been too focused on making sure I had time for a fast douche of my ass in hopes of getting fucked again. I'm definitely interested in topping too, but maybe tonight we can take turns. We haven't made specific plans about what we're going to do together, and visions of various options for physical pleasure stretch out in front of me like an ocean of delightful potentialities.

My dick grows thicker, and my heart thumps rapidly. Dizziness floods me as the door to the van slides back to reveal Dan, shirtless in just his boxer-briefs and nothing else. Fuck, yes. He wastes no time, and I'm all right with that.

I get out of my car, locking it behind me in a daze, and start toward him.

His muscles are unreal. Each one is long, sinewy, and striking, and they stand out with every movement he makes. I actually choke on my own spit at the sight of his six-pack and the muscles encasing his ribs. Holy beautiful body, Batman. Holy bruised and scraped-up face, and arm, and hip and…

"What happened to you?" I ask, stopping mid-step into the van. "You look like you were dragged around the parking lot."

Dan winces and rubs his purple-red jaw. "Took a rough fall."

"Climbing?"

He nods.

"How?"

"Things happen."

"I…wow. You look like hell." I circle him in the tight space of the van, trying to see all the various injuries. "Have you put Bactine on this?" I ask, sliding a finger on the feverish skin next to one of the bigger scrapes on his thigh. "Have you put anything on any of it?"

"I poured some alcohol on earlier. It's fine."

"Do you have a first aid kit?"

Dan stares at me, his hazel eyes seeming to glow in the low light, and I can't figure out what he's thinking. Maybe I'm being too intrusive. Maybe he doesn't want me here after all. Maybe I should just offer to suck him off and go…

"It's here," Dan says, turning to a cupboard and quickly undoing the locks that keep the doors from swinging open when the van is in motion. He tugs a medium-sized plastic toolbox out of the way, and then grabs a slightly bigger white box with a red cross on it. Popping it open, inside is an entire drugstore's worth of first aid supplies. He removes iodine, Bactine spray, and a few bandages, both the stick-on kind and wrap.

Taking it all over to the bed, he sits down with a little wince, and then meets my gaze again, but this time with a quirked brow. "Wanna play doctor?"

I huff a laugh, close the van door behind me, and turn back to him. "If you're down for that, sure."

"I might not be able to go quite as hard tonight, not like I did last time, but I can still eat your ass and suck you off."

I lick my lips. "Why, Mr..." I stop. "What's your last name?"

"McBride."

"Ah, Mr. McBride, that's a very dirty thing to say to your doctor."

His smile is sharper than expected, but it cuts into me. It's pleasure, and hurt, and desire all at once. Huh. Pretty weird reaction to some random hookup's smile, but what can I say? This Dan guy does it for me. In every fucking way. What that means about my taste in men, I don't know, but it can't be good.

I'm probably going to break my promise to my mama. I mean, he lives in a van for fuck's sake. He doesn't want to be friends for even fuckier sake. But...his smile, and his body, and those eyes...

Unf.

I play around at being his doctor and given how hard his dick is by the time I've dabbed, sprayed, bandaged, and wrapped his various injuries, all while trailing my fingers up and down his skin, and occasionally licking and biting his nipples, I think he enjoys my doctoring skills very much.

"Want to get rid of these?" I whisper, tugging on the waistband of his underwear. "Because I really think I should inspect your dick. Make sure it's all right. It seems in distress..." I rub my thumb against the material stretched over the head of his cock, enjoying the wet patch that soaks through. His tanned skin is flushed, his breathing rapid, and his nipples tight. My head spins that he wants me this much.

"Yeah," he says. "Get rid of them."

I work them carefully over his injuries and throw them to the floor. He groans and reaches toward me as I bend for a kiss. Just like last time, I'm blown away by how fast the kiss escalates from our lips barely touching to wet, deep, and hard. I feel like I'm going to die if he pulls away, but I also want to get my own clothes off.

My cock aches against my now too-tight jeans.

Dan breaks off to whisper, "Take your hair down."

I oblige, and the dark tumble seems to mesmerize him. He reaches up to thread his fingers into it before pulling me in for another kiss. He's completely in control, even though I'm the one still dressed, still half-standing, and ostensibly the "doctor" in our game. But he's got hold of my hair, and he might as well have hold of my balls because I'm at his mercy. He guides me through the kiss, altering the angles with tugs against my head and groans into my mouth.

I'm startled by how much I like it. Because, while I enjoy some good hair-pulling, I don't typically like being at someone else's command, and yet nothing about this feels demeaning or like Dan is using me. More like Dan knows what I want better than I do, and he's giving it to me.

"Suck me," he whispers.

"Now?" I ask, dazed. My lips ache from the intensity of our kisses, and my cock is throbbing. I want to get my pants off and get naked so we can rub skin to skin, and he can eat my ass like he suggested earlier…

"Now," he says, using his hands in my hair to push me down toward his cock. It's a gentle push, more of an urgent suggestion, and I don't fight it because a wet burst of cum against my tongue suddenly seems necessary and right. Dan's good at this sex thing. He might be horrible at making small talk when taken by surprise in a coffee shop, but the man knows how to make everything about sex seem like an imperative for life, and that's a beautiful thing.

His cock fits well in my mouth, though from this angle, the slight curve makes it hard to deepthroat. It doesn't seem like he minds, though, given how he groans and tightens all over. His balls draw up before I've done more than swallow a few times around the head and get his shaft fully wet.

"Fuck," he whispers. "I'm gonna come pretty fast. But that's good, Doc, because then I'll be ready to eat that ass for hours."

Hours? Is he serious? I really don't know. I wouldn't be surprised, though, because he *had* made an art form of eating my ass during our first hookup, and I haven't forgotten that for more than a few minutes at a time ever since. I mean… the way he'd used his tongue? And moaned? And acted like my ass was his favorite dessert in the world?

I might come in my pants just remembering it. I focus on sucking his cock again, pleased at the way he's shoving against my tongue, leaking jizz into my throat, and fuck, *fuck*… I reach down to squeeze my balls and try to hold on to my own orgasm. It's a close thing, but I manage it.

Dan releases my hair, whimpering as it cascades all around his hips and thighs. "Fucking hell," he murmurs. "Doc, your hair is its own sex toy."

I have more control now, so I wrap my hand around the base of his cock and start sucking. My hair swirls and moves around his thighs, stomach, and hips as I twist my head and work his dick in and out, around and around, letting saliva wet his balls as I do.

"That's…that's…I'm coming," he says softly, almost a whimper, and then he's exploding in my mouth, a heavy, salty load that I almost choke on, but manage to swallow. His hips twitch and work even after I've released his dick, and he jerks over and over as aftershocks rock him.

As soon as he recovers, he tugs me up to his mouth for a kiss, and then breathes against my aching lips, "Get your clothes off. I want to taste that ass."

I don't hesitate.

Within moments, I'm naked on my back, hands cupped behind my knees to hold them open and wide, and Dan is examining my cock, balls, and hole like they're something new and special.

"Great length, Doc," Dan says playfully, leaning down to lick all the way from the root of my cock to the head. "Love the way you've trimmed around it. Easier to play."

He glances down at his own hairiness. "I leave mine alone for the most part."

"I like your body hair," I say, breathing hard, feeling a little anxious and anticipatory since he still hasn't touched my hole. After his promise of prolonged rimming, I'm pent-up and desperate for his tongue. "It feels good grinding against my hole while you're fucking me."

Dan growls and the sound is so deep, like his voice, that I feel it in my nipples and cock. His rumble reminds me of those ASMR videos on YouTube where the noise is so good it's almost bad. It feels like a shivery, pleasurable scrape all over my body, especially in my most sensitive places, and all from just his voice.

"Fuck," he grunts, and then squeezes his eyes shut for a moment before he opens them again and peers down at me. "Yup. You're still the hottest thing I've ever seen. Jesus Christ."

I feel pretty ridiculous with my hair splayed over the pillow, my knees drawn up next to my chest as I hold my legs spread, but his eyes burn with lust despite having just come in my mouth a few minutes earlier.

"Your hair," he whispers, reaching out to slip his hands through the long ends that dangle over my chest, using one to tickle my nipples. "It's beautiful."

I don't know what to say because I really want him to get his mouth on my hole, but if we're going to compliment each other now, I've got plenty to offer up for him too. "Your body..." I smile up at him. "Is fucking hot."

He smirks. "I know. I'm going to lick you now, okay?"

"Okay..." I whimper.

Then he finally—*fucking finally*—bends over and twirls the end of his tongue over my anus. No further commentary, or preparation, or teasing. He just gets to work on my hole like it's his dinner. I have never, ever, *ever* been rimmed by another man like Dan rims me, and I'm honestly not sure if I love it, hate it, or love it so much that I'd commit murder to feel this again. It's almost as intense as the way he fucks.

I arch my neck, grip the backs of my knees, and flex my feet over and over, trying to keep my noises soft enough not to disturb the other campers around. I'm losing the fight, though, and Dan sits back on his heels, leaving me gasping for air and trembling. He appraises me with a wicked eye, teeth digging into the flesh of his bottom lip. "I could gag you," he says finally. "I have a ball gag. But only if you want."

I swallow convulsively. I've never in my entire life played like that before, and I've never considered it with a relative stranger, but he's not saying he's going to tie me up. I'll still have my hands and feet free. I can still leave if I need or want to. He's just talking about plugging up my mouth.

"Alright," I choke out.

He nods, hops down, and rummages in one of the stacked plastic bins of drawers wedged and roped into the van. He lifts the ball gag, and my mouth fills with saliva. I swallow again.

"I've never used it on anyone else. I just use it myself sometimes for the hell of it. Sit up for me so I can put it on."

"On yourself?" I sit up like he asked, surprised that I sound like I'm far away. Maybe I am, because as he approaches, I'm somehow simultaneously entirely inside my body—all my nerve endings alive and alert—and outside of myself, watching as I open my mouth for him to slide the ball in. It's thick on my tongue, and it feels like a lot to accept. My cock throbs and I lose a small pulse of pre-cum. As it slides down, I close my eyes, heart pounding, and he clasps the gag behind my head. It tastes and smells like silicone and the straps smell of new leather. I'm not sure what I think of having my jaw held open like this.

"Is it pulling your hair?" he asks, checking that the straps aren't hurting me. His cock is hard and brushes against my arm and chest as he leans over to make adjustments. "Does it feel all right? If you don't like it, you can take it off at any time. And if you can't get it undone, I'll help you."

I realize I can't verbally answer him now with my tongue weighted by the ball and my lips spread so tightly around it, so I reply with a nod. The gag feels weird, but also now that I'm about to get my ass eaten again, it also feels necessary to keep me from screaming in ecstasy. I lean back, pulling my knees up and begging with my eyes. Dan bites his lip, strokes his dick a few times, and with a whispered, "Fuck," he moves back into place.

He teases me first, playing with my cock and sucking the head of it into his mouth. I twist and moan. It's good, *so good*, but I want him back at my hole. Now that I know rimming can feel that way, I don't want him to stop. Especially when I'm not sure if he's going to want to ever hook up again. I want all I can get.

His mouth moves down to my balls, sucking at them, and then licking down over my taint to breathe against my hole.

"I like how you squirm," he murmurs. "And your hole is so fucking pretty. Has anyone told you?"

I groan and flex my feet, dying to feel his tongue again.

"Have you ever looked at your hole?" he asks.

For someone who'd been so awkward in the coffee shop, and not exactly great with words both times we've talked before fucking, he sure knows how to talk in bed—getting consent, spinning me up, praising me. If he's not careful, I'm going to fuck around and fall for him. At the very least, I'm going to get addicted to sex with him. That seems inevitable.

"No?" he asks.

I shake my head.

"Mm. It's hot. It's a really nice color." He glances up at my chest. "Basically the same as your nipples, and it's shaped really tight."

He presses his lips to it, and I writhe, anxious for more. Saliva pools in my mouth around the ball, and some of it drools out the side of my lips, and some of it I swallow down with effort.

Dan teases my anus with fluttery kisses and then pulls back. "I don't know why I love assholes so much, but I do. Lots of guys are super into dick, but I'm really into ass—holes specifically. And yours is one of the nicest I've seen."

Okay, so maybe I've gotten ahead of myself saying his bedroom talk is smooth. It's definitely gone a little off-track now, but at the same time I feel strangely proud of my asshole being one of the nicest he's seen. Like how many holes has Dan seen anyway? Five, a dozen, a hundred? It doesn't matter, because *mine* is one of the nicest.

But there's no more thinking about it now because he's back at his work. I groan and shout against the ball gag, and it's not exactly quiet, but it's definitely more muffled than if I wasn't wearing it. My balls draw up, and my cock dribbles constantly. If he starts fingering me while still licking my rim, I'm going to shoot my load everywhere.

Shaking hard now, riding small spasms that grip and release me, I push my tongue against the gag as tears gather behind my squeezed-closed lids before slipping down my cheeks. The sensation of his tongue fucking in and out of me, licking my hole, and working me over is overwhelming. I'm on the verge of either coming or kicking Dan away when he sits back, grabs a condom and lube, and asks, "Can I fuck you?"

I nod, lifting my knees further back, presenting my saliva-wet hole to him, begging with my body.

He gets himself positioned, and I realize just as he's pushing against my hole that I'm about to be full on both ends—stuffed with the ball gag and stuffed by cock. The thought makes my eyes roll up and my dick spurt needily.

He thrusts in slowly, carefully, darting glances between my face and hole, checking on me as he works his way inside. I grip the back of my knees, nails digging into my skin, and my legs twitch as the curve of his cock rubs my prostate perfectly. When he lets out a low, deep growl, I tremble all over.

My nipples ache, and my hole burns with the stretch. I throw my head back once he's fully seated inside, his hips flush against my butt. He grinds his pubic hair over my sensitive rim while he digs in hard. I want to curse, but I can't with my mouth full, and my tongue shoves against the ball gag again as I leak more tears and start shaking in earnest. My legs quiver, my body jitters, and Dan stares down at me like I'm the best thing he's ever seen in his life. He glows with lust and a soft fondness that's addictive.

I suddenly realize I'm not sure how I'm supposed to move on from sex with Dan. Like...this is just a hookup. But no lover, no other hookup, and no boyfriend has ever brought me to this sort of intense madness. Just like last time, I realize Dan can do *anything* to me right now and I won't stop him. I'm under his spell and his command, and I need it like air.

Speaking of air, I'm pulling it through my nose hard as I prepare to be fucked into the stratosphere. Dan seems to be gathering his energy for it, grinding against me, breathing slowly in and out like he's preparing for something difficult.

Catching my eye, Dan's expression grows even softer. He leans forward, carefully pushing some hair away from my face, unsticking it from where my tears and saliva have it plastered to my skin. His calloused fingers scrape over my chin, over my lips stretched around the ball gag, and then up to my cheekbones, and over to my ears, just touching my face gently while roughly grinding against my hole down below. The juxtaposition is exquisite and maddening. I want to beg him to fuck me hard with long, deep strokes, but I can't say anything at all. Just whimper, grunt, moan, and leak tears.

Which has never happened with any other guys either. He's making me a wet mess all over—dripping cock, leaking eyes, lubed-up hole. But before I can get self-conscious about that, he pulls his hands from my face, grips my hips, and forces me even harder onto his cock. "I'm going to fuck you really goddamn hard now. Shake your head if you don't want that. Nod if you do."

I only nod once before he's fucking into me like a wild, bucking horse.

I scream against the ball gag and toss my head on the mattress. His strong arms lock next to me, holding him up off my body so each thrust gets maximum force as he strokes in and out, and my cock gets no stimulation from his taut belly. His cock rams across my prostate with each thrust and I convulse hard, losing my grip on my legs so that my feet jerk against his hunching back.

Pushing up to his knees, Dan effortlessly tosses my calves over his shoulders and bends me in half before somehow, some way, ramping up his slamming thrusts. Faster. Harder. I scrabble against the bed, grabbing hold of the sheets and gripping them for all I'm worth. I'm sure I'm going to come any second, but I don't.

As the blissful tension builds and builds, Dan shoves my hands up by my head, holding them there as he begins to perspire. The heat and warmth grows between us, the scent of sex and sweat. I groan and writhe, desperate now, working hard to reach orgasm from his thrusts against my prostate alone, shaking all over as chill bumps race over my skin, but I don't come.

Dan, for his part, drinks me in with a greedy, smirking expression, like he's nowhere close to climax and can keep me like this forever if he wants to, and *fuck* I want him to. I'm pretty sure every stupid choice in my life that has led me to this moment of sheer, utter, insane physical bliss has been worth it because I hadn't ever known this level of pleasure exists.

Until now. Now I can never forget.

Dan's hazel eyes are burning hot, eating me up with his gaze as greedily as he'd eaten my asshole. My cock is neglected between our bodies, straining toward him and getting no contact. I guess because he's not a cock man? But I can't bring myself to give a shit when I'm losing it like this from being fucked like a goddamn rag doll. As if I'm not six feet tall. As if I'm not a grown man. Dan fucks me like I'm tiny, and he's going to break me with his dick.

I convulse again but this time the pleasure doesn't release, it just intensifies and grows. My cock goes harder than ever, and my balls tighten so much I feel woozy. I pull air in and out of my nose, sounding like a racehorse, and sweating like one too. I want to come, but I can't get there. I twist my hands around and struggle against Dan's grip on my wrists, trying to fight this orgasm out of my body. Dan releases me, but bats my hands away from my cock when I go right for it.

"Shh," he says, pushing my hands to my sides and stopping his thrusting. "Shh, now. Don't touch yourself."

His voice is throaty, deep, and rough, and it feels like it's stroking over my skin, running its vibrations over my cock, and I cry out, wanting to come so badly I can taste it.

"I'm going to take your gag off," Dan says, and I barely hear him as I hang there on the edge of orgasm—so close and yet so far.

He leans over and flicks some kind of safety and pulls the gag from my mouth. Strings of spit slide over my cheeks as he tosses it aside, and then he leans down to capture my lips with his.

Jolting in shock, I *explode* in pleasure as his tongue slides over mine, a sudden brutal orgasm stealing my sanity. I shout into his mouth, my body pulsing around his dick still shoved so deep inside.

My jizz flies over my stomach, up to his chest, into my hair, and all over the sheets. Dan kisses me through it, holding on to my chin and eating my wails of bliss.

Then he thrusts twice, grunts in that deep, almost soundless way he has when he comes, and jolts hard against me. He stops kissing me as he climaxes, but he nuzzles my tear-and-saliva-wet cheeks, rubs his face in my hair, and kisses my neck, almost wallowing in my body as his prolonged orgasm shakes him. I'm still shaking too, with hard little aftershocks that stun me.

"Holy fuck," he whispers as it finally ends. "You are the best fuck I've ever had."

"Same." I can't say more. I'm at my wits' end because I don't think Dan can be a seahorse, but he's definitely someone I can't just walk away from now. At least not this part of him. Because *this* part of Dan makes me feel like I'm a universe being born and he's my maker.

And that's terrifying.

And beautiful.

I want to fuck him for years.

As he pulls himself out of my body, leaving me empty and a little sore, I only know one thing: I need more of him, as much as I can get.

Unbelievably, after only a short rest and some water, as well as some sweet words of praise from Dan for what he calls my "unholy fucking skills," I get more.

This time we sixty-nine our way to less intense, but still won-derful orgasms, before he smears liniment from the first aid kit over my hole and collapses next to me.

"It was great fucking you, Doc," he says. "You can stay and rest a while if you want." And he promptly falls asleep.

Feeling unsure of how to feel about what he's said—so dis-missive and lacking intimacy after what we've just shared, what he's given me, and what I've let him have in return, I lie next to him, listening to his breathing. I consider getting dressed to go, but before I can, Dan throws an arm around my waist, and presses his entire body tight against my side.

So… I stay.

Dan

I WAKE TO the ping of a phone alert, but it's not my phone because my notifications tone is different. I blink my eyes open and see a mass of black hair sliding over a sleek, naked back as Sejin reaches for his jeans and fishes his cell phone out of his back pocket.

"Oh," he says in a cute combination of sleepy and happy. "It's a VLive notification."

"Mm." I flip onto my back and gaze at him as he clicks something on his phone, and then scoots back against the padded van wall, yawns attractively and eyes his screen. The tinny sound of voices speaking another language reaches me through his phone speakers.

"Is it okay if I watch?" he asks. "I missed the last one."

I yawn too, and sit up a little, curious about how it is that I've apparently let some man, this man in particular, sleep over in the van with me. Did I ask him to? I can't remember. I just remember coming three glorious times after a long, hard day of climbing, not to mention that brutal fall, and after busting that last sweet nut into Sejin's hot mouth just…sort of falling asleep.

Damn, it'd been good, though. I remember that much for sure. The best I've ever had. The way he moans and moves, the way he shivers and writhes, the way his asshole tastes and flutters against my tongue when I eat him…

Damn.

I really don't think last night is going to be enough. I'm going to need to fuck him again.

Plus, there's the whole smile thing.

I've seen him cry, and grimace, and come. I've seen him laugh, and yawn, and smile warily, even happily, but I still haven't gotten that purely joyful smile like I saw in his dating app photo or like I saw him give to Jeanie and those little kids at Tater Tots.

After last night, I really don't think fucking him is going to earn me that smile, though. Powerful orgasms just seem to leave him stunned, not smiley. I'll have to figure out another way to get it…

And I'll fuck him a few more times too, for good measure. Because if things go wrong on Heart Route on D-day, then I'll want to have banked plenty of magnificent orgasms like last night's before I go. Sejin is the best source of those I've ever found.

So, Sejin it'll have to be. Assuming he wants to fuck again too.

And why wouldn't he? He'd practically sobbed in pleasure last night while I'd eaten and screwed him. No, not practically. *Did.*

There's no way he's going to be against doing this again.

I gaze at him, taking in his handsome face and gorgeous hair. Smiling at the video on his phone, he's kind of adorable. My heart does a funny flip-flop in my chest, and I rub my breastbone, still watching him. His lips are swollen from the blowjob, the ball gag, and the kissing last night. My cock stirs.

What is it about him that makes me so hot?

Everything. *Everything* about him from what I can tell. I even like his voice. It's so…warm. Like a pot of maple syrup in sunshine. Kind of like his eyes. They're a glowing brown that I'd pour over pancakes any day.

What the fuck am I thinking? Good lord. Orgasms make me dumb.

Sejin sees me watching and scoots over, showing me the screen.

"What's VLive?" I ask, trying to get my mind off all these

strange thoughts and onto the phone in Sejin's hands. There are five Asian guys on the screen, all wearing sweats or t-shirts, and all seeming pretty hyped up about something. I can't really say what since they aren't, you know, speaking English. Which is pretty much the only language I know, unfortunately.

"VLive is a service that a lot of KPop idols and other celebrities use to broadcast live videos to their fans. I mainly use it to follow KPop groups, though."

"KPop. That's Korean pop music, right?"

"Yeah."

I tilt my head. "Why don't they use Facebook Live? Or Instagram?"

"Because not everything is about American companies," Sejin says casually, eyes still on the screen. He points at one guy. "This? This is Cha Eunwoo. He isn't my bias—um, my favorite—in this group. That'd be Moonbin." He points at another guy. "But Cha Eunwoo is Cha Eunwoo no matter who your bias is. I mean, look at him."

I look, and the guy's handsome, but so is Sejin and he's right next to me, so I'd rather look at *him*. But maybe I just don't know enough about what's going on with the VLive thing, so I ask, "What are they talking about?"

"Not a clue. I don't speak Korean."

"Then why are you watching this?"

He shrugs, still smiling. "I just like seeing them talk to each other. I like the sound of their voices too. Not just the language, which I find fascinating, but also I like hearing them laugh together."

"Mm."

Sejin looks up. "If it's bothering you, I could go finish watching it in my car before I head home."

"Nah," I say, observing the men on the screen tease, shove,

poke, and talk over each other. They're all wearing makeup, surely. Because their skin looks like it's made of spun glass, it's so perfect. "It's fine."

For some reason, I don't want him to go yet.

It's possible, likely even, I could get hard again and we could go another round before he heads out. I'd like that. Still, my balls are pretty sore and the rest of me is really feeling that long-ass fall from yesterday. It was a gnarly one. A real whipper. I hadn't placed a piece of gear properly, and so it'd been nearly a full pitch's worth of distance. The rock rash is stinging like a motherfucker now that the endorphins of sex and the oblivion of sleep have worn off. The bruises throb too.

Besides, if I'm being honest with myself, I don't want him to go because I kind of like having him next to me. His skin against mine is soft, and the brush of his lightly hairy leg over mine is agreeable, and I like how he smells. His sweat, and shampoo, and the lingering odor of our cum is heady. Rye would probably be very smug about this if he could see me now, cuddled up beside Sejin, soaking in another man's company just because I want it.

So the fuck what? I'm human, aren't I? Not some alien. No matter what my foster families seemed to think. I deserve moments like this, don't I?

I shove the doubts away, along with the surging mental whispers that this isn't safe or smart, that this is a distraction. I'm not distracted. I'm just at peace. Relaxed and attracted and wallowing in corporeal comfort with another man. That's all.

Fuck, Sejin smells good, and I like how his breathing is timed with my own. There've been men I haven't kicked out of bed directly after fucking in the past, and the way their breath didn't hit evenly with mine always made me crazy. But Sejin's intake and outtake syncs with my rhythm perfectly. It's like we're one unit right now, breathing and existing together in my cozy van, warm and snug.

I've rarely felt so content in my life, and never with another person. That's what great sex will do, I guess. Leave you limp and soft, willing to accommodate and accept almost anything. Like this VLive thing. I don't get why he's watching a livestream of young men from a KPop group who all speak and sing in, presumably, a language he doesn't know. But I'm curious about what's going to happen, or not happen, next. Will they sing songs? Dance? What?

Before I know it, I've been watching these dudes for about ten minutes, and I haven't hated it. It's been…enjoyable? Leaning against Sejin, resting my cheek on his shoulder, and just absorbing this sparkling bit of human interaction from across the globe.

"Who are those guys? I mean, what KPop group are they?" I ask when it's over, and Sejin closes the app.

"Astro," he answers. "Fans or staff will translate what they said later, and I can rewatch it then if I really want to know what they're saying. But the important parts will be live-translated by fans on social media." He opens an app and taps in a few search terms, showing me how various fans have been posting translated snippets from the broadcast. It seems that some members of the group like mint chocolate ice cream and others don't and, for some reason, that is a very important divide, requiring debate and noogies. It's beyond me, but Sejin smiles his particularly gorgeous grin *at his phone*, and I'm simultaneously thrilled to see it and disappointed that, once again, it isn't for me.

"You're a fan of them in particular?"

"Yeah, I'm really into their music right now. They just released a new album, and I can't wait to teach the dance for their comeback song to the kids. I'm still learning it myself, though. Then I have to kind of dumb it down for them."

"Comeback song? Were they on a hiatus?"

"No, that's KPop slang for a new lead single on an album." He shrugs. "And they call the lead single a title track, even if it's not the title of the album. It's a thing."

But I have more questions. "You're a dancer? Were you trained or self-taught?"

Sejin laughs. "I'm *not* a dancer. I'm just a KPop fan who likes kids." He stands up, and I'm afforded a full body, naked view of him stretching. God, he's gorgeous. I don't want him to go yet, and I reach for him.

"Sorry, I have to work this morning," he says. "I need to find a shower and…" He glances at his phone again. "I'll still be late, but whatever. What do you recommend?"

"For a shower?"

He nods, gathering his clothes and sadly covering himself so that I can't see his pretty butt and the sleekness of his back or the sexy way his balls nestle under his cock. I really want to get my hands on him again, but I guess I have to wait because consent has been withdrawn now, and he's on his way out.

"The campground showers are that way." I gesture with my hand. "But they're pretty gross. If you head into the woods,"—I wave my hand the opposite way—"you can find a fresh waterfall, and I prefer it. The water's cleaner, believe it or not."

Sejin stares at me, glances at his phone again, and seems to calculate. "A waterfall?" he says uncertainly.

"It's not far. Not that much farther than the shower block."

That's not entirely true, but I want to show him the waterfall and see him wet and slick beneath it. No idea why, but I do.

"You'll have to show me another time," he says. "I really do have to get to work. Campground showers seem like the best bet."

"Okay."

"But, hey, I mean it," he says, his eyes earnest and intent on mine. "Next time? I'd love to see it. I've never used a waterfall as my shower before."

Next time. *Yes*, he said next time. I smile, feeling like I've won a prize of ice cream, pancakes, Jolly Ranchers, and every other yummy thing in the whole world.

"You're in for a treat," I say about the waterfall. "An ice-cold treat."

Sejin's eyes go wide and he looks like he wants to ask more questions, but then he glances at the time on his phone again, grabs his pants, and says as he puts them on, "Do you have a towel I can borrow?"

I point toward three folded into a cubby. "And take that bar of soap too." I point to one of the half-used soaps on a rope hanging on a hook next to it.

"I'll return these to you next time we..." Sejin pauses and uncertainty washes over his face.

"Next Friday?" I suggest.

He nods.

"I'll be looking forward to it, Doc."

After Sejin leaves, I sprawl back in my bed and feel something hard under my hand. I grab it and smile. The ball gag.

I can't wait to see him again. I should have said Wednesday.

No, I should have said tonight.

CHAPTER SEVEN

Sejin

"WHOA, DUDE, YOU look rough," Gage says, appraising me before returning to mopping up a spill by the door to the patio. Caramel macchiato by the looks of the mess.

I run my hand over my unshaven face. I don't have a ton of stubble, but what I do have just makes me look like there's flecks of dirt on my chin and cheeks. No sexy morning growth for me, alas. Thanks, genetic lottery.

"Yeah, I had a long night."

Gage snorts. "Uh-huh. Gay guys. Man, you dudes have it all."

I quirk a brow, curious what he means by that given the fact that gay guys do not, in fact, 'have it all' in a lot of really important ways.

He flushes and says, "Never mind."

"Girls have casual sex too, you know."

Gage glances toward the counter where Celli is helping a customer. "I know."

He's mumbling now, indicating he's not going to say much more than that. Which is fine. I don't really want to see him dig his own grave with me or with Celli. I'm quite sure he's getting plenty of action from her, but straight guys always think queers are getting sex right and left. But Gage knows I've been hard up for months now, and all I can think is that he's horny right this second and frustrated about it.

Given the fact that Celli is wearing a cute sundress that makes her look like a sweet snack, I guess I can't blame him. Poor dude. She'll probably blow him in the back, though, if she gets a chance. Those two can't keep their hands off each other.

Speaking of the back, there's a full-length mirror so employees can check their uniforms and once in front of it, I check myself out as I pull on my extra Papa Bear shirt. I keep it stuffed in my locker in the break room for emergencies. It's old and faded and has a stain on the back from where Celli dumped a mug of strong Turkish brew on me by accident, but it'll get the job done.

Wow. I do look rough. Gage wasn't kidding.

My hair is up, per the health codes, but it's heavy and still wet from the damn cold shower I'd scrambled through back at the campground. It can't have been much warmer than the waterfall Dan had mentioned. I know my hair will still be damp when I let it down later. It takes forever to dry.

My jeans are the same ones I wore last night, and they smell just so-so. I hadn't done anything strenuous in them before arriving at Dan's van, but the kinda sexy, sweaty funk of the vehicle's interior has permeated the fabric, making me feel like I still have Dan all over me.

My eyes shine in a delirious way, like I'm sleep deprived—I am—or hopped up on drugs—hopped up on sex, more like—and the dark circles under them aren't very attractive.

I look exhausted, but I feel wide awake. Cold showers will do that. I'm surprisingly warm too, like the jolt of icy water woke up a furnace inside me, and now it's in overdrive. My head, hands, and feet tingle with heat.

I'm just about to head out to start my shift thirty minutes late—thank goodness Pete isn't in this morning—when my phone pings.

My heart jumps and a dizzy rush of anticipation hits me. Is it Dan?

Martin talked to his dad today.

No, it's just Leenie.

He thinks Uncle Buck is lonely. Sejin, you really ought to call him.

I swallow hard. A flash of irritation rises in me, and I put the phone in my pocket without replying. My dad has my number, plus he's the dad. He can call me if he's lonely. And he will. Won't he? The nagging doubt is almost as irritating as Leenie's text.

When Mom was alive, my calls with Dad consisted of him picking up the phone, recognizing my voice, and saying, "Let me get your mother." It was always Mom who called and texted, and I always talked to her about my life, plans, and problems. Dad has never participated in that kind of parenting. He was always busy at the chemical company and too exhausted when he got home.

We don't have a lot to say to each other. Martin and his dad have a different relationship. They're tight. They talk every week. It's just the way they are together and always have been. When I was a kid, I thought it was weird how much time Martin and his dad spent with each other because Dad and I weren't that close. But now I know that different people have different relationships with their parents, and I don't appreciate Leenie, or Martin, or Uncle Verny making me feel like there's something wrong with mine. Or to be specific, with the way Dad and I don't talk.

But as I go about my day, chatting with Celli, fielding her intrusive questions about who I'm hooking up with, serving customers, bussing tables, cleaning messes, mopping, sweeping, pouring coffees, and checking supplies, Leenie's texts linger in the back of my mind. If Uncle Verny says my dad is lonely…

What if he is? He and Mom were married for twenty-eight years before she died. She handled everything relationship-wise, including friendships and family. Dad doesn't know how to do any of that.

During a break, I step outside to stare up at the vibrant blue sky and listen to the birds chirp. I tug my phone from my pocket and send a brief message.

Thinking about you, Dad. Want to talk soon?

A read receipt flashes almost immediately, but no bubble appears. I blink and swallow hard.

Okay then. I was right to begin with. Dad and I prefer to grieve alone.

A slew of hikers and climbers, some I recognize from prior seasons, assail the coffee shop, most of them filthy from early morning outings into Yosemite, but all of them jovial. Their voices rise and fall as we fill drink order after drink order and put together plates for their food. The way they rib each other makes me think about Dan. He doesn't seem the ribbing type. I wonder how he gets along with these guys and what they think of him.

As I work, I drift closer to where they've congregated, having pushed tables together in the coziest corner of the shop. They've shoved the overstuffed chair over too. Bussing tables, I can't help but listen in on their conversation.

"Y'all heard that asshole's back in town?"

"Fuck, yeah, Lowell told me about him. He's a fucking lunatic."

"Who? Dan McBride?"

"That's the one."

They have my full attention now, and I start clearing tables more slowly, making sure they are extra thoroughly wiped down, and the chairs too, so I can hear more.

"I heard he's sending some of the hardest routes and planning something stupendous."

"He's one of those fools who climbs like he's got no future."

"Some are saying he's the next Honnold."

"Nah, no way. He's just a lil' nobody."

A guy wearing a green beanie scoffs. "Nobody? *Ha.* He free soloed Moonlight Buttress."

Raspberries of disbelief are blown by a few guys and one girl too. "Who said?"

"Peggy Jo."

"Peggy Jo? *The* Peggy Jo?"

That perks my ears up as well. I know Peggy Jo, and she's a total badass. Definitely deserving of being called The Peggy Jo, in my opinion.

"Yup."

Everyone grows quiet at that until a girl asks, "Why's she talking him up?"

"He's her protégé, and he'll never spray for himself, so she does it." Green Beanie rolls his eyes. "Proud mama."

"Proud mama? Who's proud when their kid free solos recklessly like that? Jesus, that's courting death."

"It's raw athleticism," Green Beanie disagrees.

"It's insane."

"Yeah. Well. It's both," a different guy says.

I stop next to them with my tub of dirty dishes. "Sorry. I couldn't help hearing what you were talking about. What's free soloing? And why's it insane?"

Voices overlap at first, but finally one stands out. It comes from a tightly-wound girl with a wide mouth and intense blue eyes. "It's when you go up without ropes. No safety at all. One single miscalculation, or the rock's a little sweaty that day, or your toe slips..." She drops her hand dramatically and slams it on the table. "Splat."

I jolt, the dishes rattling in my tub. "Splat?"

My mouth goes dry. Dan's body is a work of art. The idea of it flat as a pancake with the life blown out of it crushes me.

"Yup. Typically, there's no surviving it," a guy with a scraggly beard and chin-length blond hair says. "Depending on how high up a person is...well, let's just say this guy free solos walls high enough that if he fell, he'd explode on impact."

"Humpty dumpty climbs a great wall, humpty dumpty has a great fall," the first girl sing-songs morbidly. "Well, you get the picture."

"So, yeah, the guy's a maniac," another girl with a dark brown ponytail says.

I feel a little nauseous. "Y'all sound like you kind of hope he falls."

They gasp like I've just slapped them in the face, and I guess in a way I did, but they all seem way too titillated by the idea of Dan's possible "great fall," and it makes my stomach churn.

"Nah, man, no way. We'd never want that. It's just this guy's an asshole."

I think of Dan's awkward bluntness and can't help but agree. He *can* be a dick, but then I think of his consideration in bed, the playful way he'd called me Doc, and how he'd grinned when I'd taken up his suggestion of role-play. He's a young man, no more than twenty-five, like me, and being an asshole is no excuse for the way they've been talking about the possible end of his fledgling life.

"He's arrogant," another guy says, this one with curly brown hair and pale, crystal-colored eyes. "He thinks he can outclimb legends like Alex Honnold—do you know who he is?"

I shake my head.

"Look him up. He's the greatest alive at the moment, or one of them. Adam Ondra, Magnus Midtbo, and Tommy Caldwell are some others—"

"Dean Potter!" someone else chimes in.

"He's dead."

"Yeah, but this Dan asshole thinks he can outclimb Dean's record climbs. I mean, he did already free solo Astroman, and he's planning to take on a route on El Capitan, so—"

"El Capitan?" I squeak.

The Captain is one of the most majestic, iconic rock formations in the world, featuring over three thousand feet of sheer granite walls. My knees go weak at the thought of Dan—of anyone really—going up something that size without any safety gear at all. I'm scared enough of the idea even *with* ropes, and harnesses, and equipment.

"Arrogance gets climbers killed," the wound-up girl says, jittering her knee up and down anxiously.

"Again, Dean Potter." This is from another guy, different from the one who first mentioned the name, and he says it much more solemnly.

Heads nod throughout the group, others go wordless and thoughtful, and a few more look sad. The nervous girl—intense and observant, she reminds me of a spring about to be sprung—says, "Why did you ask? Do you know him or something?"

I clear my throat and play dumb. "Dean Potter?"

"Dan McBride," she says, watching me closely.

I have to lie. I don't know why.

Even though I don't really know Dan, I sure as fuck *know* him. I had him in my body last night, and I laughed with him this morning, and plan to fuck him again on Friday. But, even so, I'm just not ready to say I know this lunatic who's apparently climbing Yosemite Valley all day without ropes and then putting his body in mine at night… and holy fuck.

What the fuck?

What the *actual fuck*?

"Uh, no," I whisper. "I don't know him."

She narrows her gaze at me, but one of the guys lets out a burp, and another belches after him in a weird sort of gaseous harmony. Laughter breaks out and voices rise again, and all mentions of Dan, free soloing, or consideration for my questions are thrown aside in favor of immature burp and fart jokes.

I'm glad of it.

Later in the afternoon, my phone dings. I glance at the message, not sure what I'm hoping for—a reply from my dad, a text from the maniac I'm fucking? I don't even know.

But my stomach swoops hard when I see the preview on my lock screen.

Hey, Doc, want to meet up tonight? I know we said Friday, but I'm ready for another round if you are.

My pulse rushes. I imagine leaving the coffee shop after my shift is over, going home, taking a nap, and skipping dinner in favor of prepping myself. I imagine telling Leenie not to expect me home, heading back to the campground to the blissful seclusion of Dan's van, and sweating my way through another set of orgasms that rock the ground under my feet. Or under my knees, depending on the position...

I imagine bussing a table two days, or three weeks, or four months from now and overhearing from a callous set of climbers full of faux pity all about how Dan's body was discovered in pieces, exploded on impact, smashed below El Capitan's imposing walls. My fingers shake as I put in my reply.

Can't. I'm busy tonight

Ok. Friday then

I click like on the text, but don't send a real reply. I'm not sure I can do Friday either actually. I need to think about this before I let Dan get any further under my skin.

I need to think about it a lot.

Dan

ROPE SOLOING ISN'T as easy or smooth as climbing with a belay partner. It requires the climber to pass over the same pitch three times instead of just once, but Peggy Jo is of an age that means going up the more difficult big walls is a once-in-a-while kind of thing, and Rye is doing some volunteer work with Yosemite Search and Rescue today, so I'll have to make do.

One advantage of it, though, and it's a biggie, is that I'm able to really get to know each pitch of the wall. It allows me to move at my own pace, which can be quite slow when I'm training and don't feel hurried to move on for fear of boring my belay partner senseless. It also means that every inch of wall I cover is gained entirely by my own toil, and that's something that I need to feel confident and comfortable with when I'm free soloing.

Plus, I'm alone on the wall. My favorite way to be.

Today, my mind isn't at ease the way I'd like though. Sejin's response to my text yesterday was definitive, and I respect that, but it was also vague enough that I don't know why he said no. "Busy tonight" can mean a lot of things. It can mean he has to work—but he worked the morning shift at his coffee shop job, and preschoolers don't meet at night, so that doesn't make sense. It could mean he doesn't want to meet up because he's tired, sore, fucked out, and just not interested in more sex right now. But then why lie about it and say he's busy? Why not just say he's not up for it? It *could* mean that he's got plans with other friends or family…

Or another casual hookup. Or a boyfriend.

What if he has a boyfriend?

No, no, Rye would know if Sejin were dating someone. Rye knows everything about the queers of this little community, so he'd make sure to tell me if Sejin was already attached like that. I realize some guys are fine with their men getting dick elsewhere from time to time, so it wouldn't necessarily mean that Sejin is a cheater, even if he does have a boyfriend…

But, no. Rye would have said. Right?

Sejin does have that accent, though, that sweet, lilting, Appalachian sound that makes my insides feel a little funny when he talks. And that could mean he has a boyfriend—or girlfriend—back home, and maybe that boyfriend's in town, and he was meeting up with him last night. Or her. That's a pretty out-there prospect and, statistically, the probability is pretty low.

Which leaves the last option, the most likely one given my general run with people during my lifetime—he's already over me.

I'm typically a one-and-done kind of guy myself, but there have been a few times I've fucked guys more than once and, yeah, typically they dip out by the third or fourth fuck. Having gotten what they wanted from me, and found my personality and company lacking, they get out of Dodge. I've never cared that much before, but for some reason, with Sejin, it hurts right beneath my solar plexus to think that I'm only worth a few fucks to him. I thought I'd taken him to some pretty great heights during our first two hookups, and I'd wanted to take him to even more. My chest aches to think I won't get to.

It's…well, it's disappointing. But that word doesn't seem to completely capture the way my thoughts keep circling the brief exchange of texts, trying to figure out what I'm sensing and what went wrong. Worse, my feelings don't stop twinging worse than my healing rock rash and bruises, even as I prepare to launch myself up the next pitch of my climb.

This isn't a particularly difficult wall. I've chosen it because the route sports a gnarly dyno similar to the one on Heart Route, and I can repeatedly practice it at less height with ropes, and without having to tire myself out so much to get to it.

Unfortunately, the wall isn't empty, and there are other teams of climbers both up on the wall ahead of me and gathering at the base. Luckily, most are taking the easier route up, and using aid climbing to boot, so they'll be out of my way soon. But a few are standing off to the side at the base, eyeing the route like they're gonna scramble up after me. I'd really rather they didn't.

"You Dan McBride?" one of the guys asks as he passes me, scratching at his stubbled face. If I can shave with a hand mirror in a waterfall, then this guy can shave in whatever homey bathroom he has wherever he lives. There's no way he's a dirtbagger, not with his shiny new climbing shoes and gear. I wonder how he's heard about me.

"Yup." I finish chalking my hands again and shoot the group a hard, discouraging look. I'm not here to make friends. I'm here to climb, practice this dyno, and forget about "Mr. Can't. I'm busy tonight"… Fuck. What's his last name?

"Is it true you're planning to free solo El Capitan's Heart Route?"

My blood goes cold and my breath hitches. Who's been talking? Rye? Peggy Jo?

Gotta be Peggy Jo.

Get a few beers in her and she's spraying about her former students like a fire hose.

"I don't know. We'll see." My usual answer to anyone trying to ferret out details of my climbing plans. It's what I said the day I left my final foster home too. Mr. Anderson had squinted at my stuffed backpack, my scavenged bicycle, and my determined face before he'd said, "When you coming back home then?"

And I'd answered just like I did now: "I don't know. We'll see." I never went back.

But I fully intend to free solo El Capitan's Heart Route. I just don't want a sea of spectators watching me when I do it.

When I reach today's dyno, I steady myself and consider it. The distance I'll need to leap is a little farther than what I'll have to do on Heart Route, which is both good and bad. Good because I know I won't be practicing under-propelled, but bad because jumping too hard with too much velocity later while on Heart Route could cause me to bounce off the wall, and if I'm free soloing it, fall to my death. So, this isn't a perfect solution, but getting comfortable with the dyno aspect is key. The roof may be what I'm most afraid of, but that doesn't mean the dyno isn't still one of the riskiest parts of the endeavor.

I end up having to let even more climbers pass through as I work on the move repeatedly. I do it thirty times, and I'm wrung-out exhausted by the time I finish. Which I realize, as I start climbing the pitches to the top of the route and make my way over the cliff's lip to the flat, rocky top, is great because I'm way too tired to worry or obsess anymore about Sejin. All I can think about is how nice it is to stand up and see the view I've earned, and how good dinner is going to taste in the van. I even picked up a bag of pork pot stickers from Trader Joe's earlier in the week, and they'll taste fantastic fried over an open flame at the campground.

What had I been thinking inviting Sejin over more than once anyway? I'm not here for hookups. I'm here for *this*. For training. I need to keep my head screwed on straight and not lose it for the best piece of ass I've ever had in my whole fucking life.

I mean truly the best.

Goddamn. So good.

I stretch my arms high and gaze up at the clouds in the blue sky.

So, so, *so* fucking good.

Is his skin covered in E, and I get high whenever I lick it? Because, Jesus Fucking Christ, he's addictive. And I really do want to see him smile for me like that picture on the app. Earning a smile that brilliant would be almost as good as sending a 5.15d route for the first time. Maybe better.

Why was his text so—

"Dan." A familiar voice calls my name, and I turn to see Lowell Moody approaching wearing a harness and an unbuckled helmet. I'm glad I hadn't seen him at the bottom, or I would have been roped into climbing with him, and then he'd have asked questions. I'm really hoping to avoid a conversation with him about my plans for the season.

Other hikers and climbers lingering around the top of the cliff all move away as Lowell approaches, and I don't blame them. Lowell is a rough-looking guy. Wiry, skinny, with a messy beard, and weird, golden eyes that seem to glitter in the sun. He's otherworldly and intimidating. I don't know how he didn't scare the victims he rescued as a member of YOSAR. Yosemite Search and Rescue had been his full-time job until his recent retirement after his divorce.

I remember how startled I was when he'd arrived to rescue *me* after I'd gotten stuck up on a ledge with a badly twisted ankle. He'd descended from the top looking like some kind of alien or angel or superhero. I'd thought I was hallucinating. He's sharp as a knife too, both physically and mentally, not classically handsome in any way, but powerful. I don't know how else to explain it. He's just a force of nature and it shows all over his features.

I squint against the sun, taking him in.

His wife leaving did a number on his head. So did his last rescue attempt that'd turned into a heart-wrenching body retrieval. The details are gruesome, and even I felt gutted reading about it, and that sort of thing doesn't usually affect me much. He retired from YOSAR shortly after, unable to keep it together on the job or at home. Now he climbs full-time, as far as I can tell. At least he has a house, though, unlike me and Rye, so he still has that semblance of normalcy.

He grips my hand as I say, "Lowell, hey."

"Enjoying this early-season cool day?"

He releases my hand as I nod, and then his gold eyes shimmer as he stares out into the distance, taking in the view.

I work on collecting my gear, which is more than usual since

I've been rope soloing. I hook carabiners to loops of rope and square away everything I can in my backpack for the hike out. Lowell is next to me doing the same quietly—which I like—and quickly—which I can respect. He moves faster than I do, a sense of urgency in every twitch of his muscles. I wonder if it's something innate in him, or something he learned in YOSAR where time is of the essence in most rescues.

We head off together, almost as if we had done the climb as a pair, and I wish Peggy Jo were here so I could say, "Look! I do have a friend. Would someone who isn't a friend do *this*?" Where "this" is hiking down the back side of a mountain with me, and now that I've thought that through, it seems like a low bar. But I can't exactly have high bars for friendship, now can I? Peggy Jo would be the only one to pass. Well, and probably Rye.

"Where are you staying nowadays?" Lowell asks as we near the end of the steeper part of the path.

"In the van. Same as always. Got a camping slot, though." Which I don't know how long I'll be able to afford. I prepaid for the season just to make sure I couldn't get kicked out, but after that… I'll have to find some church parking lot to crash out in or something. Churches don't usually call the cops on you so long as you're out of their lot by Sunday when the crowds show up. Or maybe I'll beg a bit of Peggy Jo's driveway while I decide what to do after I send Heart Route.

"Nice."

"Eh, it's all right."

"Access to showers must be good."

"Typically I hit this little waterfall near the camp site. The mold and toilet stink get to me in the shower block."

"Mm, nothing like the fresh, crisp shock of a cold waterfall," Lowell agrees.

As we continue down the trail, letting casual hikers pass on their way up, I remember having suggested to Sejin that we shower in the waterfall. He'd seemed into the idea at the time, but maybe it'd been too weird for him after all. Had that been the breaking point? The bridge too far?

"If you were seeing someone—" I start.

"Mmph," Lowell mutters.

"No, not seeing someone, but fucking them—"

A passing man gives me a startled glance and puts his arm around his wife as if my curse might damage her in some way.

It's just the F word. Live a little, dude.

"Uh-huh." Lowell glances at me, waiting for the rest of my question.

"If you were fucking a guy—uh, not that you fuck guys—"

Lowell shrugs. "I don't count it out. Just because I haven't, doesn't mean I won't."

Oh, huh. Interesting.

For a second, I entertain the idea of fucking Lowell, but as soon as I imagine myself naked with all of his alien powerfulness, I lose interest. I guess I want someone I feel more equal to, even though, until Sejin, I hadn't ever given much thought to what or who I want to be with, per se. More just acted on instinct and impulse. Still, I can't imagine ever fucking Lowell. It'd be like fucking a demi-god in the midst of his midlife crisis. Too intense and too *much*.

And what do I mean by *until Sejin*?

Like how has Sejin *changed* anything? We've fucked a few times, and that's all.

"Spit it out," Lowell says. "You're being weird. Not like yourself. What's gotten under your skin?"

"A guy."

"Obviously."

"I fucked him a few times, and it was outstanding." I get animated, something I rarely do, and it captures Lowell's attention. He almost trips over a rock, lending a hint of humanity to him for a moment. "It was like boom, pow, and wow. Like, *holy shit*, did I just shoot my entire soul out my dick or what? Like is this guy made of actual *drugs* because I feel high and like I could fuck him a million more times before I get enough."

"Huh."

I wait for more, but that's apparently the extent of it. "I'm not kidding."

"I didn't think you were."

"I really want to fuck him again."

"Then do it."

"He…" I hesitate. Sejin hasn't rejected me. He hasn't declined to meet on Friday, but my gut says something is off and that he'll cancel before the day is out if I don't do something. I just don't know what that something is, or if I *should* do it. None of this is in my plans.

"I'm supposed to be training," I say instead. "He's a distraction."

"Training for what?"

I frown and consider. If I tell Lowell the truth, he's going to have opinions, and he'll probably tell them to me, because what I'm planning to do is, by all measures, dangerous, and he's a former search and rescue guy. But I hate lying. I lied my entire childhood just to get by, not that I was very good at it. I was caught out in those lies often and, at some point, I decided not to lie anymore. So I don't.

"Heart Route," I hedge, leaving out the part about free soloing it. It's a tough enough free climb, and I'll let Lowell think what he wants.

"You're young still," Lowell says, as if he's eighty instead of barely forty-five. "Let me tell you now, Heart Route will still be waiting for you later, even if it takes two, three years to send it. But the best fuck of your life? He won't wait."

I'm silent, hoping he'll say more, but that's it. I don't know if he's having regrets about the way his marriage ended, or if he's just speaking the truth, but I know with certainty he's right. I want to achieve my goal of free soloing Heart Route, but I also know there's no one else planning on doing it. No one else is as foolhardy as I am. I don't *have* to rush it. I've got time.

I mean, I still plan to hit my goals, but I can hit Sejin's hole too, and it'll be fine.

"What if he's seeming less interested all of a sudden?"

Lowell glances at me. "Any particular reason why?"

"Have you met me?"

He huffs a laugh. "Hm, well, how bad do you want this?"

"Define 'this.' Because I want his ass pretty bad."

"By 'this,' I mean whatever it takes to get that ass, even if it means something involving feelings."

"Feelings? Ugh. Fuck, no. I don't want feelings."

Lowell chuckles. "Well, maybe that's why he's less interested. Maybe he senses that."

"Do you think it requires feelings to fuck?"

"For some people, yeah. They want a little more than just physical pleasure out of their encounters."

"What do you think he wants?"

"I don't know. Could be friendship. Could be love. Or I could be wrong, and he just got his fill and is ready to move on."

"Friendship," I say, thinking back to my conversation with Rye about how living in the moment means enjoying time with friends. I remember that particularly beautiful smile in Sejin's profile picture, the one he's bestowed on the children and Jeanie and his phone, but not yet on me. "I'm not so good at friendship."

"You're not so bad at it either. Maybe just ask him what he

wants. Communication is good. Even if all he wants is fucking…or nothing at all."

Right. I agree with that. I'm always very careful to negotiate consent in every sexual encounter and not just assume that what we'd agreed to last time will be okay this time, and all that. Maybe friendship could be the same. Negotiated. In exchange for his smile and more sex, I could agree to…what? What would he want me to agree to?

I guess I should just ask, like Lowell suggests. How much worse can it get? Sejin's already losing interest. I can feel it, so I have very little at risk here.

When we reach the end of the trail and circle, Lowell chucks his stuff into the back of his Bronco, and he pulls me in for a hug. "Heard a rumor about you, Dan," he says as he squeezes me. "Tell me it's not true."

"What rumor's that?" I ask, enduring the prolonged contact without flinching, which I consider a real win.

Lowell releases me. "A rumor about your plans for Heart Route."

I shrug. "A man's gotta have goals."

Lowell stares into my eyes. "I suppose I can't talk you out of it?"

I shake my head.

"Guess I'll warn my buddies back in YOSAR about an upcoming smear they're going to have to clear off El Cap's floor."

I know he's trying to scare me, but it's not like I haven't extensively considered that possibility. "Hopefully not."

"I hope not too. Listen, about that good fuck…"

"Uh-huh?"

"Don't let him get away. Whatever your plans are for the season, nothing is worth missing out on seeing that through. Believe me. Boom, pow, and wow wins over death-defying climbs in measures of both safety and pleasure. If the worst comes—" He grimaces. "How far up is that first crux?"

"The dyno on Heart Route?"

"Yeah."

"About 1,000 feet."

"All right, so that's…hmm." He winces. "During that long, ten-second fall, at least you'll have some amazing sexual memories to have no regrets about, instead of thinking 'if only I'd banged that guy one more time…'"

I huff, but he's right. Fucking Sejin again is worth whatever it requires. Even if I do have to be friends with him. I don't want to die thinking about his sweet hole and his nice dick, and how I never got to feel it inside of me. I need to make this work. At least until it gets stale.

Back in my van, I start it up and drive out of the parking lot to head to the campsite. As I wait in line behind a half-dozen other cars to exit onto the main road, I tug out my phone and send a text.

Hey, Doc, hope we're still on for Friday. Looking forward to it.

For the next twenty-four hours, I wait for a reply.

But Sejin doesn't answer.

CHAPTER EIGHT

Sejin

LEENIE AND THE kids have crashed my place of business, and normally I'm fine with that, but I've been stressed out the last two days for a plethora of reasons.

First, my dad never texted back, which kind of hurts a little more as each day goes by. Why doesn't he at least reply with "I miss you too?" Or something innocuous like "Things are good here, son. Hope you're fine."

I miss when my mom was so excited for my every adventure. "Send pictures!" she'd demand, and then respond enthusiastically to each one when I did. "Those clouds are beautiful!" she replied once to a photo of me in front of a dingy hotel sign, sent as proof both that I was alive and of where I was staying for the night. I hadn't even noticed the clouds.

Dad couldn't seem more disinterested in my life if he tried. I know he's grieving, we both are, and I know he prefers to do it alone—we're alike like that—but I hate feeling like I've lost both my dad and my mom since her death. It sucks. A lot.

Second, Leenie and Martin had a fight last night, and I worry it was about me. I could hear them in their bedroom trying to keep it down, but words seeped out from beneath the closed door. Things like *months, how much longer, why,* and *"it's not that I don't love him too, but…"* So, yeah, it must be about me, and I really do need to get the fuck off of my cousin's sofa and figure out my life.

But where can I go? Rents are insane around here. I don't make a lot of money. Dad doesn't have any to give since the chemical companies shut their doors and left West Virginia in the lurch. It's not like I can ask him for a loan when he doesn't even respond when I ask for a phone call. But I hate that my presence is probably causing them stress.

Third, Pete is on my ass at the coffee shop because I asked him to rearrange the schedule around my work at the preschool again, and you'd have thought I'd asked him to cut his dick off and let me eat it for breakfast, because he was seriously uncool about the whole thing.

And then there's Dan.

He texted about Friday, and I haven't replied. Mainly because I don't know what to say. If I say yes, then we're going to fuck, and it's going to be *amazing*, and I'll want to do it again and again. But some day down the road, whether we're still fucking or not, someone's gonna say "Did you hear about that climber that died?" and it's going to be Dan. And I'm going to have to live with the knowledge that someone I've had sex with, that I've had inside my body and come for and with, someone I think I might care about way more than I should after just two hookups, died doing something I don't even understand.

I just don't know how to feel about that.

But right now, I *do* know how I feel about Leenie, but more specifically Jeremiah and Sarah Kate crashing out in the comfy corner of the coffee shop, settling in, screaming for me constantly, asking for multiple free refills, and Leenie asking me to watch Jeremiah while she changes Sarah Kate's diaper. All of them are basically treating Papa Bear like their home-away-from-home when I'm already in deep crap with Pete. Normally the guy's indulgent of his employees' families, but today he's short-tempered and has it out for me. If Leenie wants me off her sofa anytime soon, she really needs to pack up and go.

But I'm not sure how to explain that without Pete overhearing, and...

The door chime rings. I look up expecting a new influx of folks given that it's almost lunchtime, so I'm surprised to see just one customer. My stomach drops, and I go a little light-headed as our eyes meet.

Dan.

He looks good too. Wearing worn jeans that hang on his narrow hips, a t-shirt stretched tight across his chest muscles and snug-capped sleeves that show off how wiry his arms are. He's all...*unf.* So lean and sexy, with his big, wide eyes staring right at me full of questions and intensity. I'm instantly aware of my skin in an acute way that's hard to explain. Like I'm tingling with effervescent bubbles of anxiety and attraction popping all over the surface of me at once. It's weirdly hard to breathe.

I swallow as Dan approaches the counter.

"Small hot apple cider," he says, not taking his eyes off me as he hands over his debit card. "And a few minutes of your time."

"Look," I say, as I begin to make the drink. It's pretty easy—some apple cider, some steam, whipped cream, and *voila.* "I'm at work, and I can't really talk."

Dan takes the cup from my extended hand. "When's your break?"

"He doesn't get one today. He was late," Pete says, bustling up next to me, his grizzled voice rising with irritation.

"Alright. I'll wait until your shift is over," Dan says, going to sit at a table by the window and bringing out a worn journal and a pencil. He begins marking inside of it.

"That guy bugging you?" Pete asks warily. "Because I can handle him if you want."

"No, he's fine. I kind of owe him a conversation, I guess." I don't *owe* him anything really, but I don't feel right not giving him an explanation about why I'm going to cancel on him for Friday night.

Pete groans. "Drama, kid. Guys like him? They're drama."

I don't know if he means because Dan's a climber—evident by his build and the remnants of chalk on his fingers—or if he means because Dan has shown up at my workplace to talk and is going to just…wait. Isn't that a little stalkerish? Should I be worried?

I don't know. I feel like I should talk with him, though. He's not being a disturbance at least. Unlike the other people who came here to see me.

At just that moment, Jeremiah starts to sing the alphabet song at the top of his lungs, and Sarah Kate starts wailing like a banshee, and Leenie calls out, "Sejin, can we get more apple slices?"

Pete grumbles, "Does she think I opened this place to feed her kids?" But he slaps an apple onto the cutting board and next thing I know he's handing me a plate with apple slices on it. Dan hasn't budged, and doesn't look like he's going to, and I don't actually know what I'm supposed to say or do.

"Uh, I know I was late," I say, "but, um…" I trail off. "Could I please just take a minute to talk to him?"

Pete looks up from where he's cutting almond butter and strawberry sandwiches into halves to put out for the to-go sales cooler and glances at Dan by the window. "For fuck's sake, kid, get your life together and get it out of this coffee shop."

He looks at his wristwatch. "I'll give you ten minutes…" He glances at Dan again, and then over at Leenie. "No, twenty-five ought to do it, alright? But never say I'm hard on you. After today…" He rolls his eyes. "I'm a goddamn pushover, is what I am."

I'm never going to agree he's a pushover, but this is definitely kinder than I expected. I take the apple slices over to Leenie and manage not to let her pull me into a conversation. Instead, I say, "Listen, Leenie, I heard there's going to be a free acrobatics show from that traveling troupe over in El Cap's meadow this afternoon. If y'all leave now, you can make it in time."

Her eyes light up, and I know I made the right call. She can get the kids out in the fresh air, let Jeremiah run around, and entertain them with a spectacle. I should have thought to mention it sooner, but I'd been too distracted by my runaway brain.

She starts to pack up immediately.

Jeremiah grabs my leg. "Sejinie, come with us!"

"I can't, buddy," I say, dropping to a crouch next to him. He shifts his hold to my neck. "I have to work." I kiss his sweet cheek and rub our noses together. "But I'll see you at home tonight, okay? And we'll have a game of Candyland while Mommy has a bubble bath."

"Yeah?" Leenie's eyes meet mine.

"Yeah."

"I'm holding you to that, Sejin," she says. "I'd kill for an hour alone in the bath."

"I know."

I escort them out the door of the place like it's my home or something, and after helping get Sarah Kate into her car seat and waving them off, I head back inside to face Dan.

My palms are itchy, and my tongue is dry. I decide to put it off by grabbing a glass of water for myself first, downing it quickly, and then heading into the back to check my hair and face. Pete sticks his head in, sees me brushing my hair before putting it up again, and snorts. "As bad as Celli," he mutters, and then leaves me to it.

When I finally get the courage to go break it to Dan that I'm not going to suck his dick this weekend, or fuck his ass, or let him fuck me—*woe! woe indeed!*—I look a lot calmer on the outside than I feel on the inside. My stomach is knotting, my heart is beating harder than necessary, and my dick is traitorously buzzing with a rush of blood like I might get a half-chub just sitting down across from Dan.

I take a deep breath and watch as he closes his journal and puts it away in his small backpack. "Hi," I say. "I'm sorry I left you hanging about our plans for Friday."

"It's alright. Most guys eventually leave me hanging."

I swallow. "I guess you want to know why?"

"Actually, Doc, I was mainly just hoping I was wrong, or if I wasn't wrong, that I could find a way to change your mind."

"Well, maybe I want to tell you why."

"I didn't violate your consent or boundaries, did I?" he asks, sitting up a little straighter, concern lacing into his deep voice.

"No, of course not."

"Good," he says, relief washing over his features. "I'm not always great at reading people, and I try to always keep things really clear even when it's..."

He licks his lips. They glisten and capture my attention. I remember how nice his mouth is when applied to certain sensitive places on my body, and I shift in my seat.

"Even when it's intense."

"No, you never crossed any lines with me. Not sexually anyway."

"Oh? I crossed lines another way?" He frowns. "I've been known to do that. Say the wrong thing. Accidentally be a dick."

"It's not what you said, or that you're kind of a dick—"

He laughs, and my heart stumbles over the wide spread of his mouth gleaming across the bottom of his face. Christ, he's handsome, and my body really wants to respond to him the way it has the times we've been together before. But the worrying part is that my *heart* wants to respond too. His smile is endearing and special, and I can easily get used to it and start to want it every day.

"So, what is it then?" He sounds genuinely curious and not at all defensive. An open mind waiting to hear his crime.

"I didn't even know I might have a boundary like this, but…" I clear my throat and pick at my thumbnail nervously. "I'm not judging you. I know we were just hooking up, and that's all it was ever supposed to be, but…" I meet his steady gaze and feel something inside me unlock. Words spill out. "I heard some other climbers talking about you, saying you're planning on free…what did they call it? Free…you know, going up El Cap without ropes."

"Free soloing," Dan says calmly, like I haven't just said that folks are saying he's on a suicide mission. No denial. No wince.

"Yeah. That you're going to free solo El Cap."

He nods, and his expression doesn't change much. "That bothers you?"

"Yeah. It does." I tug my hair out of the ponytail restlessly and let the cool cascade of it hide my face a little as I go on. "Maybe it shouldn't. I mean, we're just fucking, right?"

Dan shrugs. "We don't have to just fuck."

My throat clicks as I swallow again. I wish I had thought to bring another glass of water to the table with me. I could use a sip right now.

"You'd want to move past just hooking up?"

"If you do, sure. Do you want to?"

It's tempting. Horribly tempting. "I don't know? That might make it worse."

"How?"

"Look, these climbers that were gossiping about your plans, they didn't seem to think—" How am I supposed to say this to his face? "They thought you might fall."

"Ah, of *course* they think that." Dan sits back and kicks his legs out to the side, crossing them at the ankle. He looks pretty smug for a guy who's in the midst of being rejected.

"You don't agree?"

"I wouldn't be training to do it if I believed a fall was inevitable, would I? I'm not suicidal. People just want to believe anything *they* are too afraid to try is impossible."

"But it's not like you *can't* fall," I say.

"It's just not something I worry about. I don't consider it the most likely outcome."

"Yeah, but you *did* fall, just the other day, didn't you? I put Bactine on your scrapes, remember?" And then we'd fucked like animals; I feel dizzy again remembering it.

Dan tilts his head, the scrape on his cheek still red and evident. "Look, Doc…"

"Look what?"

"I was about to say something, but it always pisses Rye off when I say it, so I guess I shouldn't."

"That's not very reassuring."

"You're right. I'll go ahead, but keep in mind I've never had people care if I die or not, and so I don't really get it. Falling isn't something that scares me."

I blink, trying to understand. "What does that mean?"

"No one gives a shit about me, and I'm used to that."

"I give a shit about you."

"Oh." He lets out a slow breath and meets my eyes. "Do you?"

"Well, yeah. That's the reason why I don't know if we can hook up again. I don't want to care about you *more* and have it end…" I feel sick. "Like that."

"Huh." He tilts his head again, thinking.

"Huh what?"

"Having people care whether I live or not is weird."

"Weird? It's *weird* to care whether the guy who makes you come like the world is ending and then being reborn out your ass lives or dies?"

"Okay, more like different. And it's not like I'll definitely die."

"Just likely."

He shakes his head. "I won't do it if I think it's likely either." He smirks again. "But back to what you said before—"

"Okay."

He leans forward. "You came so hard the world was reborn out your ass? I fucked you that good?"

I roll my eyes. Men, they're all the same. Even me. "You know you did."

"Well…" He shrugs again, leaning back and settling in with his feet out and crossed. His smug expression doesn't fade. "I knew that, yeah. Which is why I was so confused about why you were ghosting me."

"Now you understand."

"I understand that you and I have the same fear, yes," he says, solemnly. "Of getting attached."

"Right."

"I admit, I almost let you walk away. I don't see many benefits in attachment either. But I've thought a lot about it the last few days, and I think we should risk it."

"Because the sex is so good?"

"Yes, but also…" He scrubs a hand through his hair and then leans forward, elbows on the table. "Actually, no. Let's take sex out of the equation."

I scoff. "How? We're literally hookups. We're not even friends. If we take it out of the equation, what do we have?"

"Nothing."

"Exactly."

"And that's perfect."

"You've completely lost me."

"Stay with me now," he says, tapping his palms on the table. "I've had two goals ever since I saw your profile on that hideous app." He puts up two fingers. "To fuck your brains out. Did that." He puts one finger down. "To see you smile at me the way you're smiling in your profile picture."

I blink at him baffled. "I've already smiled at you? Plenty of times. I just smiled at you earlier when I sat down."

"It wasn't the right smile."

I'm not sure if he's a stalker, a freak, or an adorable weirdo. Inside I'm feeling the urge to run, to laugh, and to throttle him all at once. Maybe kiss him too. "What's the 'right' smile?"

"The one where your nose crinkles up, and your eyes go kind of half-moon shaped, and they shine and twinkle, and…" He pulls out his phone, taps a few things, and then shows me my own profile on the hookup app. "This one."

I snort. "Weird, but okay. I mean, not 'okay, I plan to spend time with you until you achieve this bizarre goal no matter the cost to my own mental health should you plummet off a wall later', but 'okay I'm still listening even though I shouldn't be'."

"I figure there's no way around the fact that life is short—"

"And yet you're aiming to shorten it even more?"

"Life's short, even taking my goals out of the equation." Dan sees my eye roll coming and puts his hand out. "No, wait, I know what those other climbers said got under your skin. They filled your head with all kinds of visions, right?"

"It didn't take much," I confess. "My mom died a little over a year and a half ago, and I don't have room for more death in my life right now."

"I'm not going to die."

"You can't promise that."

"Right, and neither can you. You could walk out that door right now and get smashed by a runaway semi-truck. Boom—you never fucked me again, and how sad is that?"

"I thought sex was off the table for this discussion."

"Fine, you never smiled at me like this"—he shows me the phone with my stupidly happy face on it once more—"and what an eternal fucking loss for me, right?"

"But the chances are a lot less—"

"Chances are all we've got."

Something about that sentence, issued from his handsome mouth with such finality, hits me right in the chest. It's like a boot kick that knocks my breath away. The light from the window shimmers around him, highlighting his brown, curly hair, and the fuzz on his jawline. I'm mesmerized by his big eyes. They're almost hypnotic as he gazes at me, certainty roaring out of them like a physical thing that also shakes me deeply.

"Kid!" Pete yells from behind the counter. "Time's almost up. Got that personal life cleaned up yet?"

He'd said I had twenty-five minutes, and it's definitely been less than that, but a glance out the window at the bus of tourists that has just rolled up tells me my time with Dan today is over.

"Why do you want to see me again?" I ask. "The real reason."

"I feel like I need to see this smile." He taps the phone again. "I feel like I'll regret it for the rest of my life, no matter how short or long that is, if I don't."

I smile at him. "There. Now you've had it."

"Your eyes aren't glowing."

I huff and cross my arms over my chest. "You're a real dick, you know that?"

"So I've been told."

I ponder that. Dan seems resigned to being considered an asshole. Interesting, and kind of sad.

"Kid!" Pete calls again.

Scooting back from the table, I rise. "I have to get back to work. I can't give you an answer right now. I'll text you later, okay?"

"Promise?"

He sounds so young then, and he looks it too. Far too young to die.

"I promise," I say, putting my hair back up in the ponytail for work.

He watches me keenly, and then says, "I love your hair, Doc."

"Thanks." I shift awkwardly, not sure how to break free from him. I want to say something more, something normal or funny or soothing. I don't even know if I want to soothe him or myself. Instead, I smile again. "Later, Dan."

"Later," he agrees.

By the time I've helped Pete with the influx of tourists, Dan has left the building. Again, I don't know how I feel about that. Relieved, I guess.

At the same time, I'm confused now in a way I wasn't before. I could use some advice, and it takes me a few hours to decide who to ask for it. I have a lot of friends, but not a ton of them are people who have the kind of life experience I need or who care about me for my own sake. Or should.

After my shift is over, I get in my car and drive to my favorite lookout point and park. With the vision of El Capitan looming ahead of me, I take a deep breath and pull out my phone.

And I call my dad.

Dan

PEGGY JO'S HOUSE is nestled at the back of a dead-end road. Its main feature is a giant window at the rear that shows off a view of snow-capped mountains and evergreens. Otherwise, it's a fairly normal house—one story with the bedroom, office, kitchen, laundry, and living area laid out nicely.

But my favorite thing about it is her bathroom, which is blessed with extraordinary water pressure. Waterfalls beat the campground shower block any day, but Peggy Jo's bathroom is a luxurious indulgence by my standards. One I'm definitely going to treat myself to before I leave for the campground again.

But, right now, I'm on Peggy Jo's front porch, sipping lemonade, and listening to country music jangling out over the outdoor speakers she had installed last year. She can tell I'm worrying over something, but she's got her own reasons for having asked me to come over, and so she's getting that out of the way first.

"Bella is pregnant," she says, kicking her feet up onto a wicker ottoman and leaning back in her favorite cushioned porch chair.

"Oh?" Bella's not married as far as I know. I mean, I don't always pay attention when Peggy Jo talks about her daughter, but I think I would have caught it if Bella had gotten married. That's pretty big news. Like pregnancy. "On purpose?"

Peggy Jo snorts. "I don't rightly know, to be honest, but the fact of the matter is she's pregnant and she's having the baby sometime in October. She wants me to be there with her."

"And she's just now telling you about it?"

"No, I've known. But I was hoping I could convince her to come stay with me here for the duration of it. She declined. She's happy with her doctors there and wants to bring the baby home to her little house in Georgia. But with the timing…" She touches my hand. "I hate to be away when you make your ascent."

Ah. The implications of that statement hit me immediately. I plan to free solo Heart Route in late October or early November and going to Georgia to help with Bella's new baby means Peggy Jo won't be around to support me in the lead-up to that. "Don't worry about it. It's fine. It's all good."

And it is.

The fewer people around caring too much about the outcome of my climb, the better. If Sejin decides to stick around and do some caring in my direction—and I really hope he does, which is super weird in and of itself—then having Peggy Jo gone for the big event will be a load off. I can only take so much worry directed at me. Rye, Lowell, Peggy Jo, and maybe Sejin? That's a lot. How can I fly up the rock with all that extra weight?

"I feel mighty torn about it," she says. "For a lot of reasons."

"Don't be. Of course you'll want to be there when a screaming new life comes into the world."

"You're right. I do. I want to meet my grandbaby as soon as they arrive. But I don't want to miss your feat either. You've worked so hard for this, for so long. I feel like I might just be the only person on earth who really knows all the preparation and effort you've put in to send this route. Crazy as I think this particular goal is, Dan, when you step over the lip, triumphant, ready to tell me and everyone else 'I told you so,' I want to be there to hold you."

I smile into my lemonade. A woodpecker swoops close and then up over the roof of the house. "I don't need to be held, Peggy Jo."

"I know you don't think you need it, but you do."

A cat meows from within the house, and Peggy Jo sighs, standing up to let it out. I can't remember if this one is Romeo or Julio, or maybe it's Muggs. Peggy Jo has three cats; they all hate me, and I can't tell any of them apart. They're some mixture of orange and black and white, but damned if I know which one has the white patch by its tail, which one has it by its eye, and which one has no white patches, but just streaks.

The cat steps daintily through the pebbles by the front porch, going around to the side garden, where it disappears into a thicket.

"Don't worry, he'll be back," Peggy Jo says.

"Mm," I say, rather than announce my complete lack of worry about the cat. Whichever one he is, he'll be fine. Those cats are terrors, and I have the scars to prove it.

"But, unfortunately, I can't be two places at once," Peggy Jo says, continuing with her line of thought regarding Bella's baby and my free solo of Heart Route. "And as much as I consider you a son—"

"You need to be with Bella," I say. "Don't apologize. I don't want you here for it. You know I wouldn't have even told you before I went and did it anyway. I'll go when I'm ready and when no one knows."

Peggy Jo stares at me, and I don't dare look at her face. I don't want to see if my words have hurt her, made her angry, or worse, made her sad. A few birds chirp, the cat comes creeping back around the side of the house looking both guilty and defiant as he shifts his way over the pebbles to settle in the sun.

"I have one last problem," Peggy Jo says, "before we can talk about yours."

"I don't have anything to talk about," I deny.

"Mm-hm, well, whatever you say, but I figure it'll come out sooner or later. First, though, let's stick with me."

"Happy to."

"The house and the cats," she says. "I can't leave the cats with the boarder for two or three whole months, and Grady Houser, my neighbor who usually takes care of them when I travel for long periods, is wintering in Australia this year—lucky bastard—and leaves a few days before I do."

"Hmm."

"So, I was wondering if you would stay here with them? It'll help with your money problems too. I'd pay you for cat sitting, and you could stay here for free. Remember what Henry said about your funds? A year max. This could really help with that."

I don't like the idea of living this far out from El Cap, but it's true that my biggest expense, by far, is the camping slot. I could get my money reimbursed for the weeks I don't use. I feel strangely superstitious, though, about the idea of living in a house like this when I'm training for the biggest climb of my life.

Maybe it's silly, but it feels too soft. Like if I were to live here instead of in my camper, I'd lose focus, become a couch potato, and do nothing but watch television all day. I can already hear her counterarguments—I'll rest better in a real bed, and that alone will make my training more efficient and help me retain the strength I've earned.

But still I resist.

I have an idea, though, of who might want to stay here in exchange for feeding the cats.

Rye's in a living situation that prevents him from having even partial custody of Jeanie, and so he might be interested in a house-sitting gig, even if it's only temporary. Maybe Andrew would be more likely to let Jeanie spend the night with her Mommy from time to time if he was out of the tent. So long as it benefited Andrew, of course.

I decide not to say anything about that, though, until I've felt Rye out on the situation. People too often don't react the way I expect them to, and then I'm left looking like even more of a jerk.

"I don't need a commitment right now," Peggy Jo says, reading my expression in that way only she seems good at. "But I'll need one soon. I need to make some kind of plan. I'd rather help you out than someone else, but I need to know whoever is watching the cats is reliable."

"The cats hate me," I point out.

"They don't need to love you. But after you feed them for a few weeks, they sure will."

"Ha."

That's the last we talk of it for now. I know I'll have to give her an answer or counter-solution soon, but I'm relieved she doesn't try to pressure me. That's one thing Peggy Jo rarely does, and probably one of the main reasons we've stayed friends.

"So, tell me what's bugging you," she says.

My nose wrinkles. "I'd rather not."

She gets up, goes inside, and comes back out with a bowl of chips and another cat on her heels. This one has the white spot on its nose. She calls it Julio as the door falls shut behind her, telling him to watch his tail. He darts out just before the door slams. So that's one cat identified, two to go.

"I like a guy," I say.

She sighs in satisfaction, like she's known the whole time I was going to spill. I'd kind of known it too, but I like to make things hard if I can. I mean, why give anyone the idea that I need them or whatever? Because I don't. It's just…

I don't get people, and I don't get what's going on with me and Sejin, and Peggy Jo's smart. She's *good* with people and might have some insight that'll help me understand.

"I don't think it's a wise idea for me to keep seeing him, but now that *he* thinks maybe it's not a wise idea to keep seeing *me*, I'm trying to talk him into staying." I sip the lemonade, watch Julio collapse next to cat number one in the sunshine, and then say, "Why?"

"You don't like to lose?"

"No. I don't normally care that much when a guy or girl moves on."

"So, it's this particular guy then."

"Yeah."

I let silence fall for a few moments, watching as a moth flaps near the cats. Julio bats at it before it flies off and away from danger. Neither cat chases it.

See? That's what I should do, not try to get Sejin to fly back to me.

"We've hooked up twice. I've talked to him two… Yeah, two,

maybe three times outside of those encounters. I should be willing to let him walk."

"Why don't you then?"

"Here." I dig my phone out of my back pocket and pull up Sejin's profile on the hookup app. I enlarge the photo and hold it out for Peggy Jo to see.

She takes the phone, holds it out from her face, and squints a little before her eyes adjust. Then she smiles. "Oh, it's Sejin."

"You know him?"

"Of course. Everyone knows Sejin."

"I didn't know him."

She says nothing else, but hands me back the phone. Suddenly, I need to know. "Do you like him?"

"There's not a soul alive who wouldn't like Sejin."

"Well, that smile? The one in the photo? I *really* like it."

"He's adorable."

"Yeah, he's always good-looking, but there's something about that smile…" I frown. "I think this probably sounds creepy. When I told him about it, he looked a little weirded out."

"Enough for you to notice? Oh, lordy. What exactly did you say?"

"I told him that I want him to smile at *me* like that, and he hasn't yet. I told him I want to hang out with him and be around him a lot until I earn that kind of smile."

"He's never smiled at you? I can't imagine that. The boy's a smiling machine."

"No, he's smiled at me a few times, but never…" I bring up the photo again and thrust it at her. "Never like that."

She studies the photo. "Never like he's looking at someone he loves?"

It's a kick to the chest. I sit back in my chair. Cold. A little stunned. Holy shit, is *that* what the expression on his face is? Love?

I don't want that, do I?

Being loved is…

I don't know what it is. I haven't experienced it much. The closest thing I have to a person who loves me is Peggy Jo. I've always said I don't need love, I don't want it, and all it does is hold people down, keep them back, tether them.

A cloud shifts over the sun and a corresponding shadow passes over the cats. Coolness falls on the front porch, and a strange despair drops on me. I'll never make Sejin love me, and so I'll never see that smile directed at me. I've wanted to see it in person from the beginning, and then I wanted it all for myself, and if Peggy Jo is right about what that smile means, then I can't ever have it.

I hate not having what I want because I'm always so careful to make sure what I want is something I can accomplish all on my own. I've made a huge blunder with Sejin and his smile. I've made the mistake of coveting something I can't give myself.

"What's wrong?" she asks. "You look like I shot your dog."

"I don't know what to do now," I say. "I thought if I could just get this smile from him, it'd be enough. But…"

Peggy Jo stares at me. "It's okay to want to be loved, Dan. You deserve to be loved."

I don't reply. Love's a foreign thing. A mystery I'll never solve.

I still want to see Sejin's most beautiful smile directed at me. No matter what the cost, it's worth trying for. I know it is. I want it almost as much as I want to free solo Heart Route. And that makes no sense at all.

Not a lick of it, as Peggy Jo says.

No, not even a *lick* of a lick of sense.

Sejin

"HE DIDN'T PICK up the phone," I say to Leenie, digging a spoon into the peanut butter jar, ignoring her glares because I know something she doesn't: I bought her a new jar on the way home. All she has to do is check the cupboard for it. "I called, for the first time in forever, and he didn't pick up the fucking phone."

"Sejin, language," she says, glancing at Jeremiah playing with trucks at our feet. He's using the lines in the kitchen linoleum as roads, and the table legs as mountains. Apparently, these trucks can drive vertically and even upside down because he's zooming them up the legs and underneath the tabletop.

"Sorry." Apologizing for the f-bomb I dropped feels hollow, though, because I have a lot more of them locked up inside. "What am I supposed to do? Beg him for attention? Everyone blames me for whatever's going on with him, I guess because I'm the one who left West Virginia. But he has a phone, Leenie. He can use it to call me or, I don't know, he could pick up when I call him."

"Verny says he's been depressed since your mom died."

"I know, but what am I supposed to do about that? Stay there? Suffocate in that tiny town forever?"

"I thought you loved home."

"I love it when it's in my memory. I hate it when I'm there. Especially since Mom died."

"Do you think he might feel the same?"

"I don't know. But, again, what am I supposed to do? I can barely afford to take care of myself—who am I kidding, I *can't* afford to take care of myself at all! I can't bring him out here to join us. Your sofa isn't big enough!"

She scoffs and ignores the last jab. "You could talk to him about it. He could probably afford the move, and it might be good for him. You two could get a place together, and—"

"What part of 'he doesn't pick up when I call' did you miss, Leenie?"

I hate to sound so angry with her. It's not *her* fault my dad is now even more determined than I am to run away from our feelings after Mom's death. I just hadn't expected that when I finally really needed him, like I'd needed him this afternoon, he wouldn't be there.

"I'm sorry," I say meekly. "You've done so much for me, and I shouldn't have snapped like that."

"You're hurt. He should have picked up. Or texted. Or…maybe he's out of range?"

"Maybe."

"I'm sure he'll call. Just be patient, Sejin."

"Meh. I hate patience."

"I know you do."

My phone buzzes in my pocket and I jump. Part of me wants it to be Dan, of all people, and part of me is certain it's my dad. His ears have probably been burning. That's the part of me that's right.

"Hello? Dad?" I say, and Leenie leans back in her chair, self-satisfied relief playing over her features.

His voice is a pleasant, familiar rumble that settles my anxiety as soon as it hits my eardrums. "My phone says you called earlier. I didn't hear it ring. Not sure why."

"Do you have it set to Do Not Disturb maybe?" I wave at Leenie and stand up, abandoning the jar of peanut butter, the spoon still stuck in it, to walk out of the kitchen, through the front door, and out to the driveway. The reception is better there. Plus, there's at least a modicum of privacy.

"Beats me, son. I'm just proud I can work the damn thing at all. Your mama made me get it, and I'm glad and all but, Lord, the way they change it every time I just got it all figured out. Took me near a week to re-learn how to close the internet pages after this last update."

"It was confusing," I agree.

"Anyways, you called, and I'm callin' you back. You okay out there? Need me to come get you? Just say the word."

I smile. God, what is *wrong* with me? I've been convinced he doesn't want me around and is avoiding me, or blaming me for his grief and pain, but here he is saying he's here for me. In his own way, of course. Not in those words. But I know what he means.

"I'm still okay. What about you, though? The family's worried."

"Oh, bah. Those extroverts don't know how to leave a body alone, I tell ya. They're like your mama. Always getting together with each other and talkin' up a storm. Dang if Verny didn't come over last week, and I thought I was gonna have to just get up and go on to bed with him still yammering on the couch."

I snort. Just hearing my father's voice makes me long for West Virginia, even though I know it's not the place for me. But there's just something about that accent, that emotional warmth that persists even when I'm getting a scolding, and the friendly nosiness of every last neighbor, friend, and family member—all wanting the best for me, all prying way too much. That's not even getting into how the mountains themselves hug you like a mama. They're warm and curved, and don't loom over you like snow-capped, luminescent, wrathful giants that might decide to come alive, march during the night, and take out the human race.

Wow, just talking with my dad has unlocked a part of me I don't always embrace—the colorful, winding, wordy part that wasn't born or bred into me, but was instilled by being soaked in Appalachian culture since I was eight months old.

I fall into my accent harder as I reply. "I'm so happy to hear your voice, Dad. I've missed you so much." It's instantly true. It happens every time we talk. As soon as I hear his voice, the missing just wells up inside me. It's part of what makes reaching out hard.

"What's going on? You don't call for no good reason."

I sigh. Earlier, when I'd been sitting in the car, staring at El Cap, I'd had some sort of words planned, but now they escape me. "Boy trouble," I summarize.

"Ahh. You used to talk to your mom about that."

"Yeah."

"So, what's the problem? He a jackass?"

I laugh. "Pretty much."

"Cheating on you?"

"No. We aren't dating, really… Well, we aren't dating yet." Because isn't that sort of what Dan is requesting? We can take the sex out of the equation, but he still wants to spend time with me because he wants to see a very specific version of my smile. Which is so fucking weird and yet…I kind of get it. I want to know more of him too, and that's what I think he *really* means. But I'm not an idiot. If I say yes, I want to spend time with him too, then sex is gonna go right back into that equation, and then we'll be dating, or something very much like it.

Dad and I are quiet together for a moment, which is something I always appreciate about him. Mom would fill in the silence, and I liked that too, because I liked everything about her, but with Dad, I'm given some time to think.

"This guy I'm seeing is a rock climber."

"Tough guy, then."

"Very tough. And he does some dangerous climbs."

"Right."

I take a deep breath. "What if something happens to him?"

"You think something might happen to him?"

"I think the chances are higher than average *by far*."

"Ah." He's quiet again.

"I'm scared to get too close to him, even though I want to at the same time. There's something about him. He's kinda odd, and we don't really know each other very well." Try at all, outside the bedroom, but I'm not telling my dad that. "I just have a feeling in my gut, if I keep seeing him, I'm going to fall for him. And I'm going to fall *hard*."

"Did your mama ever tell you she had those breast cancer genes?"

"Yeah." I'm a little discombobulated by the apparent change of topic, but I'll roll with it, see where he's going. If he just needs to talk about Mom's death, then that's okay.

"We didn't know, of course, when we married. They couldn't test for it yet back then."

"Right."

"But once we found out, I thought and thought and *thought*. How if we'd known, we could have done things differently. Gotten an early mastectomy or what have you. That kind of thing. I'd have loved her, no matter what."

"Of course you would have. So would I."

"But do you know what she said to me?"

"No."

"She said she wished we'd known when we were young too, because then I could have married someone else, and not gone through all the hard times with her—the infertility, the cancer."

"Oh." I suck in a breath. *What about me?*

"I knew as soon as the words left her mouth, son, that she was telling me how much she loved me. She was telling me she'd have wished for another future for me that didn't have this pain. But I also knew I wouldn't have traded a single dang moment we had together, just her and me, or the three of us as a family, for any kind of life with another woman. I lost your mom too early, but even if I'd lost her way before I did, even if I'd only had a few years with her, it would've been worth it."

"Oh." I see now what he's trying to say.

Dad's voice is serious when he asks, "Do you love him like that?"

"No, not yet anyway. I barely know him."

"So, this is your chance to run," Dad says.

"Exactly. And I feel like I *should* run. He's not a good long-term bet."

"Right."

The Sierra-Nevada mountains loom above the tree line around the yard, hemming me in. They don't want me going anywhere.

"But even when I run, my feet keep wanting to head back to his door."

I don't tell my dad that Dan's door opens up to a converted van. My eyes fill with tears when my father speaks again. He says exactly what I want to believe and everything I'm afraid to hear.

"Trust your feet, son. Your feet have never steered you wrong."

CHAPTER NINE

Dan

I'M HALFWAY UP the twelfth pitch on Heart Route, rope soloing again, when my phone vibrates with an incoming message.

I haul myself up to a resting place with a few footholds that're slightly bigger than the nickel-edge holds I've been climbing all morning. I reach into my pocket to pull out my phone. I have it on a string that's attached to the harness, so I don't drop it and accidentally murder anyone.

The string gets briefly tangled with one of the carabiners. Once I get it free, I stare at the message preview on my screen. I can't believe it. I'd nearly given up hope after two more days of radio silence from Sejin.

Are you still interested in hanging out?

With chalky fingers, I press in a question. *Hooking up or hanging out?*

Hanging out.

I can almost hear the emphatic period he puts at the end of it.

Yes, I send without hesitation. I've had his ass a few times, and I'd like to have it again, but I want to win his smile more, I know, whether I like it or not, whether it's smart or not, this is the first step to achieving that goal.

Sejin replies with *I have the weekend off*

I do too

Wait, you have a job?

Climbing, yeah

It pays?

It could, I hedge, because I'm not sure this is the exact moment when I want to go into my "purity of motivation" speech with regard to climbing.

But it doesn't currently?

I get by

Why are we talking about money? I thought we were talking about hanging out, and now he wants to know about money? I haven't proposed marriage, for fuck's sake. I just want him to smile at me. Jesus. I wipe a hand over my sweaty face.

Frowning, I type *Does it matter?*

Not really

Then why are you asking?

Curiosity

Fair. Now he can indulge my curiosity in return. *What's your dream date?*

Wow, are you going to try to impress me?

I just want an idea of what you'd like

I've never thought about it

More bubbles appear, and I wait as he continues to type.

I guess it'd be something unexpected and exciting, but not frightening

Define frightening

Well, for example, I'm afraid of heights

What part of heights scares you?

Looking down? The one time I went climbing with some friends up a small wall, I hated seeing the drop below me.

So, seeing the exposure is too much?

Yeah.

Did you fall at all?

Yeah

Did you hate the fall too?

No. Well, it wasn't fun. But seeing the rock drop away behind me really freaked me out

Even though you were roped up?

Yeah. It doesn't make sense. Lizard brain stuff, I think

Brains don't have to make sense

So climbing isn't likely to be a good date for me

Not so long as you can see how far away the ground is

Right, but I like hiking! I like a good view

Camping?

Camping is good

I'll pick you up Friday at sunset which, according to Google, is going to be at 7:36

Alright. How should I dress?

Comfortably

Like 'we're going out to dinner' comfortably or 'we're going camping' comfortably?

The latter

Are we going to build a fire and roast marshmallows? Zip our sleeping bags together and make each other see the stars?

I'm down for that

It's kind of too bad we started out the way we did

Why's that?

It makes it harder for me to resist you

You still want to resist? Why? He's the one who messaged me, after all.

You don't seem like a safe guy for me to care about

Nothing in life is safe

Is that what you believe?

It's what I've experienced, yeah

Huh, well, I'd like to hear more about that

I'll tell you about it on our date. I'm hanging a thousand feet up and should probably get back to sending this route

What? This whole time?

I send a photo of my view. He replies with multiple exclamation points, and *Holy shit! Be careful!*

I'm always careful

Are you?

Yes

I wish I believed that

You should. I'll see you tomorrow at sunset. Send me your address

He does and I recognize the street as one not too far out from the center of town.

Sunset tomorrow, I say again.

I'll be ready He again includes a purple, horned devil emoji. I immediately feel my balls tingle and my cock chub up.

Tease, I reply, since he's already said we aren't hooking up.

Am I though?

I don't know, are you, Doc?

I guess you'll find out, heh, go climb your rock

I pocket my phone again and start back up the pitch, ignoring the way the razor-sharp crimps sting my fingertips. I feel like I'm flying up the wall. My muscles and blood are humming with something more than lactic acid and adrenaline. I feel like I'm a bird, or a song, or sunlight embodied in human form.

I think this feeling is what they call hope.

Weird.

CHAPTER TEN

Sejin

LEENIE WATCHES ME pacing by the window for a few seconds and then goes back to getting pajamas on Jeremiah. Sarah Kate's been in bed for the last hour and a half, and Martin's out back mowing the lawn before the last of the light disappears.

"Is he late?" she asks, when she obviously can't stand to see me wearing a tread into her wood floor any longer.

"Not really. He said sunset, and the sun's not technically set yet." I glance at my phone for the official time the sun will disappear behind the horizon. "Another six minutes, I guess, and then he'll be late."

"Sejinie?" Jeremiah asks, as Leenie works his feet into the footed pajamas.

"Yeah, buddy?"

"Why are you nervous?" He can't quite pronounce the word yet, so it sounds like nuhbof, and it's adorable.

"Because…" How can I explain everything buzzing around inside me to a four-year-old? "I'm excited," I say instead. "I hope I'm going to have fun, but I'm not sure if I will. Like when you went swimming for the first time. Remember? You were scared, but also excited."

"Right. Are you going swimming on your date? Don't worry, Sejinie, just hold your breath real good when you're underwater, okay?"

I smile. "I'm not sure where we're going actually. It's a surprise for me."

"A surprise!" His eyes light up, and he jerks free from Leenie's embrace. "I love surprises! Can I go too?"

"No," Leenie breaks it to him. "This is a surprise only for Sejin."

His shoulders slump and just as his lower lip begins to wobble, there's the sound of a motorcycle coming down the road at an alarming speed, louder even than Martin's mower in the back. I glance out the window and see the bike pull into the driveway in a spray of gravel and dust. Sweat breaks out over my brow. Holy smokes.

It's Dan. And he's here for me.

"Oh, wow," Leenie says, picking up Jeremiah and peering past me. "You gonna be alright on that thing?"

My hand shakes a little as I push it into my pocket to bring out a hairband. I'd left my hair loose for the date, but I'll definitely need to put it back if I'm expected to ride on that. My pulse pounds. I've never been on a motorcycle before. Do I trust Dan to be safe? Where did he even get it?

I watch as he tugs his helmet free and shakes out his short, curly hair. Leenie lets out a little sound and then says, "Oh, I see. He's strange looking, but also… damn."

"Wide-set eyes," I murmur.

"Sexy way of holding himself," she adds. And I guess it's true. I've always been so captivated by his face when his clothes are on that I hadn't entirely noticed that.

Dan looks toward the window like he knows we're in here staring out at him, and he smiles in that way where the lower half of his face transforms into a startling slash of white. He starts up the sidewalk to the front door.

Leenie moves out of my way as I go to throw it open before he can ring the bell.

Jeremiah squirms out of Leenie's arms, rushing out and toward Dan, who stares down at him like an alien has just burst onto his path.

"Can I ride?" Jeremiah asks, taking hold of Dan's hand like he's known him forever.

Jeremiah's never met a stranger.

To his credit, though, Dan doesn't pull away. He simply crouches down, gives Jeremiah a serious look and tells him, "Sorry, kiddo, but the bike is for grown-ups only."

Leenie moves past me and scoops Jeremiah up, saying, "Sorry! He thinks everyone is his pal these days. We gotta work on the concept of stranger-danger. Uh, not that you're a danger. I mean—" She blows hair out of her face and then redirects herself. "Hi, I'm Leenie."

"Dan," he says, offering his hand.

They shake, and Jeremiah puts out his little hand too, saying, "I'm Ja'miah. Baby Sarah Kate is sleeping." Which sounds like sweeping, and Dan looks around as if he expects to see an infant with a broom.

"This is Jeremiah," Leenie translates. "And my other little one is already in bed."

She gives Jeremiah a little tickle. "Which is where this one should be now too."

Jeremiah promptly starts squirming and protesting, working up to an anti-bedtime screaming fit. I kiss his head as he passes, twisting in Leenie's arms as she's on her way back inside with him. "Sleep tight, buddy."

"I will not!" he wails.

"Later, Leenie. Tell Martin goodnight for me."

"Sure thing. We won't wait up."

"Yeah, don't," Dan says. "Nice to meet you," he adds, like an afterthought. His eyes are on me now as if he doesn't want to look away. "You look good."

I lift my hair to put it back, and he watches avidly as I secure my hair away from my face. Then his gaze skims down my front. I'm wearing some older tennis shoes, a pair of faded jeans that hang nicely, but which I also don't mind ruining, a BlackPink merch t-shirt, and my windbreaker jacket.

Dan turns back to the motorcycle and retrieves a second helmet for me. There are two saddlebags, and I assume he's packed whatever else we'll need in them.

"Where'd you get the bike?" I ask.

"It belongs to my mentor."

"Oh?"

"Yeah, Peggy Jo Barton. You might know her. She, uh, seems to know you."

"Peggy Jo! She's the coolest!" I say, grinning. "In her sixties and still going strong."

"Yeah, she taught me to climb, and she taught me to drive her bike." He pats the seat.

"Amazing."

He shrugs.

"I mean, Peggy Jo is goals all day long, isn't she?"

"She wouldn't be my mentor if she wasn't."

I take the helmet he's still holding out toward me and put it on. I must hesitate a moment as I approach the bike because his eyebrow quirks up, and he glances over toward my Versa.

"We can take your car if you're scared."

"Nah," I say, a little breathlessly. "I'm good."

I adjust the lay of my ponytail in the back, and then clasp the helmet under my chin securely. He watches, leans in, and kisses my nose softly before pecking my lips. I shiver and he smiles again, that surprising, blinding thing, before adjusting my chinstrap to be a little tighter.

"There," he says. "That should do it."

I feel all fluttery and flushed, but I try to keep my cool as he climbs onto the bike and shifts forward so there's ample space on the seat behind him.

I swing my leg over, scooting close so that my crotch aligns with his ass, and I grip the unbuttoned fronts of his jean jacket. Taking hold of my hands, he shifts them so I'm holding onto him securely around the middle. I can feel his core strength and the flatness of his stomach beneath my forearms and hands, and the broad warmth of his back against my front.

"I'm good at this. Don't worry," he says, starting the bike.

The way he maneuvers us out to the road shows he's telling me the truth, and I wave goodbye to Martin, who's come around the side of the house with the mower now. With a roar, we drive off.

The roads he takes me on lead to higher elevations, and I'm familiar enough with the area to realize we're heading toward Tuolumne Meadows and Tioga Road. I'd ask him why we're going there, but the sound of the motor, the wind, and the snug fit of the helmets seem to preclude that.

As darkness comes down around us, the night feels big. The stars are bright pinpricks above, mixed with smudgy, wispy clouds, and the moon is barely over the horizon, not giving off a ton of light. The forest around us amplifies the mystery, and I hold on tighter to him, feeling the wind buffeting my body as Dan drives into the night, illuminated mostly by the headlight of the bike.

The vibrations of the engine rattle me all over, especially my butt and thighs. I'm unaccustomed to the tension required to stay on the bike, and the way I clench all over, bracing myself, when we round a curve feels like a workout. It's not that it isn't fun, but it's scary too, and something about *that* feels right when I'm with Dan. This isn't us in the back of his van getting naked and taking each other to the sky. This is us on a bike, in a forest, heading into a night of mystery, but my blood pounds with the same intensity.

My muscles are tight and tired by the time Dan slows down, turning onto some dirt paths, taking us off the main road and into the area near the meadow. I'm not sure where we're headed exactly, but like I said, I know the general location. When he slows and eventually stops, I cling to his back for a few more seconds, letting myself adjust to the way we're still now, no longer whooshing through the world. Then I lean back, and Dan climbs from the parked bike first to help me off. My legs feel rubbery and strange as I remove my helmet and give it to him to stow away. I stamp my feet against the ground.

"Okay?" Dan asks, glancing at me as he opens one of the side saddlebag compartments.

"Yeah. That was cool. I've never ridden on a bike before."

"I was kind of hoping you'd say that," he says, pulling a backpack from one compartment, and a second bag from the other. "I get the impression you like to try new things."

"I do."

He digs in the pack for headlamps, passes one to me and keeps one for himself. He lifts the backpack onto his shoulders and the other bag up on his arm. "C'mon. It's this way."

As we step from the forested area and into the meadow, the moon has risen enough to expose the land in a wash of blue and silver light. We almost don't need the flashlights, but we keep them on anyway. It's a beautiful place during the day. Leenie and Martin love to bring the kids here to play, and I've come a few times with them. But at night the fields are ethereal and eerie.

"What about bears?" I whisper.

Dan puts his hand out to me. "There'll be no bears. We'll be fine."

I don't know why I believe him, but I do. I mean, this is a

madman we're talking about, a person who climbs enormous rock walls without ropes and is planning to do so on El Cap. Why do I trust that I'm safe with him? I don't know. Maybe it's because of how he's been during our hookups—so careful to get my consent, so caring about my pleasure—I don't know. But I do trust him.

I take Dan's free hand and let him lead me across the grass, guide me over rocks, past standing water, and around uneven ground. In front of us is a moonlit, granite dome. It shines in the darkness, along with the other rock formations and mountains around us, like something brought from the surface of the moon. It's massive. Or at least it seems so to me. Intellectually, I know, given the size of other domes and towers in this glacier-carved land, this particular one isn't that impressive. In fact, during the day, Leenie and Martin have climbed up the less steep side while I watched the kids down below. But the side Dan is leading me toward is sheer and tall, and my head falls back to take it in as we approach. I'm beginning to suspect what he has in those bags.

We've walked in mostly silence so far, but as he draws me up to the base of the wall, I say, "I hope you don't think I'm going to climb that thing."

"Well, I brought the gear in case you wanted to," he says, patting the bigger bag he's got hoisted over his right arm. "And I've got the top rope already in place." He gestures at the wall. "But if, after we talk about it, you decide you'd rather not, we can always hike up the back side for our starlight picnic." He indicates his backpack.

"What's there to talk about? I'm afraid of heights."

"You said it was the exposure that really gets to you." He motions around. "It's dark, and it's only going to get darker. The moon won't rise more than it already has, and it's going to trend back toward the horizon soon enough." He indicates where it's already dipping again. "Then it'll be really dark. You won't be able to see anything except the wall just ahead of you. And this wall is, I promise, some of the easiest climbing around. Kids do it. Old people. Total beginners. I could do this wall in my sleep. It'll only take about thirty or forty minutes for you, tops. Probably less. I know you don't really know me as a climber yet, but you can trust me. We're going to do this in the safest way possible."

"In the dark."

"Yup."

"Isn't it safer in daylight?"

Dan reaches out and touches my chin with the tips of his fingers, rubbing his thumb against my cheek. "I'd never let anything happen to you, Doc."

"Because you haven't seen that smile?"

He grins, the light from my headlamp bouncing off his teeth. "Yeah. And I can think of a few other reasons."

I hesitate. As the moon drifts down into the nest of trees at the horizon, it's growing darker and darker. I can barely see a few yards away now and that's only because the light of the moon is reflecting off the white granite of the wall. My belly swoops, but when I meet Dan's gaze, I just can't say no. He's looking at me so seriously, like when he talked to Jeremiah earlier, with a gentleness that makes my heart leap. His thumb still moves against my cheek, and I feel each hot swipe of it as pure reassurance.

It's not a dare. He's not challenging me to do this for bragging rights or to push my limits and see how much he can get away with when it comes to me and my boundaries. I can tell that from his expression alone. There's nothing smug in his face right now. Just a hopeful warmth that makes me want to say yes, that makes me want to lean forward and kiss his mouth.

Admittedly, I don't know *why* he wants to climb this allegedly infantile wall with me, but it's clear that he does, and I know enough about climbing to know I'll probably be perfectly safe doing it. Well, as perfectly safe as anything can be. I'm much more likely to have been injured or killed riding on the motorcycle than doing this.

He knows it.

I know it.

I want to say yes. It doesn't make sense that I want to impress him by badly doing something he could do in his sleep, and yet that's my hope. I want him to know I'm not the kind of guy to say no unreasonably. I'm not a coward, and this situation…

I don't think this situation is a no.

But it's not a yes. Not quite yet.

"Why do you want me to climb this with you?"

"I love climbing, and I want to share it with you." He points up. "At the top, I've already stashed a bag with everything we need to camp: sleeping bags, a portable stove, and dinner."

He moves his thumb on my cheek again, and this time I do lean forward and kiss him. He drops the bigger bag and tugs me flush to his body. We waste a few good minutes of moonlight tasting each other's mouths and getting way too aroused for our own good. I'm just about to drop to my knees and offer to suck him off when he pulls away and puts both hands on my shoulders.

"Sejin," he says breathlessly. "Are we gonna climb or not?"

"We're gonna climb." Seeing that wide slash of a smile illuminating the escalating darkness, I feel in my gut I've made the right choice.

Dan

SEJIN IS A good sport about the climb. It's too bad he's afraid of heights because he's a natural at it, really. Maybe night climbing can become a sport of its own because he doesn't seem at all frightened once he's up on the wall with darkness stretching out behind him.

"It's not bad," he says cheerfully, reaching up for the next obvious hold. "I can't even see the ground. For all I can tell by looking, it's just a few feet down."

It's not even a high climb. A pitch's length and that's about it.

It'd taken about thirty minutes to get him set up with the ropes, to review how it works—which wasn't hard since he'd bouldered some bigger rocks before—and then I'd taken lead. The moon had fully set by then, and now he really only has the rock in front of him, lit by the lamp I've attached to his head, and a few feet of darkness all around to worry about.

"You're doing great," I call down to him.

I'm at the top now, feet hanging over, waiting for him to join me.

"Thanks," he grunts, tugging himself up to the next hold. "I feel good."

When he emerges at the top, he looks good too. His eyes are shining, and his skin is glowing with exertion. The grin on his face is what takes my breath away, though. It's so close to the one in that photo I'm obsessed with. There's pride, joy, fun, and laughter there, but even though his eyes are the right shape, and his mouth is too, there's something missing. I can't say exactly what, but I suspect it's what Peggy Jo mentioned. I'm afraid the missing ingredient might be love.

That's a bitter pill.

He doesn't love me. He never will. That's the way it is. I may have to admit that I'll never achieve this particular goal. It could turn out that seeing Sejin's special smile directed at me is more impossible than sending Heart Route could ever be. But hopeless as it is, it won't kill me to keep trying. Maybe love *isn't* the missing ingredient. Maybe I can still discover the recipe. It's not like free soloing. One misstep won't kill me.

I try not to let these thoughts deflate my pleasure because Sejin is actually, for real, grinning at me right now, and it's clear he's having a really good time.

"Wow, that was awesome," he says, collapsing next to me. "I did it."

"You did."

We both turn off our headlamps and just rest a minute. Sejin lightly pants beside me, catching his breath, both of us gazing out into the darkness where the trees below are just even darker shadows, and the sky above is pitch black with bright pricks of light from the stars.

It's magical and kind of lonely with just us up here. But that doesn't make it silent. The night noises of the forest below drift to us on the wind. I listen and lean back on my elbows, the hard granite digging in.

Sejin's stomach growls and it's remarkably loud. We both laugh.

I stand up, offering him a hand. "I guess that means it's dinnertime."

Using the pulley, I haul the bigger bag up from below and tug it safely up onto the top of the granite dome with us. I turn my headlamp back on and seek out a good location far from any edges and go about setting up camp.

Sejin helps, and it quickly becomes obvious that he's not a total newbie at camping.

"Yeah, I was a Boy Scout," Sejin says, helping me gather twigs to get the portable woodburning camp stove started. Once it's lit, the golden glow from the fire illuminates his features and gives us enough light to organize our things and begin to prepare for dinner.

Suddenly Sejin slaps himself on the leg.

"Damn mosquitos," he mutters. He slaps himself again. And a third time.

I again indicate the bag I'd stashed at the top earlier in the day.

"In there. There's a rechargeable lantern-bug-zapper combo-thingy."

Sejin hums as he sets it up a slight distance from the camp, drawing the bugs away from us. The first zap sounds, and he pumps his fist. "Yes. Die, fucker."

I smirk as I start cooking our meal. Nothing fancy, just some canned spicy vegetarian chili, but I know from experience it's plenty tasty, especially when camping. There's something primally comforting in spooning hot, spicy food into your mouth while taking in the pitiless stars, so cold and distant.

Or maybe that's just me, but I can't imagine Sejin is going to complain. He doesn't seem like the fussy sort.

"Mosquitoes love me," Sejin says as he comes over and squats beside me, watching as I stir the pot over the camp stove. "I get enormous welts from them. Always have. I read somewhere once, back when I was still in college, that lots of kids who've been adopted from other countries have that reaction to American mosquitoes. There's a theory that human bodies become biological-ly adapted to the mosquitoes from the area where our ancestors are from so they don't react as strongly to the mosquitoes from those areas. But if we move or are transplanted, then our bodies react super-strongly to the mosquitoes native to the new area because we don't have the resistance built in for it."

"Huh," I say. "Did you react more or less strongly to the mos-quitos back home?"

"In West Virginia?"

"Yeah."

"The same. There's been no big change. It's not like it's worse since I moved out here to California."

Sejin settles in next to me, and I want to scoot closer so I can feel the heat of his body alongside mine, but I stay where I am for now, intent on making sure I don't burn the chili. I did that once, and it'd tasted pretty foul.

"But it's all anecdotal as far as I can tell," Sejin goes on. "I mean, I'm not sure if there's any actual science to back it up. Plus, it was forever ago that I read it. I don't even remember if I saw it online, like on Tumblr or something, or in a research journal for my studies."

"What were your studies?"

"Psychology, and then Education—enough hours to get the certifications I need to work with kids—and then I dropped out."

"Ah."

"How about you? Any college?"

"No." I shake my head.

"Just high school then?"

I laugh. "Not even."

"Really?"

I shrug. "What's the point of it all anyway? I got what I needed from school, which wasn't much, and went on my way."

"Huh."

He sounds skeptical, so I say, "Don't get me wrong, education is important, but how that education is achieved isn't."

"Except when it comes to applying for jobs. I don't know how many listings I've seen that require a B.A. at a minimum and grad school if you want something that pays decent."

"Jobs schmobs. The whole thing is a scam."

Sejin laughs. "Spoken like the true rebel I suspected you would turn out to be."

"It's not about being rebellious. It's about time and how little of it we have in this life. Why waste it doing things that are pointless and useless?"

"High school is pointless and useless?"

"It can be. Just consider…when's the last time you solved a geometry proof in your life? When's the last time you needed to know the name of every element? When's the last time all those years spent at those desks, being spoon-fed information that you'll never need, felt worthwhile? Isn't there something you would have rather been doing? Listening to KPop or traveling or something?"

Sejin stares at the fire in the stove and then nods. "I'd have spent more time with my mom."

"Oh? You a mama's boy?" I ask.

"Was. I *was* a mama's boy," he says. "She died, remember?"

"Oh. Right." I recall that he'd mentioned that before and feel guilty that I forgot. I don't know what to say about it either. I never had a mother to call my own, but people seem really attached to theirs most of the time. I imagine how I'd feel if Peggy Jo died. It's not a great feeling. I put my hand on his shoulder. "That sucks."

"It does," he agrees. His black lashes glow like gold in the firelight, and I squeeze his arm. He smiles with closed lips and doesn't look at me. "What about your family?"

"Don't have one," I say, removing my hand and going back to stirring the canned chili. It's steaming now, and ready to be served over the chips I've brought, sprinkled, of course, with cheese. Impromptu camp nachos.

"No?" Sejin asks. "Like no family at all?" Again, he sounds skeptical. Which makes sense. It takes a certain amount of effort in life to end up with absolutely no family. I'm not going to lie and say there was zero choice involved for me, but at the same time there were circumstances.

"To pervert Oscar Wilde, losing one parent—like you have—can be seen as a misfortune, but losing an entire family starts to look like carelessness. Did I guess where your skepticism is coming from?" I open the chips and dump a goodly amount into two biggish bowls I've brought, and then grab the bag of grated cheese from the supplies. When we're done here, I'll have to secure all of this well to prevent any bears or other animals from moseying up the back way while we're out here tonight.

"No, no, of course not," Sejin says. "I'm just trying to imagine life with no family. Mine's pretty big. Sixteen cousins, half a dozen aunts, a bunch of uncles, and loads of meddling. You really have no one?"

"No one at all."

"How…" He clears his throat, watching me stir the chili some more. Then I guess he decides to just go for it, and I admire that he has the balls to ask. "How did that happen?"

"Ah, it just kind of did." I add as an aside, "Remember, I never claimed to be a good cook."

I use a big serving spoon scavenged from the depths of my silverware drawer back in my van to scoop the goop over the bowls of chips. "But I guess it all began when my mother abandoned me sometime after my sixth birthday, and I got passed around twelve or so different foster homes before I finally just set out on my own a few months before I turned eighteen."

"Twelve homes? Over eleven years?"

"Yup. My cute little mug didn't seem to stir their hearts enough to make up for my weirdness, I guess."

"I'm…sorry."

"Cheese okay?" I sprinkle it on liberally when he nods, and then pass the bowl over to him, along with a spoon to grab whatever the chips don't hold. "I don't remember a lot of my childhood, to be honest, so it's probably okay. I remember almost nothing of my mother, except that she had long brown hair. I think? I'm not even sure of that. In fact, I don't remember much of anything until my second or third foster home."

"Wow. What do you remember from there?"

"Eating rocks."

Sejin blinks at me as he tries to process what I've just said. "Did you say eating rocks?"

"Yeah. I used to take handfuls of the gravel from their driveway, put it in my mouth, kind of chew it around, and then spit it out again." I take a big bite of nachos, enough to keep me from having to talk for a few seconds, and he does the same.

"Was it pica?" he asks, once he swallows. "You know, some nutritional deficiency that made you want to put rocks in your mouth?"

"Maybe. I mean, I wasn't getting a lot of nourishment back then for a lot of reasons. It was hard to get me to eat. I was super picky."

"I was picky when I was young too. Nothing but my mom's PB&J would do for lunches. I must have eaten three thousand of them."

"What about you?" I ask, glad to change the topic to him. "What do you remember from Korea?"

"Korea? Oh, nothing." He shakes his head. "I was brought over when I was eight months old. My parents picked me up from the airport. They had me delivered to them, basically. They used to joke that they should have named me Air-Mail." He laughs, and his eyes do that half-moon thing. "Anyway, there was a woman who took me from my foster mother in Korea and delivered me to my parents in West Virginia. I remember none of that. My first memory is of my grandfather dangling my feet in the Pocatalico river—that's a little river near to where I grew up, and close to my grandparents' house. I was probably three."

"Were they a white family?" I ask, though I suspect I know the answer.

"Yep. Good ol' redneck white Appalachians," he says. "I was the only non-white person in my family and, like I said, it was a big family." He pops a nacho in his mouth, seeming to consider as he chews. "Another early memory I have is of being in a crowd of my girl cousins, all of them arguing over who got to pretend I was their baby, and all of them kissing me—cheeks, head, arms—until I started to cry. They smothered me with love!" He laughs, and my heart lightens.

Sejin might have lost his mom, but it's obvious the concept of family isn't the dead space that it is for me.

"Did you feel different? Growing up non-white in an all-white family?"

"Sometimes. I remember wondering why my skin was darker than everyone else's, why my eyes had a different shape, but I didn't worry too much about it. My mom and dad were upfront about my adoption—I mean they kind of had to be—so I knew that I looked different from the rest of the family because I was born in another country. I know other kids in my situation might have had more problems with the whole thing than I did, but sometimes I think that's a failure in myself, you know?"

"Explain," I say, scooping up chili with my chip, and putting it into my mouth. The flavor isn't as smoky as when I've made it over a campfire and not a stove, but it's still tasty and hot.

"Like…okay, a year or so ago, I was watching some KPop music videos on YouTube and this related video came up in my Recommended. It was called something like 'Korean Kids Adopted Into American Families: The Truth,' and I thought, 'Oh, this is about me!' So, I watched it…and, I don't know…"

He shakes his head, eats another nacho, and then shakes his head again. "It just made me feel more isolated and alone than I ever had before."

"Why?"

"Because a lot of those young people were angry about their adoption. They had all kinds of big feelings and thoughts about it that I've never had." He flips his ponytail to the other shoulder. "Like, for example, there was this one guy, eighteen or so, and he was distraught over questions about why his birth mother had given him up, and if she was okay now, and whether she was worried about him. Maybe I'm an asshole, but I've literally never thought that much about my birth mother? It'd never occurred to me until that moment that I *should* maybe worry about her or wonder if she's worried about me. I couldn't help but think maybe there's something wrong with me that I'd never considered it. Do I lack empathy? Am I selfish?"

"Ah." I can relate in a way. I never give a lot of thought to my mother or any of the foster families I've left behind. Probably for different reasons, but I don't find Sejin's lack of worry for a woman he's never met to be any evidence of a lack of empathy or a character flaw. "Maybe you were just a happy kid with a happy family, and worry wasn't something you tended to do much of anyway."

"You're right. I wasn't a very worried kid. I don't think I ever spent a truly unhappy day until my mom got sick. Even when things were less than perfect, I was just…happy inside. I shrugged things off. Moved on."

"Some people are just like that." From what I've seen of him, Sejin doesn't seem like a man bound by doubts or worries, even if he is uncertain about my free solo plans.

"How about you? Do you shrug things off?"

"No," I answer earnestly. "I sure as hell don't."

He laughs. "Ah, you hold grudges?"

"With both hands."

Sejin laughs again, and my heart flutters. It's a rare feeling for me. One more typical of having sent a particularly difficult route, and almost never due to another human being, but I can't deny Sejin's done something funny to my insides right from the start.

"Did anything else make you feel alienated when you watched the video of adopted kids?"

I've got a lot of practice at feeling estranged, but I've always assumed if I were in a room full of former foster children, we'd have plenty of resentment to bond over. I guess Sejin had assumed something similar about being a Korean adoptee.

"Ah, it's weird. I'm a little embarrassed to admit it."

"Why?"

"Maybe it means I'm not very smart?" Sejin says it like a question, and he finishes up his bowl of nachos, reaches for the bag of chips, and starts a second helping. I feel oddly proud, like I did more than warm up a can of vegetarian chili and throw it in a bowl over chips and cheese.

"You seem plenty smart to me."

He shrugs. "Or maybe I just don't have the right priorities in life."

"Priorities like?"

"Well, okay, so a lot of these adoptees were disappointed at what they'd lost, you know? A bunch of them were angry that they'd lost their Korean culture, family, and the language of their birth. A lot of them felt like they didn't fit in here in the States, and never would, because they aren't white, and they aren't Korean—at least not in a way where they can mix well with first, second, or third generation Koreans here. And I get that. I do. Because I've met plenty of Asian people now—Korean and otherwise—who assume that I've got similar background experiences as they do, but I just don't. You know, like…like this one woman made a lunchbox joke at me, sure that I would get it, and I didn't."

"A lunchbox joke? I don't follow."

"So, apparently, a lot of first-generation kids, maybe even second-generation, I don't know, get made fun of at school for having quote-unquote 'weird stuff' in their lunchboxes. Like kimbap."

"But you had PB&J."

"Right. Every day. No one ever thought my lunches were weird."

"And these other adoptees in white families wish they'd had lunches other kids made fun of?"

"They wish they had their birth culture," he clarifies. "And if that means having lunches that others made fun of, I guess they believe all the rest they'd have gained would have been worth it."

"You don't think it would have been?"

"I'll never know. Until I watched this video, I admit I'd never thought about it much. I mean, sometimes, yeah, my grandfather would be telling me about some family history like, 'Your great-great-grandpa built that house,' and it would occur to me that my biological great-great-grandpa hadn't built it, or whatever. But I didn't linger on the thought, or feel hurt by it, or wonder what my biological great-great-grandfather *had* accomplished..." He scoops more chili onto the chips, adds cheese, thinks a moment and says, "Though now that I've said that, I do wonder what he did with his life? It'd be cool to find out. But if I never do, then that's all right too. I'm fine with some stuff being a mystery. Like, I don't know where my mom who raised me went when she died—like if there's a heaven, or if there's just nothing, or if she was reborn. And there are things about her life I will never have a chance to know now that she's gone. Little things and big ones. There's so much in death you have to just learn to be okay with not knowing. Otherwise the questions can paralyze you."

"I agree. It's important to make peace with the unknown."

We sit in silence for a few seconds, both of us pondering another great unknown—the sky above.

Sejin shrugs. "Anyway, yeah, so that video was confusing to me. I think about it a lot now, how all these other adoptees are angry about being adopted, how they feel stripped of their heritage and are upset about being given to an American white family. And I have to wonder, you know? Am I doing my life wrong? Because it never occurred to me to feel that way? Was I robbed?"

"Yes, you were robbed, and no, you weren't robbed. You lost one thing and got another instead. How you feel about it—how they feel about it—it's not right or wrong. If you're not mad, you're not mad. If you *stay* not mad, that's fine. If you get mad later, that's fine too."

"But *should* I be mad?"

"I don't know. Should *I* be mad that I was passed around foster homes and—"

"I mean, I don't know the details, but I'd say yes! You should be furious about that."

"Well, you were loved. Maybe that's the difference."

"Some of these other adoptees were probably loved and they're still angry about what they lost. But, right now, in my life? The thing I'm most angry to have lost is my mom, you know? The woman who raised me."

I clear my throat. "That makes sense. It seems like she was a good mom to you."

I feel like I'm vomiting up words from some how-to-be-a-human-being-in-hard-situations manual, and I wonder if this has been instilled in me from Peggy Jo, or Rye, or who exactly gave me the training to not make an utter ass of myself right now. In the past, I'd probably have fucked this up badly enough that Sejin would get up and walk away.

"She was." He sighs. "It's okay. You can ask."

"What?"

"How she died. I know you're curious. Everyone always is, and most people ask eventually. Let's just get it out of the way."

"Alright. How'd she die?"

"It was breast cancer. She was fifty-nine."

"That sucks," I say again. What else is there to say in a situation like this?

"It changed everything."

We sit in silence again, and then I ask, "What about your dad? Are you close with him?"

"Not really. Or not the way I think you mean. But he's the reason I'm out here tonight with you."

"How's that?"

Sejin shrugs. He looks down at the now empty bowl in his hand, his lashes touching his cheekbones, and his lips curve up slightly. "What would you say if I told you that I think you and I are going to do more together than just fuck?"

"I'd say that's pretty observant since we're currently eating nachos and camping out while not-fucking."

Sejin laughs, and I think I can see his cheeks darken in the light from the portable camp stove. Is he blushing? "Yeah, we aren't fucking right now, are we?"

"No."

"What I mean, though, is if we keep seeing each other, it's going to turn into more than sex."

"It already has," I say, collecting his bowl and mine, and starting to clear up the food so that we can seal it up good and tight. "You officially know more about me now than anyone except for Rye and Peggy Jo. You probably know more than Lowell, to be honest."

"Lowell Moody?"

"Yeah."

"You know him?"

"Carried me out when I twisted my ankle a few years ago. We're not close, but I consider him a friend. I think he probably considers me…annoying."

Sejin laughs.

"*You* know Lowell?" I briefly wonder if they've fucked, but then I remember Lowell's ex-wife, and that he very recently confirmed that, while he is open to sex with a guy, he hasn't done that yet.

It shouldn't have mattered anyway, except that it does. I really don't want Sejin fucking anyone else for the time being, and some scary part of me, deep down, suggests that maybe I don't want him fucking anyone else *ever* again. That's a bit much, though. That part of me needs to calm the fuck down.

"I know everyone in this town at this point. Working at Papa Bear, it can't be helped. As for Lowell, I don't *know* him, know him. He's just an interesting person. Hot too. And straight."

"Maybe."

"Oh? Interesting. I just know he's got that scary archangel vibe going on, and if he asked me to get in his bed, I'd put out."

I waver between enthusiastic agreement about the whole "archangel" description, and a definite spike of anxiety at the "I'd put out" comment.

"Speaking of..." Sejin hesitates and gives me a very strange look before saying, "Are you still hooking up with other guys?"

"Are you?" I ask too quickly.

His eyes widen. "No. I've been way too busy. But the season has officially started, there will be offers, and I just want to know—"

"No," I blurt out. "I mean, I don't intend to hook up with other guys right now." Since when? And, Jesus, why? Just because Sejin's pretty? Because the sex is great? Because of his smile? Because of the way he just talks to me like I deserve his life story? I don't know. But I'm not fucking anyone else if I can fuck him, that's for sure. "I'd like it if you didn't either."

"Hmm," Sejin says, considering, and my gut churns anxiously. "I'll let you know if I change my mind, but I'm okay with agreeing to fuck only you for now. I mean, it's not like I have a ton of spare time, and the sex we have is great. If I'm going to spend my limited free time getting laid, I might as well do it with someone I know is gonna get the job done and do it really damn well."

"I take fucking very seriously. I won't let you down," I say, and it sounds ridiculous as soon as it's out of my mouth.

Sejin laughs and puts his hand out. I take it, and I'm surprised by how cold his fingers are. Mine are warm, and he curls his in around my palm, stealing the warmth from my skin. "This isn't a job interview, but I believe you, and I accept your proposal for a limited period of monogamy, to be renegotiated if things get unfun for either of us."

"Limited?"

"Well, you're just here for the season, right? Surely you don't expect me to stay virtuous after you've gone?" He squeezes my hand. "Or do you agree with me that if we continue on, things are going to get real between us super-fast?"

"No, I…" I clear my throat. "I kind of just thought we'd camp out tonight, and I'd get to fuck you again soon, and that would be that. But I guess what you're saying is that you and I are…what's happening between us is…" I fumble.

"It's not going to stay casual," Sejin says firmly. "I don't think there's any way. I mean, look at you." He gestures at me, and I look down. "You're holding my hand by a fire on top of a dome you made me climb, and I'm here with you despite my fear of heights—"

"Fear of exposure," I correct.

"And we're talking about our lives, and we ate nachos, and…I don't know. I just don't think this feels casual. Though, I guess if you were someone else, and I were someone else, it might still be. But as it is…I just feel like if I keep seeing you? If I keep having sex with you, or climbing with you—"

"You'll climb with me again?"

"Maybe. But if I do these things, I'm going to fall for you, and that's what I told my dad. I told him you're into danger, and your lifespan might be shorter than usual—"

"Into danger." I snort.

"And *he* told *me* a story that made me decide to go ahead and see you tonight. So, you have my dad to thank for the fact that I'm here at all." Sejin's hand clenches a little in mine. "Is any of what I just said a problem for you?"

I stare at his face in the light of the portable stove. The stars are tiny, glowing perforations behind him, and his hair is coming down all tumbled around his face, and I can't imagine him not being here or missing this moment.

"No. I don't have a problem with that at all."

"Good, that's good to hear."

He leans in and kisses me. The world dissolves in a swirl of emotion I don't understand. Feelings I've never had before swell and push against my skin and I murmur, "Oh, Christ," against his lips before clenching the front of his jacket and dragging him close.

My heart pounds like it does when I try the dyno on Heart Route and miss. Falling hard and fast through space. Crash-landing into rock, solid and inescapable.

This time, though, my inescapable crash is into Sejin and his sweet lips.

CHAPTER ELEVEN

Sejin

OUR KISS DOESN'T last very long, but when it's over, I feel like my heart's going to pound out of my chest. I don't think Dan is a wise bet, and I don't think he's the seahorse of my dreams, and yet I don't want to walk away from this anymore. Not even if…

I swallow. Not even if it all ends in a gory mess. Still, it's easy enough to ignore that possibility right here in this starry moment.

"So, what now?" I ask, as Dan strokes his fingers against my cheek, and gazes into my eyes.

"I don't know."

He's breathing a little erratically, and I again consider tossing aside my original insistence that we aren't having sex tonight by offering to blow him, but then he leans back and asks, "Want to listen to some music?" He turns to that bag he keeps producing camping gear from and holds up a small, square object. "I've got a Bluetooth speaker."

"Sure."

He powers it up, opens Spotify, and then glances at me. "Want to listen to one of your playlists?"

"We could, but I'm curious. What kind of music do you like?"

He shrugs. "A little bit of everything, but mainly I listen to more raucous stuff, you know, to get my blood pumping before a climb or during a hard push up a pitch. None of it seems right for…well, for a night like tonight."

"A date?"

He smirks, scrolling through music lists on his phone. "Yeah, a date, I guess. I mean, does this seem like it fits the mood to you?"

A ripping guitar chord tears into the stillness of the night, and it's startling enough that I yelp.

"That's what I thought," he says, laughing, and turning the song off.

"Here." I hold out my hand and he passes his phone over to me. I look up one of my public playlists and press shuffle-play. The first song is a piano cover of "Stardust" by Astro, and I check the queue quickly to make sure nothing jarring is coming up next, but the app has coughed up a nice, soft piano-focused playlist of some of my KPop favorites. "This okay?" I ask.

"Sure," he replies, and then we spend some time cleaning up the camp area and securing the food. Once everything is put away, and the twigs refreshed in the portable stove to keep the fire going a bit longer, Dan unrolls the sleeping bags.

As we crawl into our respective bags, piano notes drift from the speaker, and the night swallows them as the music drifts up into the sky. I roll onto my side and look at Dan, and he reaches out, twining our fingers together.

"When did you start listening to KPop?" Dan asks.

I stretch my hand open, and he places his palm over mine, comparing sizes. My fingers are longer, but his palm is a bit bigger. "My cousin Nevaeh, which, in case you don't know, is heaven spelled backwards—and that's important for the rest of this story because it tells you a lot about her parents… Anyway, she got super rebellious in high school and started dipping her toes into things her parents thought were dangerous. Like KPop."

"They thought Korean pop music was dangerous? Why? Because it's in another language?"

"No, they thought relatively hairless young men, wearing make-up and dancing in high fashion outfits to elaborate choreo was dangerous. Mainly because of their internalized homophobia, racism, and ethnocentrism, but they truly believed Nevaeh was being subtly seduced to the queer side by KPop, and also maybe becoming a communist. Which is hilarious since South Korea is one of the most capitalistic countries in the entire world, not to mention deeply misogynistic, and frankly not at all accepting of us homosexuals—"

"I'm bisexual, actually."

"Ah, okay. Well, not accepting of us queers, that's for sure. It's not even legal there to marry or adopt kids if you're not in a heterosexual relationship."

Dan sneers, but says nothing. What is there to say? It's not like the US is a longtime bastion of equal rights for the LGBT community either, and our rights are being threatened every single day.

"South Korea has a way to go in that regard," I sum up.

"I assume her parents hating KPop just made it more enticing for your cousin," Dan surmises.

"Of course. They hadn't yet figured out that the queer snake in the grass was me. So, she would come over to my house, where I, a spoiled only child, would have access to all the KPop goodness of her dreams. She introduced me to her favorite group, and I was a goner right from the start."

"Was that group…uh, Astro, was it? Were they always your favorite?"

"No, and even now I wouldn't call them my favorite. My ult, as the kids say"—I wink at him—"is a group called SHINee. I fell in love with their song 'Replay' as soon as I heard it. Then it was just a long, winding tumble down the SHINee rabbit hole until other groups began to make it onto my radar. Now I'm what's known as a KPop multi. I like multiple groups and solo artists. I get around."

"Can I hear it?"

"What?"

"The song that made you a fan."

"Ha!" I sit up and reach for the phone and cue it up. "Okay, but it's an old song, a bit dated."

"S'okay." Dan sounds a little sleepy as he tucks his hands under his head and smiles up at me. "I'm fine with that."

"Alright. Here we go." I press play and the familiar music starts up. I sing along lightly, the lyrics and sounds embedded in my memory.

"I thought you said you don't know Korean."

"I don't." I laugh. "I'm probably pronouncing most of it all wrong. But, yeah, I've learned a little from the songs. For example, the word *noona* means older sister or older girl in general, and it's a little flirty when used by someone who isn't a relative. So, the lyric I just sang is *'Noonan neomu yeppeo,'* which means *noona* is so pretty. So, this song is about a pretty older girl that the singers have a crush on." I do some of the upper body choreo. "And the dance is a little like this. I have the kids perform it sometimes."

"How do the kids feel about not understanding the songs?" Dan asks.

"Oh, they don't care, and a lot of them learn the Korean words to a larger degree than I've been able to. They're so young and their language centers are still wide open."

"Would you like to learn more?" Dan asks.

"Korean? I guess." I lean back and stare up at the stars. "I mean, I looked into it and there are free online resources for beginners, but I…" I trail off.

"But something's keeping you from starting?"

"Do you know any other languages?" I hedge. My reasons for stalling are pretty absurd.

"Nothing more than some basic Italian from Duolingo. I want

to climb outside of the US one day, and the Dolomites in Italy are at the top of the list. But I've heard there's some good climbing in Thailand and China, as well as Laos. There must be some good climbs in Korea and Japan…" It's his turn to trail off.

"I'd love to travel too," I say. "And, yeah, before you ask, I do want to go to Korea one day."

"I wasn't going to ask that, actually."

"You weren't?"

"No, I was going to come back to what's keeping you from starting to learn Korean. You're passionate about the music and lyrics, and you can imitate some of the sounds. That seems like a good start."

I clear my throat. "It's a dumb reason. I *should* start. I really should."

"But what's the reason?"

"Tenacious little jerk, aren't you?"

Dan smiles and shrugs again. "Sort of my calling card—stubborn, obstinate, determined. Required in my line of work."

"Is it work, though? Like do you have a sponsorship or…"

"No more trying to switch topics. Just answer the question."

I frown, a burst of rebellion making me want to tell him to fuck off, but instead I tell him the truth. "I feel like I'd be betraying my parents. Which is dumb, like I said. I mean…neither of them ever asked me to stay monolingual. In fact, Mom really hoped I'd pick up more Spanish than I did back in high school." I pull my hairband out and let my hair fall around me. "Besides, where was I supposed to find a Korean teacher in West Virginia, or here in Mariposa County for that matter?"

Dan lifts up on one elbow and pushes one side of my hair back, searches my face, and then falls to his sleeping bag again. "I have a pal…" He breaks off. "Well, okay, I met this guy once, I don't think Peggy Jo would let me call the guy an actual pal… Anyway, he teaches Greek—his mother tongue—online through some service, and he only charges about eight bucks an hour. He gets enough by teaching something he knows well to keep climbing as his main passion. Surely there's someone like that out there teaching Korean."

"Maybe…"

"If you're not interested, don't worry about it. It just seems like you're on the verge of something here. It's like when I was learning climbing from Peggy Jo. There was the introductory phase, and I could have stayed there indefinitely and just enjoyed indoor climbing with autobelays, but eventually I took the next step."

"What would I do if knew Korean? I mean, what benefit would it give me?"

"Beats me. The pleasure of learning it? You could ask me the same about climbing."

"Hmm." I don't know that I want to commit to anything right now, but he's given me something to think about. "I should probably get off my cousin's couch before I start spending money on language lessons, though," I say.

"Your cousin's couch?"

I realize I've never told him about my living situation, so I fill him in.

"So, those kids I saw you with at Papa Bear—and the boy I met—are your cousin's and his wife's?"

"Did you think they were mine?" I ask, laughing. "And Leenie was what? My wife?"

"No, no, of course not. I just assumed you had your own room there, and she was a friend or a roommate." He frowns. "I mean, I hadn't really thought that much about it. I mainly just wanted to get you away from them so I could have you to myself."

I sigh and lounge back down. The next song to come up on the playlist after "Replay" ends is one of my favorite BTS songs, and I sing the lyrics softly.

"How do you know what the songs are about? In general. You know, if you don't know the individual words?"

"I look up the translations online. The first word of this song, *bogoshipda,* means 'I miss you' and this song is about the loss of an important friendship."

"Ah. Never experienced that. I hear it sucks."

"It does."

"So you *have* picked up quite a few words, then."

"Of course. *Hajima* means stop or quit or don't do it. And *saranghae* means I love you."

"Mm."

"Are you really interested in all this?"

"Why wouldn't I be?"

I shrug. "I don't know. It's all pretty frivolous."

"It makes you happy. What's more important than that?"

"Being responsible. Making a living. Getting off my cousin's sofa."

"Overrated. All of it. Especially the being responsible stuff. Fuck that."

That makes me laugh. "Remind me not to introduce you to my father. He's all about responsibility. Spent his life on it."

"Most men do."

"Women too."

"Of course," Dan agrees. "Responsible for the men in their lives, and the kids, and their work, and so much more. Or so I hear. I admit Peggy Jo's one of the only women I've ever known who's responsible like that. My foster mothers weren't good for much when it came to me." He pauses, considering for a moment. "Though I guess Edith—my third or fourth foster mom—was pretty great. She cared about me. It's not like she meant to get sick." Dan's eyes go sad, and he shifts his gaze to the stars. "That's why they sent me away from her."

"I'm sorry."

"Yeah. And when I was older, Mrs. Crawford tried to be a good parent for me. But by then it was too late, and I wasn't having it. I made the poor woman miserable. So, I got sent off to Mr. Anderson's, and I cut out of there as soon as I could. Never looked back."

"You had a rough time growing up," I say, stating the obvious.

"Can't deny that." He clears his throat. "It's all right, though. Taught me not to rely on anyone."

"Is that what this whole free solo thing is about? Not relying on anything or anyone?"

"Just me and my body against an uncaring rock wall? Which will prevail? Yeah. Something like that. It's a battle I feel in my soul and a communion of sorts. An acknowledgement of my absolute lack of importance in the world, the meaninglessness of life. My existential crisis made manifest."

"Christ."

"Yeah."

"You say all that like I say 'I put too much milk in my cereal and now it's soggy.' You say it like it's nothing at all."

"You have to make your peace with it, you know?" Dan shifts in his bag. "To be a free soloist, you can't *want* to die, but you can't hate the idea of dying too much either. I don't typically tell anyone before I free solo something, and I don't always tell people after I've done it either. Some climbs I keep just for myself."

"Why?"

"Because they're not for public consumption. Nothing I do is for public consumption. My motivations are pure."

"Pure…"

"Untainted by the pursuit of money or fame."

"Right. But money is good, right? It's nice to have some things that only money can provide. Like shelter, food, and that sort of thing."

"You sound like Peggy Jo. Of course, those things are great, but they're for the future. Once I've achieved my goal."

I push my hair back away from my face. "What goes into achieving a free solo climb like you're planning?"

"Lots of practice and preparation. Day in and day out. This…" he motions between us. "This is a distraction from it, to be honest. I shouldn't be pursuing this. I need to keep my head in the game, and instead I find myself thinking about you. About fucking you, sure, but also just like…what your hair looks like all down and spread over your shoulders with the sun shining on it… like polished ebony."

"Dan, you're a secret romantic, aren't you?"

"Maybe. I'm just finding out these things about myself. I haven't ever…I don't typically…Like I said, you're a distraction I shouldn't be pursuing, and yet I want to. I've always told myself that life is about doing what you want, when you want, as much as possible."

"You're not going to get hurt because I'm so distracting, are you?" I feel both flattered and afraid.

He blows a raspberry in the darkness. "Of course not. I'm far too good at what I do for that."

"What happens if you fall? Do you think about that?"

"Of course. It's part of my training actually. Mental training." He sits up again and combs both hands through his hair, and then looks right at me. "The night before I free solo anything, I spend a few hours imagining the entire climb, and typically it's the crux— the hardest part—that scares me the most. So, I'll imagine myself failing at it, falling, and measure exactly how long I have before I hit bottom. I think about Peggy Jo and now, sometimes, Rye. How they'll feel. Imagine them crying. But then I imagine how they'll move on—and they will. It won't take them very long even. And if something happened to me, you'd move on too. Everyone moves on. You've learned that by losing your mom, haven't you?"

"No. I haven't." I feel a deep hurt inside both for him and for myself. "In fact, I've learned the opposite of that. I've learned that I'll *live*, yeah, but I've learned that she's the one and only mom I'll ever have. She's the one who raised and loved me. I lost a *lot* when I lost her." I pause, reach out to take his hand and he lets me. "You'd be the one and only Dan, you know. The one and only Dan for Peggy Jo, and Rye, and…well, I guess for me. Forever. I think, because of your childhood, you don't realize how irreplaceable of a person you are."

"I don't think I'm *replaceable*, just not that especially important to anyone at all."

"What if you became important to someone? To me?"

"Then…then we'd have to see."

"See what?"

"See what happened then."

I sigh and pull my hand back. "You're damaged goods, aren't you?"

"Sure am, Doc." He leans back, cupping his head with his hands and gazing up at the sky.

"Oh, man. What am I choosing to get into?"

"Hopefully my sleeping bag, because I know we said no sex, but I'm dying to just kiss you."

I roll my eyes. "Right, sure, 'just kiss me'."

"Feel free to put me to the test."

"I don't think your sleeping bag will hold us both."

"Feel free to put *that* to the test too."

It turns out I fit, but barely, and kissing Dan until we're both panting, rutting fully clothed together and dying to come, is an intoxicating way to spend the night.

In the end, I *beg* him to let us get off, and he denies me. I'm not sure how I feel about that—orgasm denial isn't a kink of mine. But I'm too exhausted, wound up, and spun out to protest much, or to do more than cuddle in next to him throbbing with desire, tired, and finally I drift off to sleep.

Sometime in the middle of the night, I feel him leave the bag, and I wake up enough to watch him climb into mine. I'm too drowsy to ask if everything's all right, and instead simply stretch into the room he's left behind.

I have a moment's wonder if that's what he means when he says everyone moves on. He leaves, and the space is filled, and no one misses him. I open my mouth to ask him to come back over, but I'm so tired and warm now that dreams jerk me back under before I can.

We sleep separately the rest of the night, and I wake in the morning with a strange, wild feeling in my heart. I want to sleep next to him. I want to feel his skin on my skin. And I want it for a long time.

I want it today, tomorrow, and the next day.

And we've only just met.

Oh, God. What if *I'm* the seahorse?

Dan

SUNRISE CRESTS OVER the eastern view of the meadows and Tioga Pass. It's egg-yolk yellow and eye-wateringly bright as I blink awake. Sejin is already up, singing softly to himself with earbuds in as he dances to music I can't hear. He looks like a dream outlined by the morning sun, long hair blowing in the wind, and his limber arms and legs making angles and arcs. He's so beautiful.

I know he thinks I'm beautiful too. I'm not sure why because, objectively, I'm a little goofy-looking, but there's just something about how he gazes at me that lets me know he sees something he likes in my features.

Not long ago, I thought he'd never gift me with that smile I crave, and last night…well, last night I think I came close to seeing it. It was dark, though, and I can't be sure. But I do know he's starting to care for me. I mean, we both said things about feelings that we can't exactly take back, even if they're embarrassing in the light of day.

I hoist myself up and onto my feet. I need to piss, and I don't want to think about all the confessions we made last night. Sejin's so absorbed in the sunrise and his music, that he doesn't notice me urinating off the cliffs behind us. My mouth tastes disgusting, so I fetch the small mouthwash bottle from the bag and take a swig before swishing and spitting.

When I'm done, I approach Sejin cautiously because I don't want to startle him. He's dancing fairly close to the edge—though not too close. He's being careful.

He must see me out of his peripheral vision because he turns, rips his earbuds out, and grins. "Look! The sunrise is amazing! I was afraid you were going to miss it."

Holding out the mouthwash, my offer is met with a fist pump, a cute habit of his when he's excited, and he takes it from me. He swishes too, and then spits over the side of the drop-off. "Hope no one's down there."

A quick glance shows us that the meadows are empty, and we're alone here in the morning light. I grab the speaker from our camping area, and when he sees what I've got in my hand, he connects his phone.

A piano-based KPop track wafts from the speaker, and Sejin takes my hand, leading me into an easy dance on the top of the rock. I'm grateful for the first time in my life for the ballroom dance portion of gym class in middle school. At least I can follow as he steps me through the movements. The sun rises higher, and the yellow breaks into a coral along the path of the mountains. Eventually he drags me close and, as the song changes to another equally appropriate for a breaking dawn, he presses his lips to mine in a soft kiss.

Some part of me is aware this is absurd and romantic, and that I should, by all rights, be alone in my van resting for Monday's training climb. But I'm swept up by the moment, charmed by the way his hair spills around his face and flies in the breeze and how his smile turns his eyes into those shimmery half-moons, and the way he somehow still smells appealing after a night roughing it.

I'm a little ripe myself, but he doesn't seem to mind as he presses against me, dotting kisses on my stubbly jaw and back to my lips. He's singing softly now with emotion and intonation, as if he knows what he's saying, though we both know he doesn't. Not entirely anyway. The gist of it, maybe, which makes me curious…

"This song, what's it about?"

"A once-beautiful thing that lives on only in memory."

"Ah."

"Sad, huh?"

But it's not that sad. I like the concept. Everything passes. Hard things, pretty things. Happiness and suffering. It all slides away like a river rushing downstream. You can't catch any of it. Memory is the one place those things can live. And beautiful memories—which are few and far between in my life—are the best, of course.

"It could be sadder. It could be a horrible thing that lives on in memory. Those are the saddest things of all."

Sejin's wistful smile fades away entirely, and I want to take my words back. I've ruined the moment.

"I mean, at least the beautiful thing happened at all," I murmur.

Sejin clears his throat and starts to turn away.

I grab his arm. "Listen, I didn't make a lot of memories growing up that I want to hold on to, so—for me—the idea of something beautiful living on in your mind is really nice, but I don't have a lot of personal experience with it."

"Ah."

"I'm sorry. I think I said something wrong."

He shakes his head. "No. You're right. I was thinking of my mom, and losing her never stops feeling sad, despite all my wonderful memories. But maybe I'm doing her a disservice feeling that way. Maybe I should be more like you—glad that I have beautiful memories to cherish."

"I had a Jewish…" I stop before I say the word friend, because he'd been a fellow newbie climber that Peggy Jo had taken on for about five weeks six years ago, and I'd met him a few times. Is that an acquaintance? Probably. "I knew a Jewish guy, and he used to say 'may her memory be a blessing' when someone died. I mean, that's what he said when Peggy Jo's mom died, but it seemed like something he said regularly in death situations…"

Sejin snorts. "'Death situations.' Oh, Dan. You're a mess."

"I like that, though. Memories as a blessing. Believe me, when you've got a lot of bad memories, the idea of a memory being a blessing and not a curse is really nice."

"I bet it is, and you're right. My mom's memory is an incredible blessing in my life."

"She'd want you to think about it that way," I say, which might be overstepping, but I feel a certainty of it, deep down in my soul. "She'd want you to remember her with joy."

"You are so weird," Sejin says, after a few moments of pondering the sunrise. Then he adds, "I'm sorry you don't have a lot of good memories."

I touch his cheek. "Here. Now. This will be a good memory."

Truth be told, I've made a lot of good memories in recent years, even if I haven't, until this moment, thought of what I've been doing in quite that way. I've always used other words for it: living in the moment, living fully, enjoying the now. But, here with Sejin, I see it for what it is. I've been creating a nice buffer of good memories to protect against all the bad in my past. All my focus on the *now* is one more giant step away from the darkness of *then*.

Even the suffering I put myself through while climbing is *my* suffering, chosen by me and me alone. The wall I've chosen. The route I've chosen. The risks I've chosen. All are protections against my ugly past, devoid of choice, devoid of victory. Devoid of love.

Tangling my hands into Sejin's hair, I pull him toward me for a deep kiss. He falls into it easily. As the sun rises high enough in the sky to mark that new day has begun, we break apart, gazing into each other's eyes.

A new beginning.

CHAPTER TWELVE

Sejin

"HOLY SHIT, IT'S cold as fuck!" I gasp as I leap away from the waterfall.

It's not a big one. In fact, most people wouldn't even pay it much attention or go out of their way to find it. But there are little falls like this all over the park from spring through the end of fall.

Fresh, clean water rushes from an overhang and splashes onto a floor of granite. It doesn't pool, but instead seeps into the cracks or rushes off away down the slope to join a creek below. I can see where Dan got the idea for using it to wash. It's very much like a shower.

Except that it's freezing cold and there's no way to adjust the temperature.

"It's not so bad," Dan says, walking deliberately beneath the water and standing there with a grin on his face. I see the goosebumps rise on his skin, though, and his nipples pebble up, and his cock and balls shrink fast.

I convulse with my arms around myself, my long hair plastered over my forehead and down my back and shoulders.

"C'mon," he says, stretching out his hand. "You'll get used to it."

I gasp again as I take hold of his fingers and step back beneath the water. I nearly leap out, but he grasps me close, and I laugh as he kisses my neck and shoulders. "Stop, stop." I giggle. "I'm drowning. I'm dying. I'm getting hypothermia."

He releases me immediately, but I don't go anywhere, pressing up against him instead. He doesn't grab me, though, so I wrap my arms around his waist and kiss his lips. He licks into my mouth as the water comes down around us, cold as hell and making us both shake. We stop kissing long enough to shampoo ourselves and each other with the Dr. Bronners that Dan has stashed in his endless bag of supplies.

Once we're clean-ish, I duck back out from under the water, grab the towel Dan put aside for me, and wrap it around myself. My legs are shaking, and I feel colder than I've been in years, yet I'm filled with a sense of invigoration and vibrancy.

I dress recklessly, eager to get layers on, and my jeans stick to my still wet legs as I pull them up. Tugging on a relatively clean flannel shirt from Dan's bag, I find it's a little short on my arms.

I watch as he washes himself more thoroughly than I'd dared. By the time he finishes his shower, my core seems to have lit a blaze in me that's got me warm and snug like I've been sitting by a bonfire instead of dousing myself in cold mountain water.

Dan towels off, puts on his clothes, and then grins at me. "Fun, huh?"

I laugh because I don't know what to say. It's definitely a new experience for me, and one I wouldn't swear off doing again, but I'm not sure it was *fun*, per se. It was…it was wild. I feel wild and free and like I'm new in my skin.

"What's on your agenda for the day?" Dan asks when we're back where we parked the bike, packing up the saddlebags with the gear we brought to the waterfall.

"Not much. You?"

"I need to go back to Pothole Dome later with the van to re-trieve the camping gear."

"Wouldn't that be easier in my car?"

Dan looks up at me. "Yeah. It would actually. You don't mind?"

"No."

"It won't take the magic from the memory?"

I grin. I knew he'd borrowed Peggy Jo's bike to impress me, and I won't lie, I'm impressed, but even if we go back in the light of day to retrieve all the gear, I'm sure the memory of our night and morning at Pothole Dome will remain plenty magical for the rest of my life. "Not at all."

"Alright. I'll take you up on that ride." He rakes his gaze over me now that I'm dressed, and then checks his watch. "Want to go get breakfast first?"

I spot a familiar hunger in him, but I don't think it's *that* kind of hunger unfortunately. A sliver of disappointment bites, but then I remember I'm the one who'd said no sex during this date. But surely that was just for last night, right? Today's a new day. A new date. Literally.

"I'd like that." I step forward and take hold of his jacket to haul him close. "But I don't suppose you want to eat something else?"

"Your ass?" He swallows hard, eyes lighting up.

"Sure. If you think I got it clean enough in that waterfall."

"I'm not picky," he whispers. "I'll eat your ass any day, anytime, anywhere."

"Filthy boy."

"Mm," he says, and his hands are in my tangled, wet hair before I can think. We kiss, and I'm starting to think he's going to bend me over the motorcycle, take my pants down, and rim me right here, when a Toyota pulls up and a small family of hippies piles out.

"Let's go," Dan says, adjusting himself. "Breakfast, then sex, and then we get the stashed gear."

It's not far, but the way he drives the motorcycle into town like he's in a rush to get on with our plans has me gripping hold of him in terror and excitement.

I can't wait to see what we do with this new day.

Dan

PAPA BEAR IS crammed full of people, but Sejin uses his employee privileges to skip the line, pop into the back, and return with stale cinnamon rolls with the icing a little congealed on top and two cups of coffee.

"I know this isn't exactly a healthy breakfast, but it should hold us over until the place clears out enough for me to convince Pete to make us his special turkey-and-egg sandwiches with extra-*extra* bacon. It won't be on the house, but it'll be twice as much food as he usually gives out."

Sejin leads me to a table by the front door, and we bite into our gooey, sweet pastries and ignore everyone as the place fills even more. It's clear by the way we're staring at each other that we'd both rather be sucking face than licking the icing off our fingers, but the nachos from last night were a long time ago, and the demands of the body temporarily outweigh our lust.

We've just finished up the last of our cinnamon rolls when Rye drops into one of the two open seats at the table, a to-go boba in his hand, and a wide smirk on his face. "What's up? Is this a morning-after or a morning-before?"

"Both," Sejin says, his eyes twinkling. He's so handsome my heart skips a beat.

"Uh-huh, well, good for you guys." Rye grins. "I had a nice night, myself. Even got paid for it."

I waggle my eyebrows, but Sejin looks around to see if anyone's listening. "I'm pretty sure this isn't Nevada and sex work isn't legal here," he murmurs.

"If it were Nevada, I'd have to be registered and all kinds of nonsense." Rye shrugs. "It's not like it's a felony. I mean, what's a misdemeanor in this day and age?"

"So long as you don't let Andrew know about your side-gig," I remind him. "He'd sic his lawyers on you like white on rice, and you'd *never* see Jeanie again."

Rye eyes me with irritation. "Has anyone ever told you that you're an asshole?"

"Regularly."

He turns his attention to Sejin, who still looks uncomfortable with the conversation. "C'mon," he says. "You're saying you've never accepted money for it? Get real. I know you have."

Sejin sputters, coffee hitting the table. He wipes it with his napkin and again looks around to ensure privacy. "How'd you know about that? I never told anyone," he whispers.

Rye points two fingers at his own eyes and then at Sejin's. "I see you. Like recognizes like."

"I'd hardly say you two are very alike. You're a Dom and he's…not," I say.

Sejin leans over the table and explains, "I only took money a few times while I was traveling across the country. It was never the only reason I slept with them. But when they'd offer, I'd accept. I was super strapped for cash, and I really needed the help. So…" He shrugs. "I took it."

"Take out the traveling part and the not asking to be paid part, and I'm the same," Rye says. "I don't Dom men unless I want to, but it's a lot of work and I deserve to get paid." He grins again. "Even if it's all very pleasurable labor which I enjoy very much."

"How did you get into that work?" Sejin asks, running his finger over the crumbs on his plate before bringing it up to his mouth to lick clean.

I lean back. This is a long story and a salacious one. "Go on, tell him," I urge.

Rye rolls his eyes, but he has a smug little smile on his lips too, giving away that he enjoys blowing Sejin's mind like this. "Before our divorce, Andrew and I had fallen into a kink-based sexual relationship. He got off on submitting, and I got off on making him submit. Both of us had been raised in the Mormon church, so it was all *very* naughty and taboo, of course. Which made it crazy-hot for him—and for me."

"Ah."

"That worked well for a little while. We were both happy with at least *that* aspect of our relationship, if nothing else. Until I decided that I wanted to transition…"

"Oh."

"Yeah. He's straight and not into men. That's reasonable, but he also thought what I wanted was a crime against God and that I was setting a horrible example for Jeanie. Things got ugly."

"Oof," Sejin says. "I'm sorry."

"What made it worse was how mean our divorce and my transition made him. He became very cruel to me and, well, in general. Though I think he's still a good dad to Jeanie. He's gone back to the church—except in the ways he hasn't—and he tries to do the right thing by her, even if it's doing the wrong thing by me. Maybe even especially if it hurts me."

"Yes. I remember."

Rye shakes off the bad memories and rouses a smile again. It looks effortful, but not insincere. "Now, I'm finally at home in my skin. I'm not ashamed of who I am. And Andrew? Well, he's looking for just the right woman to be his secret Dominatrix. Because Andrew *will* keep it secret even from the Mormon women he dates or marries. I think at this point he prefers it to be illicit, you know? It's more fun for him that way."

"Andrew," Sejin says on a sigh. "He's…" He shakes his head.

"Oh, believe me, I know."

"Seat taken?" The deep, resonant voice is followed by the last empty chair being scraped back and Lowell sinking down into it. His eyes are brighter than usual, and he's not as scruffy-looking as he has been the last few months. He looks shiny, well-scrubbed, and almost like he's something close to happy.

"Hi," Sejin greets him. "Join us."

"Yeah, join us," I say.

Rye lifts his boba in a greeting. "Lowell, long time, no see. How's it going?"

Lowell's brows do a strange little dance—surprise, maybe? I can't tell. "Going well."

"Good. I'm glad to hear it."

"Speaking of your dick of an ex," I interrupt the boring pleasantries and turn back to Rye.

"I don't think we were, actually."

"We were before Lowell sat down," I remind him. "Anyway, do you think you'd want to housesit for Peggy Jo and her cats? It might make Andrew go easier on you for visits with Jeanie if you had a real place to live."

"Where's Peggy Jo going?" Lowell asks.

"To Georgia. She's visiting her daughter, Bella. She's having a baby."

"Sorry, I can't," Rye says, chewing on a tapioca bubble. "I'm allergic to cats."

"You could take allergy meds," Sejin suggests.

"That's okay for a few hours from time to time, but I can't take them every day. Plus, with my new YOSAR volunteer position, I'm required to stay closer to the park. Peggy Jo's place is too far out."

That's not the answer I was hoping for. I sip my coffee and try to think of counter-arguments, but there are none to be made.

Lowell stretches his arms up high, shifting in his seat, and he makes a soft, pleased sound that gets my attention. He's looking less "archangel" fierce today and more like a confident king of a man, soaking in the sun from the window. I haven't seen him like this since before his divorce, maybe not even then.

"You're relaxed," I observe, wishing I had another cinnamon roll. They were good. "Finally get laid?"

Lowell's lips tug up at the corner. "Maybe I just got a good night's sleep. How about you?"

"Everyone at this table *knows* I'm getting laid." I gesture at Sejin meaningfully and take his hands. "And he is too."

Sejin's cheeks are flushed when he pulls his hands away, but we stare at each other and the heat flies between us. Rye starts making gagging noises, while Lowell chuckles under his breath. I'd like to get out of here, but we still haven't eaten anything substantial. I'm starting to wonder if we really need to… I have chips and salsa back in the van if we need sustenance later. Getting Sejin naked and underneath me feels way more important than good nutrition.

Lowell mutters, "It's always hard to think about anything else when it's new, isn't it?"

I pause, realizing that he's right. I've barely thought about Heart Route since I picked Sejin up on the bike last night. I watch as Sejin catches his hair back in another hair tie he's fished from his pocket, and my heart catches in my chest. I'm gonna grab that hair, hold it tight, and do unspeakable things to Sejin's mouth and dick and ass. My pulse flutters as our eyes meet again, and he smiles softly. His shy little dimple is too much for me.

Sejin's stomach gurgles loud enough to be heard over the clank and clang of silverware and murmurs of the crowd.

"When are you going to get Pete to make that turkey with ba-con-and-bacon sandwich?" I don't want him keeling over on me mid-sexcapade. I need him to have some stamina so I can do all the things I want to do to him today. I have to try to get him out of my system enough to focus on Heart Route tomorrow.

"Are you two hungry?" Sejin asks Lowell and Rye.

They both shake their heads. "I had a big breakfast," Rye says.

"Me too," Lowell agrees.

Now it's *my* stomach's turn to protest, and it growls loudly. "Wait here," Sejin says to me, and darts into the back of the café again, ignoring his boss's loud gripe that he shouldn't be there if he's not working.

"You're smitten as a kitten," Rye teases as soon as Sejin disappears behind the swinging door. He shakes his boba at me, rattling the ice and tapioca beads.

I shrug. "If you kissed him at sunrise on top of Pothole Dome, you'd be smitten too."

"Ooh, is that *romance* I hear you describing?"

I grimace. "Yeah. I think so. Gross, huh?"

Rye laughs.

"It sounds like a good morning," Lowell counters, his gaze going distant and sad again. "It's been a long time since I've watched the sun come up with someone special."

"You enjoy sunrises?" Rye asks.

"Sure." Lowell's shrug downplays it. "I also like sunsets, and dancing, and kissing."

"Noted," Rye says with a firm nod. Why he'd be making note of that, I don't know, but then Sejin's sweeping across the room again, his ponytail streaming behind him.

"Here," he says, shaking a take-out bag he's brought from the back room. "Pete's in a mood, so I didn't bother asking him for anything special. I got turkey sandwiches from Gage."

We sit again, both of us stuffing the sandwiches in our mouths like we're in a competition and the winner gets to top. Or bottom. Depending on whatever the winner wants to do. I'm down for either.

Lowell brings up a new route on the Dawn Wall a friend is trying to send. Rye asks pertinent questions, and I tune them out. The Dawn Wall is an impressive feat, but trying to veer off Tommy Caldwell's route is foolish.

Instead, I watch Sejin eat. His throat bobs as he swallows, his long, pretty fingers grip the sandwich lightly, and his pink tongue darts out to lick mustard from the corner of his shiny, wet lips. I catch his gaze, and he's peering at me too.

I go hot all over, and my heart flutters as he pops the last bite into his mouth.

"Come on," I say, shoving the remains of my sandwich at Rye, certain that he'll either eat it or throw it away for me. I reach my hand out for Sejin to take. "Let's get out of here."

Sejin's fingers are soft and a little cold, but the look in his eye as we rise from the table is eager and hot.

"Enjoy yourselves," Rye calls, shaking his nearly-finished boba our way. "Don't forget: condoms, lube, consent, and safe words."

A woman near the table coughs and glares at Rye before pointedly nodding toward her teenage son, who is quite obviously listening. Good! Let him hear about condoms, lube, consent, and safe words. If he's lucky, he'll need them sooner than later.

Sejin's cheeks darken with a blush, but I just pull him out of Papa Bear and back to the waiting bike. Clambering on, both of us are overeager and I, for one, am already hard and aching.

Based on the way Sejin thrusts his crotch into my backside when he sits down, I'm not the only one.

As we tear out of the parking lot, and I point the motorcycle toward the campground, I think about how Lowell is right. My mind is full of sex and Sejin, and right now that's all that matters. That's all I even *want* to matter.

Heart Route can wait.

CHAPTER THIRTEEN

Dan

THE VAN FEELS like a welcoming, warm hug as I pull Sejin in and slam the door shut. I should ask him if he needs anything before we fuck, but I'm impatient to get him naked and keening. I know it won't take much. I had him spun up so high last night that I almost came in my jeans just from the noises he was making.

Sejin doesn't object as I start divesting him of clothing. His pulse beats visibly in his throat, and I lick it, loving the sweet taste of his skin.

"How do you want to do this?" I ask, open to whatever he suggests, but hoping he's serious about letting me eat his ass. It's my favorite thing to do with a guy, and with Sejin I find it even more arousing than usual. He squirms so nicely when I push my tongue in, and his noises—eager gasps, breathless whimpers—get me so hard.

"Yeah, um, so…" he groans as I unzip his jeans and bite a nipple at the same time. "Can I top? I wanna feel you like that."

"Yeah, that works for me."

He huffs a laugh, and then we're silent as the heat between us escalates. I end up naked on my back, head propped up by pillows, sixty-nine-ing with my cock in his mouth, as he lets me eat his ass. He shakes as I work him open with my tongue and fingers, and his throat vibrates around my cock as he groans. I'm certain I'm going to shoot and end this way too early.

"Off," I say, tugging at his ponytail until he releases me. "I'm not ready to come yet."

"Want to get inside you," he whispers, but then he collapses, open mouth against my thigh, breathing hard on my cock and balls as I go back to eating his hole. I love how he twitches, his dick dripping on my chest as I work him over.

Eventually, he heaves himself away and almost topples off the bed onto the floor of the van, but I catch his leg and keep him from going over.

"Holy shit," he says, flopping beside me. "I'm horny as fuck. Get on my cock."

I grin. This is the first time he's been bossy in bed, and I'm eager to see more of this side of him. I grab the bottle and condom from where I put it next to the mattress. He rolls it on as I uncap the lube and work it over my own hole.

"Let me…" he says, reaching between my legs and under my balls to press his fingers at my entrance.

"No," I say, pushing his hand away. "I'm good."

"You sure?" he asks. "It was your tongue on my ass, remember, not the other way around. I don't want to hurt you."

"Doc, no offense to your ego—I'm not saying you're small— but you're not gonna wreck my hole. So just lay back and let me get on your dick."

"I feel like I should be offended, but…" He lets out a groan and grips the tops of my thighs as I push down. The head of his dick breaches my ass. It's not an easy entry, the lack of prep makes me tight and he really isn't small, but with some effort from me—and a lot of curses from him—I sink down onto him until his base stretches me wide.

"Fuuuuuck," he says on a rush of breath. "Don't move. Don't…don't move." His nails dig into my thighs and I sense that he's about to come, so I do exactly as he says and barely breathe.

"Oh, God," he whimpers. "I swear…I'm…*fuck*…"

I wait a few more seconds and then the temptation is too much. I lift up and ride him while he jerks and spasms beneath me. Orgasm rips through his body, contorting his features, and making his abs tremble as his legs begin to shake.

"S—sorry," he stutters, as I lift off with a grunt to check out the full condom. "That's…that's never happened before."

He covers his face with his hands, and I say nothing as I tug the condom free and add it to the small plastic bag I keep by the bed for trash.

"Fuck," he says again. "Dan, I…"

"Shh," I say, sliding down next to him. "We have all day."

"Do we?" he asks.

"We do." I kiss his chin, and then his nose, and sit back to stare at his flushed face. "I like how your eyes hook at the edges," I say, pointing to where the epicanthic fold makes the inner corner of his eyes turn down sharply. "It's pretty."

He makes a weird little sound and then draws me down to kiss. My ass feels empty, but he slips his fingers into me after a few moments, and I spread my legs, letting him finger me until he's hard again.

Round two takes longer—a lot longer—and being fucked by Sejin is like on-sighting a route up a wall: a wonder and a surprise.

I hold on and let him take me higher.

Sejin

DAN'S LIKE A furnace inside, and my cock is held by the hottest, most vibrantly beautiful man ever. He clings to me as I drive in and out, and my balls draw up tight, threatening to make my promise that this time will last into a lie.

Shorter than me, Dan's in the perfect position to bite my nipples as I fuck him and so, of course, he does. I cry out, shoving his knees up against his chest and grinding in deeper. It's not even hard to slam in and out of him with all my effort. Dan takes me like he does everything else—with full commitment and concentration. As I stare down at his wide eyes, boring into me as I plow him, I feel, in some ways, like he's the one fucking me.

He stares with such clarity and determination as I take us both higher and higher. I could become lost in all this lust, but he's right there, dragging me back to his eyes and body whenever I start to vanish into the sensation. It's different from when he's on top, when he drives me out of my mind until I'm drooling and shaking. With me inside, he keeps me reeled in, hooked on him—a fish on the line of our mutual pleasure.

"Dan," I whimper.

"Yeah, Doc?" he grits out.

"Can you come like this?"

He smirks. "Ready so soon?"

"Your ass is too good."

He laughs. "Yeah?"

"I can't hold off." I hunch into him again. "Help me," I whisper. "Help me make you come."

He takes hold of his own cock and strokes it a few times. "Shift up," he says, and I do. He grunts. "Yeah, right there. Just…like…"

I pound into him, and he quivers beneath me. I keep my gaze on his face, watching avidly for the signs of his climax. He peers up at me too, that soul-baring look that undoes me. Suddenly, his eyes roll up. I squirm all over as he clenches around my cock, and his feet pound against my sides in a quick convulsive flex—and then cum flies from his dick, hits his chest, the bottom of my chin, and coats his stomach. He's quiet, but he spasms all over.

I cry out, my balls tightening and my elbows locking up as I shove into him again and again. His brilliant eyes flutter, and then his gaze is on me again, small grunts coming from him with each of my thrusts.

The way his ass clenches around me is too much, and I fill the condom as I stare down at his luminescent eyes, his wide mouth, and his high cheekbones. He's beautiful and he takes my dick like a dream.

"Dan…"

"Mm," he says, sweat standing out on his skin and his hair a mess.

"I don't think I can do the waterfall again today."

He laughs and tugs me down to kiss. "We can use the campground's shower block. Though it's not much warmer."

"And not nearly as clean."

"No."

His lips are swollen from all the kissing, and he has a red mark from where my incoming light beard has scraped his chin. I feel the beard burn on my own chin too.

When we exit the van on trembling legs to head to the shower block, I'm sure we both look like fucked-out messes, but I don't care what the families in the tents and campers around us think. I only wonder how I'm going to report to work tomorrow when I'm sore from climbing, sore from sleeping on a rock, and sore from fucking Dan's ass into next year.

"Hey," Dan says later, as we climb back onto the motorcycle to go get my car.

I tighten my grip around his middle, rest my helmeted head against his back, and sigh. "Yeah?"

"You okay?"

"Yeah."

"You sure?"

"Just thinking about last night and today. I don't want it to be over yet."

"Don't worry, Doc," Dan says. "There'll be more days like this."

He starts the engine and we're off, driving into the unknown future where I don't know how long I get to have him. I have to believe that no matter what...

Beautiful memories always stay.

CHAPTER FOURTEEN

Dan

5 weeks until free solo ascent

"WHAT ON EARTH is that all about?" Peggy Jo asks as I climb into her truck.

I look to where Peggy Jo is staring at Sejin dancing to KPop—a song from girl group called Twice, I think—with some kids from a few campers over. The two oldest look to be around eight or ten years old, and the little ones are between three and five, probably. I'm not great at kids' ages, but that's my best guess.

They're dancing by the open door of my van, from whence the music is streaming, and my van's keys shimmer in Sejin's hand as he shakes them in time to the beat.

"He's showing them some choreography," I say, adjusting my seatbelt and settling my backpack at my feet.

"Yes, I can see that."

"He slept over."

"I can see that too."

"He'll lock up the van, and I'll get the keys from him later at Papa Bear." I pause. "He works there."

"I know." She looks at me and then back to Sejin. "He's slept over a lot lately."

"How do you know?"

"Rumors," Peggy Jo says. "Lots and lots of rumors."

"What are people saying?" I don't know why I'm asking. I don't really care. At least not for me, but I do worry for Sejin. He probably won't like people talking shit about him or us. *If* there's an us—and it seems like there is, just like he'd predicted back on Pothole Dome.

"Let's see, what are people saying?" She pretends to think about it. "Mainly that you're losing your focus on climbing because you're so absorbed by this thing you've got going with Sejin."

I scoff. "I'm as focused as ever on climbing. I just do something other than hang out alone on my rest days."

"Are they even rest days now?" Peggy Jo says, insinuation lining her voice.

"Sometimes," I hedge.

Sejin and I have been seeing each other at least three times a week for the last three weeks now. Sometimes it's a date, like Pothole Dome or a movie at the theater, and sometimes it's fucking in the van until we can't walk straight, and sometimes it's just hanging out. It's not the best use of my time, but I can't seem to make it through more than a few days without asking him over again, and he can't seem to say no.

I suspect Sejin isn't *trying* to say no, though. Aside from his mostly unfounded fears about my imminent death, he has no real reason to resist this pull between us. Unlike me. *I'm* the one who has goals that could be sabotaged by my fixation on him.

Peggy Jo and whoever's spreading these rumors are both right. I *should* be more focused on my climbing plans right now and not primarily on seeing Sejin's smile, and secondarily on hearing him laugh, and tertiarily on fucking him senseless.

But, in my defense, the fucking has slowed down a little in the last week or so. We've spent more time cuddled up in bed watching our respective YouTube videos on our phones—climbing videos for me, KPop stuff for him—than we've spent having sex. Like, one day last week, it rained and there was no way I could fit any climbing in.

So Sejin wrangled an early shift dismissal from the coffee shop and headed over. Physically, we barely did anything. We just made food and ate it in my bed, listening to the rain, talking about our lives, and then kissing before napping. I hadn't known what to make of that except that it'd been fun, low key, and just what I'd needed.

But it's not like we're over each other already either. On another day, I tied him down with some old climbing rope I had lying around, and he'd squirmed helplessly as I ate and fingered his ass for a long, tortuously hot afternoon. I was out of my mind with lust just watching him tug at the ropes and drool around the ball gag.

And on yet another day, we played doctor again. He re-earned my nickname for him with some very dirty applications of an ACE bandage. My balls have never felt so well-wrapped, and my orgasm has never been so hard won. It'd been a fun day.

But so was the day we went on a light hike, and the day I swung by the coffee shop to watch him work while I read Tommy Caldwell's memoir on my phone, and the day I met him at the preschool after he'd finished up with the kiddies so he could drive us in to town for a movie and dinner together. That was the most traditionally date-like date I'd ever been on. The restaurant even had white tablecloths.

The least fun day with Sejin was when I made the mistake of agreeing to hang out with him while he took care of Jeremiah and Sarah Kate. And…well, let's just say Jeremiah isn't a fan of me. He's very attached to Sejin, and it seems he blames me for how often Sejin is away from the house these days. I accept that blame heartily and even told him yes, Sejin *is* going to spend a lot more time with me in the future too, so he'd better get used to it. It'd been all downhill after that. The kid actually bit me. Sejin scolded him, and Sarah Kate cried.

In the end, I'd left early to let Sejin watch the kids by himself. It didn't seem fair to rile Jeremiah up with my presence when he just wanted Sejin's attention all for himself. I can relate.

Later Sejin came by, though, and we watched the stars from the top of my van, and then slept—without doing more than kissing again—side by side down below.

In between seeing Sejin, I am still training. Which is what I'm going to do today with Peggy Jo. She's going to belay for me while I work on the lower-stakes dyno again. Normally I like to do this practice alone, but I feel like I've got a handle on the jump these days, and I want to show her how often I make it to put her mind at ease. I should take Rye up Heart Route again sometime soon, show him the real deal, and then maybe the rumors about me will change from "suicidal idiot climber distracted by pretty man" to "crazy talented, totally gonna free solo Heart Route climber *falling* for pretty man."

Because, yeah, I've fallen for Sejin, and I'm not ashamed to say it. I still haven't seen *that* smile, though. I've come close. So, so close. But there's always something holding him back. I'm pretty sure it's the knowledge of my plans and his fears for my future, but I'm not going to give up trying for either one of my goals. It's just not who I am.

I tell Peggy Jo the truth. "I might be a little distracted right now, but you were the one who encouraged me to go after him. Now you're not happy that I did what you said?"

"Oh, no, I'm pleased as punch," she says, as she makes the turn on the road that will lead us to where we'll park before hiking in. "I just think if you're not as focused as you once were, maybe you can dial it back. Put this free solo ascent off another year. Let things settle with Sejin and see if a relationship changes your outlook on your Heart Route plans."

"You're hoping he'll convince me not to do it."

She shrugs. "He can't love the thought of you taking the risk."

"What is 'risk,' Peggy Jo? We're putting our lives in jeopardy on the road right now."

"Save your risk analysis bullshit for Sejin when *he* asks. I've already heard it."

"What makes you think he'll ask?"

"That boy is plumb gone for you. He'll ask."

"What makes you think he's—" I can't bring myself to say 'plumb gone,' so I just wave my hands around. She gets the drift.

"Rumors again," she says with a sigh. "Reliable ones. Plus, my own eyes. I saw how he sent you off just now. A smile like some kind of shy sunshine, and a tender kiss, and how happy he looked when you gave him your keys—"

"Only because it means he can get back in bed and—"

"Wallow around in your scent? Like a man in love?"

"Peggy Jo, what do you want from me?" I frown. "I thought I deserved love? You said I did."

"You do! And he does too, and my heart is glad to see you together, but I also hope you take *his* heart into account when you're planning your future."

"Did you take anyone's heart into account when you drove over to pick me up today?"

"Much more likely to die in a car crash, blah, blah, blah. I know. I know. And don't get started on your whole 'free soloists rarely die while free soloing' because Exhibit A—Bachar, and Exhibit B—Bailee Mulholland, Exhibit C—Michael Spitz, Exhibit D—Nathan Roberts—"

"Don't list everyone, Jesus." Hearing the names does make me feel oddly superstitious. All that bad energy.

"Those aren't even all of them from *that one year*, Dan."

I focus on the name I can possibly cast doubt on. "About Bachar… some think he could have had a heart attack because he wasn't even close to climbing at the top of his ability when he fell, and—"

"You're going to argue this based on a 'coulda?'"

"It's not like they could really tell from the state of his body."

"Dan, what am I going to do with you?" she murmurs. "Or the better question is what is Sejin going to do with you? Bless that boy."

"Yes, do bless him. He needs it."

She rolls her eyes. "Speaking of things people need," she goes on. "I really do have to find someone to take care of the cats and my house when I go to be with Bella next week. You mentioned you might know someone?"

"Yeah, at first I was thinking of Rye. He needs a good place to stay if he's going to have any hope of getting partial custody of Jeanie again. But he says it won't work. Cat allergy and YOSAR obligations. But I have another idea now," I say. "Sejin. He's been living at his cousin's house, sleeping on their sofa for over a year, and I get the impression his cousin's wife—"

"Leenie," Peggy Jo supplies, because of course she knows everyone.

"Yeah, Martin and Leenie. I think they'd like it if he moved on. They sure don't complain when he stays in the van with me. The kids, though…" I look at the place on my arm where Jeremiah had sunk his teeth. There's still a small scab from one particularly sharp tooth. "They'd like him to stay."

"It'd just be for a month," Peggy Jo says. "He'd need to have something lined up for after."

"Sure." I don't mention that I have a plan for that too. It's way too early to bring it up to Sejin, but if things keep going well between us, I'd like him to tag along on whatever my next adventure is after I send Heart Route. He wouldn't have to continue inconveniencing his cousins, and I'd get a sexy traveling companion.

By stealing Sejin away, I'd become a permanent villain in Jeremiah's mind. Oh, well. You win some; you lose some.

"If he says no, you'll have to stay with them," Peggy Jo says with finality.

"Alright," I agree.

But I know Sejin will take up Peggy Jo on her offer, and I can't say the idea of us having somewhere bigger than my van for some regular privacy doesn't sound appealing. Even if the space will be bedeviled by cats who hate me even more than Jeremiah does.

Once I send Heart Route, I could crash with Sejin at Peggy Jo's, plan my next adventure, and convince him to come with me. As much as I'll miss her, the timing is perfect. Her absence will reduce my stress for the ascent of Heart Route and allow Sejin and me a chance to play at temporary domestic bliss. All the comfort, none of the commitment.

Well, almost none of it.

I like having Sejin around. I can see us continuing on this way indefinitely. I hope he can too.

"What's your plan for the day?" Peggy Jo asks.

"Gonna show you how I can take this dyno. No sweat."

"Hmmph." She doesn't sound skeptical so much as stressed. "*This* dyno is not *that* dyno."

"I know, and I've been working it too."

"How about the roof?"

I shudder against my will. "Still gives me the heebie-jeebies."

"Have you practiced on the similar roof you found in Tahoe?"

"It's a bit of a drive…"

Doing serious practice with the roof on the boulder in Tahoe would require me pulling up stakes, so to speak, at the campground and leaving town for at least a few days. It's not that I can't go that long without seeing Sejin, but I just haven't wanted to…

Alright. Maybe everyone's on to something with the rumors that I'm losing focus.

"I'll go this week."

"What about Sejin?"

"He can go too if he wants."

"He has a couple of jobs, doesn't he? Plus, he helps his cousin's boss over at the plumbing business now and again, *and* he babysits those kids," she reminds me, like I don't know my own boyfriend's situation.

Wait. Boyfriend? *Boyfriend?* Maybe…maybe that's what he is…

"Yeah, so?"

"He can't just say 'sorry, I'm not coming in to work or helping out around here today because I'm taking off with my itinerant lover.' It's not how real-life works. Not that you'd know anything about that, living in a van and barely scraping by. If it weren't for that trust fund from your grandfather, you'd be eating stolen Saltines and ketchup from the Lodge for your meals and foraging for berries in the forest."

"Lover," I say out loud, ignoring the rest, especially the mention of my biological grandfather and the surprise of his money. "Hm. Lover. I don't know about that." I test the word in my head again: *lover.* Is it worse or better than *boyfriend?* I'm not sure. I should ask Sejin his opinion.

"Well, what do you call him?"

"Sejin. Or Doc."

"Doc?"

I shrug. "An inside joke about some games we play."

Peggy Jo chuckles. "Oh, lord, you've got a nickname for him?"

I shrug.

"I really think you oughta consider putting this climb off a year."

"You're telling me other climbers are celibate? Bullshit. Alex Honnold was notorious for his appetites before he married—"

"I don't know about notorious, but the man had relationships off and on, yes. But when did he get hurt? At the start of a new relationship, that's when."

"And when did he free solo El Cap? In the middle of that relationship."

"So, you're in a relationship with Sejin?"

"I don't know. We don't fuck other people. We agreed to that. We hang out a lot. We like each other. I don't see why we have to nail this down right now. I kind of have other things on my mind? Like Heart Route. Just as an example of, you know, where my focus is."

"Right. Look at you, getting all sharp with me." She clucks her teeth. "I regret taking you under my wing most days, you know that?"

"Then stop spraying about me all over town."

Peggy Jo laughs. "If I can't spray about my obnoxious protégé, what good have all these years of mentorship and endless anxiety done me?"

I snort, and we both let the subject drop. She turns on the radio and some old-timey country music fills the cab of her truck. It's not horrible. I kind of like the banjo and the harmonies. But I also wish Sejin were here, and he could introduce her to the charm of KPop.

Weird how I miss him, and it's been less than an hour since we've been apart.

I wonder if I can teach him to overcome his fear of heights. I'd like to have him on the wall with me. I'd like to have him most anywhere if I'm being honest.

Maybe that's love? I don't know.

But it's definitely something new.

Sejin

"DOESN'T HE KNOW it's your birthday?"

"To know that, I would have had to tell him," I say, licking the spoonful of icing I'd filched from Leenie's mixing bowl.

"And why didn't you?" She pulls Jeremiah's hand out of the bowl, but that doesn't stop him from popping his icing-laden finger into his mouth and sucking it clean with an excited little "ooooh."

"Because we aren't there yet."

"Alright, but where are you then? You spend most nights with him now—"

"Not most. Some."

"Most. And you—Jeremiah, no, that's enough." She lifts the mixing bowl up and away from his little reaching hand as I stick my spoon in to snag another dollop. "Sejin, you're a terrible role model."

I shove the spoon in my mouth before she can snatch it back. The icing melts over my tongue and I moan. "It's so good," I say around the glob. "And it's for my birthday cake, so…"

"So, you can eat it when it's on the cake." Leenie darts a glance at the clock. "Which I really hope I can finish up before Miss 'Misery' Sarah Kate wakes up from her nap. She's been a nightmare with those teeth coming in. Ugh."

"Did you remember to put the teethers back in the freezer?"

"No, can you grab them for me? Wash them off first!"

I leave her with the mixer and Jeremiah to quickly pick up around the living room, wash off the two teething rings I find in the sofa cushions, and pop them both in the freezer so they can numb poor Sarah Kate's gums later.

"You never answered my question," Leenie says, covering the mixing bowl and putting it in the fridge to chill while we wait for the layers of the cake to finish cooling.

I make sure the colored icing and sugar decorations are out on the table and ready for the big event. Jeremiah's been looking forward to helping with that part all day. "What question?"

I'm going to make her work for it, because I'm a jerk, and also I don't quite know what to say. She's already plenty skeptical of Dan and his place in my life. She'd been a little too happy when she'd thought he'd forgotten my birthday altogether, not that he didn't even know about it. And I get the impression she'd love it if he just upped and went away.

Not that she doesn't want me to be happy. She just wants me to be happy with someone who's not Dan. Someone who doesn't free solo, and who Jeremiah doesn't hate—though I think he'd hate anyone who gets so much of my attention—and a guy who isn't a little less-than-charming when he doesn't like the direction a conversation is going…

Someone with a job. Someone who doesn't live in a van.

Someone who puts me first. Someone who wants to build a future with me. Someone who fits her idea of a "good choice for a life partner."

You know, not Dan.

And I get it. I do. If Celli was dating someone like Dan instead of someone like Gage, I'd tell her to run for the hills and find herself a good man with a stable job and a solid future. Not that Gage has a stable job or a solid future, but he's at least not climbing up giant walls without ropes, and he's not living in a van. I mean, he lives with his mother, but he's only twenty, give the kid a break, alright? The point is, I get why Leenie isn't into me seeing Dan, and I get why she keeps poking at me about the state of things with him.

I genuinely don't know what answer will bother her more. The one where I'm honest and admit I don't know what we are to each other really, but I also know I'm not walking away yet. Or the one where I lie and say Dan has asked me to be his boyfriend and that we've both committed to finding a way to make this thing work long-term.

I go for honesty because it's always the best policy, and anything else is just a test of her reaction, and that's not really fair.

"Leenie, didn't you ever date someone and just…let it happen? Did every guy before Martin have to promise love and eternal devotion to get into your pants? Didn't you just have some fun with a man or two?"

She glances at Jeremiah who's begun playing with the cake decorations, zooming the packages around on the table like they're cars. "I'm not saying I didn't have my share of fun, but you're not 'having fun' with Dan, Sejin, and you know it as well as I do."

"Last night was plenty fun."

She rolls her eyes. "You care about him, and I just don't see the evidence that he feels the same way. You've made so many changes for him—"

"I have not!"

"You go climbing with him—"

"I'm challenging myself. And it's at night, on easy walls. I don't even really see how high up I am, and he never makes me rappel down. He always agrees to hike out the back way."

She points a finger at me like she has me now. "You watched a Marvel movie with him because that's what *he* wanted, and you don't like action films."

"Like you've never seen a movie with Martin that you knew you wouldn't like?"

"Martin's my husband. This is just some guy you—" She breaks off and looks at Jeremiah and then back to me before she mouths the word "fuck." "Or that's how he treats you anyway. You go out of your way for him. But what does he do for you? Other than insist that his goals are more important than your feelings, and—"

"Aren't they though? This is a lifelong dream of his, Leenie. If he met me and within a few weeks just walked away from it? What would that say about him? What would it mean that I even asked him to do that?"

"Did you ask him?"

"Of course not!"

"Does he know it bothers you?"

"Yes!"

"But he does it anyway." She points at me again like this is her victory.

"Leenie, I know he rubs you the wrong way, and I know you just want what's best for me, but I think if you really look at what you've just said, you'll see for yourself how unfair you're being to him. It's his life's work."

"Work—ah, now there's something he doesn't do. He has no job, Sejin. He's basically homeless."

"Unhoused. Yes, but that's the lifestyle of a professional climber, you know that."

"Professional implies he gets paid to do what he does, which according to him, and according to you, he does not."

"He doesn't *yet,*" I clarify. "I mean, if he feels like it's important to keep money out of his motivations for free soloing, or whatever more difficult climbs he chooses to do, in order to feel like he owes nothing to anyone while going up those walls—if that makes him safer—then what does it matter one way or another?"

"It matters when *you're* working two and a half jobs and sleeping on my sofa, and the man you're seeing semi-seriously, no matter how you want to pretend otherwise—has no means of helping you into a more prosperous future."

"I know you want me off your sofa—"

"I don't!" Leenie exclaims. "I just want you to be happy. And, honestly, Sejin, how can he make you happy in the end? At best, you'll live in poverty together. At worst, he's going to get himself killed and then you'll be miserable. Think about how hard it hit you when you lost Lisa. You don't want to live through that again."

I want to snap back with "you only lose your mama once," but I keep my mouth shut. I know she doesn't want to fight with me, and she only has my best interests at heart. But I also know I'm not walking away from Dan. Not right now, and maybe not ever. Like it or not, it seems I'm the seahorse, and I'm on this ride with Dan until the end—bitter or sweet. I'm sorry it upsets her, though, and my silence seems to break through her burst of anger.

"I'm sorry, baby," she says to me, moving away from the counter to take my face in both of her hands. I look up at her and she smooshes my cheeks so that my lips pout out. "Let's not fight on your birthday. We just love you so much, don't we, Jeremiah?"

"Sejinie loves me too!"

"Yup, he does." She pushes my cheeks out, flattening my lips, and then smooshes them together again, a laugh coming into her voice. "We love you, Sejin. We just want everyone in your life to love you like we do."

She kisses my forehead and then turns back to the fridge. "Okay, let's see about that cake. Ready to decorate, Jeremiah?"

"Yes!" he says, standing up on the chair and cheering. "I'm ready!"

I seize his little legs to make sure he doesn't fall and smile at Leenie as she brings the layers over, grabs the mixing bowl of icing, and we start to assemble my birthday cake.

Jeremiah only makes a little bit of a mess when he dumps the entire contents of the yellow sugar sprinkles over the top. But I tell him I like it and turn it into a round sun over the white icing. It reminds me of a certain egg-yolk sunrise I saw on Pothole Dome. Like that morning, the cake is destined to be a beautiful memory and, like I've tried to achieve with my fears for Dan, I resolve to let the disagreement with Leenie go.

Love—if that's what the tide of life is bringing in as it rushes between us all—can't be dealt with logically. Love is just too powerful for that.

CHAPTER FIFTEEN

Dan

T HE TEXT FROM Sejin is unexpected, but welcome. It's strange how just seeing his name on my phone screen makes me feel like birds are fluttering in my heart. It's also kind of gross. But I like it.

Papa Bear gave me the afternoon off. I have your keys with me at my place. Text me when you're outside, and I'll bring them out to you.

I reply with a thumbs-up and turn to Peggy Jo. "He's not at Papa Bear. He's back at his cousin's house. I'll have to grab my keys from him there."

Peggy Jo doesn't hesitate in her change of direction. She's so familiar with the area and everyone in this town that, of course, she knows where Martin and Leenie live.

"I was impressed today," Peggy Jo says as we near the gravel drive that marks their small house. "You didn't miss on that dyno even once."

"Told you."

"But that dyno's not—"

"Not the Heart Route dyno. I know."

"What're your stats on that one?"

I clear my throat. I don't really want to admit it. They aren't as good as she's going to want to hear, and so I shrug and say, "Not bad."

"Stats, son."

I open my mouth to say that I'm not her son, but instead I just cough up the number. "Around seventy."

"Around?"

"Give or take."

"It's either seventy or it's not."

"Okay, sixty-nine these days."

"Sixty-nine out of a hundred tries you make it."

"Yup." Honestly, it's a pretty impressive stat. That dyno is ridiculous. But when you're talking about free soloing, it's miserable. No one wants those odds.

"What's your timeline for this again?"

"I want to go up late October or early November before the weather moves in and the rock gets too slippery. I really don't want to wait until January or February, though the friction might be better then. But…well…the winds."

"The winds make that a no-go," she agrees. "Fuck, Dan."

"I know."

"This is stupid."

"So you've said before."

But then she goes and sprays about my accomplishments all over the town. I don't know what to make of that. Mixed messages have always screwed me up. That's why I rely on my own inner compass the most in life. It's never guided me wrong.

"You can't possibly consider it with a rate of less than ninety-eight."

"Hmm." I know Honnold has done some climbs he couldn't get better than a ninety-five percent chance of success, but that's way better than sixty-nine. And I don't have a ton of time left.

Maybe Sejin really is too much of a distraction. If I'm going to make this timeline, I need to be up there drilling the roof and the dyno every damn day. And my rest days should be for rest, not fucking, not going on dates.

I grit my teeth together. I don't want to walk away from this, though. I've never wanted to know so much about another human being in my life. I've definitely never wanted to bang a guy over and over and over again…

Do I really have to choose?

"Well?" Peggy Jo asks. "What's going on in that head of yours? You're not so pretty when you frown, you know."

"Maybe I have to let him walk."

"Sejin?"

I nod.

She sighs. "He's a wonderful man. Once in a lifetime."

"So's this climb."

"This climb can be done next year. It's not like there are others scoping it out. No one's nipping at your heels trying to steal this crown away from you."

"It's not about that, anyway." Though I'd be super pissed if I found out someone free soloed Heart Route before me. After the time I've put in? After the effort? All the planning? But even if that happens, I'd still want to do it. I'd still have to prove it to myself.

All I need is me and my own endurance up on that wall. I don't need anyone else.

Which means I don't need Sejin.

"I should just end it now," I say. "Rip the Band-Aid off. Move on. Let him get his dick wet with other hot guys traveling through, and *I* shouldn't get my dick wet at all until I've accomplished this."

Peggy Jo doesn't say anything to that. I get the impression she doesn't want me to let Sejin walk, but I also know she thinks I have to if I'm really going to send Heart Route this year. I've lost too much time already on him. Sixty-nine represents great sex but terrible odds, and I'm not suicidal.

"Alright. I'm going to end it now," I say as she pulls into Martin and Leenie's driveway and the house comes into focus in front of me. "I'll tell him when he gives me my keys."

"Right now?" she says, eyebrows doing wild things. "Right here?"

I nod.

"Isn't that a little brutal?"

"Brutal's good. Brutal's final." My heart is pounding. I feel sick. I have to do this, though. Sixty-nine percent when at this stage? It should be closer to ninety at least. I've got to get focused for real.

"I see." Peggy Jo sounds stunned, but I don't give her a chance to voice her opinion. I get out and walk toward the front door. I know Sejin said to text, but I feel like I should knock, get the keys from him, deliver the news, and get the hell out of Dodge.

I lift my hand just as the door flies open on its own. Jeremiah runs out wearing a party hat and holding a fistful of multicolored balloons. He squeezes past me, squealing with laughter, and Sejin's right behind him.

"Dan!" He's wearing a party hat too, there's white and yellow icing on his face in the shape of a baby's handprint, and his hair is down, all brightly black and messy. He's so damn pretty I catch my breath.

"Hey!" he exclaims, a wide, amazing smile on his face as he steadies himself by grabbing my shoulders so he doesn't run into me.

I gulp.

Holy shit.

It's the smile.

The smile. The one I've always wanted to see directed at me. And it is. Now. Here. It's *mine.* That toothy grin, those upside-down moon eyes, that messy joy and affection.

It's all mine.

He's mine.

"What—what's going on?" I say after Sejin presses a sweet,

sticky kiss to my mouth and then moves around me to chase after Jeremiah zooming around the yard with the balloons. They aren't helium-filled, and they drop to the grass with soft bounces as Sejin tackles him and tickles his sides.

"It's his birthday," Leenie says from behind me, arms crossed over her chest, smiling fondly at her son and Sejin wrestling in the yard.

"Jeremiah's?"

"No, Sejin's."

Martin appears behind her and comes out to clap me on the shoulder. "Good to see you again, Dan." He's holding Sarah Kate, who chews on a teething ring and stares at me with big, brown eyes that seem to look into my soul. "Sejin's gonna need a rescue, I think," Martin says to Leenie. "I'll handle it."

Sarah Kate starts to wail as she's passed off to her mom, and the squeals from Jeremiah and the cries from the baby mix with Sejin's laughter and Martin's chiding attempts to pry his son off Sejin's squirming body.

I stand stock-still, trying to process the chaos, vaguely aware that Peggy Jo is waiting in the truck. I'm even more distracted when Sejin lurches up from the ground, birthday hat askew on his head, grass stains on his shirt and jeans, and still wearing that gorgeous smile that I've been wanting so badly. It makes my head light.

He rushes toward me and grabs me in another kiss. "Hey, I'm happy to see you," he says. "Want to come in for cake? We have plenty."

"Uh…" My mind goes fuzzy taking in all that perfection aimed right at me. I've wanted this since I first saw his picture on the app, and now I have it, and it's even better than I thought it would be. "Cake?"

"Yeah. White on white," he says, indicating the smear on his face. "And some yellow sugar to make a sun."

"Oh. Yeah…um, I…" I stare up at him. I'd been planning to do something, hadn't I? Planning to tell him something important.

"You okay?" He asks, his smile shadowing with concern, shifting from one kind of perfect to another. "Did you hit your head today?"

"No, I'm…I'm fine." I glance toward the truck. "Peggy Jo—"

He immediately turns and waves to her, motioning for her to get out of the truck and come on over.

"We have enough cake for her too," he says.

Peggy Jo exits the driver's side with a smirky grin, but as she approaches, she only says, "Who's the party for?"

"Sejin!" Jeremiah yells, coming at us full speed with his balloons back in hand. I don't know what they're making balloons out of these days, but it must be strong stuff because he's tossing these around like they're dodgeballs and, no matter what, they don't pop.

"Happy birthday to Sejinie!" he sings. "Happy birthday to you!"

"Yes, it's mine," Sejin confirms, and catches Jeremiah up in his arms, blows a raspberry on his belly while he squeals, and then puts him down again. He turns to me.

At that, Jeremiah narrows his eyes, snarls, opens his mouth, and lunges my way. Lightning quick, Leenie grabs hold of his arm and leads him inside with a firm scolding. "No biting, young man."

Peggy Jo laughs. "Do the kids bite you too, Dan? Not just my cats?"

I nod dumbly, staring at Sejin. I'd meant to tell him something. I even remember now what it was, but…

"Come on in," Martin says to Peggy Jo. "Long time, no see, and we've got chips, dip, and lots of cake to spare."

Peggy Jo follows him into the house, and I'm left gobsmacked on the front stoop with Sejin gazing at me with all that joyful affection that makes my heart feel like it's been taken over by nesting songbirds in love.

"It's your birthday?"

"Yup. Twenty-five this year. I'm getting old."

I slip my fingers over his cheek, grazing over icing and sugar, and then I take hold of a hank of his hair and tug it lightly. "Why didn't you tell me?"

"You needed to train today."

"But—"

"No buts. You had things to do. I don't want to get in your way."

I lick my lips and tell a massive lie. "Don't worry. You're not in my way." I kiss him. "Happy birthday, Doc."

He grins against my lips and kisses me again.

I can't end things with Sejin. No matter if I should, I just can't.

But I *do* set him up with Peggy Jo to go look at her place and meet her cats. If all goes well there, he'll move into her house by the end of the month, much to Jeremiah's chagrin. The kid glares at me the entire conversation, and when his mother isn't looking, he sneaks over and opens his mouth to expose his baby canines my way in a wordless threat.

I nod at him solemnly. Threat received, buddy, and entirely understood. I'd bite someone if they tried to take Sejin away from me too. With that thought, when no one's looking, I surreptitiously press my own forearm against my teeth and bite myself hard enough to leave a mark. A reminder not to be a fool.

What had I been thinking? I almost lost him. I almost ruined everything. I take a deep, determined breath. I can do this. I can send Heart Route *and* be with Sejin. I'd be an idiot not to find a way to do both.

I run my fingers over the teeth marks on my arm.

An absolute idiot.

CHAPTER SIXTEEN

Sejin

"THE CATS ARE great," I say, curling up at Dan's side and listening to the rain pound the top of the van. Another day lost for his training schedule, and this time I can see that it bothers him.

"Time is getting short," he'd said earlier as he glared ominously out the open van door at the gray sky. "This weather is bullshit."

I agreed, but hadn't known how to soothe him other than by taking his pants off and sucking his cock. So, I did that and some of his tension melted away as he wrapped his hands into my hair, fucked into my throat, and then come with a hard grunt.

Afterward, he'd licked my hole and fingered me while watching me jerk myself off. Pretty low-key for us, but it was relaxing as the rain had dumped against the metal roof.

Now we're naked and cuddling, discussing my visit to Peggy Jo's house yesterday and whether I plan to take her up on the offer to housesit for a month while she goes to be with her daughter during and post-delivery of her grandbaby.

"Be careful. Those cats are assholes."

I raise a brow. I'm in pretty far with Dan to be discovering this red flag now, but it's a big one. "You don't like animals?"

"Love animals. Hate cats."

"Cats are animals."

He looks skeptical. "Okay, I don't hate cats. Cats hate me." His expression shifts to embarrassment. "Probably because I'm scared of them."

"Why? They're so adorable."

"Exactly. My fourth foster mother's cat was very cute. She liked to lie on her back and show off her fluffy tummy."

"Oh, no."

"I reached out to pet it—" He shows me a scar on his arm, one I'd assumed was from a fall while climbing, like most of his others. "It was a trap. One of many of that fiend's tricks."

I laugh.

"Cats aren't trustworthy," he says like it's an indisputable fact. "So be careful. Don't let Peggy Jo's lure you in with their cuteness. It's all a front. They'll bite if you give them a chance."

I blink at him. He's so earnest and strangely vulnerable and so, so wrong.

"Are you going to take the job?"

"Obviously," I say, rolling over to grab my phone so I can check the notification that dinged a few seconds ago. I'm relieved that he has a decent, if sad and distorted, reason for disliking cats.

"Is Astro live?"

"Nah. Just BTS Official making another announcement," I say, putting the phone aside for now. I can always see what the members of the most famous KPop group in the world are up to later.

"You have notifs turned on for KPop groups?" Dan asks.

"Yes? *You* have notifs turned on for Ice & Rock's account," I point out.

He lifts his hands in surrender. "I was just curious."

I kiss his cheek in apology for my defensiveness. "Anyway, I'm going to do it. Take on the house and the cats. The real question is what to do when she comes back. I can't move out of Martin and Leenie's place and then ask to move back in. Though maybe they'll appreciate me more once I'm gone. No more free babysitting and helping out when the plumbing company overschedules Martin."

"Can you really fix plumbing?" Dan asks, once again not staying on topic and instead darting off down some side rabbit hole.

"Of course. Why wouldn't I?"

"I don't know." He twines his hands into my hair again. He loves playing with it, and I like how it feels when he does. "I just don't see you as the kind of guy who likes being on his knees."

"Excuse me? I get on my knees for you all the time."

He kisses the side of my face. "You know what I mean."

"You don't think I can do dirty work or something? That it?"

"No, I…" Dan tilts his head, pondering a moment and then says, "I guess it's because I've never seen you in that mode. Like how you've never seen me up on a big wall. I'm sure you have a hard time picturing me there."

I wince. "I can picture it far too well."

I've spent way too much time imagining Dan up on a wall, no ropes, fingers slipping…ugh. It makes me nauseated. I've made a point of never taking him up on his offers to do any day climbs. I've agreed to other night climbs, though, so long as it's no more than we did before. But I can tell he really wants me to go up a bigger wall with him. See him in his element. Show off for me.

But I don't know if I want to see that. He can show off for me plenty here in the van—show off his body, his passion, his strength, his intelligence, his focus. I can experience it all without having to see him do something that terrifies me.

"Anyway," I try again. "I'm excited about the housesitting. Muggs loved me. He was purring in my lap for half the conversation."

"That demon took a chunk out of my hand once." Dan shows me a scar at the fleshiest part of his palm. "It got infected, and I couldn't climb for two weeks."

"What did you do to him?"

Dan huffs. "I sat down? I don't know? Cats just hate me. Like Jeremiah."

"Jeremiah's not a cat. He's more like a puppy."

"He's an adorable little brat," Dan says. "I want him to like me, but I stole his favorite Sejin away, and he can't forgive me for that." He smiles up at me and touches my hair again. "I can't blame him."

"Peggy Jo's the one taking me away from Jeremiah. You just borrow me." I smile and then remember. "Have you seen her backyard view? It's so beautiful. Mountains on mountains, and that shimmery ribbon of creek down below. I could sit there all day drinking coffee and staring at it."

"When will you move in?"

"Sunday."

"She's leaving so soon?"

"Her daughter is feeling anxious, and Peggy Jo wants to be with her to help prepare the apartment for the baby."

"She'll be a good grandmother."

I study Dan for a long moment and finally ask the question that's been niggling at the back of my mind for a few weeks now. "Danny?"

He doesn't react to me using the cutesy version of his name. "Mm?"

"What are we doing?"

"We're resting while it rains."

I shift to a seated position, and he hoists up onto his elbows, his brows wrinkling in understanding that there's something else I'm trying to ask. I go on, "I mean, we're together almost every night now, and sometimes we don't even have sex—"

"Are we not having enough sex? We can have more—"

"That's not what I'm saying. I just…want to know what we're doing. You and me. Together."

I can see his brain snapping through my words and trying to

sort out the meaning of whatever expression is on my face, studying it like a slow-mo film ticking by. "Oh," he finally says.

I flinch slightly but then shrug. "Yeah. I've been wondering. No pressure. I just want to make sure we're on the same page. What are we?"

Dan's face quickly shifts, like he's considering different possible responses, each problematic in some way, until he finally settles on, "I guess we're a couple. We're boyfriends."

"We are?"

Dan frowns. "I think so? Unless you don't want to be?"

I laugh. "I want to be."

"Cool." He takes hold of a length of my hair and uses it to pull me down again. He kisses my lips, my neck, and then scoots down to suck on my nipples. "You're so easy," he murmurs as my dick rises up between us. "I like that about you."

I shift so I'm between his legs and thrust my hips against his. "You're pretty easy too."

"Doc?"

"Mm?"

"I've got a pain in my ass—"

I snort. "You *are* a pain in the ass."

"—and I need you to check it out for me."

I slide a hand down over his hardening cock, slip my fingers over his taint, and gently touch his asshole. "This where it hurts?"

"Inside," he murmurs, making his eyes go wide and innocent. "Awfully bad, Doc. Deep inside. I don't think your fingers will reach."

I chuckle. "Lucky for you, I have something a little longer we can use."

"Hurry up, then," he says, pulling his legs up around my sides, and hunching so that his cock rubs against mine. "I need your doctoring skills. You've got such a great bedside manner, Doc," he says, not breaking character. "Firm, knowledgeable."

"Knowledgeable? Oh, I know all about your asshole," I say, still laughing a little, but Dan doesn't seem to mind that I can't keep our role-play serious in any way today. "Let me examine it before we start the procedure."

I scoot down, pushing his legs back and up, and study his tight hole. He's lightly hairy around it, and he flexes his feet in anticipation when I lean close and blow. Then I set about giving him as good as he gives me, and the way his legs shake, his cock leaks, and his silence turns to low moans tells me I've learned a lot about rimming from his enthusiastic assaults on my ass.

"Fuck," he says, tugging me up to kiss me again. "Get inside me."

I reach into the drawer and pull out the last two condoms and the lube. "We need more," I say, holding up the two packets for him to see.

"Do we?" he asks, his eyes burning hotly.

I swallow hard. "What do you mean?"

"How long has it been since you fucked someone else?"

We both know the answer. We've talked about our sexual history on and off over the last month and a half we've been doing this, and we know that neither of us has any STDs, and it's been more than enough time since we were with anyone else at all.

"Are you saying we could…" I shiver. It's such a delicious thought. Being in Dan, having him in me, bare and raw and real. "I've never done that before with anyone."

"Me either."

I look at the condoms in my hand. I lift my eyebrows as I put them back in the drawer I got them from, holding eye contact with him. He doesn't even blink; instead he starts stroking his own dick and grinning.

My hands shake as I get back to what I was doing. I apply lube to my cock, biting into my lower lip at the sweet slick of it on my skin, and then press against his asshole. He's still wet from my saliva, but the lube makes everything nice and slippery down there.

"I, uh, don't want to wait," I say, breathlessly as I line myself up against him. He holds his legs back for me, limber as ever, and I gaze at where the head of my cock presses against the straining rim of his entrance. I take in the whole picture—his cock standing hard and proud out of his curly, dark brown pubic hair, and my own straight, jet-black pubes framing my aching dick. I push gently and he bears down…

"Holy fuck," I murmur, my eyes half-closing as hot, tight pressure kisses the crown of my dick. "Oh, my God."

I don't know if it's the fact that I'm doing something so new and somewhat taboo, or if it really does feel so much better without the barrier between us, but I'm not sure I'm going to get fully seated inside him before I blow my load.

I pull back out.

"Not good?" he says, but he's laughing. I know he can see on my face just how fucking amazing it is and that I'm desperately trying not to come all over the sheets and his legs so that I can get another shot at getting back in.

"Fuck you."

"Please do, Doc."

"Lame," I mutter, but then I close my eyes, take some slow breaths, and get myself together. When I open my eyes, Dan is staring up at me with a fondness that makes my heart crack open, and I gasp with emotion as I line up and push again.

Dan's asshole seems to pull me in this time and, as I sink into his gripping heat, I let out a groan that fills the entire van. "You're so hot inside."

"Not outside?"

I pinch his nipple and he laughs, which makes him squeeze

around my dick, and that just about sends me over the edge too. "Just let me catch my breath," I say, rocking in and out slowly.

Dan relaxes back and takes my slow thrusts easily. His hands roam up and down my chest, tweaking my nipples, and then he twists his fingers into the lower hanging parts of my hair again. He tugs lightly, like he's got hold of reins, and says, "Ride me now, horsie."

"I prefer Doc."

"No animals in the bedroom?"

"Please no."

"Not your kink?"

"Not at all."

"No problem." He lets go of my hair and goes back to my nipples, teasing them with the callouses of his fingertips, something he knows drives me crazy in a good way. I shiver as my nipples spark with pleasure with every careful swipe. "So, Doc, how's it feel in there?"

"Tight," I say again.

"The pain's all gone now," he says with a smirk. "You're massaging my insides perfectly."

"Here?" I shift to peg his prostate.

His legs quake. "Yeah." He's breathless now. "There."

"Seems you have a condition known as Homosexual Prostate Horn—"

"Bisexual," he reminds me.

"Right, sorry. You're suffering from Bisexual Prostate Horniness. It requires regular massages from a penis or dildo"—I thrust hard, and he grunts in that near-silent way that I've come to love—"on your prostate until it stops feeling so painfully horny."

"You're ridiculous, Doc," he says, and rolls his eyes. Like this whole role-play thing isn't his idea, and like he's not flushed from his chest up to his neck and into his cheeks with lust and pleasure as

I vigorously fuck my cock against his prostate.

"You're about to come," I point out, lifting his cock from where it strains against his stomach and smearing the copious amount of pre-cum around the head with my fingers. "I could probably just stroke you once or—"

"Don't!" he says, reaching down to still my hand. "Let's switch."

"Now?" I'm just getting into the swing of fucking him, and I'd planned to tease him for a few more minutes before making him shoot.

"Yeah. I want to come inside you."

My head spins. "Oh." I don't know what to say to that. I hadn't even thought yet about what it would be like to come inside Dan. I'd just been too busy enjoying actually being in him bare. "Yeah?"

"Please. I want you to let me. I want to come inside you so bad. Please let me."

It's not like Dan to beg. That's typically my job in the bed, so I pull out of him slowly, savoring the last of his heat before the cool air of the van hits my throbbing dick. My balls tighten, and I fall onto my back on the mattress, lifting my legs to expose my hole.

I know what's coming. Dan can never resist getting his mouth on me. And sure enough, he dives down to suck and lick my hole for what seems like forever and only a few minutes all at once.

I toss my head around on the pillows, my cock pulsing with heat and need and my asshole gripping around his tongue. If it weren't raining so hard, I have no doubt he'd get the ball gag out to muffle my cries, but the roar of the downpour is enough to cover all my noises.

And then he launches up, his cock already slick with lube— which he must have managed while still eating my hole—and I bear down to take him in. It doesn't feel that different from my end, but the sound he makes as he slides inside makes my tummy flip, my nipples ache, and my balls draw up tight and hard.

"Oh," he whimpers. "I see."

I laugh, and he goes very still over me, his hands clenching and unclenching a little too hard on the back of my thighs, holding me down and open, and I know I'll have some nice finger-shaped bruises there when this is over. A sweet reminder.

I don't think I'll ever be able to recall this moment or the sound he made as he entered me without getting instantly hard, though. There's such a raw, rare expression on his face—total awe and, maybe I'm crazy, an affection so deep that I'd almost label it love, except it can't be. It's too soon.

But his cock is perfect for my body. Every little twitch of his hips seems to push against my prostate, and I'm gasping with pleasure before he even starts to fully stroke.

"Sejin," he whispers.

"Yeah?" My voice cracks, and I swallow trying to get a grip on myself.

"I'm sorry for teasing you before." He ducks his head and quakes all over. "I'm about to come."

"Then come," I say. "Fill me up. Like you wanted."

He puts his hand over my mouth and squeezes his eyes tight. "Shh. Shut up, Doc. I want to enjoy this for more than…" He grits his teeth and then breathes in and out of his nose slowly. "Just lie back and take it for a minute, baby, alright?"

Baby.

I like Doc. It's fun, it's sweet. But, holy shit, I *love* baby. My cock flexes and I reach for it, but he releases my mouth to knock my hand away.

"No," he says. "I'll control it."

I squirm then, unable to stop my body's needy reaction to those words, and he groans, "Ohhh, fuck you, baby," but it sounds like a tender declaration more than anything else.

His hips snap, and I reach to hold onto his straining shoulders as he fucks into me. His mouth is open, his eyes are on mine, and little sounds unlike any I've ever heard hitch out of him. He clenches my thighs, and he digs in deep with his dick before grunting in that quiet way that signals he's going to come.

"That's it," I encourage. "Come inside me."

Dan groans and gives over to a rolling thunderclap of orgasm. Sweat breaks over him as he shakes and convulses, his eyes roll up, and his breath comes in stuttering, quiet gasps. I feel his cock thud, shooting his load as he pushes deeper, straining with aftershocks.

I breathe hard, my cock aching and asshole clenching around his throbbing dick. I think I can feel the heat of his cum inside me, and maybe I can. All I know is that this feels different, special, and I know I'll never forget this moment for the rest of my life. I commit everything about it to my memory—the strain of the tendons in his neck, his scrunched-up face, and the way he jerks like he's going to empty his entire being into me.

"Don't come," he grits out, his eyes still squeezed closed. "Not yet."

I feel like I'm going to shoot anyway, because knowing his cum is inside me is hot as hell, and I'm on the verge, but I hold back with difficulty.

Slowly he releases my thighs, and I feel the bruises blooming on them already. Even more slowly he eases out of me. The sense of emptiness is profound, until he slides three fingers inside and hooks them against my prostate. I whimper, and he meets my gaze. "Good, baby?"

I twitch all over, wordless but encouraging him with moans. He rubs against my prostate hard with the pads of his fingers, and then he leans down to kiss me. As he fingers me, making my muscles jerk and twitch and my cock leak and flex, he nuzzles my cheek and rubs his face against my messy hair.

"Doc," he murmurs. "I think I'm gonna have to keep you."

I can't say anything at all. I'm so close to coming and yet so far, and my dick is in serious need of friction so I can get off. As usual, though, he concentrates on his favorite part of me, and I can't complain about the pleasure radiating from my hole. I shiver and shake, my legs twitching on the bed as he keeps finger-fucking me. Harder and harder, and I groan as he speeds up.

"Fuck," I shout as my body tightens, and every bit of my consciousness seems to center around my hole and pelvis, and then I break into convulsions of lust and bliss that I can't seem to control. My hole spasms again and again around his fingers, my body shakes and my nipples hurt blissfully, and then my cock suddenly grows so hard I feel faint.

"Oh, fuck!" I scream. That's when I shoot gobs of cum all over myself.

"Yes," he whispers as he avidly watches white streaks paint my stomach and chest while he rubs inside of me so hard I see stars. "Yes, give it to me."

I reach down to stop his hand, the sensation too much. I twitch and convulse through so many aftershocks that I lose the ability to do anything more than moan and cling to Dan, who doesn't let me go.

Later, after he's cleaned me up, given me water, and settled in beside me, he pushes my legs back and looks at my hole again. "My jizz is up there," he says, so matter-of-factly that I laugh. He meets my eyes. "I'm gonna lick it out."

"What?" I gasp, and start to protest, but when he leans down and his tongue touches me, I just give up and let it happen. Because, fuck, it feels so good.

I card my trembling fingers through his hair and quake as he urgently cleans me up down there. I feel tears prick in my eyes, and they slide out. I haven't cried while being fucked in a few encounters, and I'd thought I was past that. But this is different. These tears are something more.

When he leans back, wiping his mouth with the back of his hand, he seems to know these tears are special too. He seems to grow worried. "Was that all right? Are you okay? What's wrong?"

I shake my head and pull him down beside me.

He doesn't settle, though, concern etching his features. "What's wrong? Tell me." He nuzzles my cheek again. "Sejin, talk to me."

"I think I love you," I say. "I'm sorry. I know you don't want to hear that. But I think I do."

"Well," he says slowly, his lips flattening into a bit of a frown and then relaxing again. "It's not that big of a problem."

"It's not?"

"Nah. Because I think I love you too." He kisses me, and his mouth tastes of his cum and my ass, but I don't care. Another tear slips out and trails down my cheek.

"I didn't mean to make you cry," he says. "I just can't get enough of you. I won't eat it out of you again if you don't like it."

"I like it," I whisper. "I'm not crying about that."

"Then what are you crying about?"

I laugh. "I just told you."

"You're crying because you think you might love me?" he asks, looking baffled.

"Yeah, and I don't quite know what to do about it."

He frowns. "You don't do anything about it. It changes nothing."

I swallow even harder. "I know. I guess that's part of it. It changes nothing."

Dan touches my chin, then my cheeks, and he says, "I mean, I guess it changes what you might do after Peggy Jo comes back…"

"Let's not talk about that yet," I say. "I'm still stuck on what we just did and what we just said. Let's let that sink in first."

"Sink in." Dan smirks. "I can't wait to sink into you again. Give me two hours. Then we're gonna flip-fuck the opposite way, and you can come in me this time."

"Alright," I agree, exhaustion sucking me under.

He tucks a warm blanket around me before grabbing a book from the shelves behind his head. "Go to sleep," he says, like it's an order, and cracks open the book.

The rain hammers the top of the van, and I watch his eyes move over the pages for a few minutes before the heavy pull of sexual satisfaction, emotional upheaval, and the lull of the rain tugs me into sleep.

I dream of climbing a tall, white wall of polished granite. It's dark and I can only see a few feet above and below me. I'm scared to look down, and I know that Dan's somewhere up ahead, free soloing. He's left me behind as he forges on. He's climbing so fast that I know I can't reach him.

I'm alone on the wall.

Dan

WE FUCK BAREBACK two more times because neither of us can believe how good it feels or that we're actually doing it. To me, it's probably the best feeling I've ever experienced outside of that brief burst of delicious victory when I've sent a difficult new route without a single fall, or the first time I ever saw that special smile of Sejin's aimed right at me.

These feelings I have when I'm inside Sejin, when he's open to my cock and open emotionally too, are the wildest things I've ever experienced. I feel utterly high from them. Like I've licked meth off Sejin's skin and heroin from his leaking dick and molly from his asshole. I feel like I'm going to lift up into the sky and fly, but at the same time I don't want to stop wallowing in the earthly flesh and taste of him and the sounds of his pleasure.

I also like *not*-fucking Sejin—being alone with him, reading together, cuddling, laughing, and listening to him rattle on about whatever he wants. But I am absolutely *in love* with fucking Sejin, especially raw. I might also be in love with the way he says "Oh, fuck, I love you" when I'm plowing him so perfectly he leaks pre-cum and tears in equal measure.

And the way he clings to me when it's over.

And the way he rides my fingers because he feels empty without my dick.

And the pulse beating in his throat, and the silky sound of his fucked-out laugh, and…ugh, so much more.

Rye was right when he said I shouldn't do something as risky as free soloing Heart Route without letting myself truly enjoy Sejin first. I can't imagine if the worst happened and I'd never gotten to feel this way, to experience this sloppy, messy, layer cake of emotions. Because that's what this time with Sejin is—cake. The delicious part of life that makes the rest worth enduring.

I hadn't been lying earlier when I said I was in love with him, though I never intended for him to know that. Now it's out there. He thinks he loves me. I think I love him. We're boyfriends. We fuck raw. This is a real thing that's happening. And…well, it hits me a little belatedly that it's kind of a lot of responsibility. I have Sejin's body and heart in my hands.

He has mine in his.

What does it mean if I fuck up out there on Heart Route and leave him empty-handed?

I'm terrified I might only find out the answer as I'm plummeting to my death and no one wants that. Least of all me.

CHAPTER SEVENTEEN

Sejin

"WATCHA READING?" RYE asks as he sits down across from me in Papa Bear.

I check my phone and note that I have another half-hour before I start work. Gage and Celli have the counter under control, and Pete isn't here to try to convince me to take up any slack without pay, so I've got time to chat. I hold up my book—*The Impossible Climb* by Mark Synnott.

"Ahhh, that's a good one for an overview of climbing. Lot of history and plenty of gossip about the assholes of the sport." Rye smiles. "Mr. Synnott clearly had some grievances to air."

"He dishes on a few climbers, yeah. There's one guy he seems really careful not to be too negative about because he's dead now, but he obviously didn't adore him, to say the least."

"For sure," Rye agrees. "I know just who you're talking about. Most of the best-of-the-best are mentioned in that book, though. It's a nice place to start."

There's no mention of Dan, of course because a—he's newer to the game, and b—he's determined to stay out of the culture of the gig. Something I haven't quite pried into as much as maybe I should. Mainly because I want his attention on *me* when he's not climbing, and if he's part of this whole *thing*, a member of a select but still fairly thick crowd of climbers, then he'll have a lot less time to loll around in his van with me. Or so I tell myself.

"I picked it up off Dan's shelf," I say. "He has a lot of books, but this one seemed like the one he'd be least likely to miss." I indicate the spine. "It's not very creased. Not like the ones he goes over again and again."

"He doesn't know you borrowed it?"

I shrug. "He wasn't there at the time. He'd left with Peggy Jo, and I was just hanging out on my own—"

"In his van?" Rye's eyes take on a glitter.

"If he heads out really early, I hang out before I leave for work. You know, it takes some time to warm up from those freezing waterfall showers he likes."

"He makes you bathe in the waterfall?" Rye hiccups a laugh. "There's literally a shower block right there."

"I know, I know…" I wave it off. "He likes the waterfall, and I like it too."

"Weirdos."

"Yeah, so I was there alone, and my eyes landed on the books. I got curious, chose this one, and just…took it."

"I'm sure he'd let you borrow it."

"Yeah. Me too." Yet I don't want Dan to know I'm learning about climbing. I have my reasons, and they aren't the ones he'll want to hear. Namely, I want to know what drives people to do the things Dan does, and what their lives are like…and their deaths.

"What've you been up to? Seems like I haven't seen you in ages," I say to change the topic because I'm not sure I want to get into all that with Rye either. He's a great guy, but I know he's tight with Dan. Plus, I'm not sure I'm ready to share the inner turmoil I feel when I think about the man I'm in love with doing something as insane as climbing up El Capitan without ropes.

"True that. It has been a while," Rye agrees. "Hey, check it out, I've got some real stubble coming in." He takes hold of my hand, leans forward, and presses it against his cheek. I rub lightly and feel the new roughness. "Cool, huh?"

"Super cool," I say. I don't have a ton of facial hair myself, so I remember all too well how excited I was when the wisps I do manage to grow started coming in. "When you're ready to learn to shave it, let me know and I'll be happy to teach you if you need help."

"I'm not shaving this for a long time," he asserts with a grin. "It's hard-won, and I'm going to enjoy looking at it in the mirror."

"It's definitely impressive," I say, though it's really thin. He needs a few more years of hormones working their magic before he'll have anything like a real beard.

"Yeah, I think so too. Amazing what the right amount of T can do, huh?" He rubs his hand over his face. Then he smiles at me again, his nose crinkling a little. He's pretty cute and looks even younger than his already-young years—which is pretty typical of the trans men I've met in my life. "Anyway, let's see. What have I been up to lately… I've been busy with that new job."

"With YOSAR?"

"Yup. And climbing with Dan."

It's funny. I know Rye spends a lot of time helping Dan with training, and I spend a lot of time with Dan when he's *not* training, but we don't actually see each other despite that connection. We haven't ever been *friends* exactly, more like casual, chatty acquaintances.

"Yeah…Dan…" I say, and my eyes go unfocused.

I don't know what's gotten into me today; maybe it's reading about how another famous free soloist, a guy named John Bachar, died while doing a really easy climb without ropes.

I've been fixated on it all morning to the extent that I had a hard time concentrating on teaching the kids during my time at the preschool. I'd been planning to start them on the Twice choreo for their hit "Can't Stop Me," which actually has an English version, but had ended up just letting them dance out their wriggles to old, familiar songs and in freestyle. They'd all been exhausted and went down for naps easily, so Heather hadn't minded—not that she ever cared what I taught them so long as it was age-appropriate—but I'd been confused by my inability to stop thinking about Dan falling and exploding on the rocks below.

In fact, I'd come into Papa Bear early to continue reading and hopefully to get some other stories in my head, or some kind of reassurance that free soloing isn't as dangerous as it seems.

When Rye walked up, though, I'd just read about teenage Dan's hero Alex Honnold's justification for why free soloing isn't that dangerous. Driving 80 miles per hour on the interstate is dangerous too, and you can't control all the factors around it either. One slip of the hand on the steering wheel, or one slip of someone else's hand on another steering wheel, and you're toast, and yet people do it every day.

It's true, but…

"Hey, you okay?" Rye asks. "You know you can talk to me about Dan, right?"

"Sure."

Rye puts an elbow on the table and rests his chin in his palm. "He's a lot to handle."

"He can be, I guess." But he isn't. Not to me. "Actually, there's nothing about Dan *as Dan* that's hard for me to deal with? It's just the free soloing that's a lot."

"Ah. Believe me. I get you on this."

I swallow. Rye truly cares about Dan, and he's going to know more about climbing than just about anyone else I can talk to about it. I'd considered bringing up my fears to Peggy Jo when I'd met up with her alone to discuss me moving into her place, but the timing never seemed right. And Peggy Jo is like a mother to Dan. Too close. Too invested.

Rye, though…

"I guess I'm reading this to try to understand, you know? Not just why people do this, but what the real risks are. How dangerous is free soloing really?"

"It's very dangerous," Rye says. "No doubt about that. And don't let Dan or any other free soloist tell you differently. But, if it makes you feel any better, free soloists aren't typically suicidal and not that many have actually died *while* free soloing. Most go out doing something completely different."

"What about that John Bachar guy?"

"Yeah, he was older, and it was such an easy pitch he fell from." Rye frowns. "It could have been that the rock got slippery, or for some reason he pumped out—that's when your muscles get too overexerted and your grip releases against your will—but… well, there's evidence that he had some medical stuff going on with a shoulder injury too. It could have led to muscle weakness that prevented him from getting as good a grip as he'd needed. Apparently, he made some posts in a forum asking how to deal with that sort of thing not too long before he died. Or maybe he had a heart attack or a stroke. We'll never know since he was alone, and his body was…" Rye rubbed a hand over his eyes. "Well, let's just say an autopsy would have been impossible."

"But a lot of other free soloists have died, right?"

"Yeah, but most weren't even free soloing. Like Dean Potter died doing a wingsuit BASE jump. And Michael Reardon died while doing an easy climb near an ocean and a huge rogue wave swept him off the rock, a completely unforeseeable event. Charlie Fowler died in an avalanche, not while rock climbing at all. It's obviously not impossible to die while free soloing—and more and more climbers are trying it, so more deaths have happened in recent years—but it's also not inevitable. There's no getting around that it's wildly dangerous, but most people agree that successful free soloists are actually very methodical people."

"And Dan's successful?"

"So far, yes."

"So far. Ha. That's the quandary, right?"

Rye smirked. "He'd tell you that so far you're a successful motorist…"

"A justification he's picked up from his hero." I lift the book.

"Yeah."

"Part of me wants a list of things more dangerous than free soloing—"

"BASE jumping, wingsuiting—" Rye starts to tick things off.

"Another part of me just wants to find a way to get all Zen inside and not care. Just live for the moment. Enjoy him while it lasts. My mom died a few years ago, and I wish every day I could have another hour with her, with both of us carefree and neither of us knowing she's sick."

"I'm sorry. That's rough."

I ignore the platitudes. "I try to live like that with Dan, but sometimes I feel like this climb is my mom's cancer. It's always looming over us."

"Does it tarnish the good times for you?"

"I try not to let it." I flip my hair over my shoulder and lean forward, getting serious with him. "I was doing okay with that until I decided to reassure myself by reading this book. Now I've got too many vivid pictures in my head. It's easier to pretend nothing scary is happening since I don't climb with him—"

"You don't? Ever?"

"I'm afraid of heights so he takes me up sometimes at night on smaller walls when I can't see the exposure, but otherwise no. I don't see him do it, and I don't participate, so it's all"—I wave my hand—"something that's out there somewhere. You know, like how people feel about their parents' places of work growing up. They don't see it often, so it's easy to forget it even exists."

I rub a hand over my face. "Until the chemical companies shut down and leave your town in poverty, but that's another thing entirely."

"Sejin?"

"Yeah?"

Rye takes hold of my hand and squeezes. "I'm up there with him and let me tell you, he's the best of the best, or one of them. He's good. He's *more* than good. He's inhuman on those walls. But even I can't promise you anything."

"No. No one can." I shove the book across the table. "Maybe I don't want to read more of this."

"Maybe you don't. Or maybe you do. And maybe you should come up on a wall with me and Dan one day."

"I can't go up a wall like that. No way."

"No, not this route he's training for, anyway. But maybe another, less challenging one, and if you see how good he is, how it's like breathing for him, then maybe it might ease your mind some."

"He'll be roped in, though."

"Of course. He always is when he's with me."

"So, you've never seen him free solo?"

"Once. We went to the Grand Tetons, and he free soloed up a chimney. I just sat on the roof of the van and watched. He was amazing. Like watching a monkey climb a tree. Natural. Easy."

"I don't know…" I shiver. "I really hate heights. When we climb at night, it's not so bad, and I do see how good he is. He's really stable and reassuring. But he's only taken me to Pothole Dome and some similar climbs like that. He doesn't want to push me."

"Maybe you should push yourself then. You don't have to love it, but if you see how safe it is with ropes—"

"I know it's safe with ropes. I just get vertigo from the exposure."

"Right." Rye rubs his chin, feeling his new hair growth. "That does make it harder."

"I hear what you're saying, though. It would be good for me to see him in his element so I understand more fully what he's capable of. It'd soothe me."

"Or it could make things worse." Rye puts his hands up in a "don't shoot" position. "There's no saying what you might think or feel about it. It might give you too much to imagine at night when you can't sleep. It really could go either way."

"Thanks," I say with a smile, but can't help adding sarcastically. "This has been a very helpful conversation."

Rye chuckles. "I'm sorry. I worry about him too."

"Does he worry about himself?"

"I think so. He doesn't want to die. But maybe you should ask him about the climb, have him review the pitches with you, explain why he is or isn't worried about different parts of them. Knowledge can ease the anxiety of ignorance."

"Or ignorance can be bliss."

"Yeah."

Pete comes in the front door and sees me sitting with Rye and checks his watch. "Don't you have some hours to make up from when you took off early last week?"

I smile at him winningly, but he just rolls his eyes and motions for me to join him. So I press Rye's hand and say, "Thanks for talking with me. Gotta get to work."

"No rest for the wicked," Rye says.

I don't think I'm wicked, but as I gather my things and go change into my work uniform, I wish I were a witch or wizard who could put a spell on Dan to keep him safe on the wall as he climbs.

He'd hate that, though. He wants to send the route completely on his own.

Me? Well, I just don't want to lose him.

Dan

"YOU'VE NEVER BEEN interested in this before."

I'm a little skeptical. It's not that I don't want to show Sejin my plans for Heart Route, but his sudden interest is noteworthy, and my experience with people is that when something is "noteworthy," it also means "trouble."

"It's important to you, and I'd like to know more about it."

"Hmm."

I go ahead and get out my notebook with all the topo and beta for the route, and also my Yosemite Big Walls Guidebook. I crack it open first. "So, this is Heart Route," I say, running a finger over the line on the photo showing the twenty-six pitches that I've etched into my own heart and mind through repetition over the last three years.

I've gone over the same terrain again and again, usually alone on the wall since most people have little to no interest in this magical route for some reason. Probably the difficulty with the dyno and the roof, and probably because there are more famous routes to master first.

I explain all of that to Sejin. "That's part of why I picked this one. It's ignored."

"Twenty-six pitches? What does that mean?"

"A pitch is a section of rock, basically the length of one rope. A single pitch climb is one rope length, and a multi-pitch climb is multiple rope lengths."

"So, this is twenty-six rope lengths?" Sejin touches the red line on the photo of El Cap.

"Yup. And what you and I have done together, when we've gone out at night, have all been a single pitch or less."

"Ah." Sejin frowns slightly, touching the line again. "What are the hardest parts?"

"Well, the first seven pitches are known as the Heart Blast, and they're pretty tiring; I'm not going to lie. That's why fitness and consistent training is key. You can't afford to get up past Heart Blast and then be so exhausted you pump out—" Sejin says, nothing, but I go on to explain it anyway. "That's when your grip muscles get weak from lactic acid due to overwork, especially in your hands and arms, and you let go against your will."

Sejin's breath hitches.

"That's almost never happened to me."

"Right… Almost."

"And never while free soloing," I say soothingly. "Obviously. Because I'm alive."

Sejin's body tenses, and I forge on ahead. "Pitch 6, which they call Dub Step, has some of the most difficult moves of the entire route. A down climb—which is when you climb down instead of up, obviously, and a dyno."

"Dyno?"

I know he knows this term, because I've mentioned it before, but I explain it again. "It's a dynamic movement—in this case, basically a sideways leap."

"A leap."

"Mm, and once you've started it, you're committed. You can't change your mind midway."

"Ah."

"So that's rough stuff, but I've been practicing that move a ton this season, both up on the route itself, and with similar dynos elsewhere. I built out the exact dimensions of this dyno on a climbing wall I installed at the barn I was staying in last winter—"

"You were staying in a barn?"

"Yeah, I guess I never mentioned it. It was cheap—as in free—because it was abandoned, and I put a climbing wall on the side of it. I built a model of this dyno and worked my ass off on it. Got to where I was about ninety percent with it, but…" I cluck my tongue. "The exposure changes things. Obviously."

"Obviously…" Sejin's throat convulses as he swallows.

I point out the next pitch. "This is the slab that leads to Heart Ledge. It's a tough section. The first team to free climb it—that's going up with ropes but not using any aids—thought at first it would be impossible, but they found these tiny holds about the width of the side of a nickel. Sharp holds. Good thing my fingers are calloused all to hell, huh?"

"Yeah," he says faintly.

"The steepest climbing is here, starting with the roof pitches." Here my voice falters a little, and I hope he doesn't catch it. "It's spooky, but doable. It's rated 5.14d which is…well, the rating says it all."

"Difficult."

"Very." I move past the roof pitches and sweep on to the next bit, a crazy flake at a rough angle. "After that, it's a section of smooth granite with nickel-sized holds, but then you take Golden Gate right on up to the top." I don't emphasize the true difficulty of the section directly after the roof.

"Well," Sejin says, leaning back away from the photo. "None of that is extremely reassuring."

I can't help the laugh that barks out of me. "Doc, this is hard stuff, but it's not impossible."

"Maybe it *should* be impossible."

"It just takes training—"

"And luck."

"Mostly training. As they say, 'shit happens', but my job is to make sure I'm in a position to have the climb of my life before I even start up."

"The climb of your life," Sejin repeats, and I hear a bit of bitterness. "The *final* climb of your life, maybe."

I sit back, jaw tensing. I don't want to fight with him about this. "Any moment of any day could be the final one."

"Sure, but statistically—"

"Look, when I was nine, this kid at my school's dad died, and do you know how?"

"How?"

"He was parked at a stop sign when a massive limb from a tree collapsed onto his car, crushing him."

"Yeah, but—"

"And when I was in middle school, this kid named John died after getting allergy shots. The anaphylaxis didn't start until he and his mom were on the highway, far from the doctor's office, no EpiPen in the car, and boom…dead."

"Jesus."

"And Peggy Jo's husband Ivan died when he was only thirty-two—Bella was just nine—while swimming in the ocean. A freak riptide grabbed him. Look, we don't know what's going to happen."

"So why bring extra danger into your life?"

I lean back, frustrated. "Because I can't live out an existence where I don't at least see how far I can go against a completely unfeeling, uncaring world—in this case, the rock."

Sejin swallows and looks back down at the map. "I'm going to make peace with this," he says quietly. "I am. I don't want to be the guy who couldn't handle the enormity of his boyfriend's dreams. I'm just scared."

I take hold of his hand and kiss his fingers. "I get scared too."

"Do you?"

"Of course. I'm not a robot."

"No…" Sejin says, leaning forward and burying his face against my neck, kissing the skin there softly. "You're not a robot at all. You're flesh and blood. You're fragile."

"Not as fragile as you think. I'm made of tough stuff. So are you."

Sejin doesn't argue, but he does push me down to the mattress and climb on top of me. His weight is comforting and warm, and he says nothing, does nothing, for a very long time.

We just hold each other and breathe.

CHAPTER EIGHTEEN

Sejin

P EGGY'S JO'S PLACE is in the high-country forest and about a thirty-minute drive from town. The house itself is basically my dream home, except I'd probably have a dog instead of three cats. But I like cats too, so I'm good with caring for them. Plus, they seem to adore me.

Or they *did,* until Peggy Jo started moving her luggage out to her truck. Now they're hiding beneath beds and in cubbyholes, glaring balefully, looking worried, or somehow, mysteriously, both.

The kitchen is an open-concept with a counter separating it from the living room, which feels massive with its gleaming wood floors and floor-to-ceiling glass doors along the entirety of the back wall. These show off a stunning view of the mountains, and I can't wait to see how the light plays over the land at all different hours of the day and what the stars look like at night. The light pollution must be low out here. There's so much space to wander and what seems like unlimited privacy.

The living room is cozy, with a big sectional sofa, a large television screen mounted on a wall, and a rug that's nicely fuzzy against my bare feet. The décor isn't any particular style, but just Peggy Jo personified into a living space. There are photos of her daughter—a slightly plump, dark-haired little girl—and then woman—with a wide smile, and photos of Peggy Jo climbing at various ages. There's a wedding photo of Peggy Jo with her husband, a tall, handsome man with heavy, dark eyebrows, and, most interesting to me, a few photos of Dan.

In one he's probably not even twenty yet and hasn't grown into his eyes. They look enormous—like dinner-plate large—and they're full of skepticism and mistrust. As the photos of Dan progress, he begins to look more and more like himself, and that mistrust gradually fades. I decide to take a closer look at these pictures, and the photo albums she has sitting out in plain sight, later when I'm alone.

In the middle of the living room, there's a wood-burning stove that Peggy Jo assures me will heat the entire room for most of the cold months of winter. There's central gas heat too, but she says the stove will warm things up more quickly and efficiently, so she keeps a big pile of wood just around the corner of the giant glass doors. She asks only that I keep up with it, replacing what I use every few days or so. It's not hard, she says, given that there are plenty of downed trees and limbs along the edge of her property, many quite big.

I've never chopped wood before, but I figure it can't be that hard. There's probably a YouTube video demonstrating best practices for it.

There's also a big hot tub, the barrel-shaped kind that requires climbing a ladder on the outside to get in. Peggy Jo says I can use it any time, just to be sure to test the water regularly and to keep the lid on to prevent pine needles, leaves, and critters from getting in.

After showing me around the property one last time, Peggy Jo and I take the last of her luggage out of the house and strap it onto the racks of her truck bed, cover it all with tarps, and then come back inside for a cup of coffee before she heads out on the road.

"Sure you don't need my help moving your stuff in?" she asks.

"Nah, I've got it."

"I want you to feel comfortable here. Please don't hesitate to make yourself at home," she says to me for the five-hundredth time since I pulled up this morning with the entirety of my worldly belongings in the back seat. I don't even have enough to warrant using the trunk.

When I left West Virginia, I also left the concept of accumulation behind. More for the sake of lack of space than out of any decision to try to save the planet or anything. Dan has more stuff in his van than I own, despite his lifestyle seeming much more on the fringes.

"Don't worry, I will," I say, laughing a little when she slaps my arm gently.

"I really do appreciate you staying here to look after my brats." She gazes around sorrowfully. "I said goodbye to them all this morning because I knew they'd hide when it was time to go, but I wish I could give them all one last kiss."

"I'll give them one for you."

She grins, and it makes her wrinkles stand out in a wonderful way. "Thank you. And, I have to say, I'm glad it's you here. As much as I thought it would solve a few of Dan's financial problems to move in, the cats really do hate him."

I laugh.

"Which maybe isn't a problem in terms of keeping them fed and watered, but if something happens and one of them needs to go to the vet, Dan would have a hell of a time getting them in their travel crates."

"I'm not sure I'll have it much easier if it comes to that, but I'll totally give them loads of love every day, I promise."

"That's another thing Dan wouldn't give them. He's not a fan." She eyes me speculatively. "Speaking of Dan…"

I brace myself. I've suspected for some time that Peggy Jo is curious about our situation and that getting information out of Dan about us is probably as useless as digging for coal in a played-out mine.

"Does he treat you right?"

"Of course." I'm surprised she needs to ask that. She knows him plenty well to know he'd never mistreat anyone, much less someone he cares about, and I think she knows he cares about me.

"It's not that I think he wouldn't want to, but sometimes Dan is…" Peggy Jo sighs, turns sideways on the sofa, and faces me more fully. "Dan is so used to being alone in the world, he doesn't always consider how things affect other people who care about him."

"Yeah," I say, smiling and hoping to hide my raw vulnerability.

"Dan is a good man," she says, like I might not know. "I've grown to love him as my own."

She rolls her eyes. "Of course *he* didn't come to see me off today, but I'm not too surprised by that. He struggles with goodbyes. He typically sees it as abandonment."

"He doesn't seem to think you're abandoning him. If anything, he seems—" I bite off the end of my words.

"Glad I'm going?" she says with a laugh. "Oh, there's a part of him that is most definitely glad I won't be around for the big climb. The pressure of knowing someone down on the ground cares about him is…well, not necessarily too much for him, but he feels it's a burden. Which brings me back to you…"

"You worry I might be a burden to him?"

"I struggle with my own feelings about this part of who Dan is," Peggy Jo says, frowning out the massive windows at the big lawn. "I admire his drive, his athleticism, his bravery, and his determination. I spray about him constantly—"

"Spray?"

"Climber slang for bragging," she clarifies. "He'll never spray about himself, and he isolates so much from the community that very few will spray on his behalf. Which leaves me and Rye for the most part doing the bragging about his various accomplishments."

"He doesn't want people to know what he's done?" That seems odd to me because I get the impression Dan is very proud of what he can and will do.

"It's not that he doesn't want them to know, so much as that's not why he does it. Public accolades or external validation doesn't play into his motivations. It's internal for him."

"But why? What's he got to prove to himself?"

"I've been trying to understand that for years. How are you handling that aspect of who Dan is? Emotionally, I mean. You alright?"

I clear my throat and chew on my lower lip, trying to think of how to answer. "I try not to think about the free solo too much. He showed me his plans the other day. I asked to see them, and he explained the...the pitches?"

She nods.

"He explained the pitches to me, and I believe it's safe to climb it all with ropes—barring things like rockfalls or freak accidents. Challenging, yeah, and maybe you bust your knee on a fall or whatever, but not deadly. Without ropes, though..."

"Without ropes reduces the room for mistakes to zero."

"Right, and mistakes happen." I twist my hands in my lap. "I remember when I was just a kid riding my bike down the same street I always rode down..." I laugh. "I don't know what happened, but I took a corner too fast and wiped out. Cut my knee. I still have a scar. If Dan's up on the wall and he 'takes a corner too fast,' he's *dead*, and there's just exploded body bits to scrape off the...the...what do you call the ground? The deck?"

"The floor."

"Right. Well, it's not like I can stop him from doing it." I try to smile, but it feels shaky. "I don't even think I *should* try. If he tried to stop me from..." I pause. "I literally cannot think of a single thing I do that's half as dangerous as what he does, so that doesn't work. I just know in my heart that if I forced his hand… Well, he's been in love with free soloing a lot longer than he's been in love with me—if he's even really in love with me—"

"He is."

"So, what he's doing might seem unhinged to me, but the choice is to lose him for sure or just lose him maybe."

Peggy Jo watches me with such empathy in her eyes that tears well up.

"Oh, sweetheart," she says, reaching out and dragging me close. "You're very brave. Braver than he is, actually."

"I don't think so. I'm terrified of heights."

"But you're the one choosing to stay with him knowing that you might have to *live* with the pain of his consequences…and he wouldn't. He'd get maybe a dozen long seconds to make peace with it, and then it'd be over. You, though…you'd have to live with it for a very long time. And I get the idea you're familiar with grief."

"My mom," I choke out.

She pats my shoulder. "Ah, I see. But you're willing to risk that to be with him."

"My dad says it's worth it?" I say it into her shoulder, and it comes out like a question.

She lets out a small laugh. "It might be. I hope we never find out."

"Me too."

We pull apart when the sound of a heavy vehicle coming up the drive, kicking up gravel, breaks the silence. A cat meows and darts out from beneath the chair and into a bedroom.

"Well, well, speak of the devil," Peggy Jo says with a twinkling smirk as she stands up and starts toward the front door. "Seems like Dan isn't going to let me go without a final goodbye after all."

I stand and follow her, my heart ricocheting between exultation at seeing his face and a feeling of guilt that he might somehow know

Peggy Jo and I had been talking about him, that we'd shared our mutual love, fear, and pain. As if by discovering Peggy Jo also shares my mix of worry and pride in him, I've gone behind his back. It's silly, I know, but I hope she doesn't mention it to him.

Peggy Jo throws open the front door and calls out, hands on her hips, "'Bout time you got here, you ruffian."

Over her shoulder, I see Dan striding from the van. He stops in front of her for a silent moment and then throws his arms around her and gives her a hard hug.

"Now, don't act like I'm never seeing you again," she says. "You'll scare your boyfriend."

Dan's eyes lift and meet mine, but he doesn't let go of Peggy Jo. I swallow and then smile at him. His brows furrow slightly. He squeezes her hard one more time and releases her.

"You flatter yourself," he says. "I thought you'd already be gone. I was just coming up here to schtup him on your sofa."

Peggy Jo snorts, and I feel my cheeks heating with embarrassment. "As if I believe that's the only reason you came."

None of us do, not after that hug.

"Well, when do you leave?" he asks, glancing at his watch. "If you're going to make it to Fresno-Yosemite for that 12:10 flight, you need to get going."

Peggy Jo agrees, and we run through a few final things about the cats, double-checking that I know where the emergency vet is located, and where the number is for her preferred regular clinic.

By the time I convince her I'm absolutely prepared for any event with the cats, she's out in her truck. She kisses Dan's cheek through the window, waves at me where I stand in the doorway to the house, and then makes a three-point turn to pull down the drive.

Dan rounds on me, nods once, and says, "Okay, that's done. Get your clothes off."

Dan

WHEN I ARRIVE, I can tell Sejin and Peggy Jo have been talking about me. Sejin looks guilty and Peggy Jo is smug. But I don't really mind or care what they've been saying, so long as I get one last hug from Peggy Jo, and then get to bend Sejin over the back of her sofa and fuck him raw.

So, I do just that.

"I haven't been able to stop thinking about this," I grind out, watching my unsheathed dick plunge in and out of him. There's something so carnal, so erotic in being inside him without a condom that I feel my balls draw up and my hips stutter. I might shoot any second. "Love fucking you bare."

"*Unf*," he grunts, and I shift my gaze from all his loose, inky-black hair spilling everywhere, and the way his slim hips move to catch my thrusting cock, to stare out at that gorgeous view of the mountains, trying to make it last.

But it's not long before my gaze drifts back down to watch his hole swallow my dick. His little squirming movements show how much he loves taking it, and as I pummel his ass, he grows deliciously loud.

The cats act like spooked little demons who scamper from one hiding place to another, yowling angrily. That could have been a mood killer, but it's entirely offset by how nice it is to be fucking Sejin in a place with plenty of privacy and lots of room to move. There's a kind of intimacy to fucking in the van, sure, but there's a fantastic freedom to fucking literally anywhere else.

"Danny," he moans, and I note again how his West Virginian accent deepens charmingly as his lust rises. "Talk to me. Tell me more. How much you like it."

He's gripping the seat cushion of the longest part of the sectional sofa, white knuckled and panting. He writhes and whines as I shove in hard again. I brush his hair off his back and lean over to take hold of his shoulder to slam in even harder.

"Fuck," I whisper. "You feel so good on my dick." I moan as his asshole clings to me with each pull out. "You don't want to let me go, do you, baby?"

"No," he whimpers. "Stay with me."

"Mm, I'll stay." I thrust into him repeatedly until his knees start shaking, and then give out.

He's limp over the back of the sofa. It's no doubt digging into his stomach, but he just keeps convulsing and crying out, clenching and releasing the sofa cushion. I know he's going to start leaking tears soon too. I've come to recognize the sounds he makes before he gets so aroused and overstimulated that he starts to cry. I shouldn't get so turned on by it, and I wouldn't if I thought he was in pain, but he's not—he's just in too much pleasure.

"Oh," he lets out with a gasp, and his hips gyrate uncontrollably, his asshole squeezing and releasing around my plunging dick, goosebumps break out on his skin in waves, and I sense the intense bombs of climax going off all along his nerves. "Fuck," he whispers, his whole body jittering like a living jackhammer, and I recognize *that* now too. The reverberation of a massive anal orgasm.

I feel a bit smug. I've only had an anal orgasm twice. Neither time was with Sejin. Both were with this one guy a few years back who had a monster of a cock that left me with no choice but to lose myself on it. My dick's big, but it's not hole-wreckingly huge, and yet I've managed to give this pleasure to Sejin at least a half-dozen times since we started fucking. He's a drooling mess afterward too, especially if I give him more than one.

Which I aim to do today.

Sejin goes non-verbal as I wrap my hands up in his hair like it's reins, tugging him back on my dick. His head is tilted back, his gaze staring ahead out the windows. I wonder if he sees anything at all through his haze of lust. I fuck him like I have no other plans for the rest of my life. Steady, hard, determined—like how I climb when I'm in the zone. He has no defense against this, not now anyway, if he ever did, and I notice tears falling from his face to the sofa, splattering and leaving dark dots on the upholstery.

I think of his cock, trapped on the back side of the sofa, and wonder if it's hurting now, aching for stimulation and touch. I should take it in hand, but I know this will all be over in a heartbeat if I do. And I love making him either ask for it or come despite my negligence of his dick.

It's a powerful feeling to fuck a man until he comes hands-free. But maybe I'll take mercy on him and let him shoot his load after I've wrenched another edgy anal climax out of him.

Tugging his hair back, I jackknife into him again and again, and he takes me like he's made for this. His skin blotches red and hot up and down his back, his breathing staggers, and he squirms frantically, goosebumps breaking out over his skin again. His asshole squeezes around my dick, and his hips convulse hard as the jitters commence. "Fu-u-u-uck," he grits out, overwhelmed, his voice shaking with his body.

"That's nice," I say as calmly as I can, given that my nipples are tingling, my balls are hard with the need to release, and my cock feels like it's being sucked by the sweetest, hottest hole in the world. Even better—that hole is attached to the most delicious man, and I'm desperately, wildly in love with him. "That's a very nice compliment. Coming on my cock like that."

His breath hitches hysterically, and I let go of his hair to reach around to check his dick, finding it wickedly hard and hot. The tip is drenched, and I smear the pre-cum around with the tips of my fingers before releasing it. Sejin hangs his head and whimpers, and I don't know if it's in disappointment or relief that I'm not done fucking him yet.

"Want to go for another?"

His asshole tightens around me, and he breathes erratically for a moment before nodding.

"This position okay? You comfortable?"

He hesitates and then nods again, which I take to mean that he's *not* comfortable, but he also doesn't want to move. Still, I clarify, "You're good here? We can switch to another—"

"Now," he says urgently. "Here."

I get the impression from the pressure behind his voice that he can't express much more than that.

I dig my fingers into his hips to hold him steady, and I smirk as he thrashes his head when I begin to pummel his ass again. He loves being fucked. I do too, of course, but Sejin loves it like it's reason enough for living. He gives so much of himself while bottoming, and always has, even that first night we hooked up. I can't imagine giving that much, even for him. Even when that one guy's massive cock forced those anal climaxes out of me, I didn't give him all of myself, not the way Sejin does for me. I held something back, but he never does.

"Danny," he warbles, turning his head so that I can see his tear-streaked cheek. "It's so good. You're so good."

If he can say that much, I'm not fucking him well enough to get that third anal climax. I twist one hand up in his hair again—he seems to love that as much as I do—and hold him in place with the tension between my strong hand on his hip and my grip on his hair. I ride him until I'm sweating. He's damp with sweat too. The slap of our skin is loud in the room, almost as loud as his cries.

And then—like a beautiful dream—he hits a wall of pleasure. Going perfectly rigid, he accepts my ramming cock like a sheath as his body locks up. A spasm rips through him, knees collapsing under his weight, elbows going out so that I'm holding his torso up by my grip on his hair, and he screams.

I feel his cum paint my bare feet as his anus grips wildly, and I realize he's hit both at once—anal climax and penile orgasm. He quakes like he's having a seizure while I shove my cock in as deep as I can, hold tight, and grunt. I twitch all over as I shoot my load into his perfect, beautiful, writhing body.

I imagine my jizz coating his insides and I groan, shaking as this orgasm steals my sanity for gloriously long bursts of pleasure. It's intense, and it takes time for me to return back to myself. I pant against his heaving back, blinking wetly as he hauls in breaths beneath me. Wow, weird, I've got tears in my eyes too. I kiss his shoulder blades, his spine, and his wet cheek before I heave myself back onto my heels and tug free of his body.

"Fuck," he says, reaching back to spread his ass open for me, showing off how I've left him fucked open.

I grin as his hole clenches helplessly on air and a dribble of my cum slides out. I use my index finger to push it back in. Irrationally, I want it all to stay inside, to be absorbed into him, to be part of him forever.

"Oh, God," he whimpers, and trembles some more. I finger his hole lightly until he's closing up around me, and then press my thumb against the twitching pucker of it as if I'm sealing it closed.

I help him stand up, and he leans against me, our height difference making it so that he has to wrap his arms around my shoulders while I steady him with an arm around his waist. His hair swings around us both, soft and tickly. I love it. "Let's go clean up. Peggy Jo's got great water pressure."

"Can I walk?" he mutters, huffing against my hair. "I don't think I can walk?"

"I got you, Doc," I say, squeezing him tightly. "I got you."

"Yeah," he agrees, a small sob seeming to wrack his body as he leans more heavily against me. "Yeah, you do."

I fight back a weird lump in my throat. I hope I have him. In every way. It's a lot of responsibility, and...

I don't want to let him down.

CHAPTER NINETEEN

Sejin

I N BED WITH Dan the first night at Peggy Jo's is a little strange. The sheets smell different from the ones in the van or the ones I'm accustomed to at Martin and Leenie's, but I suppose I can get another brand of detergent and wash everything I use if it bothers me. Which I'm not sure it does. It's just different.

Another oddity is how I feel after playing house with Dan all afternoon post-fuck over the sofa—which, holy shit, how does sex with Dan keep on being so stupidly good? I'd have thought we'd start hitting a rut by now, but I come for him like that's what I'm put on this earth to do. It's ridiculous. But, yeah, after we'd showered and cleaned up our mess and then napped on the sofa to recover, we'd woken to three mad cats yowling for dinner. Once I'd fed them, Dan and I got wildly domestic.

We made dinner together and watched a TV show. We built a fire in the woodstove. We chatted and rubbed each other's feet, and we cuddled. We brushed our teeth next to each other at the vanity sink in the bathroom, and we climbed into the queen-sized bed in Peggy Jo's bedroom with a series of yawns and goodnight pecks on the lips.

It feels right. Like we've shared space like this a thousand times before. I mean, I've slept over in his van, but it's hardly the same thing. It always feels so temporary, so much like a break from reality for me, as if when I climb into his van I'm stepping outside of time.

Today in Peggy Jo's house, though, it's more like a vision of what could be. A future that I don't know if I have the guts to hope for, but I want to try for anyway. But how? Dan's a climber, and I'm an overemployed-but-broke prodigal son with no real life plan.

I might be terrified of Dan's willingness to risk so much, but at least he has a goal. One that *could* earn money if he were willing to take on sponsorships.

I turn onto my side and watch him sleep in the light of the nearly full moon pouring in from the crack in the curtains. I wonder about the possibility of a future for us. A real one. With a home. And little rituals. A way of being that's *us*.

I start to list all the things that would have to happen for a dream like that to come true:

I'd need a real job.

Dan would need an income.

We'd have to find a house we both liked.

We'd have to want the same things from life.

Dan would have to survive his Heart Route free solo.

My eyes fill with tears. It's amazing how much hinges on that. Only everything.

Dan

Waking up in a soft bed in a big room, with the scent of coffee and the sound of bouncy KPop drifting in from a full kitchen is new. I wallow in the warm covers, listening to the sounds of breakfast being made, and smile up at the ceiling.

I can imagine Sejin in there, moving around Peggy Jo's kitchen, hair up in a messy bun, and his cute little ass wiggling to the music. He'll probably occasionally break out into the choreo for whatever song is playing. Something by Astro probably.

I could get used to this, I decide. And that thought is underscored in gold when I suddenly smell bacon frying.

"Merowrrrr." I hear it a mere half-beat before a small, furry demon pounces onto the bed and hisses in my face, showing me his terrifying fangs, and then darts off out of the room through the slightly open door.

"Devil," I mutter, rubbing a hand over my sleep-crusted eyes and trying to still my now wildly beating heart.

"You're up," Sejin says cheerfully when I come out to join him in the kitchen, after I've taken a leak, shaved, and brushed away the morning breath. He gives me a long up-down, and I feel my cock stir. How does he do that? Make me want him with just a sly grin and a coy look? "You look sexy."

I look down at myself. The night before I'd been reluctant to go out to the van and rummage for a clean t-shirt and boxers to sleep in, so Sejin had pulled out some things from his own luggage for me to wear. They aren't anything more than a pair of soft athletic shorts and a t-shirt, but they smell like him and that's nice.

"Mmph," I say. I'm not really a morning person like he is. I don't take forever to get out of bed or drag ass, but I do sort of hate to be cheerful in the morning. That's more of an afternoon mentality. Or maybe nighttime.

After considering my taciturn personality…

Maybe never.

"Sit," he says, pointing to the table where I've shared many a meal with Peggy Jo. I pull out a chair and a cat scampers off all offended like I moved it just to irritate him.

Sejin bends down to stroke the angry cat and whisper something to him. I narrow my eyes, looking for any sign that the little horror might bite Sejin. These cats have been known to pretend to want my attention, only to strike when I actually do reach out to pet them. But Romeo—Julio? Muggs?—simply rubs against Sejin's fingers and then twines around his ankles like it's his job to trip Sejin.

So that's his diabolical plan.

"You're really suspicious of these cats, huh?" Sejin says, as he turns back to the bacon, eggs, and toast he's assembling on plates for us.

"They're suspicious of me too," I point out.

Sejin snorts but doesn't say more. Though I do notice he drops some eggs to the floor and the two cats that have come to watch him cook dive for the bits. Aha, he bribes them, huh? I could try that, but it seems beneath my dignity. Plus...*cats*.

We've just started eating when Sejin's phone pings. I figure it's another VLive alert for one of his KPop bands, and we'll eat breakfast watching people speak Korean, and we'll enjoy it though we have no idea what's going on. But, instead, Sejin seems surprised by what's on the screen, and then he starts to type quickly with his thumbs.

A ping, ping, ping of back-and-forth texting begins. I eat my breakfast and leave him to it.

"My dad," Sejin says after a few minutes, finally putting his phone aside. "He's curious what the plans are for Thanksgiving this year. I'd promised to spend it with him, and he's..." Sejin blinks and shakes his head. "He's offered to fly out here instead of me flying home to him."

"Why's that?"

"I don't know. I usually like the holidays back home, but I haven't been back to West Virginia since I left..."

There's a lot of weight behind those words, and I know there's a lot Sejin isn't saying about that. I sip my coffee and ask, "Do you want to go home for Thanksgiving?"

"I don't know." He picks at his food. "I hate the thought of walking back into that house knowing she'll never be there."

"So long as you don't go home then she can still be there in your mind?"

"No," he says quietly. "I know she's gone. I saw her body. I can't call her on the phone when I need her. I don't have my mom in my life. It's just…I don't want to look back like that. I don't think she'd want me to. She knew me. She knew I wanted to travel and move away, and live the kind of life where I'm not in one place forever. Going back isn't moving forward, you know? Not for me."

"Mm." I don't have anything to say to that. I'm not the person to talk to about family stuff. Surprise trust fund money from biological grandfathers doesn't count as having family.

"But I feel guilty too. Like, am I wrong to abandon Dad there with all the memories? Does that make me a bad kid?"

"Your dad's a grown man. If he wants to leave West Virginia, he can. In fact, from what you just said, he's suggesting he do just that."

Sejin's eyes widen and I point at him with my fork. "For Thanksgiving this year."

"Yeah."

"No rush. There's over a month to decide."

"He wants to plan ahead. He saw a good deal for plane tickets."

"Mm."

Sejin meets my eyes. "Would you, uh, would you want to meet him?"

"Your dad? Sure." I shrug. "Why not? If I'm still around, that is."

Sejin's jaw flexes. "You better still be around. What kind of talk is that?"

I realize he thinks I'm referring to the Heart Route ascent. "No, I mean, I might head out of here for destinations unknown after I've sent Heart Route." I sip coffee again and lean back in my chair.

"I've been thinking about asking if you'd want to go with me."

"Really?"

"Yeah, but heads up: I'll basically have no money by then, and we'd live like nomads in the van."

"I've been living on my cousin's sofa," Sejin says, quietly. "I can handle being with you in a van for a few months."

"You think?" My heart leaps.

"Yeah. Of course." Sejin frowns, the laugh lines by his lips deepening in the opposite direction. "But what about Thanksgiving and my dad? Where will I be staying by then? Peggy Jo will be back, and I'll be…" Sejin shakes his head and the little wisps of hair that have fallen out of his messy bun dance around his face. "I'll be where?"

"You just said it. You'll be living in the van with me."

Sejin pokes at his food. "I hope so."

I tilt my head. "You just said you would be?"

"I know. It's just…I wish he hadn't asked right now, you know? I don't want to go back to West Virginia, but I don't want him to buy tickets to come out here if I'm going to be with you somewhere else. It's bad timing."

"We could stick around here."

"Then where will Dad stay? In the van with us?"

"With your cousin? In an Airbnb? A hotel? The lodge? There are a lot of options."

Sejin frowns and I don't understand his worries. "Right. Yeah. Of course."

I look at my watch. "I gotta go. I'm late for my training already."

"Meeting someone?"

"Yeah. I'm supposed to pick Rye up from the campground, and he's gonna belay today. I think I'm going to work the roof again. Gotta nail that down tight."

Sejin pales and his dark eyes look luminous as he gazes up at me. He says nothing. I stand up and come around the table to kiss his forehead, then his nose, and then his lips. "I'll see you later, Doc."

"Later," he says, a little tiredly.

"What're your plans?" I ask.

"I took today off to get settled in here. Will you be coming back here tonight after your training?"

I should say no and return to my slot at the campground. But I push a wisp of hair off his forehead and say, "I'll be back by dinner."

Leaning close, I whisper in his ear, "Don't tell anyone, but I think I love you." Then I kiss his earlobe and turn to go.

I'm almost out the door, boots in hand to lace up on the porch, when Sejin says, "You can tell everyone, Danny. I *know* I love you."

My throat goes tight, and my heart beats like a wild horse running in the valley. I should look back at him, but I don't. I step out into the blue mist of morning, lace up my boots, and get in my camper van.

As I drive away, I whisper, "Doc, I know I love you too."

I probably should have told him that to his face.

Sejin

"SO, WHAT DID he say exactly?" Leenie asks, cradling her cup of tea and gazing over to where Papa Bear has set up a new play area for kids off to the side of the parking lot.

It may or may not have been inspired by her son, and it might have been my idea. We set it up with some old railroad ties, a couple of low-to-the-ground slack ropes, some tires to jump in and out of, a few low hammocks, and a wooden teeter-totter that Gage put together for us.

Pete loves it because it keeps the kids out of the cafe proper, and it draws more families in who spend loads of money on snacks and sweets while they suck down their coffee and let their kids romp. So now he loves me too. I've been on his good side ever since the new play area went in.

And today I'm just here as a guest. I'm not working at all for a change. It's kind of nice.

"Dad said, and I quote, 'I'd like to come out to see you for Thanksgiving instead of you flying home.'"

"Wow, that's…I know you might not see it this way, but, Sejin, that's actually great. It's the first time your dad's shown interest in doing anything new since your mom passed."

"I know, but maybe I should face the house without her. Face it *all* without her."

"Your mom wouldn't want you to be sad, Sejin. It doesn't honor her to go back there and pick through her stuff and feel miserable. That's what your dad's been doing, so I'm relieved to hear that Uncle Buck is ready to do something adventurous."

"What if he thinks he *has to* come out here? Because I won't come home?"

"What if he wants to get the hell out of that house before the darkness of the holiday season and all its memories consume him?" Leenie counters.

"What if he comes out here and he doesn't want to go back?"

"What *if?*" She lifts a pointed brow. "You've been running away from her death, just like he's been wallowing in it. This is a good thing for both of you. Tell him to come. Tell him he can stay with me and Martin—"

"On the sofa?"

"We'll have a blow-up bed by then."

"He can stay at a hotel or an Airbnb."

"Sejin…"

"Yeah?"

"Don't overthink this. Just be your sunshiny self and let this happen. Don't fight him. Tell him you're excited he's coming. Tell him you can't wait to show him your new life and for him to meet your new friends." She snarls slightly. "Even Dan, I guess."

I chuckle. "You're so hard on Dan."

"He hasn't shown me yet why I shouldn't be."

"Ah, Leenie, stop. He's just not that kind of guy."

"What? The good kind?"

I roll my eyes. "He's definitely a good person. He's just not charming…or personable. Or the kind of guy to have an office job or a regular income."

"He must really blow your mind in other ways because I just don't get it."

"It's okay," I say, and I mean it. "You don't have to."

I don't share with her that Dan's offered to take me off in his van as soon as he's sent Heart Route. I don't tell her how much I want to go with him.

"Sejinie!" Jeremiah yells from where he's hanging by his knees from the hammock. "Look at me!"

"I see you, buddy!"

"I'm cool, right?"

"You're always cool!"

He grins proudly and then does a backflip off that makes Leenie gasp, but he lands on his little knees and then claps for himself.

"Daredevil," Leenie whispers. "Gonna give me a heart attack one day. Just you wait."

I can relate all too well. I smile thinking of Dan. I have a daredevil of my own.

And he thinks he loves me.

I *know* he does.

CHAPTER TWENTY

Dan

I HANG BY my fingertips and toes from the roof of the large Heart Formation in the side of El Capitan—the formation that gives the main route I'm doing its name. I'm focused entirely on levering myself up over the lip, which will put me in the next part of the climb—the straight up, vertical granite with tiny, razor-sharp finger holds. It'll be the most dangerous part, aside from the dyno and the roof itself, because I'm not going to be able to rest from that point onward to the top. If it starts to rain, if I've misjudged the weather and it gets a little too humid, or too hot…

Well.

I tug myself up over the lip, and grip the sharp, narrow crimps enough to hook my toes into the good footholds I've located at this juncture. They were necessary to find because I do need to stop here, catch my breath, and get my wits about me before carrying on. The problem with choosing this location to mount the lip of the roof is it leaves the "safety ledge" I've scoped out below a few meters too far to the left if I pump out.

But it's all a mental game. In some ways, I realized a few weeks ago, the safety ledge is holding me back in confidence with the roof. I haven't wanted to leave the range it allows for, knowing that if I fall and land on the ledge, I'll only be very badly hurt and not necessarily dead. In refusing to leave that area, I've limited myself in terms of my choice in holds starting up the next pitch.

This limit placed on my choices is a nod to the kind of caution Sejin, Rye, and Peggy Jo want me to embrace, and it's keeping me from realizing my dream. I see that now as I rest for a long moment, cheek to rock face, breathing in and out, taking in the evergreens and the vast exposure below.

"That was sick," Rye enthuses. "You're such a badass, Dan. A terrifying, mind-blowing badass."

I grunt before giving him the signal that I'm ready to come back down. The rope keeps me safe as I start the treacherous downclimb back over the lip and the roof, and even though I'm on the rope, and thus safe as houses, I still breathe a sigh of relief when I'm positioned over that ledge again. So, yeah, a security blanket. I need to ditch it entirely.

"Let's talk risks here," Rye says, as I draw in above him to start the pitch again. I want to run through it one last time before calling it a day. "This is the second crux of the route. What's your plan if you start to pump out on the climb over the lip? I see you've got a nice place to rest there, but…" Rye bites his lip and squints up at the roof. "Maybe the thing to do, just to be safe, is—"

He looks down below where the ledge is a traverse climb less than a full pitch away. "Just take a little detour on the way up."

"You mean extend the route to rest?"

"Yeah. I think if you go into these pitches directly after those below, the risks for a mistake, or pumping out, go up exponentially. A cozy ten-minute rest on that ledge would go a long way to alleviating that. Hell, you could stash some water and food there, enough to refuel. Take a piss off the side. That sort of thing."

I consider it.

"There's no reason to rush up the route," Rye points out. "There's no one trying to do what you're doing, no record to beat, or even to set. This will be the first—and possibly last—free solo of Heart Route in history. You don't have to try to beat Honnold's time on Free Rider."

I blink at him. How he knows that Alex Honnold's time is currently flashing in my head as the goal to beat, I don't know. I guess Rye knows me better than I realized. But it's not like he's wrong. He has a good idea. It's one I've considered in the past, but written off as somehow…weak.

But it's not weak to need food, water, and a little rest to perform your best. I know this when I'm taking a rest day from training, and I should know it on the route too.

"Yeah," I agree. "That's a good plan."

Rye's eyes light up like he hadn't expected me to agree to it at all.

"What? I'm not an idiot, and I've considered it before. I just…" I point at the traverse. "It's not like it's an easy jot over to the ledge. It might make more sense to overshoot and then do a downclimb to it."

Rye's throat bobs with a convulsive swallow. Downclimbs are always difficult—fighting the pull of gravity like that—and during a free solo they're considered exceptionally risky. But what about this route *isn't* exceptionally risky?

"What's the problem with the traverse?" he asks, cupping a hand over his eyes to look more closely at the route. "It's got a decent-sized flake."

"It's not a stable one, though. The last thing I need is to pull the rock off and—" I use my hand to demonstrate my plunge to El Cap's floor.

"It can't be that unstable," he insists. "Not as inherently unstable as downclimbing."

Then he tries to demonstrate this to me by heading out onto the traverse. I watch quietly and don't argue, but he's not even six feet out there before the flake creaks ominously, and he looks up at me with wide eyes. "Fuck."

I nod. "And I weigh more than you."

"Yeah. Okay, so...the downclimb." He makes his way back across with shaky hands. He might be strapped in, but pulling a rock off onto yourself can do real damage no matter the stability of the ropes.

"Is it worth the risk or do I just need to trust my training?" I ask.

"I don't know. When I thought you could do the traverse, it made sense, but now..." Rye shakes his head and chalks up his fingers. "I just don't know. It's like eggs sunny-side up or over easy, you know? They're both eggs."

"Mm."

My phone begins to vibrate, and checking the screen, I smile. It's the photo Sejin set for his number, a photo of us from that first sunrise on Pothole Dome. It's wild how that seems both like forever ago and just yesterday. Sejin and I have only been seeing each other for a little over a month and a half, but I feel like he's already become the most important part of my life outside of climbing. It's a vulnerable feeling, and so new too.

No doubt about it, Sejin's a liability, and I don't fucking care.

I check that my phone is secured before I answer. "Hey, Doc, what's up?"

"Are you safe to talk?" he asks, like always when he knows I'm out on the wall.

"Yup." I wouldn't answer if I wasn't, but he's always going to check, and I don't mind the feeling of affection that comes over me when he does.

"I just got back to Peggy Jo's and it's so nice and quiet. No screaming kids."

"Yowling cats, though."

"No, they're all asleep. Muggs is on my lap."

"Mm." I look out over the exposure. The evergreens are so far down they look like a swath of fake Christmas trees for dollhouses. I do wish Sejin could stomach it up here. I'd like him to see this view and love it the way I do.

"Anyway, remember how you have that toy? The one you showed me a few weeks ago for, uh, orgasm denial? And I said no, but you said yes?"

"Yeah? The ball stretcher?"

"Uh-huh."

"Do you want to try it now?" I glance down at Rye who's got one eyebrow cocked up with amused interest.

"No. But I bought a toy today from that new shop on the outskirts of town…"

"Oh?" I try not to be disappointed. I'd thought about suggesting he and I go there together to pick something out, but I hadn't gotten around to it. I'm definitely not disappointed by the idea of another new toy, though. I'm all for having fun with a naked Sejin in any way possible. There's literally nothing he could have bought that I'd be unwilling to play with when it comes to him.

"Yeah. So, I want *you* to use the ball stretcher at the same time as this new toy."

"Is this your way of saying you want me to come home now?"

He laughs, and the little bells ring up and down my spine again. I can imagine him ensconced on Peggy Jo's couch with a cat on his lap, his eyes squeezed in laughter, and his wide smile taking up the bottom half of his face. God, I want to be home so I can kiss him.

"It's my way of saying be careful up there and don't get too banged up. I have plans for us tonight."

"I'm all for these plans, baby," I say quietly, looking anywhere but at Rye as I use the cheesier pet name that seems to tumble out of my mouth whenever my heart squeezes with affection like this.

"When can I expect you?"

I glance at the sun in the sky, then back at the rock. I'd intended to attempt the downclimb we'd just discussed, and then the roof again. But now…

"What kind of toy is it?"

Rye laughs from down below.

"Trying to decide how much of a hurry to be in?" Sejin giggles.

"You know it."

"It's for me to know, and you to find out."

"Tease."

Sejin giggles again, and I want to reach through the phone and lay kisses all up and down his long throat and beg him to never stop laughing like that for me. "I'll be waiting here for you."

"I'll be home by sunset. There are a few things I need to do first."

"Home," Sejin says. "I like the sound of that."

I swallow and blink up at the bright sun, blaming it for the sudden, odd prickle in my eyes. "Me too," I admit, and I must have surprised him as much as I surprised myself because he gasps lightly.

"I'll be waiting," Sejin says again, and I feel almost dizzy with the rough lust in his voice. It's a good thing I'm strapped in today—the ropes hold me up as my knees go weak.

"I have to head back," I say, pocketing my phone and not meeting Rye's knowing gaze. "What's your schedule like tomorrow? Want to try this again?"

"I'm open. Assuming you can climb after whatever Sejin has planned for you."

I smirk. "I'll meet you back here tomorrow then. Let's pack it in."

Rye doesn't protest as we start to rap down the wall. It'll still be hours before I'm back at Peggy Jo's house and in Sejin's arms, but my heart is thundering giddily at the prospect all the same. I feel young, and stupid, and like I'm scrubbed clean with joy. It's a strange feeling. Like all my outer layers of protection have been sloughed off. That's what loving someone will do, I guess. Leave you peeled raw and shiny like garlic.

Speaking of garlic, I'll pick up some pre-baked lasagna from Italian Stallion on my way home tonight. Sejin loves it.

Sejin

"I COME BEARING gifts," Dan says, coming into the house with a bag of takeout in one hand and the ball stretcher from the small box of toys out in his van in the other.

I'm still on the sofa with Muggs pressed against my thigh, and a sleepy sort of hard-on aching in my pants. I was having some very erotic dreams during my long nap.

Dan swoops over to me, bends down to give me a kiss, and then jumps back when Muggs takes a swipe at his exposed arm.

He looks good in the t-shirt and track pants he usually climbs in, but he's chalked-up and filthy too.

"Demon, begone," he mutters when Muggs darts away and under the bookcase by the wide glass doors to the patio. Dan turns back to me, leans down for his kiss, and the bag of food bangs against me.

"Sorry," he says, standing back again. "You look good like this. All mussed up. Mm. Let's forget the food and fuck first."

I laugh and stand, my knees creaking a little, and I arch my back in a stretch. That draws Dan's eyes down to my crotch, which is still horned up, and he smirks. "I see you're down with that plan."

"No. I'm hungry." I take the bag of food and direct him toward the bathroom with a nod of my head. "Besides, you're filthy, and you stink. Take a shower, and I'll get this on plates."

Dan sniffs his pits. "I smell like roses. What are you talking about?"

"You smell like onions, more like," I say, my West Virginia accent more pronounced after my nap, and he grins to hear it. "Which I sometimes like, but today I want to be the one to make you sweat."

"Mm, that won't be a problem. You've already got me hard." He takes hold of my free hand and presses it to his crotch, and I squeeze his thickening rod. "Let's sixty-nine," he says. "I know you want my mouth on your dick."

"Dan," I say in my most strict voice, but it's pretty laughable even to me, so we both giggle. "Go shower."

He rolls his eyes, but lets go of my hand and starts off down the hall.

"Oh!" I call.

He stops and turns back to me.

"If you can, go ahead and put the ball stretcher thing on?"

He nods. "No problem."

When he comes back from showering a few minutes later, he's got on a fresh pair of loose pants and a t-shirt, and I can tell by the way he's walking that his balls are bound up in that contraption he'd once thought would be fun to put on me. I can't really blame him for thinking that because I think it's going to be really fun on him.

"Let's eat light," he reminds me as we sit down at the table. "Lots of ass play is happening tonight."

"Mm-hm," I agree, and pick at my food. Italian Stallion makes for great leftovers the next day, so I'm not worried about it going to waste. "Show me," I demand after a few silent moments of us trying to act like we want to eat and not fuck. "I want to see."

He stands up and pushes his pants down so that the elastic waistband is mid-thigh, and I study the contraption on his junk. His balls are pulled down and away from the base of his dick by a thick black band of something rubbery, and they look strained but not painfully so. "That'll keep you from coming?" I ask.

He shrugs. "I mean, I can still come, but it's not as easy. This holds my balls down and away, so I'll have to work harder for it, and it'll be…" Here his mouth twists into a savage smirk "…explosive. Like each pump is almost painful, but also fucking amazing."

So, he's played with this on himself before. Or maybe with other people. I don't entirely like that, but I also don't care that much either. He and I are so good together I know what we do eclipses all other men for him. I see it every time he comes. His eyes go wide with awe, his face slack, and afterward I get to hear him say *I love fucking you so much.* Some might not think that's all that romantic a declaration, but I hear it for what it is—*I can't do without you now.*

And I feel the same way.

"Sit down," I order breathlessly, and I'm pleased when he does.

We fall quiet, both of us obviously thinking a lot more about our crotches than our dinner, until I push my plate aside and say, "Let's put it away for tomorrow."

"Finally," he says. "About time. My dick is ready to find out what your big plan is for the night."

"It's…" I feel my cheeks heat up, and Dan startles as a cat gallops past and into the bedroom. "It's a little slutty."

"Perfect," he declares. "Where's this slutty toy?"

"Let me…let me get it." My heart pounds. I've never been with anyone I could be this open with about my fantasies and wants. I've had lots of sex with lots of guys, some of it good and some of it bad, but none of it as intimate as what I've had with Dan pretty much from day one.

The toy is in the bedroom, and I have to dislodge Romeo from where he's batting at the rope handles on the paper bag and rolling around beside it. I bring the bag back to the kitchen where Dan's already put our food into the refrigerator for later and is standing with a raging hard-on pushing out the front of his pants. Mine isn't much more subtle.

I hand the bag to him, tongue-tied and hungry for this.

He opens the bag and lifts out the contents. The toy is in a black box that obscures what it is at first glance. Cocking his head, he tosses the lid on the kitchen table. The room is quiet now as he looks at the contraption inside. Not even a cat goes skidding past. No yowls or purrs.

"Mm, this looks hot," Dan says after several agonizing heartbeats pass. "Tell me what it's for, baby."

I step closer, and he reels me in, sliding an arm around me and then down over my hip and into my pants to take hold of my cock. I groan as he squeezes it and humps his own against my other thigh.

I hold the toy up, but then he takes it back from me.

"Ah. I think I see. This slides over my dick like this," he says, demonstrating how the cock sleeve works on his fingers. "And these"—he rubs his fingers over the gummy, ridged nubs that stick up from the exterior of the sleeve—"work your prostate extra hard as I thrust."

I feel my knees go weak, and I lean harder against him, which he takes as a signal to keep rubbing his cock on my leg. "Yeah. The sales guy told me it…" God, I feel so dizzy and breathless. "He says it makes him lose his mind. But, on the other hand, his co-worker said *his* boyfriend doesn't like it because it's too intense. I…" My voice hitches. "I think I can handle it. I think I'll really like it."

My mouth is dry with lust as I consider the sleeve. I really hope Dan's on board for this. I've been half-hard ever since I first spotted it displayed on a dildo on a shelf at the back of the store.

"I'm sure you will," Dan says. "I bet this is going to be next-level."

"But, um, first," I say, turning toward him and letting him nuzzle my neck. He kisses my throat and blows at the loose pieces of my hair as he strokes my cock. "I want to fuck you because I've been missing that, and somehow you always get me on my back with your persuasive tongue on my hole."

"You know I'm good with you fucking me whenever you want. All you have to do is ask."

"I know. And I want you to suck my dick tonight too. Like you offered."

He shrugs. Sucking dick isn't his absolute favorite thing, but he's not bad at it, and he'd offered to sixty-nine which means he'll be able to finger me at the same time, and he loves that. "Happily."

I lick my lips. "I'm ready when you are."

"Let's go."

We don't go far.

The sofa is better for fucking than the bed in some ways, and so we cover it with sheets and start kissing. Dan systematically checks off every last item on my wish list, and my dick is still wet from being in Dan's ass when he slicks up the inside of the new toy with lube and pushes his dick into it.

"Fuck," he groans. "It's tight. Definitely gonna keep me hard as a rock."

Not that Dan's ever had trouble staying hard, but between the ball stretcher and the toy, I can see he's really going to ache. Luckily, his cock is long enough that the head sticks out the other end of the sleeve, so he'll get plenty of stimulation to make all this worthwhile.

As for me, if the sales guy was right, and if Dan's ball stretcher really does delay his orgasm, I'm about to have the ride of my life.

"The sixty-nine was good?" Dan asks, as he lubes up the outside of the toy next, and then presses his slick fingers to my asshole. "You liked it?"

"You know I did," I huff as he hooks his fingers inside me and rubs my prostate.

"Good." He pulls his fingers out and then lines up to push inside, but before he does, he asks, "And you liked fucking my ass?"

I groan. "Get inside me."

"Answer my question."

"Danny, please fuck me. I'm going insane waiting for it."

"You're the one who wanted to top me before we got to this part, and I just want to hear some nice things about my ass. I don't know why—"

"I love fucking you. I was afraid I'd come and ruin it all. That's the only reason I'm not fucking you still. Get inside me, for God's sake!"

He grins and slides in. I go super still as I try to process the extra girth the sleeve adds, not to mention the intense sensation of the gummy ridges going past my tight rim. "Hold your legs back," Dan says, and I hitch them higher, which allows him to slide home. I shudder as the nubs hit my sensitive prostate, already so nearly over-teased by Dan's fingers.

"How is it?" he asks, pressing in tight, but not moving at all except to breathe. "Okay?"

I nod, feeling too shaky to respond verbally.

"It's good for me too. Tight along my shaft, but it's like sliding through hot velvety butter with my cockhead. All the sensation is focused there."

I whimper.

"Alright for me to move?"

"Yeah." I sound breathless and already a million miles away. My nipples tingle, my cock is hard and leaking, and my asshole feels stretched wide. I'm a little nervous, but I also can't wait to feel this. "Fuck me, Danny."

The ridges hit *boom-boom-boom* over my prostate on the outward slide, and then in a rush again on the push back in. I squirm but Dan grabs my hips and holds me firm. He thrusts again, and I throw my head back.

"Mm, should have brought that ball gag in," Dan says once he really gets moving, and I'm calling out to God and heaven and all the angels because it's *so fucking good.* "You're scaring the cats."

But he doesn't slow down or try to ease the intensity of my pleasure. Instead, he says, "Do you want me to stop?" and when I shake my head, he snaps his hips forward and back, again and again, the slapping sound of skin on skin rising in the room, and the grunting noises that come out of me are somehow familiar and yet very new.

"That's it," he says, as he keeps on fucking me and the tears start to prick in my eyes. My asshole flutters with the warning sensations of a climax ahead. "You're almost there. Show me, baby. Show me how good this feels. Let me see."

I can't pry my eyes open to return his gaze, but I feel his awareness of my every reaction, the intense rush of what he's doing to me echoing in his voice and strength, and I let him see everything I'm feeling. I let him see me crumble as he works the nubby sleeve over my prostate. I feel my cock shrink as my asshole becomes my focus, and Dan touches the crown lightly asking, "This good or bad?"

"Good," I cry out. I can't reply with more words, so I just squeeze him closer with my arms and urge him to keep fucking me. I wrap my legs around his hips, and I climax—nipples tight, soft cock shaking, and my asshole quivering as I gyrate and convulse on his cock.

Suddenly, he pulls away and out of me, and I'm left gaping and cold for a second, until he sinks down and pulls my cock into his mouth. I run my fingers through his curly hair, taking the break he's giving me and enjoying the way my dick plumps up in his mouth again. Then, just as I'm starting to feel like I could shoot, he pulls away and tests my hole to see if it needs more lube. It must be okay, because when he pushes back into me, I take him in easily.

"That's good," he encourages me, as the nubs rock my world again. "Just breathe. Let it happen."

But breathing is impossible when he starts really thrusting, and as the intensity mounts higher and higher, I see why the salesman's co-worker's boyfriend isn't into this at all. It's *a lot*. And I'm about to ask for another break when I feel a stirring deep in my pelvis, and I know...

I've had this happen before.

It's going to be big, though, and I go still, trying to catch the feeling the way I'm catching Dan's cock, and then it comes. Pulsing, shaking, back-bowing, and long-lasting, I fall apart as I climax and come at the same time. My cock goes painfully rigid as my asshole clenches, and I almost black out as Dan presses back in one more time. Shattering pleasure washes over me and pumps out of my dick in hard, strong spurts.

"Fuck," Dan says, pushing forward to kiss me through the orgasm. "Oh, baby, fuck, fuck, *fuck*."

That's when I realize he's coming too. I feel him jolt against me, and he cries out with the pleasure-pain of releasing a long-denied orgasm. I've never heard him be so loud when coming, and I want to ask him if it's good or too much, but then he pulls out of me. That nubby bit goes *boom-boom-boom* over my now insanely-sensitive prostate, and I shout. Not in a good way.

"Sorry, sorry," Dan says as tremors still wrack him.

"S'okay."

He stares down at his dick for a second and then looks up at me. "You're amazing," he says, and then reaches to wipe my wet cheeks. I hadn't even realized I was crying again. I do it so often when we fuck that Dan generally acts like it's completely normal, and so I don't think too much about it anymore.

He collapses down on top of me, and I hold him close, feeling the pounding of his heart against my chest, and our sweat and semen-slick skin glides together. "Was it worth what you paid for it?" he asks.

I choke out a laugh and kiss his soft hair. I don't even bother answering. He knows.

We both do.

Being with Dan like this is worth any price.

CHAPTER TWENTY-ONE

Dan

2 weeks until free solo attempt

"CELLI'S NOT CHEATING on you, Gage," Sejin says into the phone as I drive us in the van down CA-247 toward Park Road and Joshua Tree.

Sejin's got his bare feet kicked up on the dashboard, and his long hair is buffeting about in the wind from the open windows. We've been listening to a Spotify playlist he's created especially for our trip, and it still plays in cheerful undertones as he talks his co-worker down from some interpersonal ledge he's gotten himself out on.

"How do I know? Because she's crazy about you? Maybe that?" He huffs and pops a Flaming Hot Cheeto into his mouth and then licks his orange-coated fingers. "Did you ask her? No? Then just ask her."

He blows a raspberry as I maneuver around a particularly slow-moving truck. "Use your words like a big boy. Look, I have to go. I'm in the middle of something." He chuckles. "What am I in the middle of? *My weekend off.*"

Sejin ends the call after thanking Gage for watching the cats for us and offering him a few more reassuring sentences and insistences that Gage give Celli a call if he's so worried. He sets the phone to Do Not Disturb and grins at me. "Children, am I right?"

"What's he worried about Celli for?"

"She's in Vegas with some girlfriends, and he's worried she's going to hook up with someone there or something boneheaded. I don't know. He's being an idiot."

"Haven't they agreed to be monogamous?"

"Probably."

"Then he shouldn't worry."

Sejin pulls his hair up and into a ponytail low at the nape of his neck. "You know some people don't keep their promises, right? Like some people would say they're going to be monogamous and then just not be."

I frown as I turn onto Park Road. The brown desert and greenish-gray scrub dotted with stubby, iconic Joshua trees stretches out on either side of us. "But you wouldn't do that, and neither would Celli."

"I know." He reaches out and squeezes my forearm and then slides his hand up to rub the back of my neck for a moment. "How much longer?"

"Not too long now."

"Cool."

Sejin turns the volume back up on the music and sings along to what I think is that girl group Twice's latest release. It's an autumnal-sounding song that doesn't entirely fit the sunny-sharp weather we're driving through, even with the dirt-brown of the desert. But it'll be nice to listen to another time when we're traveling somewhere with deciduous trees in the fall.

Maybe we'll spend an autumn in Korea even…something I've been considering more and more as Sejin has been looking for Korean language instructors online. If he wants to go, then I want to go with him. There are some killer climbs in that part of the world.

As for the song, Sejin's enjoying it now, so that's all that matters.

The Hidden Valley parking lot comes into view after passing by dozens of piles of big rocks. The tall, curved, protective stone rise sits beneath a swipe of big blue sky with one fluffy cloud right in the middle of it.

"What's the plan?" Sejin asks, taking his feet off the dash and leaning forward to look out the windshield at the half-ring of rock. There are three spires around the parking lot, and plenty more good climbing spots just a small hike away.

"For what?"

"For me. I know you're trying to trick me into going climbing with you on this trip."

"Not trick," I deny. "Persuade."

Sejin's lips quirk up. "Alright, so what's the plan to persuade me?"

"You'll find out."

Sejin puts on his sandals and shoves open the door. The arid breeze flows in, and he sighs. "Ahh. Fresh air. Dust. Sun. This is living."

I hop out with him, and we both stand a moment looking up at the rock formations and the sky. The brown on the blue makes me think of a particular shirt in similar shades Peggy Jo wore a few seasons back and also of the turquoise jewelry a Navajo woman was selling at a roadside shop during my travels last spring.

"You're going to be safe on this trip, right?" Sejin asks, taking hold of my hand and pulling me close. The parking lot is crowded with cars and trucks, but no one is looking our way since most people are looking at the pillars.

"I've been thinking about the meaning of safe," I say, and Sejin squeezes my fingers and presses a kiss to my temple. "Do you know how many people are killed or terribly injured every year in skiing accidents?"

"Oh, no," Sejin says on a sigh. "This again, huh?"

"Forty-five per year, and another forty-five—give or take—are catastrophically injured. How many free soloists die per year?"

"Dan, there are millions more skiers than free soloists."

"Right, but when someone gets injured skateboarding, or skiing, or biking, people just shrug."

"They don't just shrug."

"Well, they don't sweat it every time their loved one goes out skiing or biking or skateboarding. They assume they're coming home. They assume they're going to be fine."

"The chances of a single mistake meaning death are so much slimmer."

"No, it's always the single mistake that leads to death. The single step back that takes someone over the ledge. The single glance at a text message that causes the car accident. The single—"

"What if you sneeze while you're up there?!"

"What if a skateboarder sneezes mid-jump? No one asks that."

"A jump takes a moment. A climb can take hours."

"What if you sneeze on the interstate while driving?"

"Everyone's done that."

"Some people have died from it."

"Let's not fight," Sejin says, pulling his hand away and taking a step back, squinting up at the rocks in the sun. "I don't want to fight."

"Doc?" I need him to understand this.

"Yeah?"

"I'm always safe. I'm safer than at almost any other time when I'm free soloing. When I'm strapped in? I take risks. Big ones sometimes."

"You can't tell me that dyno and roof aren't big risks."

"They're risks I believe I've minimized with practice."

Sejin's chin wobbles.

Fuck, he's going to cry. I reach out for his hand again and

thankfully he gives it to me. Tugging him close, I whisper in his ear, "When I'm up on the rock and it's just me and the universe, it's like everything is so big, every breath is so focused. I don't lose concentration, not even for a moment. I'm dialed in like a telescope. I'm so alive."

"So alive." Sejin squeezes my hand. "I get it. Life is more than breathing."

"Exactly."

He says nothing more, but I can tell he's thinking about my words even as he turns back to the van, opens the side door, and peers in. "What do you want to do for lunch? Ham sandwich? A salad?"

And just like that I know our conversation is over for now. I hope that's a good sign.

Sejin

AFTER A DAY hiking all around Hidden Valley, clambering up low rocks with Dan, and even letting him rope me—literally—into a very small climb in daylight, I'm exhausted. Covered in dirt, all I can do is wipe myself down with some wet towelettes and hope I'm not actually as dirty as I feel.

Dan, for his part, seems to relish being dusty and stinky, but that's somehow sexy as hell on him, and *that* seems very unfair. I watch him peel off his sweat-soaked shirt, tossing it into the back of the van. We've set up an awning to provide shade and a few chairs for us to rest in outside as the sun finalizes its descent, all fiery orange and purple against the horizon.

I'm having a lot of fun despite my fears. Dan never pushes me more than I can handle, and today I ended up loving the daylight climb. We were able to snag a really pretty view from the top of the route, and my joy in it seemed to catch Dan with shared happiness too. He'd smiled with an innocence that I haven't ever seen in his eyes before, and it made me think of what he might have been like if his childhood had even a little bit of love in it.

Now he's in the van putting together an egg scramble for dinner, while I rest and hold my hair up to let the breeze rush over my hot neck. Dan is tan all over from his days in the sun, but he's got some pink in his cheeks and on his arms today. My skin grew darker as the day wore on, and I smirk remembering Dan's wide-eyed disbelief that I've never had a sunburn in my life. It's not that I'm incapable of getting one, but so long as I put on a little sunscreen, I've never been exposed to strong enough rays for a burn to take hold. Today is no different.

"Here," Dan says, and hands me a plate of eggs, greens, and other veggies.

"I'm going to free solo that one before we leave." He nods at a spire I know is called Pillar Two. "I'll take it from the back side and come out on top. You don't have to watch, but it'd be nice if you did."

"Do you really want me to?" I know he doesn't like the pressure of having people on the ground observing when he's free soloing.

"I think I do," he says after a few moments of chewing and taking a swig from his water bottle. "I think it might help if you see me do it once."

The food's suddenly a lot less appetizing when I'm thinking of Dan going up the side of one of those enormous rock towers without ropes or a harness. "I don't know..."

I get that he thinks it'll help me to watch him do it and *succeed*, but what if he does it and *fails*? Then I'll see him die, or at the very least get really fucking hurt. I can't handle that.

"I'm serious when I say I could climb that in my sleep," Dan says. "It's a breeze. Not even a challenge really."

"It's so smooth, though. The rock, I mean."

"It's a simple climb, I promise. Look, let me show you." He ducks back into the van, leaving me with the plate of food and a pit in my stomach.

When he pops back out, he's got one of his climbing journals, and he flips through it with one hand until he finds what he's looking for. "Right here. These are my notes from when I free soloed it a few years ago." He tilts the journal toward me. "Easy peasy, lemon squeezy," he says, showing me those exact words scrawled on the page.

"Okay, so maybe going up is a piece of cake, but how do you get down?" I ask.

He smiles. "Carefully."

He flips the page and I see another scrawl of notes about the downclimb. "Have some faith in me."

"I don't suppose I can stop you?"

"You could," he says, but he sounds like he really doesn't want me to. I feel like, if I do, I'll be taking something precious from not only him, but from me too. This isn't a test, but it's a moment when I can either expand or contract, when I take from him or give to him. I sit with it for a long time before I say—

"Alright. So, is it going to be tonight or tomorrow morning? We have to leave fairly early if I'm going to be home in enough time to do laundry and be ready for my afternoon Movement class."

"Tomorrow," Dan says. "At dawn."

"Okay," I murmur.

"The weather looks good for it."

We drop the subject and clean up the dinner mess.

Afterward, we climb up to the roof of the van with a small Bluetooth speaker and toss some soft blankets down to cushion our backs on the hard surface. We lie there staring up at the stars while my favorite soft KPop playlist spins out songs, and Dan starts to hum along to some of them.

I hadn't realized he'd grown fond enough of some of the music to learn the melodies, nor had I realized how deep his singing voice is. He has to hum everything an octave lower, providing a warm harmony. We don't talk much, but that's one of the nice things about being with Dan. It doesn't always require conversation.

We hear voices and music from the few other cars and campers still in the parking lot, and yet it feels like we're in our own little bubble.

"Is your dad coming for Thanksgiving?" Dan says at the end of a song.

"Yes. We talked again the other day, and he's booked the hotel Leenie suggested for him."

"Mm."

"So, we have to stick around for that…"

"Of course. We can leave after the holidays."

"We'll live in your van?"

"Sure."

I take a deep breath. "Do you really want to meet him?"

"No, but I guess I will because that's what boyfriends do, right? Meet families."

I huff lightly, offended despite having asked, and also having already known the answer. "Why don't you want to meet him? He's a good guy."

"I'm sure he is, but A—I'm fucking his son, and B—I live in a van, and C—I'm weird, and D—I don't have a job. I might not really understand people all that well, but I know how that looks from the outside. He's gonna hate me."

I sigh. Dan's not wrong, entirely. "He won't hate you. He'll just be confused and worried."

"Which will worry you, and I prefer it when you're not worried."

I almost say *then stop free soloing*. But I clamp my mouth shut against it.

As much as I hate what he does, I also know that I love it too. Free soloing is part of who Dan is, and I love Dan. I love this weird, fragile life we're building together. I love nights on top of his van, and his tasty egg scrambles, and the showers in a fucking waterfall. I love it all.

I love *him*. So I have to make peace with free soloing.

"Did you hire that guy?" Dan asks after "Spring Day" by BTS plays, and I've half-assed my way through the Korean lyrics. "The one from Seoul, but who's living in LA?"

"We agreed to start the first week of November."

Dan kisses my fingers again. "Good."

"I told him by email that I'm adopted and that I've been raised by a white family, so I know nothing. He seems eager to help introduce me to the language of my birth country, and he didn't seem judgy about it. I think it'll be fun."

"New things are always fun for you."

"Aren't they for you?" I ask.

"Of course. But I also like the tried and true. When I find a good thing, I like to stick with it."

Astro's song "gemini" begins, and Dan sighs happily. "This one makes my chest ache." He kisses my fingers yet again and asks, "Sejin? What makes you feel alive? The most alive?"

"You."

"Ah."

It feels like the wrong answer, and I think about it harder. I've felt alive before Dan, and I know he's right that even if he leaves my life, I'll eventually feel alive again after him. I consider the stars and I think about the times when I've felt the most sharply aware of the magnificence of living and all of them do have something in common.

"Love," I say. "Love makes me feel alive."

Dan touches my cheek.

"I think that's what life's about. Grabbing hold of love. Laughing with my mom, listening to KPop, dancing, being around kids, touching you, traveling… They're all precious experiences I hold with love."

Dan turns on his side and I do the same. We kiss tenderly, nothing intense, and then roll onto our backs again to study the stars and hum along to my playlist.

Eventually, I say, "Alright. I'll watch you."

"You'll watch? Really? That's brave, Doc." He's more impressed with my willingness to watch him risk his life than he is with himself for risking it.

"Don't mess up and make me regret it."

"I'll do my best. I always do." Dan takes hold of my hand and holds it against his chest. I can feel his heart beating there, strong and vibrant. I think about the night we met and how he'd fucked me silly—and how I'd let him.

He kisses my fingers, and I remember the day he came to the coffee shop determined to talk me into giving him another try, despite my fears—and again, I'd let him.

He lifts his finger to the sky to point out a falling star, and I think of the ways I've tried to guard my heart, but he's kept on effortlessly, guilelessly coming for it—and I've let him snatch it.

There isn't much I haven't let Dan do. There isn't much I *won't* let him do in the future either. And there are reasons for that.

I didn't fall in love with a flawless man. I fell in love with *this* man.

I need to remember that whenever I get scared. I pull his hand to *my* mouth and kiss *his* fingers this time.

The stars soar above us, a canopy of tiny lights.

Dan

THE MORNING BREAKS open with pinks and corals, and I'm halfway up the pillar as the sun crests the horizon.

I've left Sejin on the ground below, wrapped in a blanket in a lawn chair, sipping hot coffee and pretending not to be scared out of his mind. I have my back to him, so I can't see his reactions, but I'm moving easily and well. I hope it reassures him to see me so thoroughly in my element.

Acid Rock, the name of the route up Pillar Two, begins with a steep hand crack from the inside corridor. Easy, but it takes concentration even when hooked into ropes. But today I'm out here just me, the wind, the rock, and my strength. I'm dialed in to every crevice, every hold, and thinking about every shift of my body. As I climb up to a sturdy ledge and step onto it, I chalk up again and take a moment to turn to Sejin.

He's sitting with his head tilted back, his hand over his eyes to block the sharp rays of the morning sun and obstructing any hope of reading his expression as well. I give him the OK sign with my hand and then a thumbs-up. He gives me one back, and my heart thumps. It's not the most enthusiastic thumbs-up I've ever seen, but he's not frantically waving me down either. So that's a win.

I turn back to the rock. At this point, it's a little harder, but nothing I can't handle. It's just up the main pillar, past the horizontals, making note of, but not touching, the equipment left in the rock for those coming up on ropes, and then I'm at the crux to the top. It feels like magic. My fingers lock on the grips, my toes find their holds easily, and I'm climbing like I do this route every day. I'm sweating, but only barely, and when I come out on top, hands on hips, and the sun shining in my eyes, I let out a sigh of satisfaction.

It's quiet up here.

Birds, wind, and the sound of my own breath.

"Whoo!" drifts up from the ground, and I see folks in the parking lot watching as they climb out of their cars and vans, applauding for me. I turn to where Sejin is waiting and he's standing up clapping too. No whoops coming from his lips, but he's smiling. I can see the glint of the sun on his teeth, and when he waves at me this time, it's full of excitement…and probably relief.

I take the view in, savoring the clouds, the blue, pink, and yellow sky.

After deciding to head on down, I chalk up my hands and give Sejin another thumbs-up before directing him to go on down to the parking lot area where I'll descend like we planned. This direction is an easier downclimb, but what I didn't tell Sejin is that downclimbs are always the most dangerous part of any free solo. A lot can go wrong when gravity's tugging you down faster than you want to go.

But I've done this one before, and it's easy enough, and when my feet touch the floor, I'm grinning.

There.

Done.

Just as I told Sejin, it was easy peasy, lemon squeezy, and I'm not even tired. I've got plenty of energy for the drive home.

"You're amazing," Sejin says, as I step into his arms. He holds me tight. "Terrifying, but amazing."

"You should see me climb something hard."

Sejin squeezes me even closer, nuzzles my cheek, and says nothing. I hold him tight too, and all the gawkers disperse at the sight of two guys being all couple-y. Except for one family with some little kids. They stay, and I brace myself for some kind of confrontation from the very bro-dude-looking dad when we finally break apart and start back toward our van.

Instead, one of the kids runs up to me with a paper and pen, saying, "Mister! Excuse me! Can I get your autograph, please?"

He can't be more than nine or ten and Sejin bites his lip, looking to me for my answer, and my heart thumps at his adorable attempt not to smile.

Squatting down, I accept the paper and pen, and scrawl my name on it along with a crude drawing of the sun, and a smiling mouth. The kid shifts from foot to foot as I do it, and his mom—a redheaded lady with freckles on her nose—approaches, leaving the father behind with the other two kids. She says, "Laken here wants to be a pro climber one day too. Any tips?"

"Yeah," Sejin says. "Tip number one—let someone pay you to do it."

I feel Sejin's hand slip into my hair and tousle it. "This one's a purist. He does all that crazy stuff for free, believe it or not."

The woman laughs. "Is that so?"

"Yup," I agree, and the kid asks, "What's it say?" as I hand him the paper.

"My name. Dan McBride."

"Never heard of you."

"Yeah, well…"

I don't know what to say to that, and his mother scolds him lightly.

"That's by design," Sejin offers. "He's private."

But his mother's disapproval doesn't keep the kid from saying, "It's alright. I'll keep this until you *are* famous. Then I'll sell it on eBay."

"Mercenary," Sejin says with a chuckle. "I like it."

I stand up, wiping my palm on my pants before shaking hands with Laken's mother who then guides her son away with a firm grip on his shoulder. Laken keeps looking back and waving. I stand with my hands in my pockets until the family has unloaded their gear for the day and started off down the nature trail.

As they pass us, I hear the dad ask, "So, what's he like? Is he batshit?"

"Yes," Sejin murmurs under his breath. "Yes, he's absolutely batshit insane."

But then he kisses me and strokes his hands over my cheeks, his eyes wide, and awestruck. "You really are amazing."

"You think so?"

"Seeing you up there? Holy shit, Dan. You climbed like it was nothing, like that pillar was put there by the universe as a plaything just for you. And when you reached the top? Seeing you up there backlit by the sunrise? I don't know. It was like you were exactly where you were supposed to be. You looked like an angel. It took my breath away. What a wonder. What a terrifying thing to do."

"Do you really want me doing it for money? Like you told that lady?" I ask, turning back to Sejin, and throwing my arms around his neck, reeling him in for a quick kiss.

When we break apart, Sejin rubs his nose against mine and says, "I want you to be alive, *really* alive, like you were talking about last night. I want you to feel it in your bones and in your soul. If it takes free soloing to do that, then okay. And if you have to do it for free in order to feel that way about it, fine. Money isn't everything."

I kiss his cheek. Money isn't everything, it's true, but it's a lot. And the life I lead is going to have to change before long. I was lucky to have that surprise trust fund from my biological grandfather for the last few years, but it's almost run dry and I can't continue on this way.

That's a bridge to cross when I eventually come to it.

For now, I need to focus on sending Heart Route and putting my goal to bed. Then I can move on in whatever direction I want to go.

I just know, no matter what, I'm taking Sejin with me.

CHAPTER TWENTY-TWO

Dan

1 day to free solo ascent

"CHEERS! TO AMELIA Rose!"

Sejin and I clink our beer bottles together and stare up at the night sky. It's obscured by the light and smoke from the small bonfire we built in celebration of Peggy Jo's daughter going into labor. It's also an anniversary of sorts, though I think I'm the only one who realizes it. It's been exactly two months to the day since Sejin and I first hooked up. It's hard to believe, but it's true.

"You know, when I met you, I didn't think we would ever be like this," I say, pushing Sejin's hair away from his neck to nuzzle in and kiss him there while he wraps his arms around me and stares up at the stars.

"Me either."

"I thought I'd fuck you, see your smile, and be done with you. Now I have to figure out how to keep you with me all the time, even when Peggy Jo comes back. Even when I've sent Heart Route. Even when I get old and arthritic and can't climb anymore."

"You can see a day like that? A day when you don't climb?"

"Easier than I can see a day without you."

"Dan…" Sejin shakes his head.

"Shh," I say. "I know. That's too much."

"What is it about you and me being out under the stars that makes you declare all kinds of wild things?" he asks.

"Must be the moon making me crazy."

"Must be." The light from the fire glows against his skin.

"What about you? Can you see a life without me?"

Sejin grows stiller than still, and suddenly I know the answer, but it's not because he's thinking of leaving me. It's because he's afraid I'll leave him.

"I'll send Heart Route," I whisper. "I promise."

"I know you will."

"When I do? Will you be waiting for me?"

Sejin clenches me close and kisses me hard. "Yes," he promises.

The fire snaps and crackles. "Just promise you'll come home to me."

"I love you."

He shivers in my arms, and I hold him tighter. There are a lot of things we don't talk a lot about, and Sejin's experience of loving a person who didn't come home to him one day has always been one of them. Someday soon, though we'll have to dig into it more. The mother he lost, the father who's coming, and the future in front of us.

But I have to send Heart Route first.

And there's no time like the present.

0 days to free solo ascent

I WAKE AT dawn. I don't know why or how, but I feel it in my bones. Today is the day. The culmination of years of hard work, and months and months of training. The culmination of my very life until this moment. It's like a whistle in my cells, a rising call I can't ignore.

This might not be the day I'd planned to do it—that was next week—but it's the day I'm meant to do it. There's no other way to put it.

It's time.

I leave Sejin sleeping in bed, all tousled and beautiful, and I bypass several sleeping cats to head out to my van. I briefly worry the van's wheels on the gravel might wake Sejin, but my phone doesn't light up with any texts questioning where I'm going so early.

I leave my phone on for the duration of the drive and the entire approach hike in, but I turn it off when I reach the base, so no texts or calls will come in while I'm climbing. I can't afford even the smallest distraction today.

At the start of the route, I sit down on the ground and breathe in and out. I allow myself to imagine everything that I'll otherwise try to put out of my head during the climb. In detail, I imagine falling. I imagine the fear as I plummet. I imagine dying. I think of my body on the ground—or what's left of my body after impact. I imagine Sejin getting the news. That makes my gut churn, but I force myself to envision it all as fully as possible. His heartbreaking sobs. The pain he'll feel.

I breathe in and out.

I imagine him moving on. Learning to live a different kind of life, making new friends, finding new love... Forgetting about me most of the time.

Then I change out of my approach shoes and into my rock shoes, clip on the chalk bag, and shake out my hands and feet. My heart pounds. My blood feels effervescent. Life roils inside of me with a vibrancy I only feel at moments like these. Potent. Powerful.

This is it. I step forward with determination.

It's time.

CHAPTER TWENTY-THREE

Sejin

"WHAT TIME IS it?" I murmur, feeling draggy and strange. There's no answer from the other side of the bed.

"I think my alarm didn't go off, but, fuck, I'm still so tired," I whimper, and I push my foot out to touch Dan's leg. All I feel is cool, smooth bedsheets. I sit up and squint through my tangled mess of bedhead. He's not there.

Coldness seeps through me.

But before I panic, I listen carefully for sounds in the house. Is he making coffee? Doing kettlebells or a club bell workout in the living room?

I hear nothing. Not even the sound of the cats bounding around looking for breakfast.

Shifting to find my phone on the bedside table, I check the time and see that it's just after six. My alarm is set for seven-thirty, so I haven't missed it. I climb out of bed and pull on some sweatpants, hoping Dan is just out in his van doing some hangboarding or reading, or God knows what.

But I already know.

As I open the front door and stare at the empty space where Dan's van is supposed to be, my heart seems to slow, along with my breathing, and the cold morning wind lifts my hair and races over my bare shoulders and chest. Romeo slides past me out into the pearly glow of dawn, and I don't try to catch him. He'll be back meowing for breakfast before long.

But will Dan be back at all?

I feel like I should have a stronger feeling about it all, some sort of sick dread or wild terror. Instead, I feel an almost deathly calm.

I shut the door, retreat to the bedroom, and pull on a t-shirt and a blue hoodie. I make eggs, but I don't eat them. Muggs jumps up to the counter to try for a few bites.

I put him down on the floor and go to let Romeo back in before scraping the eggs into the cat bowls and putting the bowls on the floor for them to pounce on. I turn and stare through the windows at the Sierra-Nevadas outlined in the rosy glow of morning. The clock over the stove says it's nearly seven now. I'm supposed to be at the preschool by eight-thirty, and I imagine myself there, singing songs with the kids, dancing, as Dan climbs—alone and ropeless—up Heart Route.

I've paid more attention to the route than he thinks. Studied the maps when I'm alone in the van. Even taken a peek at his notebooks, scanned his plans, his comments, his strategies, seeing no mention of me in his journals anywhere.

It was wrong to look. I've invaded his privacy. But I needed to know his chances in his own eyes.

He feels they're mostly good. But when it comes to the cruxes, he'll need to have a very good day. The best day of his life. In his notes, he said he'd wait until he felt a strong certainty that such a day was ahead. It seems like he must feel that way today.

How can a man know if he's going to have the best day of his life in advance?

How can he be willing to risk not having a tomorrow here with me? With these dumb, finicky cats? To risk attaching his death so closely to the day of Peggy Jo's new grandbaby's birth? How selfish is that? How can he…

I rub my hands up and down my arms. The hoodie feels nubby

against my palms.

Without much thought, I put on my coat, socks, and shoes, and grab my car keys. I don't have a pair of binoculars, but I know that climber aficionado Tom Reed will be in the Meadow by eight in the morning to note and track the climbers on El Cap, and if I leave now, I'm sure he'll let me use his telescope.

It's not that I want to see Dan climbing.

It's that I need to confirm for myself that he's *still* climbing. That he's on that wall, alive and well, breathing and sticking.

According to the app on my phone, the temperatures are supposed to remain low today, but the sun will start baking the upper part of the Heart Route before long, making it more treacherous and slippery. I'm not sure if I can stomach watching whatever's left of the climb, but I know I can't stomach sitting at home feeling dead, numb, and strange. I can't go to the preschool and dance like nothing out of the ordinary is happening.

I have to go see for myself.

Dan

ON THE WALL, ascending without the weight of gear or an audience, my senses dial in to the highest degree. My breath is like an ocean, rushing in and out with a heaving effortlessness that relaxes me. The wall of rock in front of me is huge, yes, but every inch of it seems perfectly outlined in my mind.

A hold that's no wider than a matchbox edge seems enormous to me, plenty of stability to hang from. The nubs I rest my toes against appear giant and secure. Each movement is accurate and strong. A peace settles over me, and I can see every shadow and edge on the wall, and even the rock itself seems to breathe along with me.

I'm in the flow zone. It's all easy.

I'm easy.

I'm free.

This is the state of being I live for and nothing comes close to it…except being with Sejin. When I'm with him, I often feel high, and dizzy with affection and lust, but this hyperawareness on the rock is something different. A solitary journey. Me against the uncaring, blank surface, and my certainty that I will prevail. I feel like a superhero or a madman. I feel the truth of my place on earth—meaningless, pointless, a speck against the rock of this planet.

It's freeing and beautiful.

This sensation lasts until I reach the dyno, and then as I steady myself, taking deep breaths, the hold seems like it's just a hop away. An easy leap. As I soar through the air, time and space stretch out forever, and yet it's only a moment. I grab the holds, and I'm safe. My spirits rise even higher. I'm invincible now. I can do this. I'm *going* to do this.

My certainty doesn't waver as I approach the pitch leading to the roof of the Heart Formation. I feel strong enough, so certain that I decide to bypass the downclimb to the ledge for the rest stop Rye and I had agreed on. I don't need it. Not today.

Instead, I start up toward the roof. A rock falls from above. I don't know where it came from or what might have kicked it down, but it hits me in the face and I wince as pain explodes on my cheekbone.

Fuck.

Sweat breaks over me, but I'm not in a good position to chalk my fingers. A hot, slick sensation slides down my face, but I can't risk letting go or touching it if it's blood or sweat. It doesn't matter anyway. I have to move on.

As I surge forward, another crumble of rock from above comes down. These are smaller pieces, more like clumps of dirt and gravel. Despite squeezing my eyes shut as soon as I hear the rocks popping off against the wall, some dust still gets in. I shout in reflexive pain and gravel pieces fall into my open mouth. I spit them out.

Mamaaaaa! He's doing it again!

The memory rises unbidden, along with a flipbook of terrible recollections from each foster home I hit along the way to adulthood. I spit and spit, unable to get the grit out of my mouth or to open my eyes. I breathe in and out, feeling streaming tears wash the dirt from my eyes. Fear knots in my chest.

The beautiful, singular focus has slipped away from me. I have to get it back. But I can still hear that brat screaming in my brain.

Mamaaaaa! He's doing it again! Mamaaaaa!

I take deep breaths, shake my head slowly. This isn't the time. I'm safe. I'm on the wall. I almost laugh. Safe? Free soloing thousands of feet up, getting ready to tackle the roof of the Heart Formation? Hilarious.

I'm absolutely fucking hilarious.

I feel the edges of my peace unravelling. I can't open my eyes, and even if I could, I can't move forward with this mindset. I have to get my head back together.

I blink, relieved when the dirt or dust seems to have slipped from my eyes with the tears. I can see, and what I see is good news. I'm right where I'm supposed to be. I know the next moves like the back of my hand.

Now I just have to make them.

So, I do.

As I move toward the second crux of the ascent, I can't seem to shake the disturbance from the small rockfall. My toeholds feel tenuous, the finger grips that I've trained on seem smaller. Even the light seems sharper, bouncing off the granite, making my tender eyes ache. Worse, the telltale throbbing in my forearms and fingers tells me I'm getting pumped.

Quickly, I find a familiar nub and a foothold that look secure enough to rest on so I can switch out hands to shake my arms one at a time, trying to free up the lactic acid.

Heart pounding, eyes still tearing, I gaze out at the exposure. It's peaceful and quiet down there. The world's oblivious to my frantic pulse and the sharpness of my fear.

The meadow stretches out all misty and beautiful, the frost shimmering in the morning light. The river sparkles in a familiar ribbon, and the falls roar with their usual white noise that always accompanies my climbs. I take more slow breaths. I try to pull the meadow into me. I need peace. Focus. Peace.

Mamaaaaa! He's doing it again!

I shake my head. I try to think of something calming, something to ground me.

Sejin.

I exhale slowly. The way his black lashes touch his cheekbones in his sleep. How his eyes hook down at the inner edges. The shape of his mouth when a smile is about to break over his face. That smile.

The smile.

I breathe in deeply.

The smile that captured my attention in that photo on that stupid app and which I've now seen directed at me, *because* of me, a total of thirteen times. I've counted. Each one is an achievement. Each one is cherished.

As I take more breaths, I think of the lesser smiles too. The ones that are rewarding, yes, but always show that he's holding something back—a thought, a fear, a sadness. I hate when he's sad. And if I fall, he'll be devastated.

I squeeze my eyes closed. No, damnit, I shouldn't be thinking of this now. But suddenly I am. I'm thinking of what happens if I can't shake this lactic acid out, if my hands won't hold on, if they let go. I think about the moment of falling itself. The horror of the descent through the air. The bone-shattering crash into rock. I've imagined all that a million times before, but now I know the worst is what happens afterward.

Sejin's smile…that beautiful, gorgeous, hard-won smile that I've wanted so selfishly, and chased so passionately these last months, will be gone. How long will it be before anyone sees it again? Before he feels joy enough for it to bloom on his face? I can't kid myself that he won't be destroyed if I fail at this. I can't lie to myself and say it won't matter.

I shake out my arms one by one again. Another little fall of rock comes down from above, but this time none of them hit me. I can only think a large bird or small animal is doing it.

On the wall without ropes is no place to rest. I can't just *hang* here. I have to move forward, and once I do, I'm re-committing to this climb. I have no choice but to move from this spot, to carry on. This is it. I'm alone on this wall, and there's no one to call for help who could ever come fast enough.

I must go on. A downclimb is riskier than an up climb. And that fucking roof looms ahead. But it's okay. I can adjust my trajectory, I'll move over to my old route, keep that safety ledge beneath me. I should have downclimbed to rest on it like Rye wanted. I should have—

I stop myself.

Should haves are for losers who end up smears on the ground. I'm not a smear. I'm still alive, still moving forward, and Sejin's smile depends on me making it up the rest of this pitch, over the roof, and up over the lip. I surge forward, moving up as quickly as I can. My hands are still feeling pumped. My forearms throb. My calves ache.

Gritting my teeth, I command my body to obey me. I've got

this. I've trained. I've worked hard. I won't be afraid. I won't.

Determined, I push ahead.

My only way back to Sejin's smile is onward. The flow will return to me. It has to…

I just have to get over the lip of the roof. That's all. Then I'll be on the wall with razor-edge holds and no time to rest. *Fuck.*

I'll make it. I must make it. But first things first.

Get up over the lip…

Sejin

IN A STRANGE daze, I park my car and start the hike across the wet meadow toward Tom Reed. I feel like I'm not real. Like the morning isn't real. Like maybe I'm dead and this is Hell, or I'm asleep and this is a dream-almost-nightmare.

The morning is beautiful. The birds are singing.

Tom is there alone with his scope already trained on the wall. He's typing into his phone, probably updating his social media and website with the details of what climbers and teams are on the wall and what routes they're taking. I walk toward him without any attempt to disguise my approach, but he still seems startled when he notices me.

"Good morning!" Tom calls out. "Here to watch some climbing?"

I nod. My throat is tight. Words won't come out, much less a smile.

"You're in for something special," he says, and I can't tell how much of his tone is admiration and how much is anxiety. "There's a free soloist on the wall."

He points at El Cap, his finger drawing the now-familiar line of

Heart Route for me. "I think he's taking this route up. It's a rare one to begin with. Only been free roped-climbed a handful of times by some of the best…including this guy. We've all been speculating that he's been training for it, but… well, we all thought he'd be crazy to try it. But there he is. Guess this is his day. Hopefully." He gestures at his scope. "Want to see?"

I nod and carefully place myself against the eyepiece as my fingers steady the cold metal.

"There are a few more teams on the wall too," he says. "But I admit, I probably won't be watching them much until this guy sends this route…or doesn't."

I wish he wouldn't keep qualifying his remarks. His doubts feel like kicks to my numb body. Bruising, even though I can't feel them.

Because I can't feel anything.

I spot Dan easily. He's hanging in one spot on the pitch below the Heart Formation's roof, shaking out his hands. I stare at him, wondering what he's thinking. Wondering if he's going to pop off the wall and die. Wondering why I love this nightmare of a man.

"This fellow is different from some of the others," Tom says. "Name's Dan McBride. He's a secretive sort. No cameras for him. I hear he's been offered some sponsorships, but is too invested in the 'purity' of the sport to accept them. Though how he lives is beyond me. Probably in a van or car like most of these dedicated climbers, but there's always a question of how they afford the campgrounds and gear. Maybe he has family money."

"No," I whisper, but I'm pretty sure Tom doesn't hear me. He prattles on.

"Not many friends or fans amongst the regulars for this guy either. He's not much of a sprayer—that means he doesn't brag about what he accomplishes much."

"Yeah," I say, because I know this, but the fellow doesn't care.

He keeps talking.

"Not bragging is sort of an admirable quality, which you'd think the other climbers would like, but mostly they think this guy's an arrogant dick. Maybe he is, but he's always been nice enough to me when I've talked to him. Well, maybe 'nice' isn't the right word, but he hasn't been a jerk either. He's got the energy of a man on a mission."

I stare at Dan through the scope as he launches ahead on the route. I swallow hard enough my throat clicks.

"What's he doing now?"

"Climbing," I manage to get out.

"Ah, yes, well, that's better than the alternative." He chuckles.

I feel some vomit rise in the back of my throat as Dan makes his way toward the roof. I remember his voice, the hitch in it, the uncertainty, whenever he's described this part to me: "It gives me the heebie-jeebies," he's said more than once.

I watch as Dan hesitates again and then moves forward.

I watch as he climbs to a point where he's hanging by just his fingers and toes.

And then I turn the scope back over to Tom because I can't watch anymore.

Dan

FUCK.

My arms are pumped. My grip loosens against my will, and I know I either have to make a mad dash for the lip—crazy and reckless, because above the lip is a relentless climb of polished granite with razor holds—or risk an insane downclimb back to where I'll have at least a chance of falling on the ledge, the way Rye and I have discussed before.

I have about two seconds to make my choice.

Three, if I'm lucky.

And I'm wasting those seconds stuck looping on thoughts of Sejin. Thinking of his fear when he wakes and sees that I'm gone. Of his expression when the news comes of my fall. Of his tears. Of that beautiful face without that perfect smile for far too long. He'll be fine without me one day. It's the getting to that one day that seems brutal and unfair now.

I can't think of him, though. I need to make a choice… or this is over.

I glare up at the lip ahead, and the sun pours into my eyes. The rock will be hot. I know this. I've trained for it.

But my arms are giving up on me.

I need to rest. It's possible, if I'm wildly lucky, I could still downclimb all the way to the ledge and sit there for a breather.

I *know* that's not possible. I won't make it.

I start down anyway. I feel my grip weakening. My hands and arms throb. My shoe skids instead of clinging, and it happens.

Falling is nothing like flying.

In case anyone ever asks.

Sejin

"OH, *HELL*," TOM says vehemently. "He fell. Oh, Christ."

My numbness shatters, and I shove the man aside to look through the scope. I hear Tom beside me speaking quickly, naming the place, the route, and giving Dan's name. He's calling 9-1-1.

I stare at the blank space on the wall. My knees go weak. My heart lurches and I turn and vomit into the grass. It's in my hair, it's on my chin, and I stare at the white, foamy bile splashed over the green, my heart burning in agony, and my breath coming in quick gulps.

"No, no, he's hit the ledge," I hear Tom say. "I can't tell. He's not moving. How long? Yeah, yeah. I'll stay on the line."

His hand touches my back.

"You alright, kid?"

I straighten and wipe the back of my hand over my vomit-wet mouth. "He's on the ledge?"

I lurch over to the scope and look through. Tom has adjusted it to point at the ledge. The bright orange of Dan's shirt is visible. But it's true; he's not moving. Not even a little bit. The scope isn't good enough to tell if he's breathing. There's red, though.

Blood.

There's blood.

I turn and heave on the grass again, and Tom talks to the 9-1-1 operator. "Might want to send someone to the meadow too. Got a spectator here who's sick. I think he might know the guy." He touches my shoulder and I shrug him off. "You know him? You know Dan McBride, son?"

I nod. Because I can't speak. I can't say the words—he's my boyfriend, the man I love.

And I can't bear to ask if he's dead.

I slump down to the ground, staring at the cold, gray rock of El Capitan, focusing on the Heart Formation. I clutch my chest, feeling the pounding of my own heart, and I wait.

The sound of helicopters and sirens lifts into the air.

Tears run down my face, the heat of them turning cold in the cool morning air. I think of Dan the night before, his warmth, his strength, his declarations. I think of the future he wants for us—the adventure, the stupid virtuous poverty, the love-enhanced, giddy dream of it. I think of his fingers on my skin and his mouth on mine.

The Heart Formation looms.
My heart continues to beat.
But does his?

END BOOK ONE

Find out about BOOK TWO at Leta Blake's Patreon.

Author's Note

First off, I want to warn readers that this novel is not intended as a book of best practices when it comes to rock climbing. In fact, it is anything but. At no point should the climbing activities of any of these characters be seen as the author advocating for any reader to attempt to replicate said feats. Let's keep these climbs fictional!

Regarding the Alternate 2021 Timeline

When I began writing this book, we were still in the thick of the pandemic and lockdown, etc, but I needed a break from all of that. I wrote this book as though the pandemic was not happening, thinking that it wouldn't matter because I wouldn't have to set the book in any specific year or time. However, as discussed later in the notes below, I ended up needing to set it in 2021 exactly. So, for the purposes of this book, this is an alternate, pandemic-free timeline.

Regarding Heart Route

Many liberties were taken with the details of Dan's chosen free solo route for the sake of the story. Heart Route is a real route up the side of El Capitan. It is incredibly treacherous, and anyone familiar with the route would, undoubtedly, have trouble believing it were possible to free solo it. The reasons I chose to go with this route anyway are:

a) Most importantly and perhaps superficially, the name was perfect for a Romance novel: Heart Route! Absolutely divine! Impossible to resist!

b) At the time, only a handful of people had ever completed the route. Thus, I believed fewer readers would have firsthand knowledge of it, and therefore would be more willing to suspend disbelief about the plausibility of Dan's attempt. I also hoped they would be able to ignore authorial changes made to the specifics of the route for the purposes of this story.

Recently, however, the famous free soloist Alex Honnold himself did free rope climb (not free solo!) this route and posted about it on his Instagram. Since then, the route has gained in popularity. But I feel confident no one is going to be foolish enough to attempt a free solo of it anytime soon. (Sorry, Dan!)

If you are familiar with the route, or with El Cap itself, you may have to work to suspend your disbelief or forget what you know in order to enjoy the story. To those readers, I apologize.

Regarding Adoption from Korea

I understand that adoption is always a fraught topic, and that international adoption is especially so. There are no doubt many international adoptions that have taken place under questionable circumstances. The views expressed by the adoptees in the video Sejin reports watching are legitimate and common feelings and thoughts. The fact that Sejin claims to feel differently should not be seen as a dismissal by the author of these legitimate and complex issues, nor should it be seen as being a preferred or better way to feel.

When it comes to Korean international adoptions in particular, there are a few things of note:

1. Korea has closed international adoptions for many years now as they grapple with population decline, but at one point in the 1990s, they were adopting out thousands of babies per year.

2. While not addressed at length in the book, it's interesting to understand that adoption itself within Korea has very different social implications than it does in Western culture. The repercussions of being an adopted child, even within Korea, are considered more severe due to the historical and ongoing focus on the importance of patrilineal bloodline. You can read about the issues surrounding in-Korea Korean adoption HERE for further understanding.

When it came to the character of Sejin, I chose to base his adoption experience on very candid and open conversations I've had with my niece, a Korean adoptee. In 2004, my niece was adopted from South Korea into our white family at eight months of age. It wasn't until she was in college that she began to more closely consider the microaggressions she faced growing up as a non-white kid in predominately white Southern Appalachia, and the lack of understanding around that within the family and within herself.

However, she also reported to me that, like Sejin, she didn't experience a lot of angst about her adoption as a child or as a teen or even now. For what it's worth, I believe my niece felt safe enough to tell me differently if she wanted to, and I do not believe she was reporting a falsely happy experience for my sake. She is currently seeking to know more about her birth culture by spending a semester of her college experience in Seoul.

Again, please do not assume that just because both the character of Sejin and my niece have relatively low-angst adoption experiences that I, as the author, believe that others do not have justified grief at what they've lost or what trauma they've experienced through adoption. I simply wanted to give some representation to my niece, who has felt alienated from not only the white Appalachian community she was raised in, but also from the organized Korean adoption communities she's come across.

Regarding KPop references
(2021 timeline, Moonbin's death)

When I started writing *Free Fall* in the spring of 2021, Astro had just released their album *All Yours*. The character of Sejin resonated with that album, and I listened to it repeatedly while writing *Free Fall*. I wrote Sejin as a big fan of the group and included references to many of their songs.

In April of 2023, Moonbin, a beloved and talented member of Astro, was found dead in his apartment in circumstances leading police to believe he took his own life. Fans the world over mourned his death, and his talent and presence will always be missed.

I faced the question of how to handle this situation. Should I remove all mentions of Astro? All mentions of the music? The reference to Moonbin himself? In the end, I decided that it would be a discredit to his memory to take those references out. His inspiration should remain behind, and I hope that you will take the time to listen to some of the Astro songs mentioned in these books, especially the song "gemini."

This is one of the main reasons the book is set in 2021.

Thank you for inspiration to: *Free Solo*, a film by Jimmy Chin and Chai Vasarhelyi, Alex Honnold's book *Alone on the Wall*, as well as *The Impossible Climb* by Mark Synnott, *Big Walls, Swift Waters* by Charles R. Farabee, *The Dawn Wall* film focusing on the life of Tommy Caldwell, the film *Meru*, also by Jimmy Chin and

Chai Vasarhelyi, Reel Rock, Dean Potter, Adam Ondra, Magnus Mitbo, James Braithwaite, and so many others. Thank you to the Bearden High School climbing team, as well. I've read, watched, and absorbed so much climbing over the last many years as I've worked on these books, and I love that the community is so eager to share their passion.

Thank you to Mia for offering climbing guidance as a beta reader.

Thank you to my niece, Clara, for being part of our family and for sharing her experience with adoption so honestly with me. Thank you to Aimee Curameng for providing an honest and occasionally painful alternate view of adoption. Thank you to Astro, BTS, SHINee, Twice, OneUS, Enhypen, and all the KPop groups that I studied so diligently with my daughter.

Thank you to Willow for going above and beyond, as always, as a beta reader.

Thank you to the readers out there who make this all possible. I write books for *you,* and I am grateful that you love to read them.

Discover more about the author online

Gay Romance Newsletter

Leta's newsletter will keep you up to date on her latest releases, sales and deals, future writing plans, and more from the world of M/M romance. Join Leta's mailing list today.

Leta Blake on Patreon

Become part of Leta Blake's Patreon community to support her indie publishing expenses and to access exclusive content, deleted scenes, extras, and interviews.
patreon.com/letablake

Leta Blake's Shop

Find special editions, book-inspired spicy art, merch and more! Leta's shop is growing, so check back regularly.
payhip.com/letablake

Other Books by Leta Blake

Contemporary

Will & Patrick Wake Up Married
Will & Patrick's Endless Honeymoon
Cowboy Seeks Husband
Bring on Forever
Stay Lucky

Sports

The River Leith

The Training Season Series
Training Season
Training Complex

Musicians

Smoky Mountain Dreams
Vespertine

Dark
The Difference Between

New Adult/Coming of Age

Punching the V-Card

'90s Coming of Age Series
Pictures of You
You Are Not Me
Only You
My Skin Begs You Please

Winter Holidays

North's Pole
My December Daddy

The Mr. Christmas Series
Mr. Frosty Pants
Mr. Naughty List
Mr. Jingle Bells

Omegaverse

Heat of Love Series
White Heat
Slow Heat
Alpha Heat
Slow Birth
Bitter Heat

For Sale Series
Heat for Sale
Bully for Sale

Fantasy

Any Given Lifetime

Re-imagined Fairy Tales

Flight
Levity

Paranormal & Shifters

Angel Undone

Omega Mine

Horror

Raise Up Heart

Audiobooks
letablake.com/audiobooks

Discover more about the author online

Leta Blake
letablake.com

About the Author

Author of the bestselling book *Smoky Mountain Dreams* and fan favorites like *Training Season*, *Will & Patrick Wake Up Married*, and *Slow Heat*, Leta Blake has been captivating M/M Romance readers for over a decade. Whether writing contemporary romance or fantasy, she puts her psychology background to use creating complex characters and love stories that feel real. At home in the Southern U.S., Leta works hard at achieving balance between her writing and her family life.